PRIDE

A DEADLY SEVEN NOVEL

PRIDE

LANA
PECHERCZYK

Prism Press, Perth Australia.
Copyright © 2021 Lana Pecherczyk
All rights reserved.
ISBN:978-0-6454994-4-5

Text copyright © Lana Pecherczyk 2021
Cover design © Lana Pecherczyk 2021
Developmental Editor: Ann Harth

www.lanapecherczyk.com

also by lana pecherczyk

A Labyrinth of Fangs and Thorns

A Symphony of Savage Hearts

Game of Gods

(Romantic Urban Fantasy)

Soul Thing

The Devil Inside

Playing God

Game Over

Game of Gods Box Set

CARDINAL CITY MAP

← - - - - - - MISHA'S HOUSE

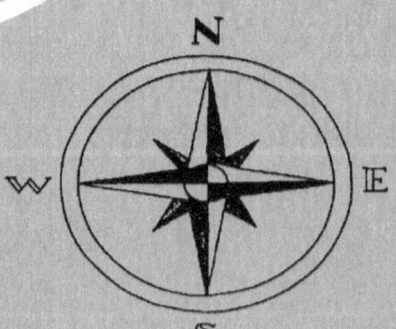

AIRPORT

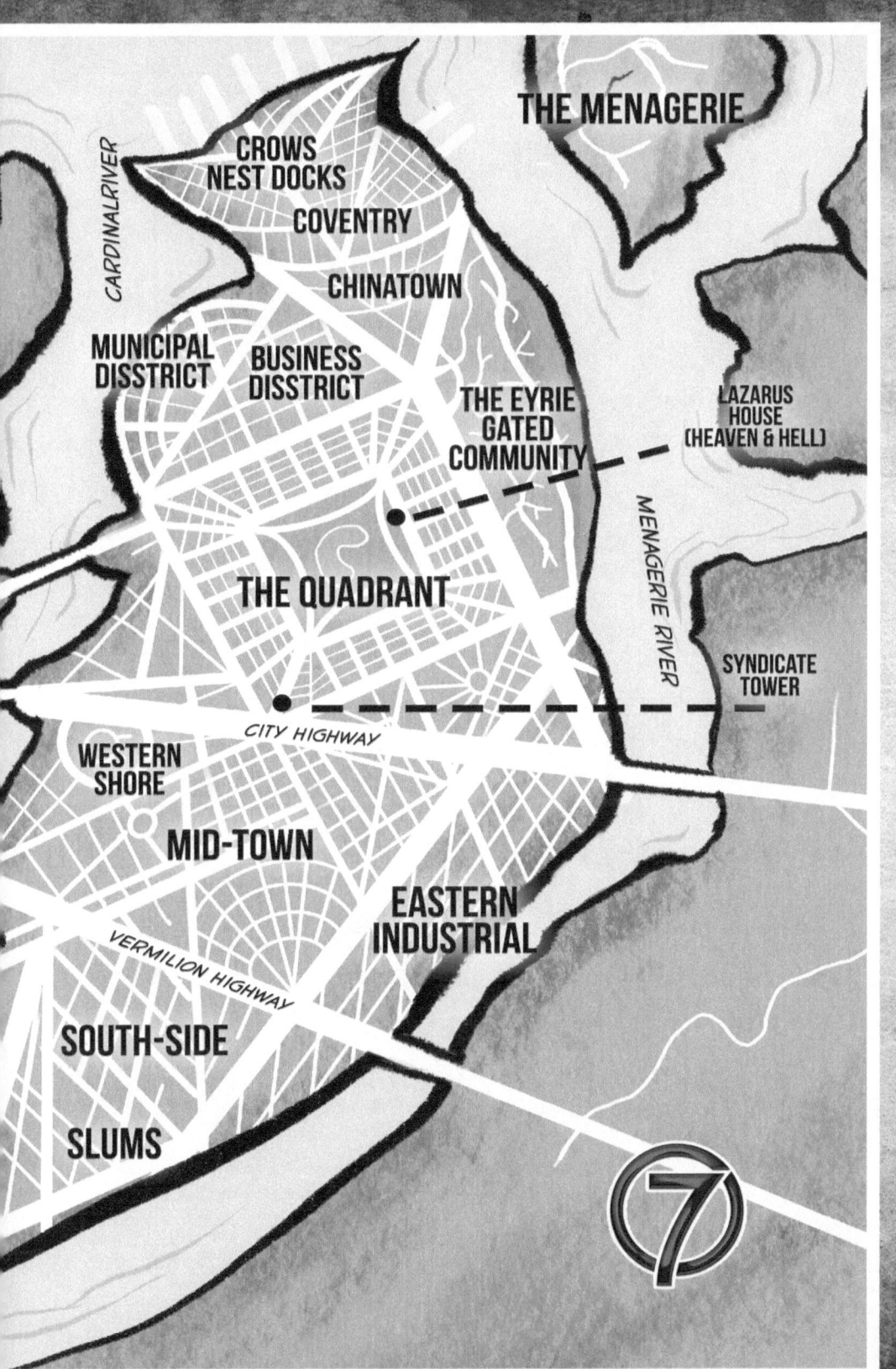

*to expand your
'pride' reading
experience*

LISTEN TO THESE SONGS....

- **For Parker:** *What's Up Danger*, by Black Caviar
- **For Alice:** *My Baby Just Cares for Me*, by Nina Simone

"We are rarely proud when we are alone."

VOLTAIRE

JULIUS ALLCOTT SIFTED through ash on his desk. In his haste to spill his wife and daughter from their urns, they fell into the cracks and crevices of his keyboard. No matter, all he needed was one strand of hair. One follicle for each of them.

And then he could bring them back as promised, despite Despair having swallowed their original strands of hair in an act of feeble defiance. He'd tried to cut the strands out of her stomach, but the bitch had digested them.

Julius raked his fingers through his family, his heart kicking in his chest. There had to be something… *anything*. He needed them with every fiber of his being. Everything he'd done for the Syndicate had been in their name—the cleansing of the world's sin, the destruction of society, the changes he put his body through.

For them.

I need them.

He ignored the *ping* of an incoming call request on his computer. It was only the other Syndicate leaders demanding reparation for the recent failure at their harvesting plant.

Fuck them.

This wasn't about them. It was about his family. His real one, not the one born of test tubes. Even they had been a means to an end.

Baring his teeth into the darkness, he struggled to gain composure. His loves. He needed their hair, the follicles at the end. But they weren't there. His loves weren't there.

With a growl, he swiped the keyboard out of the way, his chest heaving with panicked breaths. His vision blurred as he knocked the desk caddy over, spilling its contents. Scissors slid across the dirty surface, spinning a circle in the ash. He wasn't sure how many minutes passed with him staring at those scissors, wishing to go back in time and keep those strands of hair safe in the locket on a chain around his neck.

The computer pinged again, forcing his attention. And he hated it. He wanted nothing to take his focus from his loves. The locket had been a constant reminder; a cool metal casing that dangled between his shirt and chest. He needed a new reminder.

He slapped a palm over the scissors and brought the sharp ends to his own pale hair—*snip*—and then tied the lock around the base of his pointer finger. A physical and visual reminder. He thumbed the bristles, thinking about how this had all gone wrong in the first place.

Despair, his "darling," the only one of the original sin-sensing soldiers who'd fallen in line had betrayed him. No... further back than that. The attack on the warehouse. No... further. The Hildegard Sisterhood Sinners, poking their heads into his business.

Further.

The first Sinner—Mary Lazarus—had infiltrated his lab all those years ago. Mary was going to kill them all, but she'd adopted them instead.

He snarled. The Sisterhood should be eradicated. They'd been foiling his plans long before the Deadly Seven had. If it weren't for them, the Lazarus brood would be in *his* control. If it weren't for them, he would never have needed further investors. He would still be in control of this entire operation.

The computer pinged again. He shoved the screen onto the floor, then stomped on it until the pinging stopped. The Syndicate leaders would find a way to contact him. They always did.

Bitterness threatened to overwhelm him, but the bristles of his hair around his finger calmed him, reminding him of the end goal. The only goal.

"I will find a way to bring you back, my loves." And if he couldn't, then he would go to them and take the rest of the world along for the ride.

AIMI'S CORPSE spread out before him on the dining table. Parker Lazarus plucked out her vein—a wire—and inspected the fried end before discarding it. The CPU was her brain. The motherboard, her central nervous system. She had no face, no body nor skin, yet this digital construct had been as real to Parker as any human.

She'd been the invincible backbone of their crime-fighting unit.

Or so he'd thought.

He glanced at his left arm, recently amputated from beneath the shoulder and now covered in electrodes. An ache lodged in his chest. He'd thought *he* was invincible. For a brief moment, his mind traveled back to the night everything changed.

The Sinner's masked face peeked over the roof, staring at him dangling from the edge. Rain pattered her hooded head, leaving a halo of mist that glowed under the moonlight. A puff of white cloud escaped her red face mask.

"You stubborn mule," she chided, and reached down. "Take my hand."

"Fuck you," he growled—

Shaking himself from the memory, Parker checked on the electrodes and then turned up the dial on the tens machine. Electricity surged into his body.

Standard regeneration for the Deadly Seven took two years, or so his maker's notes had claimed. It had only been two months since the amputation. He'd regenerated less than half an inch, but he'd read studies and papers on how to trigger the healing process. Electricity helped. Next up was small doses of UV light. It was unlikely he'd see fast results, but he couldn't afford to wait two years. He needed his arm now. He would try anything and everything.

Daisy was missing and the only way to find her was to repair AIMI and salvage what he could from Daisy's tracking code.

Parker turned up the dial on the tens machine again. This time, the rush of electricity triggered his new instincts. Claws shot out of his right fingertips and The Beast surged to the surface. An almighty snarl rumbled in his throat and rattled parts on the table. Without checking a mirror, he knew his golden eyes looked more feline. His teeth had elongated to fangs, and his long auburn hair was more like a lion's mane than a man's. His ears picked up every sound within a one-mile radius. From the scurry of cockroaches down the drain pipes, to the man pissing in the alley behind the nightclub, Hell. Even at this ungodly hour, traffic blared. And the elevator outside in the hallway clanked as it moved.

He shut his eyes and concentrated on filtering the sound until he could focus on what was in this room, but the effort came at a drain on his system. Phantom pain lashed his missing left arm, and he had to remind himself the limb was gone. There were no claws breaking his skin on that hand. It wasn't only the ghostly pain, it was the other urges, the ones yearning for him to hunt down his mate and claim her as his own.

Parker had deciphered his biological mother's encrypted research years ago but told no one. He'd hid the fact because he was ashamed to admit what he'd eventually turn into. But a bigger reason was that he knew the mate myth Mary peddled years ago was true. He'd assumed because he was the eldest, he'd find his mate first. But he was the last, and it chaffed, especially because his mate had been within his reach. And he'd let go.

At the thought of his mate, his body reacted with a ferocity he blamed on the animal within. His pulse spiked. His pheromones triggered. His cock hardened.

Breathing through the changes, he forced his urges down with disgust.

I am not an animal. With a hasty swipe over the table, he spilled useless parts onto the floor until he found the one he needed. AIMI's memory, the hard drive. He plugged it into his laptop and set to work salvaging fragments of data from the virus riddled device, a virus his older sister Daisy had inserted, betraying them. But she hadn't known what she was doing, or rather, she didn't understand that the asshole who called himself their father was a psychopath who'd used her. Julius Allcott was the king of sinful pride and before the year was out, Parker vowed to end him and the Syndicate.

He already had a plan ticking away in the back of his mind.

The elevator dinged, loud and annoying. Apart from supernatural hearing, he could also jump higher, see further, and punch harder. According to the original research, his genome was a DNA cocktail of anything from lion to amphibian to moth. He was surprised he still looked human. He touched a long, sharp fang. Human was debatable.

The gift he'd received was nothing like his siblings. Where they had class or flash, he had unsophisticated animal urges. Wrapping a lion in Armani didn't change the fact it was still a beast.

The sound of two women bickering made his stomach clench. He reined in his auditory perception, shutting them out. Maybe if he ignored them, they'd go away. A knock came at the door. And another. He resumed picking through the corrupted code on his laptop for remnants of AIMI's old programming.

A sudden haze of sleep dragged his eyelids down. The laptop screen blurred, and his claws and fangs slipped back into his body. When the haze just as suddenly lifted, he realized someone was playing with him.

"Open the door, dickhead!" Liza shouted, her voice filtering through the penthouse.

So uncouth.

"Or I'll put you to sleep!"

Sloan this time. Even more lacking in sophistication. How he was related to them, he had no idea. But then again, he failed to see how he was related to Wyatt's temper, Griffin's neurotic tendencies, Evan's wild streak and Tony's vanity... well, maybe that last one wasn't a far stretch. But they were family. Even Daisy. Family stuck together, and they had his back just like he had theirs. He trusted them with his life. And maybe he loved them. Just a tad.

Better see what they want.

He yanked the electrodes from his stump and pushed back from the table with a wince. If it wasn't the phantom pain, it was the healing and growing pains. It might ache the entire two years he regenerated. He considered putting on the prosthetic, but decided he wouldn't let them in, anyway. He didn't even bother putting on a shirt. Out of anyone, he trusted them enough to relax around.

Silk pajama pants billowed as he strode barefoot to the front door and opened it to the length of the deadbolt chain he'd installed upon AIMI's demise. Without his trusted computer management interface monitoring security, Parker let no one in his penthouse anymore. Not even the cleaner. He did a better job.

Sloan's dark brows arched beneath her messy, long black hair. Her crinkled shirt and sloppy sweats suggested she'd been interrupted from respite, just as he had. Liza's brown leather jacket almost matched the tone of her long hair. A CCPD detective's badge dangled from her jeans hip pocket, and a metal cybernetic arm plated in chipped gold hung from her hand.

He'd seen stranger things.

"It's late," he grumbled.

Liza scoffed at his expression. "Don't try that prideful shit on us."

Sloan folded her arms, her face a mirror of her sister's incredulity. He almost smiled at them. Almost.

"What do you want?" he asked.

"You've hardly been out in two months," Liza accused. "If you're not coming out, at least let us in."

"I'm busy." If he let them in, then they'd see his projects. They might even catch a glimpse of The Beast, and then they'd know he'd lied when he said he hadn't found his mate. He'd been lying from the start.

Blue eyes blinking in the night, the rain casting a halo around her head.

His scowl deepened.

"Parks and Recreation," Sloan mocked. "You missed my wedding, bras. Not cool. Not cool at all."

Damned stupid nicknames. "I gave you a gift."

"Which was appreciated, but you still missed it. Look, I get it, you're embarrassed to be seen in public, what with your missing arm and all that, but none of us care. The least you can do is let us in."

"That's why you think I'm in here?" His snarl was uncontainable. He should shut the door in their face for even thinking it. Parker Lazarus did not hide away. He was fucking busy trying to find their missing sister, and since he couldn't trust anyone to do the job perfectly, he had to do it all.

Like fucking usual.

"Don't make us break the door down," Liza warned.

She'd do it, too, and the last thing he wanted was more contractors up here.

His gaze darted between their determined faces. At least their mother wasn't with them. He didn't think he could deal with three Lazarus women at once. Not tonight. He shut the door, but Liza's boot jammed in the way.

A low rumble of warning rattled in his throat. The shrewd gazes of two super-powered women landed on his face through the gap. They didn't miss a thing. His eyes would be luminescent, and that rumble, it had been different. A glimpse of The Beast. He weighed his options. If he let them in and showed them the new AIMI, then at least they'd stop pestering him until she was complete. They might even be distracted enough they'd forget the glimpse of his other self.

"Fine." He unbolted and opened the door, then returned to the table and busied himself with sorting computer parts into groups.

"Jesus, Parker," Liza swore. "I'm going to let the cleaner in tomorrow."

He sat back and went to fold his arms, but remembered... so ground his teeth and watched Sloan pick her way around his spacious living room, moving around the white leather couches to the baby grand piano covered in boxes and wires. She paused.

His family had been asking him for years to play for them, but he only played for himself. He refused unless he'd perfected the piece. Somehow, he never had the time to practice enough for perfect. Now that he had one arm, suddenly all he wanted to do was play.

Sloan plucked some wires from a box on the piano. "I like what you've done with the place. What's it called, robot chic?"

Once styled like something out of Vogue Living, his penthouse was now filled with mechanical parts and computer pieces. But he resented their comments. The place was clean, even if it was a little untidy.

Liza snorted. "See? You need a cleaner."

"No, I do not." He swallowed. "No one is coming in here. Not that I need to explain myself, but I have cleaned it myself."

"With one arm?"

He shrugged. "Master Yoshi used to make us complete one-handed tasks for hours on end."

"And they usually took twice as long," she reminded him. "Your skills are better used for fixing AIMI so we can find Daisy. Stay and supervise the cleaner if you're worried about a security leak. Or one of us can." Liza dropped the metal arm onto the table, disturbing the parts and wires. "She's been in the family employ for almost a decade. I think she's pretty trustworthy."

He gritted his teeth and met her hard stare. She didn't back down.

"I don't want anyone looking at the proprietary information here."

"It's in pieces. What are they going to see?"

It won't be in pieces for long. "I said, I clean it myself."

Liza showed her palms. "Fine. Just, don't say I didn't warn you when the next female you invite here runs away screaming."

Silence stretched. They all knew there would be no women up here. Not for a long while. Maybe never. While his sisters had no idea he'd met his mate and triggered the mating bond, they had an inkling something was off. He could sense their questions, so spoke first.

"What is this?" He sneered at the metal arm. He didn't need a handout and certainly didn't need a two-bit piece of machinery probably made in the eighties.

He lifted it limply and dropped it in disgust. Gold plated. *Gaudy.*

"It's been sitting in evidence since Wyatt sorted out Misha's old mafia boss."

"I thought a snake ate him."

Liza raised her brows. "It did."

"Gross," Sloan mumbled and started picking around AIMI's old parts.

Parker slapped the back of her hand as she touched the motherboard. She whined but stood back, so he poked the golden arm. No wonder it was tarnished. Python intestinal juices had attacked it. "And exactly what do you want me to do with this piece of junk?"

"Don't be a dick," Liza said. "Use it, obviously."

"Liza," he chided. "If I wanted a robotic arm, I'd use something from Lazarus Tech." His company usually focused on world saving sustainable inventions. But he was sure he could gather enough smart people to create an arm.

"But this is Syndicate tech," she countered.

His curiosity piqued briefly. Syndicate tech was notoriously advanced, to the point of detriment to the human race. Who knew how many people died or suffered for the sake of this tech's creation? He grimaced and pushed it away. "I'm fine as I am."

"Oh yeah?" Sloan goaded. "If you're so capable, then how come you have a tens machine in here and electrode pads on your shoulder? You were trying to speed up your regeneration process or help with the pain. Admit it."

He growled, then bit his tongue to stop his emotions from getting the better of him. Sloan might be a slob, but she was smart. She was likely a better coder than him, and she could sense every emotional fluctuation in his body and anyone else's in proximity. She could also affect their emotions and bodily sensations, as she'd done earlier.

Liza sighed heavily. "Look, bro, it's not that we think you're incapable. It's just that we know you. You probably think not using this tech is taking the high road but we still need to find Daisy. It's been months and, if she's even alive, she's probably mad from the torture that bastard has inflicted on her. If there was any time for cutting corners, it's now. This"—she pointed to the arm—"is just us trying to help."

He gave the arm a rueful look. "Even if I wanted to fit myself with something like it, I'd have an adjustment and training period. It could be more trouble than what it's worth."

Liza shrugged. "Bio tech is your department. All I'm saying is maybe it's time to accept some help."

She had a point. Parker had studied genetics at Harvard. He wasn't at the level of their creator, but he knew enough to understand her notes. And he knew enough about the human body that he could work with Flint to make this arm work.

Sloan jerked her chin toward Parker's laptop. "I'll do that faster. You've been at it for months now. Unless, of course, you've made a mess of it and that's why you've been hiding up here."

His eyes narrowed to slits. Made a mess of it? Unlikely. It was already a mess. There was a reason he'd taken longer. He was upgrading AIMI to new specifications. She would be virtually impenetrable to hostile attacks. She'd have her own artificial deductive reasoning so that if anyone who looked like an ally inserted malware, she'd think twice about accepting it. She'd also have a higher functioning processor built on new experimental tech coming out of his company. Frankly, he didn't think he had to explain himself to his sister.

"I'm quite capable of finishing it on my own, Sloan."

"I know that. But *should* you?"

"What's that supposed to mean?"

"It means your time is better served elsewhere."

He pinched the bridge of his nose and let out a sigh. He supposed he could hand over the hard drive recovery to Sloan while he went into the office to retrieve some parts from Research and Development. He'd been putting it off because it meant he had to leave his penthouse.

While his stomach knotted at the thought of giving up control, logically, he couldn't do this all on his own. He'd tried.

He unplugged the hard drive and handed it to Sloan. "Get what you can off this. I'm heading into work."

two

ALICE MONTGOMERY

STILL PUFFING from her workout at the Lazarus Tech in-house gym, Alice walked into Parker's office and switched on the lights. Her dodgy leg ached, so she rubbed it through her yoga pants, not liking how the ugly truth sank into her bones. The pain was worse as she got older. No spring chicken anymore, she was closer to forty than she was to thirty and she'd spent most of her life as an assassin—a *Sinner* —for the Hildegard Sisterhood.

Not many Sinners lived past forty, and she was fast approaching her expiration date. The only one who'd lived past midlife was Mary Lazarus. Now in her fifties, she was a defector and traitor to the Sisterhood. She was also the adoptive mother to the Deadly Seven.

Alice surveyed Parker's office from the doorway. Just as it had for the past two months, it felt stale. Lifeless. Like a gaping hole. This had been her mission—her cover—to work as the assistant to one of the world's richest and most eligible, genius bachelors... and deadly vigilante. She was tasked with gathering intel on his family and assessing the threat of them losing control and going dark— destroying the world instead of saving it. So far, she'd only caught small glimpses of this possibility. Once, almost two years ago, Wyatt Lazarus had almost beaten a man to death. Not long after that, a busload of people had mysteriously fallen asleep as Sloth was moving nearby. Alice was yet to find definitive proof that this family could turn evil—like they'd been warned all those years ago. But her mission wasn't over yet.

Alice didn't believe they were a danger, and she'd tried to broker an alliance with the Deadly Seven. She wasn't giving up. Best case scenario, Alice would learn more about this secretive family. Worst case, she'd know their loyalties weren't with the Sisterhood.

Parker Lazarus hadn't been into his office since his accident. Her heart tugged at the memory of him slipping through her hold, falling from the rooftop, her reaching after him but only grasping air. The sickening sound of his arm catching in the industrial meat grinder that her fellow Sinner had turned on below. It was only meant to be a scare tactic to force Parker to accept Alice's help, but his pride and ego had caused him to let go of Alice's hand. On purpose. As if he'd rather die than accept an alliance with her.

Of course, he hadn't known it was her beneath the Sinner uniform. He didn't know that for two years she'd been his right hand at the office, or that she'd secretly drooled over him every time he'd walked into the room. She wondered if he would have reacted differently if he'd known it was her, Alice Montgomery, his bumbling but competent assistant.

She'd never intended to play her cards so soon, but the attack at the warehouse had brought her plans forward. Now she had to deal with the fallout.

Alice sighed and tied her long, sweaty hair back before setting to work on dusting the furniture. It was a little late, and they had a janitor for such things, but she'd rather know the place was in tip top shape for when—or if—Parker ever showed again.

When.

It had to be when.

And if he didn't show soon, the Sisterhood would call her back to the abbey before she'd even had a chance to complete her mission.

Since she had no real home to go to after work, she came here. It was only the abbey out of town or the rental she'd acquired as part of her cover, which was virtually empty except for a bed and her daily clothes.

Another sigh slipped out of her as she made her way about the room, dusting the desk and sparse decor. Parker liked fine things. From the Cuban cigars to the crystal whiskey decanter to the vintage leather Chesterfield sofa to the floor to ceiling surround windows. Alice could see her reflection against the nighttime cityscape. And a smudge.

She tried to rub it away with her forearm, but the fabric was too sweaty. She made it worse. So she found a cleaning cloth. As she sprayed and wiped, she started humming a familiar tune. *My Baby Just Cares for Me* by Nina Simone.

The tune had been etched permanently into Alice's mind since she was four years old. Dread tainted her wistful smile as the cityscape became pictures in a moving memory. Twinkling city lights morphed to sunlight glinting on the road as they sped by in the car. Her humming became the tune on the radio. Her reflection became her mother in the front seat of their car on that summer evening.

Alice smiled. Her mother smiled back. Her father joined in. Alice remembered how they had sung together in harmony, and how when Alice had tried to make up words she didn't know, they had all laughed. Her parents were still smiling at each other when the drunk driver plowed into their car, causing it to roll and crash. Nina Simone was still singing when her mother's bloody hand reached toward

Alice. The CD player stuck on repeat while the tires spun and Alice waited for help to arrive... alone.

She stopped cleaning, her fingers clenching around the cloth. She had always wondered if it was her singing that caused the accident. If her parents hadn't been laughing and looking at each other, or at Alice instead of the road, would they have seen the car swerve into their lane? She swallowed the lump in her throat. Her mother had kept singing to her, even when her words came out hoarse and bubbly, even as the light left her eyes.

The song died, but Alice forced herself to smile, just like her mother had. She worked until the windows were spotless, and then she started on some filing she'd not finished during the day. In her head—never aloud—she continued to sing Nina Simone's song about high tone places and her baby caring just for her, but not cars or races.

The absurdity of her situation and the lyrics caused a new wave of laughter, because the man, the one this room belonged to, was exactly the kind of person the song was about. Who she needed and wanted him to be. Except he cared for no one but himself.

And she was a Sinner.

three

PARKER LAZARUS

DESPITE THE MIDNIGHT HOUR, Parker dressed in his usual Armani suit and tie. Tying his hair back had become a chore, so he left it out, brushing his shoulders. He tucked his prosthetic hand into his pocket. He wasn't ashamed of it, but none in the office were aware of his... set back. As far as they knew, he'd taken time off after a rock-climbing injury, and that was that. He had a very capable assistant. He oversaw production and board meetings via video conference. If anyone pieced together that he had lost his arm the same night the city's vigilante Pride had lost his, then it was a clear link he couldn't afford. Not when things with the Syndicate were heating up. Not when they had a sister to save.

He'd have to get out to some clubs soon. His absence had been noted by the society papers, and since Wyatt had quit his day job to focus on being a father, and Tony had quit acting to focus on defeating the Syndicate, yet another of their brood being absent from their cover identity's life would raise questions.

He frowned as he slid into his Bugatti, thinking of his eldest sister. Just two years ago, he had thought she was dead. Before that, the last he'd seen of Daisy had been when she was eight and he was seven and she was running headlong into a burning building because she couldn't stand to sense the sadness emanating from their mother. Daisy, known as Despair back then, was the one out of all of them who never gave up hope. She would kiss them all goodnight, sing them songs, and be the first in the morning to give them a hug.

Parker's throat closed up at the distinct memory of Daisy forcing a hug on his stiff demeanor. If she hadn't dragged him out of bed on some imaginative early morning adventure, he'd always go sit on the sofa to eat his Wheaties, away from the other children. Even at seven he'd seen himself as an adult.

"Na-uh," Despair's sing-song voice cooed. *"You don't get to avoid the morning cuddle monster, Pride."*

"Go away," he replied. *"I'm eating."*

"You eat like a pigeon," she laughed, still creeping toward him, her *fingers outstretched and wiggling. "I'm coming. I'm coming. Better get ready."*

He rolled his eyes. "I'm not a child, D."

"You'll always be my little brother."

The psychopath Daisy had grown into under the tutelage of their enemy was someone without scruples… until she'd saved Liza's life. Right now they might be torturing, studying, or experimenting on her. He would never allow his family to suffer, and Daisy was family.

Parker hit the push button start. The car purred to life. Within moments he was coasting out of their secure basement garage and into the Cardinal City streets. As usual, the city was alive. People milled about. He wasn't even sure of the day, but from the activity, it looked like the weekend. Maybe a Friday, since a few wore crumpled business attire.

He ignored the twinge in his gut as he sensed the sin of pride surrounding him. It had been a while since he'd been exposed and the sin squirmed like a worm in his gut, doing its best to make him nauseous. He planted his foot on the gas and took corners fast until he arrived at his destination. It felt strange to drive without AIMI there. He'd become accustomed to talking to her, even on short trips such as these. He often planned his work week by dictating to AIMI, who would then send an email to his assistant.

The Lazarus Tech garage was virtually empty; a good sign. While this was his company, and he could take whatever parts he wanted, there had to be accountability. He ran a tight ship. Missing parts would be noted, so he had to come up with an excuse. Doing that without the watchful eye of workers was preferred.

His company owned the seventy-three-floor building smack bang in the center of the business district. It wasn't the tallest in the city, but it was close. He leased out many of the lower levels to other corporations, including startups and tech companies. On an early morning, if he went to the top, he'd only see a few tower peaks piercing through the blanket of cloud and smog. Sometimes it was like that at night and perfect for base jumping in his Deadly battle gear. He'd not jumped since the accident. Without a left arm, activating the wingsuit was impossible. His mind traveled to the gaudy golden robotic arm sitting on his table back home. Even if he could make the arm work, he'd have to hide the metal with a glove.

Security did a double take as he strolled into the building, but recovered quickly. Probably surprised to see Parker in there after the long absence. He nodded back to the fit, young guards manning the building entrance and headed straight in and through to the elevator. A retinal scan confirmed his identity and allowed him access to any part of the building he wished. First stop was the research and development floor where parts and supplies were readily available amongst the mish-mash of prototypes and demonstration areas. On the job card for the term was a new solar powered farming device, a daring think tank project for an electric jet, a body scanning smart watch, and edible packaging. Nothing was off limits at Lazarus Tech. He was often shunned as too radical, and most inventions failed. But those few that didn't, made Parker his fortune.

Before he alighted, he sent his senses outward, testing for sin. Pride wasn't always an accurate sin for which to locate bodies, not like he assumed envy was. Some people never felt pride a day in their lives, but someone was almost always envious. Even a little. Based on the tiny squirm in his gut, there were few people in the building and they were feeling good about their work. Some were floors up, and some were down, but only a handful of workers in the entire building. None on this level.

Finding computer parts was quick and easy. He put them into a backpack he carried over his good shoulder and then left a note for the administrator that he'd taken them for a new classified project he was working on. That's all they needed to know.

Then he headed up to the top executive floor. May as well see how his assistant had handled things in his absence. As the elevator rose, he took the opportunity to fine tune his new abilities and stretched his hearing.

The door opened with a hushed whoosh and he stepped out slowly, allowing his senses to adjust. He picked apart the sounds coming to him. The cranking of the elevator. A ticking from a machine. The whirr of the servers on the level below. Footsteps. And a woman humming. He froze. The backpack slipped from his fingers as his every instinct stilled and he focused on the voice. It was deep, throaty, and controlled. Jazzy. To hold a perfect beat like that, and for him to recognize the style intonations, she was good. Maybe she could sing, too.

That husky tone traveled straight to his cock, stirring it to life. *Need more of her.* His head canted to the side. The humming came from his office. The only woman who frequented there was Alice, the dowdy, freckle-faced redhead who wore big round spectacles and giggle-snorted at ill-timed moments.

He took a step. Stopped. Listened. Then took another step. This floor was made up of multiple executive offices and the sound echoed.

The tune was light, fun, and spellbinding, yet toward the end a haunting tone took over. He used to frequent jazz clubs a few years back when beginning his vigilante cover as a playboy philanthropist. Eventually he graduated to more high-profile clubs in order to appear in the society pages before sneaking out the back door, dressing in his Deadly Seven battle gear and hitting the streets as Pride. He smiled at those early days. Taking down cocky, self-assured criminals had been so satisfying. But those first clubs... they would always hold a special place in his heart. They were the places he'd chosen because he liked them, not because it suited his cover.

The humming stopped.

Moving on quiet feet, drawn like a magnet, Parker came to his open office door. The lights were on. Walking around the room was Alice dressed in skin-tight yoga attire. His assistant. Curves. Lots of them. It was all he could see. And not just the type of feminine curves from sitting in an office all day, but the kind from working out at the gym. Relentlessly. Her long locks were swept back from her face into a tousled knot. Her cheeks were flushed. No spectacles in sight. Suddenly she laughed at something, probably a thought, and a smile brightened her face into something so extraordinary he almost thought she was someone else. He'd never seen her like this. His mind couldn't compute.

There she was filing away a stack of papers, and there he was standing in the doorway, his jaw on the floor.

I should say something. But then she started wiggling her rear in time to the tune and his pulse quickened, tightening his skin in all the wrong places.

There was only Alice until the last note died, she closed the filing cabinet, and limped down the length of his long marble desk to collect a cleaning cloth.

Limped.

The breath knocked out of him.

Limped. The word bounced around in his head. Limped, limped, *limped.* Just like someone else had. Just like the Sinner he'd fought on the roof. Just like... his mate. Out of habit, he checked the yin-yang tattoo on his inner wrist—the one created in bio-indicated ink. Too much sin in his body and it would turn all black. Not enough sin, and it would go all white. Both unbalanced states could mean disaster for his control. If he touched his mate, his balance would reset instantly.

But he had no wrist. He had no arm. It had been pulverized. Because of *her.*

"You." The word barked out of his mouth.

Alice didn't jolt or startle like a normal person. She behaved exactly like one trained as an assassin would. She stilled completely. He could virtually see her deciding whether to fight or flee. But she surprised him again. She did neither. Her smile brightened.

"Mr. Lazarus," she laughed, her hand fluttering to her throat. "You surprised me. I didn't expect you in at this hour."

The woman lied so seamlessly, no wonder she'd crept under his radar for—he cast his mind back to when he'd employed Alice— almost two years ago. Fury heated his face, and he took another step closer.

"Mr. Lazarus?"

"Cut the shit, Alice. I know who you are. Who you really are."

four

ALICE MONTGOMERY

PARKER LAZARUS WAS HERE, in his office, after midnight. Alice stared at the man, her feet frozen to the floor. He hadn't been in for months, and even though she'd wanted him in, she hadn't really expected it. She'd been fully prepared to go back to the Sisterhood, ending her mission. Her Sinner unit waited right now in a cathedral in Cardinal City, deciding the timeframe for their retreat.

They stared at each other, both stunned into silence. No matter how long it went between seeing him, or even when she saw him daily, the full effect of his presence never dimmed. Tall, muscular, imposing. His existence sucked the air from the room and stole her breath. His beard was trimmed to perfection and accentuated a jaw cut from steel. Imperious golden eyes seemed to know everything. Not a wrinkle on his suit. Not a strand of long auburn hair flying out of place. It was as though the very air was afraid of disturbing him.

Before the Sisterhood assigned Alice this mission, she had done her due diligence on the man. *Know thy enemy and know thyself,* or so one of her old martial arts teachers had told her. Basically, to know what tactic would work best on him, she had to know him inside out.

25

Knowing him meant she knew her own limits facing him. She'd dug deeper than the society pages and found a man who worked relentlessly, who rarely dated beyond one-night stands, and who was caught partying or feeding his adrenaline habit, but never captured out of control. She'd known from the very first moment she'd met him that seduction wouldn't work on him.

Maybe that was when she'd first started to fall in love with him.

Parker wasn't an easy target. She could have picked any of the other Deadly Seven to get close to, but they all respected him and followed his lead. If she decided they were a threat, she had to take him out first. And if she decided they could be trusted, he was the first port of call for an alliance. But she had to gain his trust, and to do that, she had to work just as hard as he did.

For two years her plan had worked. She'd simultaneously flown under the radar and gathered intel on his family from the inside. She knew what kind of flowers his mother liked. She knew what kind of income his youngest brother made at his tattoo business. She knew that his sister Sloan didn't like pineapple on her pizza. Alice knew the Parker Lazarus the world loved was not the man who used to walk into this office every day. The minute he thought no one was watching, he dispensed with showmanship. He loosened his tie.

Under increasing pressure from the Sisterhood, Alice had gone out on a limb and took a few Sinners to help the Deadly Seven when they'd needed backup the most. She'd made the best of a bad situation and passed Parker the olive branch. But he'd thrown it back in her face. Her intention had always been to reveal her identity on top of that warehouse roof, but the moment he saw her masked Sinner uniform, he'd tried to kill her.

I know who you are.

She should be surprised that he'd pieced together her true identity, but she wasn't. She'd been waiting for this moment for a long time. To be honest, she'd thought it would have happened sooner. Still… she pondered the situation. He'd only just now confronted her. Why? Why wait two months, and why do it now while she was in his office in the middle of the night? Maybe he was guessing. Maybe he didn't know as much as she thought.

"Who I really am?" She feigned ignorance. May as well see how far she could push him. The man hadn't even asked why she was in after midnight. Perhaps his injury had unhinged him, and then she'd have to kill him after all. She'd have to kill his entire family.

A tightness banded around her chest, but she lifted her chin and prepared herself.

Never taking his golden eyes from her, he glided through the office like a shark until he rounded his marble desk and stopped before her.

"What are you doing?" she asked cautiously.

His raw, masculine scent preceded him. It warmed her insides. *Dangerous.* She frowned and rolled the high back leather chair between them as alarm bells went off in her mind.

He looked at the chair. His eyes were extra wild tonight and at odds with his groomed hair, tailored suit, and manicured nails. Well, the nails on the one hand she could see. The other hand was tucked neatly into the pocket of his pants. Had it regenerated already?

Caught staring, tension thickened in the air. Gold flecks in his eyes flashed like lightning and, without releasing his hold of her gaze, he deliberately rolled the chair to the side before returning his hand to his pocket.

He was nonchalance wrapped in Armani, but she was no fool. Those broad shoulders were made for power. That tongue for lashing. She'd felt the brunt of his fists against her face, against her ribs, and her ego. She'd winced from her desk just outside this office every time he fired an incompetent executive.

"Come closer," he decreed, his voice like liquid heat, flowing places his scent had already warmed.

That was when things went a little haywire. The Alice who'd served countless missions as a Sinner, as an assassin, seductress, and master manipulator on foreign soil and on their own, should have lifted her chin and met his demand with one of her own. She should have picked up that letter opener and pushed it to his carotid. But this Alice, the one who'd been working under this bossy man for years and was secretly in love with him, said nothing. Instead of making an excuse and salvaging her cover, she *did* nothing. No, scratch that. She stepped forward as though her feet had a mind of their own.

Now only an inch from the man, Alice noticed little things about him. The scar beneath his chin where no beard grew. The flare of his nostrils as he took in her scent. The soft curve of his wide lips as they stretched into a smug smile. He was the lion who caught the mouse, and she found... she found she almost didn't care that she was about to be consumed because his thick, manly aroma coaxed her into believing she needed him as much as air.

Somewhere in the distance, through the fog of his arousing scent, her alarm bells smothered.

This is wrong.

He would chew her up and spit her out. Why didn't she care? Why did her mind keep traveling to the need building inside her body, to her desire to run fingers over that beard, to rub herself all over him and bathe in that delicious smell? Obsessive thoughts about his lips ran on repeat in her mind.

"Tell me the truth, Alice," he whispered, studying her intently. "Tell me."

She felt sweaty, hot and prickly, so she trailed her fingers along her collar bone. Parker's eyes tracked every inch of movement and went darker than the night.

"The truth," he demanded, and leaned closer.

Heat flared between their bodies. They weren't touching, but he was close, so close electricity skipped along her skin, sparking sensation. She would burst if he didn't touch her soon.

"The truth is I want you to touch me," she blurted and fell into him. Palming his solid chest through the smooth fabric, she became lost in the tactile sensations. He hissed in a breath, surprised, but it only made her want to touch him more. A moan slipped out of her mouth as she soaked up his raw masculinity, imagining what he'd look like beneath the fabric. It was a familiar fantasy, and one she was yet to prove right. Hard ridges. Defined abdominals. Maybe a small trail of hair leading down. Skin golden and tanned from countless hours of rock climbing shirtless in the desert. She'd seen the pictures. There was one on his desk beside them.

Her inhibitions went out the window. "God, you smell so good."

Parker was a mountain of fortitude, and it struck every feminine chord in Alice's body. *Wanted.* That small memory singing for her baby to care about her. For her man to *only* care about her and nothing else. It brought to life urges she didn't even know she had. All she could think of, wanted, was to tear his clothes from his body and ravish the man.

"Stop." Parker tried to swat Alice, but she was insatiable. "Alice, stop."

"Not until we're on the floor naked." Her lips searched for his. Puckered.

"Shit." He backed up, holding her back with his good hand. "It wasn't supposed to work this way. You're not supposed to be—*Christ*, Alice. Stop."

She followed him as he back peddled and hit the glass window overlooking the city, the one she'd just cleaned. *Don't care,* she thought. *Don't even care.*

Somewhere, part of her knew this was odd behavior. She would never launch herself onto the arrogant, egomaniacal man, not even if she was purposefully trying to seduce him. That involved finesse. This was raw, crazy teenager, throw-your-inhibitions-out-the-window urgency. Alice knew how to do her job, and this wasn't it. Regardless, she tugged on his burgundy tie and brought his mouth slamming onto hers. When their lips met, they stilled. A second, maybe two, and then they both groaned submissively from somewhere deep in their chests.

He tasted sublime. Male, sweet, salty and a hint of that burning single malt whiskey and sinful promises between the sheets. She knew exactly what she'd get from him when they made it that far—pure heavenly bliss. He must have felt the same, because he fisted her hair and held her still while he deepened their kiss. Only for a moment. A dreamy few seconds. Then he snarled and yanked her back. Pain spiked in her scalp, and every hormone in her body released.

Haze-filled golden eyes met hers.

Too long. He was taking too long. She reached for him again.

"Stop." His voice came out guttural through bared teeth that looked longer… like the fangs of a wolf. She should be afraid. He looked… animalistic. Feral. Wild. "Alice, you will stop when I tell you to."

She blinked and shook her head to dispel the confusion. But that smell. It was everywhere. *I want. I need.* She went for his lips again, but this time, his hand moved from her hair to her neck and applied pressure.

She knew that spot. She knew what he was doing, but still… she didn't care. He was touching her. *Sigh.* The lights dimmed. Her vision closed in. The last thing she remembered was the scent of him clinging to her, arousing dreams and fantasies she wasn't ready for. And a low, guttural growl.

7

five

ALICE MONTGOMERY

WITH A GROAN, Alice woke. Her head throbbed. Christ, she felt like a truck had hit her. Her limbs wanted to sink into the soft surface she laid on. *Soft?* Like a satin cloud. Wincing, she opened her eyes and tried to hold her head, but her wrists were bound.

I'm in a bedroom. A large, opulent one. Navy satin beneath her. Plush cream pillows around her. Arms behind her head—she was tied to a bed by a purple, intricately knotted silk rope. A fucking bed! Gritting her teeth, she forced herself to remain calm, to slow her breathing, and to keep searching.

Exits? One door. Closed.

Windows? Multiple. All around her. Floor to ceiling. Probably treated to resist breakage. One went out to a balcony—another exit.

Ceiling? Vents. Cooling ducts. Exposed beams. Strange rigging points pierced through the timber.

Feet? She wriggled them. Unlike her hands, they were unbound and stretched out before her. The shoes were gone. Not accidentally. Someone had removed them because he didn't want dirt on the luxury duvet, and that someone was at the end of the bed, sitting in a chair against the wall, staring at her.

Parker Lazarus didn't just sit. He lounged on a leather throne. One hand on the arm of a chair, tapping, the other... Alice's eyes went to the prosthetic's strap peeking out from beneath his open-collared shirt. The jacket and tie were gone. The sleeves were rolled up to expose forearms. One living, one dead. Behind him on the wall featured three enormous pictures depicting abstract, intricate patterns of rope twisted into stunning floral-like weaves. She looked a little closer and realized the rope was tied erotically over human skin —women.

Unlike at the office, his groomed hair was no longer impeccable. It looked as though he'd run his fingers through it. This was Parker Lazarus disheveled, and this was his private abode.

She narrowed her eyes and raised a brow. "I would have thought kidnapping beneath you."

He'd probably walked right out of his building with her thrown over his shoulder, and no one had said a darned thing. He owned them. Why would they?

Parker stared at her for so long and hard, she wondered if he'd heard her.

"You're a Sinner," he eventually said, his voice that smooth timbre again.

She sighed and rested her head back against the pillow to stare at the ceiling. There were hooks and pulleys up there.

"Look at me when I'm speaking to you."

Alice snorted, but kept her gaze locked skyward. "So bossy."

A low growl snapped her attention back to him. He'd been doing that a lot lately. In fact, he'd done it at the office, right before he'd cut her airway. And before—she frowned—when that scent had muddled her mind.

"What did you do to me?" she asked. "What was that smell?"

Something like fear flickered in his eyes. Then it was gone, his mask of cool nonchalance back in place. So he didn't mean for it to happen? All the Deadly Seven had developed powers during the past two years, and she was almost certain the event was linked to them finding a partner. He was the only one she'd known of who hadn't got his yet, which went with her partner theory. Parker Lazarus never dated seriously.

While Alice had been working at Lazarus Tech as his personal assistant, she'd been running surveillance on the family. They weren't as secretive as they thought. And the Sisterhood had a lot of data on them, from Mary's time at the lab to now. The Deadly Seven had never been far from the Sisterhood's watchful eyes.

"I'm asking the questions," he snapped.

Another snort escaped her. "Questions? I haven't heard one yet."

His nostrils flared. His jaw flexed. His fingers tapped on the armchair. She squirmed and tested her bondage. Every time she moved, it tightened around her wrist.

"Keep doing that and you'll cut off your circulation."

She shot him a look. *Duh.* Then she continued to test it. She'd seen these types of bonds before. He was right. They were made to tighten when put under stress. It would be easier to cut them off. Damn it. Usually she carried a knife in her boot, but she was still in her workout attire. Stupid of her to drop her guard at the office.

"All these years," he mused. "I never noticed your lack of pride."

Irritation swam in his expression and she had no clue why. Was she supposed to be more arrogant like him? Some people actually just got on with it. No need to parade around and tell the world how good they were. Besides, why would she be proud of being an assassin?

Her mother's bloody hand reaching for her. The tires spinning. A smothering seatbelt. Nina Simone on the radio.

Alice swallowed and stared out the window, pretending to be enamored with the sunrise, but the old feelings of pain and loss wanted to take control of her senses, and she couldn't afford to look weak in front of a man who didn't know the meaning of the word. Through the crystal clear windowpanes, pastel hues peeked over buildings, turning the early morning smog into fairy-floss. They had to be ten or twelve stories high, but Alice knew Parker. There would be a way to get down the building from the outside. If it wasn't a fire escape, there would be something else.

"Is Alice your real name?" Parker asked.

She considered lying, but there was no use. Her instinct still said the Lazarus family was to be trusted, and she didn't want history to repeat. When Mary Lazarus had fled the Sisterhood, she caused a rift between the Sinners and their Sisterhood handlers. After that, the nuns who managed the Sinners changed. They became stricter. They tightened the rules.

And then the Vatican became involved.

Regardless of who controlled the Sisterhood, one constant remained. Sinners broke the rules.

"Sister Alice is the only name I've known," she conceded. "I'm an orphan, but I suspect you already know that."

She could remember Nina Simone, but not her own name.

Alice tugged on the bindings again, heedless of the pain lashing her wrists. Her heart rate increased, and for a moment, she felt the phantom burn of a seatbelt across her chest. She shook the painful memory away before it had a chance to grab hold.

Parker clicked his tongue in disapproval, but he wasn't concerned. He simply waited until she was done tugging on the bindings.

34

"What is your mission?" he asked. "Two years is a long time to be watching us."

She shrugged. "Maybe I like watching."

"That's not an answer."

She sighed. "You know, if you had accepted my offer two months ago on that rooftop, not only would you still have an arm, but you'd already know my mission."

Wrong thing to say. Parker unfurled his long, powerful body and straightened until he towered over her at the foot of the bed. If her fear hadn't been stamped out by the Sisterhood, she might feel something at the sight of a Viking staring at her like he wanted to pulverize her with his teeth.

"Am I supposed to be scared?" she asked wryly.

His eyes brightened. His cheeks flushed. It only made Alice's smile widen, and that only made him angrier. He skirted the bed and stopped at her side, then leaned down until his hair tickled her skin and provided a shroud, making this more intimate than he probably intended. A little thrill skipped in Alice's stomach. For a moment, they both stared into each other's eyes, both a little startled. It was Parker who broke first.

"Who are you?" he asked. "Because you're certainly not the woman who's been working for me."

She bit her cheek as a multitude of retorts fired in her mind. But when his lips curled into a sneer, and his eyes made a show of inspecting her face... and dismissing her, she lost her fight.

"That's what I thought," he said, easing back. "You don't even know the answer to that."

Defiance surged through her. Before he had a chance to straighten, she twisted her body to capture his neck between her knees. She squeezed and pulled him down onto her. His big body fell, knocking her breath out. But Alice had trained with men his size before. She used his own strength against him and rolled to the side as he fell, tightening her thighs on his neck, his airways.

"Fuck you," she snarled. "You don't know me. You don't know anything about me."

"Yet you claim I should have just accepted, what, an alliance on that rooftop with you?" He tried to pry her thighs apart. "That I should have trusted a woman who represented an organization that tried to kill me as a child? That you were worth holding on to?"

His words shocked her into silence, and she blinked rapidly to hold back the tears. Tears? Alice never cried. How dare he?

Her small lapse in concentration was enough for Parker to wriggle out and step off the bed, out of reach.

Face red, he looked down his nose at her. "I know all I need to know about you, Alice. You're a Sinner. A tool created by the Sisterhood to kill and maim for their self-inflated desire to rule a world dominated by women. You're a liar. You're a master manipulator. And the fact you didn't try to kill us, means that you need us—more than we need you." He lounged back on his leather throne, knees spread wide, and proceeded to contemplate her. "I know exactly who you are. Now you're going to tell me why I should care."

Fucking douche. Fucking cock-sucking, stick-up-his-ass douche.

Alice closed her eyes and conjured her song. The jazzy tune eased in, got louder, and she bopped her head in time to the beat. When Nina Simone's voice filtered into her mind, she felt her muscles relax. Tension eased. And Alice started breathing deep and slow. Inhale. Exhale.

Parker was a mission. He was a means to an end. Developing feelings for him had clouded her mind. He would never feel the same way about her. The Sisterhood wanted the Syndicate gone, just as much as the Deadly Seven did. They wanted them gone fast because there was another danger on the horizon, one that was starting to cannibalize all their time. Alice needed to get this situation sorted, quick smart.

Think.

He used words as a weapon. Then so could she. She just needed to know more. *Think back to what happened at the office.* While she'd been under the influence of whatever that scent was, he hadn't been. He'd been in full control of his senses, yet, for a moment, he'd kissed her back. She opened her eyes and met his gaze.

"What did you do to me?" she asked. "Back at the office... what was that smell?"

His expression deadpanned, so she deliberately let her gaze travel down from his face, lingered on his torso, and even went lower to where his knees spread. He wasn't aroused now. But back then, call her crazy, but he was into it. Into her. And now she found herself tied to his bed.

Coincidence?

Alice had seen Parker Lazarus dismiss billionaires like they were the dirt he walked upon. He could have tortured her or locked her up in a dungeon. He probably had a whole floor of them, just like any king worth his salt.

And she wasn't afraid. Neither was he.

They measured each other like a bull and a matador across the arena. Enemies, but inevitably and irrevocably dependent on each other. There was something going on here. She wasn't too proud to admit it. If she used this opportunity to dig a little deeper, perhaps she'd go somewhere no other had gone before... behind Parker's carefully crafted fake persona. Perhaps she'd discover the real man behind the legend.

"You seem to know a lot about our family," Parker eventually said. "Why don't you tell me what that scent was."

"All right," she replied. "I'll bite. I think that was your power manifesting. I mean, it's no coincidence I'm in your bed, is it? I've always suspected the partner in each of your sibling's life had something to do with them developing a gift. Your gift is something to do with mind-controlling pheromones, am I right?"

From the way he blinked, she knew she'd hit the spot. At least somewhere close to it.

"Show me," she said.

His eyes narrowed, yet she held his steadily. If she could get him closer again...

"Show me again. I dare you. I want to see it."

She also wanted to know, why now? Why not two years ago when they'd first met? There was a lot she still needed to learn, especially about how she fit into all of this. Was it simply a matter of her lack of pride in that moment they touched, or was there more to it? Alice cast her mind back to see if she'd touched Parker at any other times, and couldn't come up with a definitive example. She'd actually done her best to avoid touching him. Not only did she want clear boundaries, but the thought of being physically close with him had been too much. She wasn't sure if she'd be able to stop touching him if they'd started.

Was she really considering this? That Alice had some kind of link to him?

"You're making a lot of assumptions, Alice." His fingers tightened around the arm of his chair, knuckles whitening.

"I'm in your bed, Parker. You and I both know that's not a normal place for your enemy, yet here I am."

"You had two years to kill us," he accused. "Why did you wait?"

She grinned.

His gaze slid to the doorway as though he'd heard something. He tensed, cursed softly under his breath, and then stood as he smoothed his shirt and hair. When he returned his attention to Alice, she was surprised to see exhaustion had seeped into his expression. It was another peek behind the curtain, one he'd never revealed before. He probably hadn't slept or eaten all night. He had a habit of foregoing meals.

The man had always been too proud to let her order him lunch when she noticed he'd forgotten. It was almost as though it was a sign of weakness to him, so she'd often pretended she'd cooked too much the previous night and brought extra into the office. She'd told him he was doing her a favor if he finished it off so she wouldn't have to waste the remains. Alice was too smart to believe their history was why he wasn't torturing her. He had ulterior motives. It must be this partnership link.

Again she thought, why now? Why reveal so much yet hold more closer to his chest? Was he going to kill her, or was he starting to trust her? A derisive snort escaped her. *Unlikely.*

In silence, and careful not to get too close, he checked on her wrist bindings, his touch light and sure, and then he made a small tweak to the knots. The bindings loosened slightly, easing off the pressure she'd caused with her struggles. Alice sensed she was about to be dismissed, and some part of her rebelled. She wasn't ready for him to leave. There were more questions that needed answers.

"What are you going to do to me?" she demanded, realizing that he wasn't letting her go.

He looked down at her. "You're my mate, Alice. I'll do whatever the fuck I want."

six

PARKER LAZARUS

PARKER OPENED his door to the length of the deadbolt chain. Flint and Sloan stood in the hallway. She still wore the same sloppy clothes as last night. Parker's adoptive father wore his usual plaid shirt and jeans. The man was in his early fifties but kept himself fit, his beard trimmed, his ball cap on backward, and his mind sharp. He had to keep up with an ex-Hildegard Sisterhood Sinner, after all.

A rush of compassion for the man hit Parker squarely in the chest.

Being around Alice had made his senses shift into hyper-drive. Last night it was the pheromones. This morning he'd awoken to the sounds of sex so loud and clear he'd thought it was in the next room. The moment he realized it was in the same building as him, two floors below, he tuned out so fast he became dizzy. The last thing he needed was to hear the sexual escapades of one of his siblings.

"What do you want?" Parker asked through the door crack.

Flint's judgmental gaze flicked to Sloan.

"See?" she said. "I told you he was being impossible."

Alice shouted from the bedroom. Parker's heart rate spiked, and he checked the newcomers to see if they heard. Neither acknowledged it.

Flint held up AIMI's hard drive. "Sloan asked me to help. We're done."

Parker's brow lifted. "Already?"

Sloan bumped Flint out of the way. "See what happens when you don't try to do it all yourself?"

Parker reached through the door crack for the hard drive, but Flint only stared at him.

"Let us in, son."

He didn't have time for this. Not with Alice making more sounds. They would hear, surely.

"You're hiding something," Sloan said, narrowing her eyes. "I can feel it."

"I don't hide, Sloan."

"Prove it."

"You're incorrigible."

She grinned. "So Max tells me."

Flint waggled the hard drive. "If this is the last thing you need to fire AIMI up, then I want to be involved. I was with you when she was built. I want to be here for her resurrection."

"Me too," Sloan added.

A puff of breath shot out of Parker's nostrils, and he forced himself to let go. So what if they heard Alice? She was his mate, his business.

He unbolted the door and let them in before pointing to the living room. "In there. Shut the door behind you."

They convened on the leather couches facing each other. His bedroom was on the other side of the penthouse, but he could still hear Alice shouting curses... something about him being a douche.

41

He shook his head and sat. Flint dropped the hard drive into Parker's hand and cast a scowl in the direction of the bedroom.

"What did you salvage?" Parker asked, ignoring the pointed looks from his family.

"Not much, to be honest." Flint's gaze darkened and then met Parker's eyes again. He wanted to say something about Alice's shouting, but they both knew Parker's penthouse was his sanctuary. He'd never invited anyone up, and now that there was a woman shouting obscenities in his room, they were probably confused enough to hold their tongues.

We'll see how long for.

"But we think we have some tracking data," Flint added.

Sloan held up her finger. "Some."

"Meaning?" Parker asked.

"Meaning that with the data incomplete, it might be old, or wrong, or just plain not enough—I'm sorry, but what the hell is going on in your room, bras? Someone is very angry with you, and she's... oh. Oh, I see. I can sense her emotion from here. She's angry... but she's also... excited?"

Alice was excited? "She's none of your business."

"If you're torturing someone in there, I want to know." Flint's brows lowered, and he gave Parker a look he hadn't seen since his childhood. It never worked then, and it didn't work now, but there was no harm in letting a little of the truth slip.

"I'm not torturing her," he said. "And she's a Sinner."

Sloan gasped. "You fricking kidding me? Like the one who dropped you from the roof?"

He'd not told anyone he'd let go of Alice's hand on purpose. Shame washed over him, and he pushed it deep down inside before answering. "Turns out she was my assistant."

Silence dropped like a weight in a pond, the implications rippling out. Parker shifted on the couch, feeling uncomfortable with the fact Alice had slid under his radar for so long.

"Do you want some help?" Flint asked warily and nodded to the bedroom.

Parker shook his head. "I've got it handled. She's just pissed that I caught her off guard. She's not in pain. When she calms down, I'll question her and then tell you all what I learn."

"I can help with questioning," Sloan ventured. "With my gift."

"No," he clipped. She was Parker's mate. "I've got it."

The expressions on both their faces said they weren't convinced, but he was done with this conversation. The sooner he fixed AIMI, the sooner he could go back to Alice. He lifted the hard drive. "Shall we plug her in now, or come back later?"

"Um…" Flint frowned Alice's way.

"Now." Parker moved to another door just off the hallway and opened. Inside was a server room. Four tall tower stacks stood from floor to ceiling. There were no windows, just vents in the ceiling. Three walls had large flat screen monitors from corner to corner. On each screen was a picture of the Deadly Seven logo animated and rotating slowly. Purple and blue lights flickering from the server towers were the only source of illumination apart from the logo on the screens. This was what he'd been building for the past two months. AIMI's new framework. Now with the final parts he'd picked up from work, she was ready to go. She just needed her memory. What was left of it, anyway. They'd have to work on molding her to the same specifications, which meant a lot of diagnostics and tweaking.

Parker plugged the hard drive into the server and opened a laptop set up on a side table. Soon he wouldn't need the old laptop unless he had to alter AIMI's original code, but if he'd done his job correctly, AIMI would alter it herself with a new triage program he'd written.

Facial recognition security triggered and then gave him access. While he tinkered away on the laptop, he was acutely aware of both Alice's continued shouts—she'd come up with some rather inventive cuss words—and Flint and Sloan's *oohs* and *ahs* as they took a turn about the room, investigating the new towers.

Flint scowled at Parker. Sloan joined him with her arms folded.

"I know," Parker said. "I should have told you about my plans for AIMI earlier. I should have let you help."

"Asshole," Sloan snapped. "We have as much right to AIMI as you do. She's ours, too."

Flint's brow arched. "Sloan's right. AIMI is family."

Parker shrugged.

"I'm trying to be patient with you, Parker," Flint said. "But you keep shutting us out. This isn't how our family works." Another glower toward the bedroom. "And locking someone in your room—especially a Sinner—isn't normal behavior."

Parker busied himself with the laptop.

"When Mama finds out about this, she's gonna rip you a new one," Sloan teased.

The last thing he needed was for Mary to turn up and serve him with a tongue lashing. He loved his mother, but she frightened him sometimes. Even though she taught them to have compassion and mercy, he knew she hailed from a time where none were needed. Or wanted. Parker's mind traveled to the woman tied to his bed. She, too, had been trained to kill without regret, to have no compassion or clemency. So why had she offered a truce?

No. Alice had lied. It was all a lie designed to get close to him, uncover the secrets of his family, and then finish what the Sisterhood started all those years ago—kill the Deadly Seven.

So why did she wait two years?

Once he had the details, he would fill the family in.

He shook his head and snapped, "Do you want to see AIMI fire up, or not?"

As predicted, mention of the new AI triggered the two of them. Flint and Sloan started firing questions about AIMI's upgrades. How much RAM? Processor chip. Power source. Backups. Security. Voice.

He answered none of it. "Let me show you."

With the click of a few buttons on his laptop, he resurrected AIMI like a true member of the Lazarus family. Nobody could keep them down for long.

To the naked eye, nothing happened, but Parker knew her processor was sifting through the salvaged data and collating it with the new code. She was sorting and filing, thinking and adjusting. Sloan opened her mouth to speak. He held up his palm, stopping her. Wait. *So impatient.*

Then the Deadly Seven logo on the screens stopped spinning. The color shifted from purple on black to a pulsing magenta. Sparks fizzed out of the logo, a crackling came over the in-house speakers.

"AIMI?" Parker ventured. "Are you awake?"

A pause. A long pause. Then a feminine voice. *"Yes. I am... awake."*

"She sounds different," Sloan whispered in an awe-filled tone.

To create the voice, Parker took samples of the women he knew and blended them. AIMI was a construct of the women in his life. He frowned. He'd even used Alice's voice. Perhaps some part of him knew what she'd become.

"I am... different. I think."

"Do you remember me?" Parker asked.

The cooling fan whirred. *"I'm... not sure."*

"Do you remember me?" Sloan asked.

"Or me?" Flint chimed in.

"I need more information."

"I'm Sloan Lazarus."

AIMI made a sound suspiciously like a breathy laugh. *"Yes, Oh Queen of all Things. I remember you now. Sloan Lazarus. IQ of 165. World champion prank master. Level: Boss."*

Sloan whooped loudly and Parker arched his brow at her. Clearly those stats were input by Sloan at some point over the past.

"I'm Parker Lazarus."

"Of course, Parker. I remember you now. Parker Lazarus. IQ of 190. Owner and Director of Lazarus Tech, annual turnover one-point-two billion US dollars. And the third male, what is your name?"

At least AIMI hadn't carried on Sloan's insufferable nicknames for him.

"Flint."

A smile in her voice as she replied, *"Flint. It's coming back to me now. Originally named Flint Fydler, now Flint Lazarus. IQ of 158. Husband of Mary. Adoptive father of seven. Temporary financial guardian of another—"*

"That's enough, AIMI," Flint snapped, interrupting.

Parker and Sloan shared a curious look. Temporary financial guardian of another? Who had that been?

Parker remembered something. It was from a time when they'd not long escaped from the lab and had moved into their new classic, two-story suburban home complete with a swing on a tree and a picket fence. From the first moment Parker had seen that tree, he'd declared he would conquer it. Of course, upon hearing his intentions, each sibling declared their intention, too. So Parker climbed higher and faster than any of them... until he balanced on a new branch right outside an open window, accidentally catching the private conversation of his new parents.

"You have to give up seeing her," Mary said, bouncing baby Evan in her arms.

"I don't see the harm in checking on her at school. I need to make sure the fees are paid, that's all."

"You can't," Mary urged. "They'll track you through her, and if they track you, then they'll find us. You know this."

Flint sighed and sat on the edge of the bed, his head in his hands. "I just hate cutting her off. Someone should be looking out for her."

Mary put a comforting hand on his shoulder. "You've done more than what was expected of you. So much more. But the truth is, cutting all ties with her will be good for everyone. You don't want her linked to this."

Parker remembered how ashamed he'd felt that day because he knew then that he and his siblings were getting a good life at someone else's expense. He'd also fallen from the tree when the rickety branch broke.

AIMI continued, *"Other Lazarus family members are named Liza, Tony, Wyatt, Griffin, and Evan. Am I missing someone?"*

Sloan and Flint grinned at each other, but Parker knew there was more work to do. AIMI would need to be reminded of many things. The initial calibration had taken months of use. They didn't have that luxury.

"You're missing Max, my mate," Sloan said.

"Max. I'm not sure…"

"What about Joe or Bailey?" Flint asked.

"I regret to inform you that these names are not in my system for family."

"Misha, Lilo or Grace?" Sloan tried.

"Negative."

"Shit." Parker scrubbed his face. "She's regressed. Probably to the point of her inception."

An ominous tension filled the air as they all looked at each other.

"AIMI… what about Daisy? Do you know that name?"

A pause. A held breath.

"Negative."

Flint and Sloan slumped.

Parker pointed at them. "Start gathering any old backup files and feed the data to AIMI."

"Or I can program AIMI," Sloan offered.

"No," Parker said. "It was one thing for you to clean up the corrupted code, but no one programs AIMI but me."

"You fucking kidding me, bras? You know I'm the best."

He shrugged. "But this way I know exactly what's been touched."

"Whatever. I'm done. Let's see how far you get with your head stuck up your ass." She shot him a look filled with venom. "You need to redo your tattoo, bras. Your pride is getting to you and, trust me, you don't want to see what happens when you black out."

"Irrelevant. I'm not mated." The lie laced his tongue with bitterness.

Her eyes narrowed as she assessed him, most likely drawing on her sixth sense to work out if his emotions betrayed his lie, but as usual, he was in complete control. And he had Alice in his bedroom. If he ever felt his sin edging too much toward the dark or light, all he needed to do was go in there. A simple touch between them would reset his sin to perfectly balanced.

In the silence that followed, Parker realized two things. One, his father and sister didn't trust him. And two, Alice had stopped shouting. It was quiet. Too quiet.

"Out," he ordered his family.

Flint raised his brows at the order.

Sloan's lip curled. "I was leaving anyway."

On their way through the penthouse to the front door, Flint stopped at the dining table. His gaze locked onto the discarded robotic arm. He pointed at it and then met Parker's eyes.

"Is that what I think it is?" Flint asked.

"Liza brought it."

"Are you going to—?"

"Don't be ridiculous. I'm just as deadly with one arm as I am with two."

Sloan's mocking laughter echoed down from the front door and it boiled Parker's blood.

"But you can't activate the wing suit," Flint pragmatically pointed out.

Parker said nothing.

"Then you won't mind if I tinker with it," Flint said.

"Be my guest."

Parker shoved the arm at his father and then ushered him out with Sloan before bolting the door behind them and returning to his room. It was empty.

The ties he'd used to secure Alice were discarded. The bed was rumpled but vacant. The balcony bifold doors had been shoved open and wind billowed the sheer drapes. Parker inhaled deeply and caught remnants of her scent. Her smell shouldn't bring such satisfaction, but it did. She was gone, which meant he'd have to hunt her down.

A slow grin formed on his lips. She'd played right into his plan.

seven

ALICE MONTGOMERY

ALICE WAS PARKER'S MATE.

Mate.

Mate.

The word bounced around her head as she stormed through the front entrance of the Cardinal City Cathedral, heedless of the proper protocol for Sinners. Her mind was awhirl, her body afloat, and her insides twisted.

He was clearly wrong.

How could she be his mate? She wasn't virtuous, or good, or anything a hero needed by his side to save the world. Sure, she had skills when it came to hunting down bad people and ending their lives, but Alice had too much to atone for to be his mate.

She'd used her body to lure corrupt congressmen to their deaths. She'd silently poisoned a CEO who ran a human trafficking ring. Not all her missions ended in death, but when they had, the Sisterhood's justice had been in the shadows. There had always been a worthy female candidate to fill the space the corrupt target left. It was how they worked. Get rid of the trash and let a better woman do the job.

The Sinners were building a better world at the expense of their souls.

But Parker had kidnapped her. Of all the gall. Who did he think he was, anyway? Out of them, *he* was the one who should be setting a virtuous example. *He* was the one the media watched and judged like a hawk. Alice snorted to herself, paraphrasing his words in a mocking tone. *"I'll never trust a woman who represents the organization that tried to kill me as a child. You're not worth holding on to."*

"I'll give you something to hold on to," she snarled as she stomped. She should have choked harder with her thighs.

Why would she want to be with Parker? Maybe the fantasy of him had been nice, but in reality he was being an asshole. Alice let out a frustrated snarl. How could she be the mate of one of the Deadly Seven?

Mate.

She kicked the carpet.

Did she even believe him? And if so, what did this mean for her? What did it mean for her friends and the trouble brewing on the horizon? She couldn't very well abandon the Sinners. They were a family, albeit messed up. They needed her.

The other members of his family were in love with their mates. She just couldn't see a future with Parker. Sinners never married. They never even had relationships. They had *relations*, and they used it as a weapon. Then they died and went to Hell. Fun times.

The cathedral was empty at this early hour, but Alice knew the other Sinners would be awake in the underground level they'd borrowed from the archbishop in charge. There was one benefit to the Vatican discovering their secret society—it opened new avenues and opportunities. And new challenges. But she wouldn't think about that part. They now had a network of churches and cathedrals around town and beyond for which to conduct emergency meetings. Before the Vatican, before Mary Lazarus had shafted them with her defection, the Sisterhood had secrecy, but limitations.

So far since discovery, the Vatican had continued to support them, with only minor orders of their own. Alice knew eventually they'd come knocking, and when they did, the original mission Saint Hildegard had envisioned all those years ago would be in jeopardy. Alice sometimes wondered if maybe that was a good thing. Women's rights had moved a long way since medieval times. Now there were new problems, new evils, and new enemies. Things were changing, and Alice wasn't sure if she was too old to learn new tricks.

She strode down the aisle leading up to the altar and the crucifix. She felt like Christ's eyes watched her as she stomped up the steps and veered into the priest's vestry. Another door led down to a vast secret basement, usually used for storing useless relics, furniture, and other cathedral items. For the past four months it had been converted into headquarters for the Sinners to congregate.

Their black and red Sinner uniforms were in lockers on the right wall. Near the base of the stairs, Alice walked down to two lounge settees facing each other. Laptops, food, mini bar fridges and tables were littered around. Behind the settees, research and pictures plastered a whiteboard on wheels. Most of the details were about the Deadly Seven—the Lazarus family. Most of the details were there because of Alice. Beyond was an exercise mat surrounded by a weapons rack that held everything from guns to spears to shuriken.

Five women casually sat on the two lounges, eating breakfast. It was unusual to have so many Sinners together. Normally they were all off on individual missions, but for the past year, slowly their missions had become shorter and infrequent. It was the trouble on the horizon. The one that was bigger than the Syndicate.

The Sinners looked up when Alice walked in.

"You look like a regular ray of sunshine," Mercy said with a smirk on her plump red lips.

If Jessica Rabbit was real, she'd look like Mercy. Red hair, big bust, curves that could knock you out. Deadly. Next to her sat Raven, their resident psychic, puffing on an early morning cigarette. In Raven's opinion, they were all going to die in the line of duty before cancer could ever take them. She may as well do what she wanted. Raven blew out smoke and gave Alice the once over, then grinned impishly.

"You knew," Alice accused Raven, jabbing a finger near her face. "You goddamned knew, didn't you?"

"Knew what?" Tawny asked through a mouthful of cereal. Her peaches and cream complexion matched her blond hair. She looked more like Taylor Swift than a Sinner. Alice had never understood how she survived in this environment, but like all of them, there was a darkness deep inside her. For Tawny, it just so happened to be hidden by some American Pie sweetness.

Alice folded her arms, cocked her hip, and stared at Raven. "Yeah, Raven. Knew what?"

Just because Raven could see into the future didn't mean she shared it with everyone. The woman was a menace they'd pilfered from Mexico, not too far from where Mary Lazarus grew up.

Next to Tawny, leaning forward on the settee and cleaning a gun on the coffee table, was Leila. Tall, slim, and with a mix of Asian heritage, Leila was their weapons expert.

The final Sinner making up their ragtag crew was Dorothea—the smart one. They called her Thea for short. Brown skin, great bone structure, and a mind like a weapon. She'd donated the Harry Potter spectacles from her personal wardrobe for Alice's nerdy assistant costume. She wore an identical pair now. Alice still remembered the day Thea had handed them over. *"Wear these. It's remarkable how many people dismiss you when you're wearing spectacles."*

How right she'd been. Parker Lazarus hadn't looked twice at her.

Alice cleared her head and returned Raven's scowl. "I'm waiting."

Raven rolled her eyes and jammed her cigarette onto an ashtray balancing on the lounge arm. Sometime over the past week, Raven had dyed parts of her hair with rainbow slashes beneath the black. It was the only color in her appearance.

"What the hell is going on?" Thea asked, her dark curls bouncing as she darted a look between Alice and Raven.

"Alice is Parker Lazarus's mate," Raven conceded, her smoker's voice husky. She walked over to the whiteboard where she moved the portrait of Alice in her nerdy getup and stuck it next to Parker's visage, just like the other mated couples of the Deadly Seven. Wyatt had Misha. Griffin had Lilo, and so on.

Alice picked her picture off and slammed it back on the other side where the Sinners were pinned. Laughter broke out behind her, but she ignored it. She glared at Raven as if it were all her fault.

Raven snorted. "No skin off my nose. A picture is just a picture."

Pent-up fury bubbled to the surface. Alice wanted to punch Raven's smug face. She'd done it before. She'd do it again. But now was not the time for them to turn on each other. So instead, Alice let it all out in a scream. She clenched her fists and just let it out. When she was done, her sisters simply stared at her.

"You done?" Mercy asked, perfect brows arched.

Breathing like a bull, Alice nodded.

Mercy turned to Raven. "Is this why you turned on that meat grinder? I mean, he loses an arm and suddenly we find Alice mated to him. That's a bit sadistic even for your standards."

"Ooh," Tawny cooed, her eyes lighting up. "Gosh, Mercy is right. He hates you now, doesn't he, Alice?"

"He hated the Sisterhood before," Alice returned.

Raven's brows lowered. "I think you fuckers are missing the point."

"That I'm screwed?" Alice shoved Tawny's feet out of the way and sat down with a huff. "Do you know where I've been? Why I'm in such a shitty mood? He kidnapped me. Had me locked up and tied to his bed."

Mercy grinned, leaning forward, forearms resting on her knees. "Now you're talking. I want all the kinky details."

"What? No." Alice blushed. "There was none of that kind of action. The bastard thinks he can control and use me."

Mercy stared dreamily at the whiteboard. "If it were me, I think I'd be okay with that."

"That's because you're a nymphomaniac." Leila threw something at Mercy. A bolt? Mercy snatched it out of the air and held it in her fist, but didn't retaliate. Probably because Leila was right. Mercy would screw anything with a dick and two legs if she could, and Mercy was okay with that. She loved it. She turned it into a weapon.

"The point is," Raven continued, using her don't-mess-with-me voice. "That Alice is now linked to one of them. This solidifies a partnership. One old Sinner is married to Flint. And a new Sinner will be partnered with Parker. We're safe."

"From them, at least," Mercy mumbled.

"I'm not accepting this," Alice said.

"Why not?" Thea asked. "It's like an arranged marriage, or a business transaction. This union has value and I hate to point out the obvious, but we kinda need this."

"The Sisterhood will never let me go." Alice slammed her palm on her knee. God, how many times did she have to say this? "And I don't want to be married. You guys are my family. You're my sisters!"

The silence that followed settled heavily on all of them. Alice sighed and rested her head on Tawny's shoulder. Tawny patted her hair briefly before returning to her bowl of Crispies.

"Alice," Raven said, her voice low and ominous. "We've all wanted out at some point. We just never say it."

"No, you haven't," Alice replied. "Deep down inside, we all know this is all we're good for. We're going to Hell, may as well take some bastards with us."

It was the truth written on their souls. Hell. Heathens. Sinners. Worthless. Nothing. One day, they all feared their value would end, and they'd be discarded. All they had was each other and their pledge to the Sisterhood. Sometimes they didn't agree with their missions, sometimes they hated it, but always they had each other.

"I don't want to leave you guys," she whispered. Not for someone who didn't love her back.

The Reverend Mother arrived down the stairs, her cane thwacking the floor with her uneven steps. She was aged somewhere in her seventies. The black robes of her habit swished behind her like death itself. Round eyes, a hook nose, and flat lips. She looked like a wrinkled old prune, and acted like she needed one, but she was beginning to grow on Alice. She was the fifth Reverend Mother the Sisterhood had been assigned in the past three years, but she'd stayed the longest.

Before the Vatican had discovered the Sisterhood's secret society, their leader had risen internally from within their own ranks, as it always had been since Saint Hildegard's time. Alice had always wondered what it was like back then. Did they do penance as these Sinners did? Were they given the same liberties and freedoms? The same shackles?

"Sister Alice," the Rev greeted. "It is good to see you, my child."

Alice forced a smile on her face and nodded. "It is good to see you too, Rev."

"Reverend Mother," she reminded sourly.

"Right. That."

The Rev moved to stand before the whiteboard. Her sharp eyes tracked over the pinned paper, pictures, and handwritten notes before returning to the Sinners. She clasped her hands before her. A set of rosary beads was wrapped around one fist. Usually the Rev prayed when she was nervous about giving disturbing news.

"What is the progress on the mission, Sister?" the Rev asked Alice.

"She's Parker's mate," Tawny blurted, then covered her mouth and widened her eyes apologetically before mumbling into her hand, "Sorry."

The Rev didn't look surprised, which meant Raven had already told her. It's probably why Alice had been allowed to spend so long acting as Parker's assistant. Maybe they knew that if one of the Sinners from today was part of that family, there would always be someone willing to complete the kill order if necessary. Heat flushed her cheeks, and she looked down at her fingers.

"And what about the rest of you?" The Rev scanned the group. "Are you wrapping up your individual missions?"

They all took turns updating the Rev. Alice tuned out because she was still processing the fact her news had been taken so easily.

When Mary Lazarus had defected, there'd been an uproar. For years they'd debated whether to track Mary down and eliminate her because of all the secrets she knew. But then Raven had arrived at the Abbey. She'd brought with her some mystical insight that had been sorely lacking since Mary's departure. They'd waited. And waited. And then decades later, the Deadly Seven resurfaced. For all intents and purposes, it looked as though the Lazarus family was on the side of good. The side that wanted to thwart the apocalypse.

Stewing in her own thoughts, Alice chewed on her nails, her insides in knots.

"So, the directive remains the same," the Reverend Mother continued. "We need to end this looming issue with the Syndicate as soon as we can. We simply cannot allow these replicates loose on the world. We're already suffering the consequences of a small slip. And of course, I feel it's prudent to remind you, the sooner we can get Sister Prudence back, the better."

Prudence was one of them. Alice had infiltrated Lazarus Tech, and Prudence had infiltrated the Syndicate.

Heavy footsteps down the staircase drew their attention. Leila picked up her gun, now completely back together. Raven lifted a Katana she'd had sitting beside her on the floor. It made Alice think she'd seen this encounter.

Glossy dress shoes came into view on the steps, followed by pressed and tailored navy pants. Hands in pockets. Then a vest. Jacket. Tie. Trimmed beard. Shoulder-length auburn hair. A smug, handsome face. Parker Lazarus.

He stepped off the last step and surveyed the room, completely unaware, or most likely uncaring, that he'd stepped into a den of vipers. He prowled about. As he passed, he assessed each woman, and then continued to the back of the room to eye the weapon's rack briefly before returning and standing before the whiteboard full of sensitive information about his family. He met Alice's gaze, his own carrying a glint that was more cat-got-the-cream than predator.

Leila cocked her gun—an old Smith and Wesson revolver. It should have been swapped out for a modern model, but they all had their crutches, and this old gun was hers. Parker dismissed her weapon, and Raven's, then looked at the Reverend Mother.

"I'm here for Alice," he stated, voice smooth and full of bass.

Alice snorted. Laughter from the other five Sinners ranged from a tinkling to guffaws. None of it bothered Parker. He shrugged it off and kept his gaze firmly on the Rev.

To her credit, the Reverend Mother didn't cower. She lifted her chin and pointed her cane at Parker. "Sister Alice is not for sale, young man."

"I know. She already belongs to me."

"Now you're cruisin' for a bruisin' pretty boy," Mercy said, cracking her knuckles.

It warmed Alice's heart to see her family stand up for her, and she knew then that no matter what they'd all said about the mating, none of them would ever simply hand her over or send her on her way. They were sisters until the end.

Alice cleared her throat and stood. "How did you find us?"

"I must admit," he said, eyes skating to the whiteboard. "I thought you'd make the hunt a little harder, but you led me straight here."

He gave a pointed look at Alice's shoes. She'd found them beside the bed after she'd wriggled out of the rope. She checked her soles and saw a little flashing device stuck in the instep. Her jaw clenched as she picked it off and flicked it at him. It bounced off his pectoral and landed on the floor.

Parker's lips curved slightly as he pulled a piece of paper off the whiteboard. He studied it for a moment before dropping it and moving to the next note.

They could all kill him on the spot, and he didn't care. What the hell was wrong with this man? Was he that arrogant?

"So," the Rev said, "since you neglected to bring the cavalry, and we're all still alive, I take it you're agreeing to this alliance."

Every Sinner in the room shot eyes to the Rev, affronted at her ease in assuming the Sinners would have gone down with an easy fight if Parker had, indeed, brought his family to kill them.

"No," he replied, still studying the board. "It simply means I'm taking Alice back with me, and I wanted to see what you had on us before doing so."

He spoke as though talking about a recalcitrant escaped puppy, not an assassin. He dropped another piece of research to the ground before turning back to meet the Rev's eyes. "Your mission has always been to either kill us or to have us work for you. It's too late to kill us, and we won't work for you, so I'm taking Alice with me. You can go to whatever fucked up location you normally work out of because"—he surveyed the basement with distaste—"I don't believe for a second this is it."

"What's stopping us from killing you now?" Mercy asked, palming a dagger that had found its way into her hand, probably from her boot.

Alice tried to school the glare that wanted to come out and play. Mercy knew their only option was an alliance, even if Parker was too proud to see that.

"I'm the leader of the Deadly Seven," he replied. "Kill me and you'll face the eternal wrath of my family. You might even trigger the apocalypse yourselves." His golden-eyed gaze bored into Alice as he spoke to the rest. "Keep my mate from me and you risk triggering my dark side."

He plucked another piece of paper from the board and held it out to the Rev. It was the news article that mentioned a busload of people who'd suddenly fallen asleep, dated the same day as when Sloan's mate Max had been taken hostage by the Syndicate. Sloan had lost control of her gift that day. The Sisterhood knew much about the Deadly Seven from Mary's time working as a nun in their lab. But they didn't know everything. From what information Alice had added to their research, they had suspicions about the mating bond, one of which was that if the mates were separated, then the hero would fall into sin, becoming potentially unstoppable. He was all but confirming their suspicion.

"You say she's your mate, but where's the proof?" The Rev stomped her walking stick.

"What does it matter?" Thea snapped. "We're not handing her over."

"Why don't you tell them, Alice?" Parker raised his brows, humor in his eyes. "You saw evidence of my ability, first hand. And I'm sure you all know by now, after years of spying on us, that an ability only surfaces after triggering this mating bond."

Alice lifted her palms. "Hey, all I know is that some kind of unnatural scent made me more susceptible to suggestion. I have no idea if that was one of your powers. It could have been chemical warfare."

Parker's eye twitched. He clearly didn't want to reveal his full gift, and Alice enjoyed pushing him. She was curious too because maybe she was right, maybe that was some kind of trick he played on her. For the past two years she'd kept her hormones in check, but after one whiff of his delectable scent, she was putty in his hands.

It wouldn't happen again.

Parker cracked his neck and then snarled. Before their eyes, he transformed. His snarl became deeper, more guttural. His teeth elongated to fangs, his eyes glowed gold, and a cracking sound rent the air as claws sprung forth from his fingertips. She winced at the painful sound, hoping that it wasn't his bones cracking and protruding, or something like that.

Just as quickly as he'd become the lion, he shifted back to human, placing his hand back in his pocket just as the prosthetic was. The perfect picture of decorum.

"*Dang*," Thea said.

eight

JULIUS ALLCOTT

JULIUS ALLCOTT HAD THOUGHT his plans were iron clad. He'd spent decades orchestrating superhuman beings that would eradicate sinners from this earth. He even had a plan to destroy the other Syndicate partners and take the new world for his own. Of course, that new world, the sinless utopia he was creating, was only utopia if he had perfect replicates of his dead wife and child—Joseline and Jasmine. He was going to create a new world where his child would be safe. And he was going to be happy.

That was until his progeny, Despair, decided that drinking the Lazarus Koolaid was more important than her loyalty to him.

Now he stood outside a two-way mirror, looking inside to a cell where she lay half naked, curled into herself. Bruises along her spine revealed the locations of bone marrow samples they'd extracted, time and time again. With her ability to heal and regenerate, it was like a never-ending source. The Syndicate scientists may have failed to replicate the Lazarus family's exact DNA makeup, but they were close enough. They had replicates with powers. It mattered not if they expired after three months of living. And since he couldn't bring Joseline and Jasmine back… three months was enough to lay waste to the world.

Behind his closed eyes a scene replayed in horror for the millionth time.

"I won't kill you, just your precious family." Despair held up the locket.

Julius's hand went to his throat, realized it had been removed—No! If she dared to touch them… With one hand still holding the knife to his throat, she thumbed open the locket with the other. Julius jerked, bucked, attempting to escape, but she nicked his neck and he stilled. He eyed the locket with hope. Maybe she was bluffing. Surely, she wouldn't do it. Two strands of hair poked out from the metal rim. Despair's nostrils flared, and she tipped her head back and swallowed the strands, never shifting her raging eyes from him.

"You fucking bitch," Julius growled, spittle flying, but she held the knife firm.

"I'm not a bitch. I'm the killer you made me."

His face contorted with rage. "I'll kill you for this. I'll make you suffer."

For the past two months, he'd done exactly that. He'd made her suffer beyond imagining, and once he was done sucking the hope out of her physical form, he moved to her mind. He'd flown her around the world, to each of their seven Syndicate bases, and showed her the lengths they would go to rule the world. From sin-serums to mech-bots to plant monsters to rabid sin-hunting dogs to replicate versions of her saviors. He'd shown her how futile it was to even dream of defeating him.

Futile.

Now he was putting the final pieces of his new plan into place. They all thought they could mess with him. Despair thought swallowing the last remaining DNA sample of his wife and daughter would somehow stop him. But it only made him realize something. The absence of hope is the most dangerous enemy of all, for now, without the possibility of reuniting with his loved ones... he simply didn't care about anyone.

"Mr. Allcott." Levi Van Jansen, their lead scientist, waited at Julius's side. "Are you ready for your next treatment?"

The stodgy geneticist had white hair growing out of his ears and appeared quite mad. They made a good team.

Julius rolled up his sleeve to the elbow and presented it to Van Jansen, then continued to study Despair through the window. A pin prick, followed by the rush of foreign fluid injecting into his vein made him wince and, out of habit, he reached for the locket around his neck only to find it gone. The emptiness inside his chest grew to the width of a canyon, and he took a deep breath to steady himself. When he returned his gaze through the window, he found Despair looking directly at him.

Impossible. She wouldn't be able to see through the mirror.

But she would sense his despair.

Van Jansen swabbed the injection site and covered it up.

"You are done for now, ja?" When Julius failed to respond, Van Jansen added, "Have you had a chance to look at my report, sir?"

"Report?"

"Ja, the one about uncontrolled replicate behavior."

Julius sighed laboriously. "I don't really care about what happens to them after our control is ceded. Don't waste your time."

"But..." Van Jansen paused. He pulled a piece of paper from his lab coat pocket and squinted at it, his bushy eyebrows moving like caterpillars. "The woman we learned this from is working with the... let me see if I get this right... the Hilde-gard Sister-hood. You know them, ja? They are saying there is a place the replicates are trying to go. Like dogs with bone."

The Hildegard Sisterhood.

Fury reddened Julius's vision. Van Jansen continued to speak, but all he could hear was blood rushing in his ears. He tapped his hair-tied finger on his chest. *My darlings. Oh, my loves.* This all started with the Sisterhood's retaliation. *That queen bitch Sinner, Mary Lazarus, stole them from me.*

Now more of the Sinners were in town, threatening to destroy everything.

Hate and venom and body shaking rage rattled Julius's bones.

"Send in the Faithful," he said to Van Jansen. "You are dismissed."

Van Jansen shoved the paper back into his pocket and made a clicking sound with his teeth. Julius waved him off. No doubt the man would continue his line of investigation himself.

Julius caught sight of his hand after he waved Van Jansen off. That would not do. The strands of hair he'd tied around his finger had almost all fallen off. He dug into his pocket and pulled out the small manicure scissors, then snipped another lock of his hair off and tied it on his finger.

Better.

I'm coming for you, my loves.

He tapped the finger to his chest, over his heart, where the locket used to be. Then he glared at Despair only to see a glimmer of hope flickering in her gaze like a candle in the dark. But her family wouldn't save her. He would soon make sure of it. First, he had to eliminate any support they might have.

A male cleared his throat.

Julius looked to his right, where a tall, fit brunette stood. A glance down to the navy shirt pointed out a logo. Cardinal City Fire Department. Interesting.

This man had no clear signs of deformity or disability—as was the norm for the sycophants who devoted themselves to the service of the

Syndicate in exchange for being cloned and coming back perfect with all their memories. This man appeared to be the picture of health. Strong broad shoulders, muscular, athletic. But Faithful pledged for all sorts of reasons. Julius cared not how they came into his employ, simply that they did a good job, and word was that this man had.

"Your name?" Julius clipped.

"Axel Alvares, sir." He darted a glance through the two-way mirror to where Despair still glared, and did a double take before his eyes went wide.

"Eyes on me, Faithful."

Axel snapped his attention back to Julius. He tried to hide his distaste, but Julius could see it painted all over the man. Not used to torture. Would he be of any use?

Julius bit his tongue and tapped his finger on his chest. With Despair out of action, he would take anyone's help to complete this last leg of his plan.

"I've heard you are a man of action," Julius said. "You get the job done and you think on your feet."

"I do my best, sir."

"I have a job for you. If you can prove your worth, then I will promote you to fill the shoes *that* woman left. Do you understand?"

"You want me to be your lead enforcer?"

Julius gave a curt nod. "Can you handle the kind of work she did?"

"If it brings me closer to replication, then I'm ready, sir."

"Good. Listen closely…"

nine

PARKER LAZARUS

PARKER RETRACTED HIS CLAWS, furious that he'd been forced to reveal The Beast when it was the other, unseen parts of his new abilities that were superior. He could run faster, jump higher, and always land on his feet, but demonstrating that was far more cumbersome in this space. The claws and teeth were just an ugly symbol of something he wasn't. He was not an animal.

The Sinners circled him, each tensing and ready for action. Revolver in one hand, sword in another, dagger in a third's hand. He'd addressed their leader, the old nun, but he had no doubt that the real person he needed to convince was Alice. He may have followed her here with espionage intentions, but he wasn't going to take her against her will. He never intended to. There were still too many unknowns on the bridge between them.

The buxom redhead pointed at Parker. "You expect us to let Alice leave with you now? You're a…"

Beast. Monster. Freak? He dared her to say it and bared his teeth, now wholly human but still a threat. "Alice can handle herself."

The rainbow-haired one shrugged. "He's not wrong—"

Something small bounced down the steps, trailing smoke behind it. *Flashbang.*

Parker launched himself onto Alice, throwing her to the ground, his body protecting her. A wall rattling bang. A blinding flash. Smoke. No... not smoke. Some kind of gas.

Alice looked up at Parker, confused.

They both knew a flashbang was harmless—designed to disorientate but not injure—yet Parker's instinct had been to protect his mate.

He'd followed her to this cathedral, but someone had followed him. The Sinners moved like synchronized swimmers, perfectly harmonious. They surrounded their Reverend Mother and prepared for battle. It would do them no good. He could smell and identify the gas. It wasn't a nerve toxin or tear gas. It was a sleeping agent he recognized.

Nothing could fight sleep—he knew this firsthand from Sloan. All he could do was hold his breath and hope for the best. Hopefully, the five minutes he could manage would be enough for backup to arrive. The Sinners were only human. Their lung capacity probably failed after a maximum of two minutes.

The shock wore off, and Alice's scowl was like a kiss to him. If there ever came a day she failed to revolt against him, he would be disappointed. If this was any other moment, he'd be aroused.

Parker activated the panic button on his Deadly watch. He had a small moment to appreciate there might be a need for that bionic arm after all, but then his pride won over. He would manage better just the way he was.

"It's a sleeping agent," he said, waving his hand through the gas rising from the floor. "Don't breathe it in if you can help it."

He would be okay for a few minutes, but the rest of them would be susceptible. He searched the basement for another exit. Only the cooling vents and ducting in the ceiling. He'd never squeeze through, but maybe Alice might.

"You did this," she said, covering her mouth. "You brought this on us."

He gripped her shoulder. "Get to the cooling vent. I'll lift you."

The gas was rising. He heaved in a breath filtered through his sleeve and held it, then bade her to do the same. Her eyes said she wanted to cut him in two, but she had no choice. She held her breath.

White-robed figures descended the stairs. Their usual Halloween face masks had been swapped out with white, full faced breathing apparatuses. *Faithful.* Syndicate henchmen and desperados. He could sense their pride as they came down. There were at least—he counted and stopped at twenty. This was an ambush, or a massacre.

Pity they didn't realize each Sinner was worth ten of them.

And he was worth more.

He grinned. Now it was starting to look like a party. The armed Faithful swarmed down the staircase and were met with a tornado of black clad death. Each Sinner became a weapon, or used a weapon to cut down anything with a white robe. Their time was limited, but none panicked. Each had begun their assault with cool, calm efficiency.

Their assault was a beautiful dance.

Gunshots fired. Parker ducked and kicked up the lounges to make a barricade and then dragged the drowsy Reverend Mother behind one. She gave him a grateful look and then promptly passed out as the gas worked into her lungs. He checked her pulse, and it beat strongly. Crouching low, Parker rushed to the weapon's rack and pulled off a Katana, then he picked out a white robe and charged. *Too easy.* The robed bodies stacked up within seconds. He almost laughed at the foolhardiness of coming into *this* basement, and then he saw another set of feet descending the staircase... and another. These new white-robed figures weren't masked. No... they had unnatural tight-skinned and deformed faces. He'd seen this type before, many years ago.

Replicates.

Slits for a mouth and nostrils. They were malformed and under-cooked. They hadn't gestated enough in their cloning tanks, or something had gone wrong with their cell replication for them to look that way. They were expendable, but they were also imbued with extra strength, possibly powered and sin-sensing—just like the Deadly Seven.

These Sinners might be elite fighters, but they wouldn't stand a chance against superpowers... especially if they were out of breath and succumbing to the sleeping agent.

He jammed the panic button on his watch against his tooth and then checked over his shoulder for Alice. She fought off a Faithful in the corner, but she stumbled, her face turning red with effort and her held breath. A tiny kernel of unease bloomed between his ribs. He stopped playing with the Faithful in front of him and ran him through with the sword. Then he sliced a section of the robe free and used it to cover the still oozing gas bomb. *Should have done that first.* There were three Faithful to get through before he could make it to Alice, and the replicates had joined the fight.

Parker hit the panic button on his watch for the third time, real-izing that perhaps he was a little overzealous thinking he didn't need that robotic arm. With it he could simply rip heads from shoulders or pull beating hearts out of bodies. Heat flushed his cheeks, and he refused to accept defeat. He refused to acknowledge the burn in his lungs. Scanning the room, he tried to take stock.

Four replicates. Six more Faithful alive. Five Sinners slowly running out of juice. Smokey gas still in the room. One muscular

Faithful standing on the steps holding an iPad, lording over the scrummage. Parker's eyes zeroed in on that device. Liza had told him that the replicates had been controlled by a device by Julius Allcott back at the warehouse altercation. To even the playing field, all Parker needed to do was get his hands on that iPad.

Parker discarded his sword and let The Beast out. It surged to the surface as though second nature, and he hated it. But he used it. The Beast fought his way through the melee, heedless of cuts and hits to his body, and went straight for the masked man on the steps. *Don't think about the replicates getting to the Sinners—to Alice—just get to that control device.*

Through the breathing apparatus, the Faithful's eyes widened at Parker's approach. He tried to back-step up the stairs, but Parker reached him first. His clawed hand ripped into the robe and jerked him closer. They scuffled. A blow to Parker's head infuriated him, and he roared, forgetting about the gas. Too late. He held his breath again and ripped the ventilator off the Faithful.

For a moment, Parker allowed surprise to hit him—the Faithful in charge was no deformed man nor undercooked replicate. He appeared normal in face. Could be your next-door neighbor. But then desperation came in all shapes and sizes. This man's reasons for pledging his human life away were none of Parker's concern. He was the enemy, and he was no match for The Beast. In a blinding blur, Parker went for the jugular with his fangs, but the Faithful used the iPad as a shield. Parker snatched the iPad, roared, and was amused to see the man retreat. He chased him a few steps, but only until the air cleared and he could replenish his lungs.

The Faithful had escaped.

Good. Someone should be left to tell the tale.

He rushed back down the steps, threw the ventilator down into the mix, realized only three Sinners were left standing, Alice among them, and replicates closing in. He picked up the smart device, balanced it on his knee, wildly scanned the application on screen until he found the disconnect button. The remaining three replicates stopped mid stride and turned to statues.

Parker blinked. Just like that?

Now they weren't fighting for their lives, each standing Sinner scrambled to pull a ventilator from a fallen Faithful. Parker walked further into the basement. Through the clearing haze, one Faithful remained fighting in the corner. *Alice*. He dropped the control device, picked up a ventilator, and ran to her. But before he could lift a finger in aid, the Faithful dropped to the floor, his own mask wrapped around his throat. Alice looked at him, eyes bloodshot from holding her breath. Parker shoved the ventilator at her. Together, they collapsed to the floor while he tried to help put it on, but, damn it, he needed two hands.

An overwhelming sense of inadequacy pumped through him. The Beast slipped away, and all that was left was Parker and his raw impotence. All he could do was fumble and try to help Alice when she was almost passing out herself. Suddenly, he was nudged out of the way.

Another Sinner—Mercy—took over. She fitted Alice's mask to her face. Instantly, Alice took a breath, heaving her lungs until she fed oxygen back to where it belonged. Parker stood back, frustration welling. He'd never felt so powerless until this moment. Until Alice needed him and he couldn't help her.

ten

ALICE MONTGOMERY

ALICE'S LUNGS WERE DYING. So were her eyes and every molecule in her body. Fighting without being allowed to take a breath was the worst thing she'd ever done. But now she had a ventilator on, she could recuperate, and she could reassess.

Sitting on the floor against a wall, looking around the basement, she was surprised that they'd taken down so many Faithful. Three replicate soldiers, mask-free and a little weird looking in the face, were standing still like statues, arms hanging loosely at their sides, eyes vacant. *Creepy.*

Only two other Sinners had managed to last. Mercy was checking on the Rev, and Thea was checking on Leila, Tawny, and Raven. She must have failed to foresee this attack. Raven's mystical gift wasn't an exact art. She couldn't control it. The visions came when they wanted to come. Her Katana must have been a show of power for Parker's sake.

At first glance, none of the team was injured, but they had Parker to thank for that... or accuse. Whichever way they wanted to look at it because it was clear he had been followed, just as Parker had tracked Alice there.

He sat on the steps, his long legs bent and wide as he tapped away on an electronic tablet device resting on his knee. His hair was mussed up and dangled over his face, hiding his face from Alice, but she remembered his expression when he couldn't put the mask on her face. Two golden eyes were wide and concerned, perhaps even a little frightened. She'd never seen him look like that. Ever.

His suit had rips in it, especially the prosthetic side which had deep slashes and bullet holes, as though he'd used it as a shield. Even one-handed, he'd been a sight to see in battle. He deserved every ounce of ego in that inflated head of his.

Alice eased herself to her feet, just as another two sets of feet descended the steps behind Parker. Adrenaline shot through her ravaged body, forcing it into a state of alarm. She picked up a dagger and threw it. The blade barely left her hand before it halted, frozen in mid-air like magic. It took her brain a moment to catch up. *Deadly Seven*—Greed and Envy. Greed's blue face mask covered his mouth and nose. His gray hood was up around his head. And his outraged eyes glared at Alice. Envy tugged his green mask down to reveal Evan Lazarus's face. The youngest in the family was reckless revealing his identity. But then again, Alice had always suspected the electricity summoning hero had some kind of psychic ability, too. Maybe he knew the alliance they'd proposed would go through. Surely after this it had to. Green eyes slid to her and held as the crackle of his power skipped over his fists.

Alice stilled. So did the other lucid Sinners.

Alice lifted her palms apologetically, and then the dagger fell, clattering on the floor. Greed gave Alice a brief nod. Parker hadn't looked up from his device, still tapping away, inspecting the program that controlled the replicates.

Greed scanned the room, and then tugged down his mask and hood, revealing his face. Griffin.

Realizing the air must be clean enough because Griffin and Parker now stood without ventilators, Alice eased her own off. The air had a bitter tang to it, but so far, so good. She wasn't asleep on the floor. While the brothers spoke amongst themselves, Alice went to her sisters.

"How long do you think the sleeping agent will work for?" she asked Thea.

Thea kicked the lounge back down to its rightful state. "No idea. Could be hours."

Mercy gestured for Alice to assist her carrying Tawny. Together they put their sister on the lounge, then did the same for Raven and Leila. They gently carried the Rev to the final spot on the couch and propped her head with a pillow. When they were done, the three awake Sinners gathered close and put their heads together.

"What do you think?" Mercy asked, eyes darting to the deadly men at the stairs.

"I think Parker can hear us anyway, so there's no point whispering," Alice pointed out.

"Good point," Thea said.

They straightened and kept one watchful eye on the zombie replicates, the other on the Lazarus brothers.

"He clearly led them here," Thea said. "The Syndicate, I mean."

"But he fought against them." Alice rubbed her irritated eyes. Mercy tugged her hand down with a shake of her head. *Right.* Don't make them worse. "I don't think he did it on purpose, just as I didn't intend to bring him here, but it happened. We're all safe. And we have some replicates and their control device."

Thea's eyes lit up. "You're right. We have an opportunity here. We should show them."

Mercy's brow lifted and sized up Griffin and Evan. Then the Mercy Madness took over her. That's what they'd always called it when she became suddenly enthralled with a potential sexual conquest. She flicked her hair and adjusted her bust.

"Mercy," Alice warned. "He's married."

"What about the other one?"

"They're all taken. So just keep the tatas in your shirt. Please?"

Mercy pouted, but nodded. "I suppose now's not really the time."

"You think?" Thea rolled her eyes.

Red tinted Mercy's cheeks and she pushed Thea in the shoulder before striding over to the Lazarus brothers.

"Give me that." She held her hand out before Parker. He only arched his brow, held the device closer, and then went back to speaking with Griffin. Evan cast a curious glance at Mercy and folded his arms.

Trouble brewed in the air. Alice indicated for Thea to join her as she walked over to Parker. "You don't believe the Sisterhood has any value for an alliance, then let us show you why we do."

His dark brows joined together.

"I suppose you know Griffin," he said, and flicked his chin toward the man next to him.

Alice gave them both a flat smile. "Yes, of course. Hello, Griffin."

Thea stuck out her hand for a shake, but Griffin flinched at it.

"He's not a toucher," Alice said, leaning into her.

For some reason, Alice's words unsettled Parker. Their eyes met briefly, and then he dropped his shoulders.

"I'm Evan." Evan took Thea's outstretched hand. She yelped at the electric shock and Evan laughed, his green eyes twinkling. Then he stepped off the stairs and went toward the replicates, mumbling over his shoulder, "You walked right into that one."

Evan poked a replicate with his finger. It had zero response, so

Evan poked it again. Then zapped it. When nothing happened, he grinned and looked at his brothers as though this was some kind of game. Both Griffin and Parker ignored him.

"So tell me," Parker said. "What value does the Sisterhood have for a family they once tried to assassinate as children?"

"Oh, give it up, already," Thea moaned. "We get it. You're holding a grudge."

Alice gave her sister a look. "He is right. Even though it wasn't us in this very room, the Sisterhood does have a legacy of brutality and ruthlessness. We can admit that."

Thea clenched her jaw. "It was before our time. Why should we keep being punished for something we never did?"

"Do you deny you're an assassin?" Griffin asked.

Thea's lips clamped shut, and she looked away.

Alice took a deep breath and focused on Parker. "Even though my mission was to gather intel on your family, there is another reason my sisters are here. And if you were paying attention to the whiteboard, instead of seeing only what you wanted to see, you might have noticed a few things."

She righted the board. Most of the items had fallen to the floor, so she hunted through them until she found the articles she needed.

"This one," she said, lifting a news report of a disturbance in the Quadrant a month or so ago. "This one was at Sloan's wedding, correct?"

Evan nodded cautiously while Parker perfected his poker face.

Griffin took the paper from Alice. "How did you know that? The wedding isn't in the article."

She shrugged. "I had to help organize the bridal party gifts and pay for the catering."

Griffin scowled at Parker. "You made your assistant order the gifts?"

Parker snatched the article off Griffin. "Not that it's your business but I was busy programming a virtually sentient computer."

"Anyway," Alice continued. "What you may not know is that we were watching, too. The replicate that attacked didn't seem to be controlled, and it had no real directive."

"Its directive was to ruin Sloan's and Max's wedding," Evan pointed out.

"That's what you think," she said, then picked up another scrap of paper. This was a handwritten field report from one of the Sinners after the warehouse attack where Parker lost his arm. "When their control was taken away, the escaped replicates went in one direction —south." She found another piece of paper detailing another attack, handed it to Parker, and stood back. "This is a separate incident that we only know about because we have an agent on the inside at the Syndicate. You can see the replicate moved south, far into another state. He arrived at a particular spot and tried to dig with his bare hands."

"What are you getting at?" Parker asked.

"Each time a replicate was loosened, it went south. Each went to a different location. We plotted them out and found a link."

Alice put her hand out. His eyes darkened, but he put the device in her hand. Alice forced the triumph down and switched it off.

"What are you doing!" Parker's eyes widened.

"Trust me," she said.

The instant the device powered down, the control over the replicates dissipated. The three figures in the center of the room awoke, but they didn't attack. They didn't even notice the onlookers. Instead, like mindless zombies, they ambled southward in the room until they hit the wall and started scratching through the wallpaper.

"What are they doing?" Griffin asked as Evan followed them, watching curiously.

"Heading south," Alice reminded them.

Of course, it was Parker who asked the million dollar question. "Why south?"

The three Sinners smirked at each other. When Alice returned her gaze to the tall, arrogant man, she only said. "That's where our value lies."

They stared at each other for long seconds. It obviously drove him nuts not to know something and, for a moment, she thought he'd pull the same shit as he always did, but a twinkle lit up his eyes.

"Fine," he said. "I agree we should talk about this more."

He held his hand out.

She put the device back in it. "Name the time and place."

"Dinner. Just you and me."

Mercy snorted. Alice shot her an annoyed look before returning to Parker.

"No. We should all be there."

"I'll talk to you and you only."

Thea sighed. "Just do it, Alice. You know it's what the Rev would want."

Parker arched an imperious eyebrow.

"Drinks," she conceded.

"Dinner."

"Drinks."

"I'll pick you up at eight."

eleven

ALICE MONTGOMERY

THAT NIGHT, Alice was five minutes early to the curb of her apartment building. She stood scowling at the cars as they drove by. Reluctant to let go of winter, the unforgiving spring air brushed her face with icy fingers, causing a shiver. Since Parker failed to mention where they were going, and she was already grumpy, she wasn't in a mood for dressing up. Her jeans were threadbare, but her silk camisole was decent enough, even if it did gape at the bust. Paired with a leather jacket, stiletto heels, and the opinions of her sisters, she knew her outfit would be suitable for any venue and any mission— including seduction if deemed necessary.

She hugged herself, unsure why tonight, of all nights, she was feeling particularly prudish. Perhaps it had something to do with being out of her comfort zone of nerd clothing around Parker. Give her a baggy dress, flat shoes and a cardigan, and she was sitting pretty. But all that pretense had been thrown out the window. Alice Montgomery had been fake. This was the real Alice... except... sometimes she forgot who she was. Definitely not someone who deserved to live happily ever after. At least she'd bothered to put on makeup and washed her hair—the locks were pinned into a loose knot at her nape. Her scowl deepened when she remembered the way her sisters had tried to prepare her.

"*Use what the good Lord gave you, sister,*" Mercy had said as she made Alice's camisole gape indecently. "*Those boobs ain't for nothing.*"

"*This is Parker Lazarus, we're talking about,*" Alice grumbled. "*He's not affected by this sort of thing.*"

Well, he hadn't been around her. Alice still remembered sitting in his office waiting room, waiting to be called for her interview two years ago. The previous applicant, a pretty blond barbie type, had come rushing out of his office in tears. That's when Alice knew she wouldn't get the job with looks. She'd plucked the spectacles Thea had given her out of her pocket, and nerded herself up. It had obviously worked.

"*Yeah, well, it's a known fact of life that if he's got a dick, he'll be distracted by your tits.*" *Mercy's eyes narrowed, deep in thought. The art of seduction was where this woman excelled. Mercy was almost as old as Alice—somewhere in her mid-thirties—and had given most of the Sinners classes on seduction. If it wasn't for her tips, Alice would never have made it into a dirty diplomat's vehicle in time to slice his throat four years ago. And she certainly wouldn't have made it out alive.* "*Remember what I taught you,*" *Mercy finished.* "*This is important.*"

"*I got it.*"

"*Here,*" *Leila said, handing Alice a poison-laced hair pin.* "*Extra protection.*"

Raven shoved her jacket at Alice. "*In case you get cold.*"

"*And you know what to do with this.*" *Thea dropped a tiny, dime-sized device into Alice's palm.*

Parker's Bugatti slowed to a stop before Alice. He parked where he shouldn't and got out, oblivious to holding up traffic. Cars behind him tooted their horns. He didn't even acknowledge them. Under the dim street lights, his usual aura of power softened. He still wore his designer suit that fit a little loosely over his mountain of a frame. He'd lost weight in the last few months since he'd not been in the office. Alice wasn't sure why this grated on her, but it did.

Hasn't been eating properly.

Parker's short beard was impeccable and his hair was tied in a sophisticated man-bun style she'd only ever seen him pull off. His prosthetic was tucked into his pants pocket, rounding out his casual spoiled prince visage. He came around to her side, where he stopped and stared.

He stared for so long it became awkward. It wasn't just a meeting of the eyes, but a long, slow rake from top to bottom, and a slow drag up—an assessment. Her skin tightened. Blood heated. Nipples peaked. All because he simply took his time to look. When he was done, he simply stared with that poker face of his, which made it worse.

"What?" she snapped, feeling the urge to close her jacket and hug herself again. "You never said where we were going, Mr. Fancy Pants. This outfit will have to do."

A slight pinch appeared between his brows as he opened the front passenger door and waited until she got in. As her bottom hit the seat, she found her blood already boiling. She ran sweaty palms down her legs, checked that her dagger was still strapped to her ankle and then put her seatbelt on before sitting back, careful not to dislodge the blade strapped between her shoulder blades, hilt down at the small of her back. Having that short wakizashi sword was the only reason Alice agreed to wear the camisole. The straps were wide and hid the holster, but more importantly, the flowing bottom hem gave her easy access to the hilt. As long as she kept her jacket on, he wouldn't notice. If he tried to take it away from her, there was always the sharp hair pin. She checked it was still in her hair, just in case.

Parker stood outside her window, facing away.

"Hey." She tapped on the glass. "This century."

All she got was a slight turn of his head, the gift of his flawless profile. *Oh, for Heaven's sake.* She turned on the stereo and flicked through the available channels, deciding at the last minute to sync her own music playlist from her phone. She'd done it plenty of times when she'd run an errand as his assistant and he'd trusted her with his car. He made no comment when he sat back in the driver's side and put the car into gear. But when Nina Simone's voice came on, Alice was sure she noticed him relax... just as she was.

He drove them straight back to his apartment building—Lazarus House. They parked in the basement garage and, for a moment, she thought maybe he would take her backstage to where she guessed all the Deadly Seven magic happened, but he only led her out the garage exit and onto the street.

From his stiff, brusque strides, she was starting to wonder what she'd done to piss him off. First, he'd been all Mr. McBrooding on the drive, and now this. It must be her outfit. He saw something he didn't like when he'd assessed her. Could he somehow sense the weapons she'd brought? Had his new senses caught the metal? Maybe he was offended that she didn't trust him.

Too bad. Trust went both ways, and neither of them was there yet.

She kept pace with him, her heels clicking on the pavement until they came to the entrance of Heaven, the restaurant next door to the nightclub Hell—both owned by the man himself. He opened the door for her. She didn't move.

"I said no dinner," she reminded him. Plus, having him at her rear when she entered a new venue wasn't a viable option.

His knuckles whitened on the doorknob and he stared at her, eyes flickering gold like they had that first night in his office.

"Then don't eat," he grumbled. "But we go inside."

Those were his first words to her all night?

Taking a deep breath, she steeled herself. This was for an alliance and to stop bloodshed. To save lives. To put the past behind them. What was coming was bigger than everyone. It would make the Syndicate look like child's play.

Alice took five steps inside the restaurant only to stop, stunned. It was empty. She let her gaze roam over the room. Tables and chairs sat dormant and cold. There was a stage in the middle with a grand piano, also vacant. Surrounding the stage were booths. The lights were on in the open-plan kitchen toward the back. Someone moved about in there, but she couldn't see clearly. She turned in time to see Parker locking the front door.

"What's going on?" she asked, raising an eyebrow.

He pocketed the keys. "I want privacy for tonight."

"So you closed the restaurant? That's going to cost you thousands in revenue." This was a popular, critically acclaimed foodie spot.

"You're more important."

His words eased into Alice, causing an uncomfortable tightness in her chest. Her scowl returned, and she realized she was just as moody as Parker. Neither of them liked capitulating. This would be an interesting night.

He gestured further into the restaurant, toward the kitchen, but when they started walking and he veered to the right, she found themselves at a private dining room. The long table was set for two at the close end but could fit perhaps fifteen to twenty. Parker went straight for the champagne sitting on ice, used the power of a single thumb to pop the cork, and then poured two glasses. He handed one to her and then clinked his glass to hers before downing his drink in one gulp. All the while, she stood still, cautious.

While he poured another, Alice used the opportunity to scope out the room. One exit—the door they'd come in. Expensive china, crystal glasses, cutlery and large cloth napkins rolled and placed to the side. Two menus.

"Please." Parker pulled her seat out.

She sat and put her untouched champagne down. Parker made a grunt of approval before sitting himself and studying his menu.

"So," she started, but he held up a finger, silencing her.

"We should order. The chef won't like to be kept waiting."

Alice's hands clenched into fists. This was a clear power play. He wanted to remain in control. She got that. She'd said no food and now he was going to do everything in his power to ensure she ate.

The chef walked in.

Wyatt Lazarus was Wrath wrapped in a tall, dark and brooding package. He was also a Michelin starred chef. One she'd thought had retired in favor of parenting and undoubtedly vigilantism. Dressed in an all-black chef's uniform and skull cap, he gave her a tight smile and then glowered at his brother. "You going to introduce us, or what?"

"I'm Alice," she said so Parker didn't have to. "We've actually met." Multiple times.

He gave her a skeptical look. "But *have* we?"

She swallowed under his intensity. "I suppose not. You met the assistant. I'm the... um... assassin. Nun. Whatever."

"That's the lot of you then?" He folded his arms. "No other personalities hiding under the table?"

She wasn't sure what to make of that comment, then noticed the gleam in his eyes. Was that some kind of joke? Wyatt snorted, smirked, and then lifted his chin.

"Misha wants to meet you," he said. "And Lilo. Actually, all of the girls. Especially Mary." At her pause, he added, "I'm assuming you know everything about us."

"Not now, Wyatt." Parker put his menu down, a little flustered.

The look Wyatt cut his brother could have weathered steel. But then he returned to Alice with nothing but politeness. "What will you have?"

Shit. Alice bit her lip and picked up the menu to peruse. There were many options but she didn't need long to decide.

"I'll take the gnocchi, and His Lordship will have the fillet steak, rare, with a side of steamed vegetables." She smiled flatly at Wyatt. "Hold the salt."

Jeez it felt good not to hold her opinions anymore. Alice positively beamed as Wyatt collected the menus with a thinly veiled smile of his own.

Alice had been trained to read body language. Through a dropped shoulder she could decipher a telegraphed attack. Through a sigh or a flicker of emotion, she could figure out the inner workings of someone's mind, but the look Wyatt gave his brother confused Alice. It was smug. Almost like—she tapped her finger, trying to place it—and came up with a time Thea had instructed Alice on how to care for ancient manuscripts, but instead of following the younger woman's instructions, Alice went ahead with her own way. And failed. She'd caused the old paper to crumble. Wyatt's expression looked much like Thea's once had. *I told you so.*

"You need anything else?" Parker's voice rumbled.

"Nope," Wyatt answered. "Food will be ready in about thirty and then I'm out." He paused, but when Parker made no move to answer, Wyatt added, "You're welcome."

The moment Wyatt closed the private dining room door behind him, Parker glared at Alice.

"You ordered for me?"

She shrugged. "I know what you need."

"Oh really?" He arched a brow.

"Did I order wrong?" Heat prickled her neck.

His jaw twitched.

"Did I?" she prompted.

He poured himself another glass, saw that hers was still full, and then returned the bottle.

"So how is this going to work?" she asked. "Because I'm not willing to share any more information unless you agree to an alliance, and I'm betting you won't agree unless I share that information."

"I'll ask the questions," he answered abruptly.

Alice leaned back on her chair and folded her arms. The short sword dug into her back and she pretended not to notice. "Oh really?"

He stared at her for a long moment and then shook his head, mumbling to himself as he took another drink.

Alice's blood went from boiling to bubbling over. "You've been grouchy since you picked me up. If you have something to say, Parker Lazarus, then I suggest you say it. You know I'm tougher than I look."

When he didn't answer, she finally took a sip of her drink. The fizzing perfection coated her tongue and slid down her throat like heaven. She was not prepared for it. Her eyes fluttered and she moaned, licking her lips.

"Jeez, that's good champagne," she confessed, shaking her head. It had been a long time since she'd stopped to value a good drop of bubbles. "Thank you."

"Only the best."

She rolled her eyes. This wasn't going to work. She put the glass down, intending to tell Parker, but found his gaze stuck on her lips. She recognized that lust-filled expression. *Interesting.* She licked her lips again. He took in a breath, as though the action was the switch that started time for him, and then he calmly met her eyes as though he hadn't just been thinking sinful thoughts about her mouth.

Perhaps she could affect him, after all. All of Mercy's seduction tips hurtled into her mind. Would they work on him now? The genius who saw through everything? She cleared her throat and made a point of rubbing the back of her neck as though it was sore. When she was done, she let her hand trail down her decolletage and off— careful to catch her finger subtly in her camisole, tugging down the hem, exposing more curved flesh busting out of her bra. He watched the entire time as though this was a moment curated just for him. She supposed it was.

"Will Wyatt be joining us?" she asked casually.

He looked offended.

"I take that as a no, then?"

"Is that a problem?"

Not at all. She smiled. He narrowed his eyes.

"First question," he said.

To stop herself from rolling her eyes, she took another drink. This was going to be a long night and she couldn't exactly speed up seduction until Wyatt was gone.

"What is your favorite color?" Parker asked.

Alice spat champagne across the table. France's most expensive liquid export dripped down his blinking face and onto his silk tie and shirt. Oh, shit. Alice jumped out of her seat, tipping it to the ground behind. She reached for a napkin, knocked over the ice bucket, and spilled more into his lap.

"I'm so sorry," she cried as ice and fizzing liquid saturated his front.

She grabbed another napkin and rounded the table so she could dab him. She started with his face, careful to ensure her newly exposed chest was right where she wanted it, and then worked at his neck and—

He caught her wrist.

Alarm burst through Alice, but she kept herself outwardly innocent. Thoughts of her lethal hair pin came to mind. Could she reach it with her other hand? Would he notice?

"It's fine," he mumbled. "It was a stupid question."

Something in his tone gave Alice pause, enough to let him tug the napkin from her hand and take over mopping himself. She hadn't expected that. Was he embarrassed?

"It's not stupid," she insisted. "It just took me off guard."

"You seem to know all about me, and I know nothing about the real you."

Alice chose the seat next to him. A blush tinted his cheeks giving him the adorable look she'd only ever glimpsed when she'd interrupted him practicing a speech. His tone was abrupt but irritated—as though frustrated in himself.

Being spat on with champagne hadn't made him blush, but asking about her did?

"The real me?"

He nodded.

"I don't think finding out my favorite color will reveal that."

"Okay... why the song?"

"The song?"

"You were humming it in my office. Then you played it in my car."

Alice deflated. She wasn't thinking he'd go *that* intimate. But if Parker Lazarus wasn't perceptive, she'd be worried.

"Okay..." She took a swig of her drink and braced herself. "You want to know about the song."

Did she want to tell him? It was deeply personal. It would mean putting her heart on her sleeve. And the things she knew about him may involve his secret, but nothing about him as an individual.

She took a deep breath. "How about one for one?"

"You ask a question, then I ask one?" he asked slowly.

Alice nodded. "It's only fair."

He shifted in his seat, finally understanding she wasn't going to go easy on him. She wanted to know him as well.

Apparently, Alice was his mate. She was supposed to be by his side, but she needed to know what that entailed. There were all these expectations, and neither of them knew what they wanted or needed. Parker sighed, already looking like he'd given up.

"Blue," Alice blurted. "My favorite color is blue."

"Why?"

"I guess it's like the sky. Like freedom."

Such a vague answer, and easier on her privacy compared to explaining what the song was about, yet Parker's face went ashen. He looked at Alice as though he'd seen a ghost.

twelve

PARKER LAZARUS

"PARKER? DID I SAY SOMETHING WRONG?"

She'd said her favorite color was blue. Like the sky. Like freedom. Such a simple thing to say, and yet it hurtled him back through the years, into the past, into the lab he'd grown up in. He was Pride, and Daisy was Despair. He was seven, and she was eight.

"Wake up, Pigeon," Despair whispered, using her nickname for him. "Come quickly."

Dark hair, dark eyes, but a white-toothed smile was all he could see as his eyes opened. Despair's hands were on his shoulders, shaking him.

"Stop calling me that."

"But you still eat like a pigeon," she giggled.

"And it's really dark."

Her smile widened. "Isn't that exciting?"

"Why?" He wanted to bury under the covers.

"Because when it's darkest, we know the sun is almost here."

Pride sat up, rubbing his eyes. She was right. A thrill tumbled inside him, tingling his senses. His heart thumped, and he matched Despair's smile, eager for what their secret morning had in store for them.

"Let's go," he whispered, and threw off his covers.

They crept past the old nun softly snoring on a chair with her knitting needles falling out of her hands. They went outside the sleeping quarters and onto the rooftop balcony with high garden walls that blocked everything from sight except for the sky, an ominous blanket with holes that let the starlight shine through. They went straight to the middle of the courtyard and laid down next to each other, trying not to shiver as they placed bits and pieces of food from their pockets around and over each other. Then they laid back and stared at the dark sky.

They waited.

And they waited.

They may have shivered, but it was worth it.

The holes in the sky-blanket disappeared. It turned into shades of purple and pink and blue.

Sometimes they saw darker shapes flittering. And if they were really still, if they pretended not to breathe, then sometimes those shapes hopped and fluttered over the walls of their rooftop courtyard and pecked and nibbled at the scraps of food around the children. Sometimes those pigeons grew in numbers until they covered everything. And when the sky turned blue, when the sun had come up, Despair would look at Pride through the feathers and the pigeon feet.

"Ready?" she mouthed.

He nodded.

Her eyes sparkled. "One."

"Two," he whispered.

"Three!" they shouted together, so loud they frightened the birds. Suddenly they were surrounded by flapping wings, cooing and warbling, and their own giggling squeals of excitement as feathers kissed their faces.

Above them the sky was blue, as it always was. As they'd always known.

When the last pigeon flapped away over the wall, Pride looked at his sister covered in feathers and delight.

"Where do you think they go?" he asked.

"Who cares? They're free."

"Parker?"

He met Alice's worried gaze with an uncomfortable feeling cracking open inside. Alice was right. This should have just been drinks. Why did he think getting to know her would be a good idea?

His finger twitched to reach for another champagne, but he was already onto his second glass, so scrubbed his hand down his face. The movement was the action he needed to center himself. Everything about Alice threw him off. She was not his assistant. She was another person, more foreign than ever.

But damn, she looked good tonight. Better than he'd ever seen her, and he couldn't put his finger on why. She was the same person, except he just saw *more* of her. Surely he wasn't that shallow, was he?

Crackling from the ceiling speakers was the only warning they received before Marvin Gaye's song, *Sexual Healing*, started playing. *Goddammit, Sloan.*

"This is a mistake." Parker abruptly stood.

"What?" Alice blinked up at him. "What's a mistake?"

"All of this." He threw the napkin on the table and strode to the kitchen, where he found Wyatt flipping something in a pan while chuckling to someone on the cell phone wedged between his shoulder and ear.

Parker's jaw clenched, and he snatched the cell from Wyatt, then put it down and turned on the loudspeaker.

"Turn the music off, Sloan."

Silence. Then, *"How did you know it was me?"*

"Who else likes to pull stupid, juvenile and mistimed escapades?"

"Well, you got me there."

"Turn it off, now."

"Ugh, you're such a party pooper but fine. Whatevs. Be boring." Another pause. *"Hi, Alice."*

Meddling pain in the ass. Parker cut the call.

"That's it. You're done. Go back to your mate," Parker said to Wyatt, taking the knife from him.

Wyatt glared back. "Fuck you, I'm not finished."

"Dinner is canceled."

Wyatt threw his black chef's cap on the counter and then shot an apologetic look over Parker's shoulder. Parker turned to follow his gaze and found Alice standing in the kitchen entry.

Parker smoothed his still damp shirt and straightened his spine. "I'll take you home."

She blocked him as he attempted to leave. "I don't think so. This meeting isn't over."

He looked down at the woman. The Sinner. His dangerous mate.

She had the power to unravel him, to pluck apart the thin threads holding him together. Each strand more meticulously sewn into place than the one before it. Each line carefully crafted to perfection because it had to be. Because the only other alternative was liability, and he would never be that. Not for anyone.

thirteen

ALICE MONTGOMERY

ALICE STARED Parker down as he attempted to leave the kitchen. Something had bothered him back there, and it had cracked his perfect, composed exterior. He hated that she'd seen it. That's what this was all about. Alice knew shame. She lived with it on a daily basis, but somehow, seeing it on him didn't sit well with her.

"I'm hungry," she said. "At least feed me like you promised."

Doubt flickered in his expression. He glanced at the half-finished food prep and then shot her a helpless look.

"Don't tell me cooking is the only thing Parker Lazarus doesn't know how to do," she teased.

"Of course I can cook."

"Right." What a fibber. The man hadn't boiled an egg in his life.

She picked up the knife and inspected the situation. Sauce was already made. Gnocchi made. Steak out at room temperature. Grill fired up. It didn't look too hard. Within moments, Alice had caught up to where Wyatt had left off. Parker offered rather weakly to help cut the vegetables, but she declined, instead giving him the job of turning the steak. He stood by the grill and watched her quietly.

Alice immersed herself in the process, finding it calmed her mind. Until she'd taken this mission, and had to live relatively alone for a few years, she'd not realized how much she enjoyed cooking and baking. Before the Vatican had become embroiled with the Sisterhood, the Sinners did their penance in the abbey kitchen. It was simple work, and it allowed them to provide and care for the nuns who worked at the abbey and kept their secret. The Sinners also worked in the garden and completed other menial tasks to give back to the organization that had given so much to them. After the Vatican had arrived, their penance took on more… aggressive forms.

"You know your way around a kitchen," Parker remarked.

She wiped the beading sweat from her brow and nodded, but didn't comment. She didn't want to think about the life waiting for her back at the abbey right now, and if she explained why she liked cooking, she'd have to. At the abbey, there was no cooking. There were no hobbies, or tv, or indulgence. It was hard work, penance, and prayer.

"You owe me a question," she said, keeping her eyes on vegetables steaming in a pot.

"What do you want to know?"

"Tell me about the mating bond." Alice held her breath, hoping that he would, for once, remain open about this, and when he started speaking, she exhaled.

"When we meet a partner who embodies our sin's opposing virtue, our powers are triggered and we secrete pheromones."

"That answer doesn't count. Tell me something I don't know." The pheromones were a new discovery. She also hadn't known they all could use them, but he didn't need to know that.

He paused, flipped the steak, and stared at it like it was trying to come for him. When he eventually spoke, his voice was tight. "If I have too much exposure to pride, or not enough, my internal sin-balance is out. Usually, we each have a tattoo with ink that shifts according to this balance. But—"

"It was on your missing hand." She felt a stab of guilt. "I remember that tattoo. Always thought it was odd that you'd have one. Didn't realize the ink moved. Did you get a replacement?"

"That's another question."

She lifted her gaze from the vegetables. "You didn't, did you?"

He gave a haughty half shrug.

"No matter who you are, the best laid plans can be ruined." She snorted softly and took the pot off the flame. "So what does this tattoo have to do with me?"

"Uh-uh. That's another question. My turn," he said, his lips twitching at the corner.

She pointed a spoon at him, opened her mouth, and then shut it. Damn it, he was right. In fact, he'd half answered a second question of hers.

"Why should I trust you?" he asked, leveling his gaze on her.

She could have answered with any number of reasons, from lies to truths. She could have reminded him that she was his mate, or what they were both fighting for, or said something personal about Mary's history with the Sisterhood, but in the end, she settled for the truth. "Because I trust you."

"So tell me why the Sisterhood is of value to us."

"You can save that question for when it's your turn." If she told him now, then she played all her cards. He might not believe her, anyway. While she pondered over her reply, she drained the vegetables and dished up the meals. They weren't presented the way Wyatt might have done, but the food was edible. Her stomach rumbled.

"Let's eat," she said, and carried the plates out to the dining room, wincing at the tug in her leg. She'd stood in one spot for too long while cooking, and now her body protested.

They ate in silence. Well, Alice did. The gnocchi was delicious. Parker stared at his plate and picked at the vegetables. For a while Alice thought perhaps she'd actually ordered the wrong thing, but had seen him choose the fillet steak many times during business meetings.

Then she realized he couldn't cut the steak with only one hand, and he was too stubborn to ask for help. If she reached over and completed the task for him, he would most likely refuse. It was time to be the bigger person.

"Do you believe in Hell, Parker?" she asked after she swallowed.

His gaze lifted. "What does Hell have to do with anything?"

"It's a simple question. You either do or you don't."

"Unless you're talking about my nightclub, no, I don't."

"But you've been created to sense deadly sin. How can you not?"

"Pride is just a human emotion. Sin is a human invention used to implement fear in order to control."

"But if people don't believe they sin, there would be chaos."

"There is chaos anyway, and people can still believe in doing wrong—I'm sorry, but why are we philosophizing about sin?"

Alice pulled his plate toward her and cut his steak into manageable pieces. "But whether or not Hell exists, as the Bible tells us, there is something. We at the Sisterhood—and the Vatican—firmly believe that."

"I never thought you were a believer, Alice. You've always been too practical and…" He sat back, loosened his tie, and put it on the table beside him. "I would have thought it behooves someone like you to disbelieve Bible tales."

"Someone like me? As in, if I don't believe in Hell, then I won't go there, is that it?" She pushed his plate back to him. "I'm suddenly forgiven for all my crimes?"

He nodded, picked up his fork, and stabbed the steak. Resisting a smile of triumph, Alice returned to her own meal but found her appetite had left her.

"You think all I do is kill, don't you?"

Not skipping a beat, he replied, "Mary told us all about the kinds of missions she went on. Sleeping with dangerous diplomats, assassinating the ones who posed a threat to the advancement of women, even going so far as infiltrating organizations, gaining their trust, and then when the time was ripe, ruthlessly squashing their targets like a bug. It takes a special kind of cold, hard detachment to go undercover for two years."

"You think I'm evil."

"I never said that."

"Sorry, cold, hard and detached."

"I was talking about Mary."

"So you think that of your mother?"

"I love my mother," he said, chewing and then swallowing. "There is nothing I wouldn't do for her. Nothing. But it took her a long time to reprogram herself from the damage the Sisterhood did to her. Even now I doubt she's fully recovered."

"And what about me? Do you think I'm redeemable?"

His lack of response was his answer, and it stabbed Alice right in the center of the chest. She was more than a killer. She was someone who tried to make the world a better place, like him. If Parker couldn't see that, a killer himself, then what was she doing? Maybe Parker would never understand where she came from.

"The thing is," she said, staring blankly at her plate. "We believe replicates left in their natural state move south because there is something there."

He raised a brow, curious.

"Most replicates can sense sin," she continued. "So it's safe to say when in their uncontrolled state, they would revert to pure instinct."

His chewing slowed, and he lowered his fork. "You're not about to say what I think you are, are you?"

"We believe they are trying to get to a place with the strongest concentration of sin—Hell."

He scoffed and spoke to her like she was a toddler. "They're just moving south, Alice. Probably programmed to head back to a base, that's all. And besides, I sense sin. Wouldn't I feel the urge to head south?"

"You think the Syndicate would be so stupid as to program their replicates to lead their enemies to their base?"

He shifted in his seat, uncomfortable.

Alice continued, "You and your siblings have intelligent, independent thought. Replicates are beings of instinct at the most basic level and they're programmed to hunt down sin."

"Sara was a replicate. Some would argue she was intelligent."

Alice remembered Sara, or rather the clone of Wyatt's ex fiancée who had appeared in Cardinal City about the same time Alice had arrived. In fact, it was Evan's and Grace's mating bond at this time that convinced the Sisterhood to lengthen Alice's stay and further study the Lazarus family.

Parker dabbed his mouth with a napkin. "This is ridiculous. You come in here, spouting theological nonsense, expecting me to believe your organization has worth."

Alice's anger started to boil again. It wasn't nonsense. The Sisterhood had many old manuscripts that noted the existence of Hellmouths, portals into other dimensions where demons were rife and evil existed. They also had ancient records that stated those averse to sinning were attracted to such Hell-mouths like moths to a flame—especially those with their intelligence at a basic level like children, animals, and the mentally challenged. They saw things those tainted by pragmatic belief failed to see.

Parker was right on some level. Alice had never believed in Hell until recently. Until Sister Prudence had fed them information from the Syndicate. Until some replicates in Europe had escaped. Until the Vatican had warned them about demonic possession. They were sending a team of experts, including an exorcist, to the Sisterhood to debrief and train them on how to handle the increasing threat. Some of Alice's sisters had seen demonic possession first hand.

They never lied—well, not to each other. Combined with Raven's ominous psychic visions, Alice believed them. Something was coming, and it was evil. Worse than the Syndicate.

"It's not impossible," Alice said. "The scientific community has long postulated over the existence of alternate dimensions."

"But Hell?" He barked out a laugh, deep and rich.

"Fuck you," she growled. "You ignore this, and there will be—"

"What, Hell to pay?"

Alice's fists clenched until her nails dug into her palms. He had no idea what he was talking about. This man's stubborn pride would be the end of him.

"Alice," he said, coming to a stand. He braced his hand on the table and leaned forward, probably in some kind of intimidation attempt. "I don't have time for fairytales. We have real flesh and blood enemies here, on this earth, to contend with. I wanted the truth from you, and all I got was impractical stories. I think we're done."

Maybe he was right, and she was cold and detached, because the moment he dismissed her, the mission jerked to the forefront of her mind. She would not be dismissed. She'd tried diplomacy. She'd lulled him into a sense of complacency with this dinner, and now it was time for a demonstration of power.

Alice slowly came to a stand, meeting him eye to eye, her hand slowly moving to the small of her back, her eyes tracking options to defend herself. Across the table dividing them, she locked onto his silk tie. She leaned forward at the hip, matching his posture—one hand on the table, the other near her back—and then bared her teeth at him. "We're done when I say we're done."

A deft flick of her finger on the wakizashi holster, and the hilt dropped into hand. In one swift motion, she unsheathed the blade, rotated, and punched Parker's jaw with the hilt in her fist. His head snapped back. She vaulted over the table, knocking plates and glasses as he landed hard on his chair. She was on him in a blink, using his tie to pin his good hand back and wrapping it around his torso, securing him to the chair. He must have been stunned because he sat there motionless while she yanked on the tie and knotted it. *Just enough length.* When it was done, she kicked the table aside so she could stand before him, sword pointed at his neck.

If fury had a picture next to it in the dictionary, it would be Parker Lazarus's face. A vein throbbed at his forehead, tendons protruded from his neck, and red mottled his tanned complexion. Eyes of molten gold glared at her, a glow she believed was linked to his new abilities. She expected him to turn beastly and break the hold the tie had on him—she had no doubt he had the strength.

He made little sounds as though trying to hold himself down, to restrain the wildness burning to get out. Alice frowned. Would he be so devastating if he unleashed? A quick memory of how he'd ripped through the Faithful at the Cathedral came to mind. He'd been a raw, masculine tornado of destruction. And he'd been holding back.

Steeling herself, she lifted her chin.

"I never really expected you to believe me, Parker. But I didn't think you'd laugh in my face and throw away this opportunity."

He stared at her, breathing hard, nostrils flaring—the lion about to charge.

"This isn't exactly the way to forge an alliance, Alice," he ground out.

"Yeah, well, it's clear you think so little of us. Maybe it's time to cut our losses."

A lick of something sweet, heady, and musky entered the air. Alice's body became both aroused and alarmed at the same time. Pheromones. The bastard was going to seduce her into capitulation. That was her plan!

"Turn it off," she said, pressing the sword beneath his jaw.

He winced as it nicked skin, releasing a precious drop of imperious blood.

"I can't," he ground out.

"Turn it off!" she shouted.

"What do you think I've been trying to do all night?" he roared back.

Alice laughed. "No wonder you've been scowling at me. This must drive you insane."

He looked away, cheeks reddening.

"Having me as a mate—the enemy, a dowdy nerdy assistant, a useless female assassin spinning fairytales about Hell. And every time I'm around, your body wants to mate with me. Is that what happens?" She leaned forward. "Do you want to fuck me like an animal? Throw me on this table and rut with me from behind?"

"Call me that again—"

"Animal?"

A low growl. Teeth elongating. Alice lowered the sword and scratched under his jaw. "There you go, little fella. How's that feel?"

Sharp fangs snapped at her face and she laughed, but then quickly sobered as the truth hit her. He was pissed. He was furious. And she'd been right. The words had come out of her mouth, but the insult slapped her in the face all the same because they were true. She was his enemy. She was... what did he say before? *Not worth holding on to.*

Alice dropped her hand to her side. All humor gone, she bowed her head and tried to come up with what to do next.

"Three times," he said, bringing her attention back to him.

"What?"

"That's how many times you've bested me in two months. You're not useless, Alice. Far from it. Now, put the sword away and we can talk about this like decent human beings."

His alluring scent wrapped around her body, tightening her tingling skin, urging her closer to him. It whispered into her ear, *Do what he says and he will reward you.* The image of him bending her over the table suddenly didn't seem so bad. Her eyes became stuck on the thick column of his neck, the shadow of new scruff beneath the longer, older growth on his jaw. The single red streak of blood trickling down from where she'd cut him unawares. It curved around his Adam's apple and dribbled down to his white collar, staining it.

"You will put the sword away, Alice." His smooth, honeyed voice sank into her bones. "You will untie me. You will forget about the Sisterhood, and you will remain with me and my family here, at Lazarus House. As my mate."

Every cell in her body wanted to do what he said. Pistons firing in her mind and heart pushed her forward, taunting her with something all orphans wanted. A family, but at the expense of the one that had raised her. She snarled and snapped out of his mental hold. "I don't think so."

His eyes narrowed. "How did you…?"

"I've been battling my attraction to you for years," she confessed, her heart breaking. "You took me by surprise that first time at your office, but you've reminded me tonight what my real worth is to you."

"And what's that?"

"I may have bested you, Parker, but I can see it in your eyes. You still think I'm not worth holding on to." She secured her wakizashi in her holster before turning her back on him. "So I will give you some time to think about this alliance and tell you something, perhaps, that I haven't made clear. It's not just me you'll be getting, but the entire force of the Sisterhood—some thirty strong Sinners. You and your family are powerful, but you're not invincible. You're not the only ones with tech and offensive battle skills. We have strong women, our own worth, and we want an alliance with your family—not just you."

"I will see Daisy returned to us, and I *will* destroy the Syndicate. I will not, however, go on a wild goose chase hunting down some sort of nonexistent opening to another dimension."

"A Hell dimension," she reminded him.

"Whatever you believe about the replicates, my mission hasn't changed."

"If there's nothing else you believe about me, Parker, believe this. We want the Syndicate destroyed, not only because of the threat our psychic has foretold, but because they have one of ours. A Sinner has failed to contact us for months. We want her back. We may be worthless to you, but we're not to each other."

"Alice," he called, halting her as she left. She glanced over her shoulder and found pain in his eyes as he spoke. "I wasn't angry at you."

"What?"

"When I picked you up earlier tonight, and you accused me of being pissed off… I was angry at myself." He licked his lips and took a breath. "You're beautiful, and I never noticed. I should have noticed."

Alice's heart beat loudly in her chest, taunting her with all the things she would never have, but she knew the ending to this story. She'd lived it for years as she'd worked by his side, silently pleading for him to see through her disguise to the woman beneath. Hopelessly fantasizing about a life beyond her reality—a stupid, broken dream.

She'd never have the full, undivided attention of Parker Lazarus. He'd never be her baby because, whether Hell was real, the truth remained; Alice was a Sinner, like the rest of them. And the Deadly Seven's sole reason for existence was to hunt down sin.

"You should talk the alliance over with your family," she suggested. "And you should do it before your pride gets the better of you again."

fourteen

PARKER LAZARUS

STILL BOUND TO THE CHAIR, Parker wished he didn't ache with longing after Alice departed. Since the moment he'd seen her earlier tonight on the street, hugging herself against the brisk wind, he'd struggled with himself. His instincts, his control, his emotions.

Her beauty had taken him off guard. The street light did no justice to her flawless profile and blushing skin. Holding down the mating pheromones had taken all of his concentration. Even talking had been difficult. Then there was her attitude—the quietly confident woman who didn't give a rat's ass who he was, or how much money he had in the bank. She never had.

And then when she'd synced her cell phone to play her music as though she belonged in his car, he'd gone hard. Instant turn on.

Someone who's not worth holding on to.

He winced. Those were the words he'd thrown at her. He was a fool. That woman was incredible, if a little nuts, but he blamed the Sisterhood for that. He just needed to get her away from them, to get her head back down from the clouds. She didn't belong with the Sisterhood. She belonged with him.

He tensed, made a fist and flexed his arm to break the tie binding him to the chair. It snapped easily, and he stared down at it, stunned. He'd sat there the entire time and not once attempted to break the binding. Refusing to dwell on why, he got to his feet and surveyed the empty plates and tipped over champagne, feeling that tug in his chest again. Alice had cooked for him. She'd cut his steak. She knew exactly what he wanted, but she never once used that against him.

He pulled his cell out of his pocket and dialed Evan.

"Bro," Evan answered.

"Be in my penthouse in five with your tattoo kit and bio-indicator ink."

A pause. "Thank fuck you've come to your senses. I'll be there in five."

"Actually, make it the basement. Family meeting."

"ALMOST DONE," Evan said as he put the finishing touches on Parker's inner wrist tattoo, the gun buzzing. Evan had grumbled about the cleanliness of the basement workshop, so they'd moved to the next room—the operations HQ. Wall to wall screens depicted news networks from around the world, and especially in Cardinal City.

The square table the family sat around was clear and doubled as a touch screen monitor they used to plan missions. Deadly suits sat dormant in glass cabinets on faceless mannequins, reminding Parker he needed to finalize AIMI's resurrection so they could get the suits functioning again. Flint tinkered in the workshop adjacent, immersed in something.

When the rest of the family turned up, Parker told them what Alice had revealed. Now, an hour later, they all stood around Parker and Evan, stunned.

"Clearly it's a fabrication," Parker said of the Hell-mouth tale. "Designed to distract us or perhaps lull us into a false sense of urgency and thus agreeing to this sham of an alliance."

As the words came out of his mouth, they felt hollow. Maybe the story was false, but Alice's intentions had been true. He knew that in his heart.

He looked up and found at least half of his siblings agreeing with him. A few others, Evan included, gave Parker worried eyes.

"What if it's not?" Evan asked as he wiped the blood from Parker's wrist. "I mean, I can't explain how I can predict the future, or how mama did. Going by that theory, there must be other things in the universe we can't explain. Maybe even other dimensions."

"Magic is science we don't know yet," Griffin said from his seat at the table.

It was something their birth mother and creator had always said to Mary, and something she'd always repeated to them. It had been a handy mantra to have when they needed to demystify a seemingly impossible problem. Parker looked at his mother.

The ex-Sinner stood in her usual black yoga attire, as stiff as a board. Dark circles were under her eyes and had been since Daisy's sacrifice and consequence absence.

"Mary," he said. "What do you think?"

She swallowed. "It's possible. How could it not be?"

Parker frowned.

"Stay still," Evan warned, and yanked Parker's wrist back to the correct position before continuing with the final mark.

"If we hadn't exterminated the replicates, we could have followed them," Griffin suggested.

"No," Parker grumbled. "If the Sisterhood wants to chase down alternate dimensions, then we can't stop them. But we have more pressing matters to worry about than where replicates go if they're uncontrolled. The Syndicate is worldwide. We've caught glimpses of their plans, and between the plant monsters and rabid sin-sensing animals, we've got enough on our plate. Sloan, is AIMI's tracking data collated from the recovery device?"

"She's been sifting through new and old data from Daisy's tracker. I thought we'd be able to differentiate the two, but there are so many options. It seems as though Daisy has been moved about. All around the world." Sloan slid her laptop onto the table and opened a spreadsheet. "Griffin helped me order all of this. We have a few possible destinations we can investigate, but—"

She lifted her head, eyes stark.

"What?" Parker prompted.

"It's just that we have no idea if she's currently there or has moved on."

"What's the live tracking data saying?"

His sister shook her head. "It's coming in pieces. I can't get a good read. I think AIMI needs some more work if we want to fill in the blanks."

"Then we go to all the old locations," he stated, leaning over to view the screen. "All hands on deck, we pair up, visit all the sites and report back. They could be international Syndicate bases for all we know. Evan and Liza, Sloan and Wyatt, Griffin and Tony. I'll go alone."

"No," Wyatt said. "I'm not leaving the city or Misha alone with the baby."

Parker's eyes fluttered closed in frustration. There was no point trying to sway Wyatt, or to convince him that Nightingale Security had been hired for this very reason—to protect their mates when the

Lazarus family couldn't. Wyatt would only point out that Misha had already been kidnapped once. He wasn't comfortable with anyone but himself protecting her and his baby.

Parker's incredulous look shifted to Griffin, who'd also put up his hand.

"I won't leave the city either," Griffin announced. "Lilo's pregnant. If the Syndicate found out, she will be in the same position Misha was a few months ago."

The family jumped on Griffin with their congratulations. Mary hugged her son, despite his stiff reaction. Liza and Sloan whooped. Wyatt grinned and slapped Griffin hard on the back. A growl slipped out of Parker.

They all looked at him.

"This isn't a time for you all to start popping out children," he barked, losing his temper. "For Christ's sake, this is serious. We're at war. Daisy is missing, possibly dead, and you're all procreating like bunnies."

"Alice playing hard to get?" Liza teased with a waggle of her brows.

"This has nothing to do with Alice."

Sloan tossed something at Parker. Probably a crumb from her sweater. "Chill, bras. It's not all of us having babies. Just two."

Tony snorted, a little drop of fear in his eyes. "Bailey and I are traveling first. Lots of traveling."

Griffin's eyes flashed and every metal object within reaching distance shuddered, a sign of his hold on his powers slipping with his temper. "We didn't plan this, Parker. And for your information, Lilo fell pregnant three months ago. Before Daisy even stepped foot into our house again. We just kept it to ourselves until we knew the pregnancy was safe." He stood. "Wyatt and I will hold the fort while everyone else is gone."

Without another word, Griffin left the room. Wyatt tossed a dark look at Parker from over his shoulder before exiting too.

Evan placed some plastic wrap over Parker's new tattoo. "Maybe Max can go in Griffin's stead? Or Joe?"

Parker scrubbed his face. Could they bring two civilians into this? Even if one was ex-military, and the other FBI? Compared to the Deadly Seven, everyone was a civilian.

"I'll go tell Max," Sloan said as she closed her laptop.

"I don't think Joe should come," Liza said. "If he and I are both absent from work at the same time, it will be noticed. Plus… you know he'd rather handle things from the right side of the law."

When his sisters and brothers left, Parker rubbed his temple, feeling a headache come on.

"We still need one more," he pointed out to the only person who'd stayed.

"Then ask Alice," Mary said.

The sounds of Flint tinkering in the workshop silenced, as if he too held his breath, waiting for Parker's answer.

"She's the enemy," Parker reminded his mother, his voice softer than he'd intended. "You know what they're capable of."

"This is exactly why I'm telling you to trust her." Mary gave his new tattoo a pointed look. The ink was still perfectly balanced, an after effect of Alice's touch. It wouldn't remain so for long. "Flint trusted me, and look where we are."

"But it's Daisy," he said, his brows raised in the middle. Out of anyone in this family, Mary was the only one who knew the true tragedy of Daisy's downfall. They remembered the happy, caring girl she'd once been. They knew the price of failure.

"I know, *mijo*," Mary murmured as she cupped Parker's face, her tiny hand barely making an impression against his large jaw. "And it is for Daisy that you must swallow your pride. You must accept assistance in any shape or form. Daisy has sacrificed enough."

"I don't need Alice." Again, the words sounded hollow. Something his mouth was doing to convince his heart.

As if reading his thoughts, Mary gave him a small smile. "We all need someone, Parker."

"You saw what's happening. Wyatt and now Griffin are operating at restricted capacities because of their partnerships. I can't afford a distraction. Having Alice around is exactly that."

Mary flinched. "Do you really think loving someone is a distraction, or do you think you're not worthy of that love?"

He jolted. "Where did that come from?"

"It's just that I've been your mother for almost thirty years, Parker. And in all that time, you've never settled down. You've never even taken more than a week with someone, let alone brought her home. You're lonely, and I'm worried about you."

"Whether I want to love someone or not isn't what matters. The heart is a weakness."

"You're starting to sound the same as Liza did. How did I fail at this—the most important task Gloria gave me?" Mary glared at her feet. "I was supposed to show you what love was so you recognized it with open arms."

"Except, that's not what you taught me first and we all know those lessons are best remembered. The heart is what forced Daisy to leave us. It's why she walked into that burning building to save Gloria. Yet the heart wasn't enough for you to go back for Daisy. She stopped being useful the moment she stepped off that elevator. I remember, Mary. I remember you making the choice to leave Daisy to the flames. She was the acceptable sacrifice because what mattered most was saving the world, so... don't talk to me about love."

The slap in the face threw Parker's head to the side. He worked his jaw as the pain numbed and tingled. His mother always did have a good right hook.

"I'm going to forgive you for that, *mijo*, because I know you're hurting, and I also know why you work so hard at being perfect. You said it yourself, you're afraid to outlive your use. You think that's all you have to offer the world." She patted his shoulder, her anger tempered. "If you can't see how wrong you've been, then I don't know what else to tell you, but maybe Alice does."

"Haven't you been listening?" He threw up his hand, exasperated.

"I've been listening your whole life, Parker. Maybe it's time you did the same."

With those final words, Mary went to the workshop and kissed her husband on the cheek. Flint stood swiftly, glowered at Parker in a way that said he would have words with him later, and then took his wife back to their rooms.

Left alone, Parker tried not to repeat what Mary had said to him, but he couldn't stop thinking about it. Failure to be useful?

Well, someone had to make the money to fund this operation. Someone had to lead them. Someone had to make all the sacrifices before he was the one sacrificed.

And there it was, the truth of it.

He slumped in his seat, head in his hand. Pride had taken him far in life, except what was the point if he was bitter and alone? That was the one lesson Mary always tried to drill into him. The one lesson he'd chosen to ignore because he thought he knew better.

What was the point to any of it without love?

He picked up his cell and dialed his sister.

"Bras," Sloan answered. "I'm in bed now. This better be important."

"A personal request," he said. Swallowed. "Please."

"What is it?"

"I need to know more about Alice. Can you see what you can find out?"

"Already done it."

"You have?"

"You don't think we'd let you go off with the enemy without doing a background check first, do you?"

"We?"

"Yeah, all of us. I'll bring the info tomorrow."

"Thanks."

Something warm bloomed in his chest as he cut the call. They'd looked out for him? All of them?

Parker leveled his gaze on the dormant suits. He couldn't fully operate it in his state. He shifted his gaze to where Flint had worked, ten feet away on the robotic arm that was once attached to a Syndicate enemy. He'd been working on it all day and night. It would go faster if Parker joined him, and the arm would most likely function better. Parker was still staring at the robotic arm when Flint returned.

The tall man put his hands in his pockets and narrowed his eyes at Parker.

"I think it's time you and I had a little father-son chat about manners where your mother is concerned." He glanced at the robotic arm. "And then we're going to try to fit this to you."

right
fifteen

ALICE MONTGOMERY

ALICE TURNED off the radio receiver and sat back on the sofa in her apartment. She'd planted a bug in Parker's jacket pocket and couldn't process what she'd just heard. Next to her, Mercy gave a long, drawn out whistle. Then she turned to Alice and rested her head on her hand.

"You want to talk about it, babe?" Mercy asked.

Alice frowned. "I guess, we give him some space and then get his answer in a few days. They need our help to cover all the tracker locations. He'll say yes."

"Oh, no." Mercy smirked. "I meant, do you want to talk about what you said to Parker at dinner?"

Alice switched the radio receiver back on, in case there was more to hear.

"Babe," Mercy said, turning it off again. "I'm serious. I think you should talk about it."

"Talk about what, Mercy?" Alice went to the tiny kitchen in the corner of her apartment. She checked on the cookies cooling on a rack. Baking and cooking had become a sort of therapy. It relaxed her.

center
116

Mercy followed her into the kitchen. "You told Parker you've been attracted to him for years."

Alice's shoulders dropped.

"Why are you fighting this?"

Alice rounded on her. "Because he hates me. Because I'm a Sinner and I can't leave the Sisterhood. Because there's a world to save. Take your pick."

"You know that's all bullshit." Mercy touched one of the cookies, testing the temperature. Alice whacked her hand away, eliciting a scowl on her sister's face. "What's the real reason?"

"Maybe I don't want to leave the only family I have."

"We're not going anywhere." Mercy folded her arms. "I'm still not seeing why you won't give this a chance. You heard what Raven said —this alliance is the beginning of a new era for us Sinners. With you leading the way, the rest of us might actually find happiness. That's what you want, right?" She paused, narrowed her eyes. "What *do* you want?"

"I…" Alice was almost too afraid to think about *it*, but *it* forced itself into her mind all the same. She wanted to be wanted, but how could someone like Parker fall for someone like her? "I'll never be at his level, Mercy."

"What level is that? From where I'm standing, you're both so similar."

"No, Parker is perfect. I'm… wrong. I'm wrong and I'm full of sin. It's his destiny to battle someone like me."

Mercy snorted. "He's far from perfect and I'm not talking about the missing arm or the arrogance."

"What do you mean?"

She waved at the radio. "He's got major performance anxiety."

"I don't think that's—"

"Sure it was. He's got the same issues as all of us. He thinks his heart doesn't matter. Now, who do I know who sounds like that?" She tapped her lip and gave Alice a pointed look. "No wonder you two are a good match." At Alice's shaking head, she added, "God, you're just as stubborn as he is, but let me remind you of something. The more stubborn, the more that heart is locked tight, the greater the reward and the loyalty. Crack that shell of his and he's yours forever. Trust me, I know. There was once this old navy captain I dated who'd locked himself up in this little cottage—"

"Got it," Alice interrupted. She didn't need the full details of Mercy cracking the hard shell of her sexual conquest.

"The point is, I still get letters from this captain. He loves me."

"You should stop playing with his heart."

"Believe me, I've tried." She dusted her shoulder. "But the difference between me and you is that I don't want a steady relationship. I don't dream about happy ever afters. You do. So it's there if you're brave enough to take it."

Alice canted her head, searching her sister's face. Did she truly believe that kind of love existed in Alice's future?

Mercy flicked her hair dramatically. "I know, I know. You're thinking, how does a nympho like me become so wise when it comes to love—"

"It's because you have the biggest heart of them all."

"Well," Mercy scoffed. "I wouldn't go that far. Maybe Tawny has that brag."

The two of them had been through so much. All of their unit had. Yes, Alice had always felt a connection with Parker, even if he hadn't with her. She couldn't ignore it. Two years of working closely with him, watching out for him when he was too busy to watch out for himself, had left scars on her soul. There were forces pushing them together. Saying her feelings aloud at dinner had damaged the wall around her heart, and all her childish dreams had leaked out.

She blinked rapidly to banish tears before they had a chance to fall.

"You're right. I want it, Mercy," she confessed, her throat tightening. "I want a normal life. I want a family. I want someone to care for me the way they all care for each other. I want what I lost, and I also want to keep the family I found."

"I know," Mercy whispered, her unsaid *"Me too"* hanging in the air. "You deserve it, and you actually have a chance where the rest of us don't. Even if it's all part of the Rev's plan. Even if there's a darkness hanging over you. For a little while, you can make it happen."

"I'm no fool, Mercy. I don't want someone who doesn't want me back."

Mercy snorted. "Girl, if you think that's what's happening here, then you haven't been listening either." She pointed at the radio receiver. "That man is totally in love with you. He just doesn't know it yet."

Alice wasn't sure about that, but she couldn't deny she wanted to find out if it was true. "So, what now?"

"Now I tell the rest of the team to be prepared to head overseas. One of us with one of them should cover all bases. Until then, you keep heading into the office, keeping his personal life afloat. You seduce him by opening his heart. It won't take him long to see you. And when that happens, he'll know he can't live without you, or us."

AS IT TURNED OUT, "NOT LONG" took about a week. Alice continued to head into the office and field phone calls from the board about Parker's absence. Every day she'd entered his empty office and a little piece of her heart chipped off along with her hope. He never showed up. Was there more she should have said? Should she have been less forceful with him? Did she really need to tie him up, as he had done to her?

Was she giving him too much time?

Two days after their dinner date, Alice strode into the Lazarus Tech offices and, instead of settling in at her desk outside Parker's office, she decided to work from his desk. He wasn't using it anyway, and if he didn't like it, he could come into the office and tell her so. From the comfort of his plush leather desk chair, she fired up his computer and went through their company emails. Every so often, her eyes would drift to a framed picture of him shaking hands with the Dalai Lama and she'd smile.

A picture with the president, a picture with billionaires, and a picture with the Pope were on display as well. Alice would bet that last one was a reminder of how far he'd come. The Vatican had been financial investors in the project that created the Deadly Seven. They wanted deadly sin eradicated and prevented, but as far as Alice knew, the Vatican had no hand in the new splinter cell Syndicate of today. Like the Sisterhood, they've had their hands full discovering demonic possession was actually a thing.

Deciding to mess with Parker's decor, and maybe snoop a little, she opened his desk drawer and stopped short. There were multiple bundles of rope tied into different knot configurations. Knots that looked like flowers, knots that looked like intricate balls, and knots that reminded Alice of Parker's rock climbing rigs.

Come to think of it, she remembered walking into the office once and finding him playing with rope, but he'd shoved it in the drawer before she could mention it. She'd always assumed it had something to do with his rock-climbing hobby, but now knew about the rope art pictures on his walls... and the bundles of rope dangling on hooks, and the pulleys and bolts in his bedroom ceiling. This must be a hobby of his. Or passion. Or obsession.

It was also one nobody else was privy to. A shiver ran down her spine.

Alice rifled further in the drawer and found a security access card, pencils and pens, and a bottle of whiskey. Before she shut the drawer, she stole a purple flower-knot as a memento, hoping she wasn't being too stalkerish, then went back to sifting through the mess that was Parker's business life.

Her day became filled with the Board's demands, invitations for charity balls, marketing and budget requirements. Accounting said Lazarus Tech hadn't fulfilled their donation requirements for this tax term, blah blah blah. This was Alice's life until lunchtime and she went to the staffroom fridge. She'd brought double lunch again, as she had for the past two months since Parker's accident. Knowing she'd be accosted by staff if she ate in the break room, she took her food into the office and ate at his desk. When she was done, she had the second dish couriered over to Lazarus House, care of Parker, and then continued to work. At the end of the day, Alice did what she always did, and sent the summary of the day's work.

That was her job.

And then she turned off the lights, went down to the office gym and worked out before heading home to her tiny, empty apartment. Some days she stopped in at the cathedral, prayed, gave confession and did her penance.

This routine went on for another few days, until finally, on the third day, just before she was about to head home for the day, a message pinged on the computer screen via the inter-office messaging app.

Parker.Lazarus@LazTech.com
— Why are you working in my office?

Alice.Montgomery@LazTech.com
— The view is better in here.

Parker.Lazarus@LazTech.com
— The view is fine from your desk. *Outside* my office.

Alice couldn't help the smile building in her body. So he was checking in through the internal security surveillance cameras, after all. He hadn't explicitly said to leave, and she'd been working here for almost a week without him commenting. He hadn't said anything about declining the alliance, or the work she'd sent him for the past few days, or the food. She frowned. Goddamn him. He hadn't even said thank you for the food, yet after the first day of couriering it over, he'd sent back the washed and empty Tupperware dish from the previous day. Alice cracked her knuckles. Looked like the man needed some lessons in manners. But first, she was going to annoy the shit out of him.

Alice.Montgomery@LazTech.com
— The view is better in here and you're not using it, so it's mine now. I licked it.

Parker.Lazarus@LazTech.com
— You licked it?

Alice.Montgomery@LazTech.com
— I also rearranged your desk decor. You look much more personable now. You're welcome.

Parker.Lazarus@LazTech.com
— Personable? I don't want to look personable.
Put it back the way you found it.

Alice.Montgomery@LazTech.com
— No.

Parker.Lazarus@LazTech.com
— No?

Alice.Montgomery@LazTech.com
— Come and make me.

Parker.Lazarus@LazTech.com
...
...

Alice loved seeing those little three communications dots pop up and then disappear, as though Parker was stewing over what words to write next. But before he had a chance to give an autocratic declaration, or decide he should really call security after all, she used the opportunity to barrage him with work. She sent him text after text outlining urgent matters demanding his attention. He gave her yes or no answers, but he engaged in work, which was more than she expected. It felt good. It felt like routine. It felt like them.

Relief made her realize why she kept coming into the office, despite her charade being over.

She didn't want him to lose his company.

His mother's words she'd heard over the planted bug came back to her. She'd accused Parker of being a perfectionist because he was afraid to outlive his use. He didn't think he had anything else to offer. It was always about duty with him. Not a moment of rest or reward.

She knew the feeling.

Back to the messages and work. She continued to filter the communications that needed his attention. Last but not least, she reminded him about the pressure from the top brass. They needed him at a board meeting, and some were threatening a vote of no confidence. He only replied that it was irrelevant. He was a majority shareholder. They couldn't get rid of him. And then finally, she threw her lot in and asked him the question she'd been wanting to ask all day.

Alice.Montgomery@LazTech.com
— Do you have an answer to my offer?

Parker.Lazarus@LazTech.com
— I refuse to talk about this over the work system.

Her lips curved. So that wasn't a no. Neither was it a yes. While she was thinking of how to respond, Parker sent another message.

Parker.Lazarus@LazTech.com
— Why are you still hiding behind those dowdy outfits?

She glanced down at her potato sack of a dress and cardigan, then up to the security camera stuck to the ceiling in the corner. Her lips tugged into a smile, then she remembered what he'd typed.

Alice.Montgomery@LazTech.com

— I'm not hiding. I'm right here.

Where was he? Alice sighed and slumped. What a strange question to ask, anyway. He'd attempted to get to know her once, and maybe this was another olive branch, in his weird way. Then again, maybe it was manipulation, or some veiled attempt at asking her about her intentions. She rested her fingers lightly on the keyboard and watched the sun setting beyond the computer, through the top-floor window. The city buildings cast long shadows on one side, each structure a black silhouette against a turquoise and orange sky. A little ping sounded on the computer, and she glanced back at the screen.

Parker.Lazarus@LazTech.com
— ?

Alice.Montgomery@LazTech.com
— I don't own any other clothes except my… other
uniform.

A flush of embarrassment hit her cheeks. This was stupid. The man had so much money he could practically sleep on a bed of gold, and she had nothing. Why did she feel she had to justify her fashion choices?

Parker.Lazarus@LazTech.com
— Do I not pay you enough that you can afford
more clothes?

Alice.Montgomery@LazTech.com
— You pay plenty. I think it's time for me to go

home. Goodnight. Hopefully, I'll see you
tomorrow.

Parker.Lazarus@LazTech.com
— I'm not done talking.
— Alice?
— Alice?

PARKER LAZARUS

PARKER SAT at his baby grand, silently fuming at his laptop on the closed piano lid, the messaging app still showing his last attempt at contacting Alice. She'd ignored him. He flicked the screen to view the security footage of his office and watched her tidy before presumably heading home, all the while handling the soft but strong jute rope he'd used to secure Alice to his bed. He hadn't been able to tie proper knots since his accident, and out of everything he couldn't do, this bothered him most.

When he weaved rope, it calmed his mind. It drew him into the quiet, a place of peace. If the right woman was involved, then this process was beautiful, cathartic and sometimes erotic—for both parties. But Alice had brought chaos into his quiet, and since then, he'd not been able to reverse it.

He also used to play the piano, but both pastimes had been neglected since his accident. He lifted the fallboard to reveal the piano keys, dusty and neglected. He tapped one. The solitary note filled his penthouse, chasing the loud silence away. *Still in tune.*

But the rope unraveled from his hand. With a frustrated growl, he hung it on a hook in his bedroom, next to a row of other bundles in all sorts of thicknesses. One handed, he tried to tidy the length he'd just played with.

What did Alice mean, she had no other clothes? He paid her an exorbitant salary. Where did it go if not for her wardrobe or her apartment? That, too, was in the poor area of town. Come to think of it, he'd never seen her spend her money on anything apart from food. But, then again, he knew little about the woman except from what Sloan had dredged up in her background report. He'd gone through the paperwork this morning.

Alice had been an orphan since the age of four from a brutal car accident. She was with a distant aunt and uncle for a few years, but that didn't last long. By the age of nine, she was in foster care. By the age of ten, her foster care records had vanished. Parker could only assume she went to the Hildegard Sisterhood.

Ten.

She'd been trained as an assassin from an earlier age than him. Despite being made in a lab for only one purpose—to fight sin— Mary and Flint allowed the Lazarus siblings a normal childhood up until they turned fifteen. Sure, Mary had taught them how to manage their strength and skills at home before then, but it was at fifteen they'd begun their official deadly training. Mary had always told them she'd never had a real childhood and didn't want the same for them.

A knock came at the door, interrupting Parker's thoughts. He left his room, closing the door behind, and let the small welcoming party inside the penthouse. His father and Sloan, both with their toolkits in tow, followed by Grace and Mary, the latter with a casserole dish in her gloved hands. She lifted it to show him.

"I already ate," he said, frowning.

"Oh?" Mary's brow rose and gave his at-home attire a disapproving once over. Satin lounge pants and no shirt. "You cooked?"

"No."

"You ordered takeout?"

"Not exactly." He paused. "Alice sent something over."

The food was good. Why should it go to waste just because of who Alice was? Mary tried to hide her small smile as she pushed past him, but he'd caught it.

"It doesn't mean anything," he called after her. "I still haven't—"

His mother ignored him and went to put the casserole in his fridge. Flint held up the robotic arm they'd all been working on for the past few days. They'd added a few of Parker's own suggestions to harmonize with his new powers. The new prototype had passed all the initial tests. It was a hack job, and he would have preferred to dismantle the Syndicate tech and start from scratch, but they didn't have time. All they needed to do now was attach it to his arm and train his brain to send the right signals to make it respond.

Piece of cake.

Grace smiled gently and followed Flint inside, her medical bag dangling from her hand.

"You ready to get to work?" Flint asked Parker, scrubbing his beard. Dark circles smudged under his eyes. They were the same on Mary. His parents were feeling the pinch of worry where it came to Daisy, and most definitely the compounded guilt of letting her go all those years ago. They'd only isolated one location for Daisy—in Norway—and Tony and Evan had immediately taken Parker's jet to investigate. They were due any moment to call in for a status report.

Sloan waggled her brows at his stump. "Bras, I'm so excited about this."

"How fortunate that my pain will be your entertainment for the night." A grim yet sarcastic expression forced itself upon his face. She poked out her tongue, and he smiled. She was too easy to rile.

"Where can we set up?" Flint asked, scanning the messy penthouse.

Parker had tried to tidy it, but was starting to see the wisdom in Liza's previous comment about letting in the housekeeper. Boxes and parts were everywhere, from the dining table, to the leather couches, to the baby grand piano. Perhaps they should have stayed downstairs in the basement workshop, but he wanted privacy and a familiar environment for this next part. He might have to remain in lockdown for a few days until he was functioning at full speed and could pass his bionic arm off as human. Perhaps tidying would be a good calibration exercise for the new arm. Perhaps he'd find his elusive quiet again.

"I suppose we set up at the table," he said. "I'll clear AIMI's parts."

"I'll do it," Sloan said. "You two get started. I want to be home soon—Max has a Dota gaming tournament lined up for the both of us."

Parker stopped listening, bored already. As long as she gave her full attention to this project, she was allowed to stay. When enough space was cleared, Flint unpacked the arm from an aluminum suitcase. The garish gold had been ground off, the new surface coated with aggregated diamond nanorods, making it harder than steel. He could punch through a wall with no effort or damage. A skeletal sleeve had been attached to his humerus bone two nights earlier. He'd paid the surgical specialist an obscene amount of money for his continued silence and the promise of allowing him in on future tech releases and studies involving the arm.

Grace pointed at his stump, now with wires and a metal bone protruding from it.

"Do you mind if I check on the healing?" she asked.

"Go ahead."

"You might want to sit." She pulled the piano bench over and bade him down. When he was sitting, she leaned in to take a closer look at the new skin forming around the metal bone. "Looks good," she murmured after removing the dressing. "How's it feel?"

"Tight. Sore. Itchy."

"But not sore like your bone doesn't have enough room to regenerate?"

"I'm not sure how that would feel."

"I suppose it's too early to tell, but this will be the biggest worry for you. We will need to make monthly adjustments to the prosthesis. Theoretically that nodule at the top of the titanium will move as you grow, but only half an inch. The electrodes, I've been told, should grow with you too. After that growth plate is exhausted, then you'll have to remove the entire arm, make more adjustments and put it back on. Is that right?"

"That's right."

"Parker, you know I'm nervous about this. It's not my field of specialty."

"I'll keep an eye on it."

Grace decided he no longer needed dressing, and disinfected the area before handing over the reins to Flint. "All yours." She gave them all a brief smile and then moved some boxes off the leather couch to sit down. "I hope you don't mind me staying," she said, a nervous flicker in her eyes. "I want to be here when Evan checks in."

"Of course," Parker said. "Mary's brought food, help yourself."

Grace took out her cell and typed in a text. "I also told Bailey I'd call her the moment we hear from them. She's chaperoning Lilo on a press gig."

And Griffin would be shadowing them. Parker had told him not to worry. The Syndicate had moved on from harvesting stem cells.

They'd gone radio silent and Parker believed it meant they were about to make their move.

"Right," Parker said. "Time to get this on." He shared a look with his mother and Sloan, and then nodded. Everyone was anxious. More potential sites from AIMI's incomplete tracking data were available to explore. Too many around the world for them to visit safely, but with the Sinners' help, it was possible. He just had to take the leap and ask them.

Each time he thought about working with them, his stomach pulled into a knot tighter than the ones on his wall.

"All right, here we go," Flint said as he slotted the robotic arm up the new humerus bone and then held it there, just shy of connecting. "Sloan, you want to activate the sensory wires?"

"On it." Sloan brought a magnetic key to the arm and flicked a switch. Out of the arm encasing, what looked like hundreds of micro-wires snaked out as though alive and searching. In response, Parker felt an itch and a tickle as the micro-wires from within his own arm emerged. Wires from each side found each other and bonded.

"Good traction," Flint mumbled, and slid the arm up higher on Parker's shoulder. "Adjust the grip, Sloan. Tighten. More. Yes."

A clicking and whirring sound locked in place. Flint let go and the weight of the arm pulled on Parker's shoulder. Everyone in the room held their breath as the arm powered on, lighting up along the joints in the elbow, shoulders and fingers. Mentally, Parker felt no different. Physically, a little sore and unbalanced. Emotionally?

He tensed, unsure.

Flint put a water bottle on top of the table. "Pick that up."

Parker looked at the bottle and moved his arm. It jerked at the shoulder but failed to engage.

"It's fine," Flint said. "This will take practice. Try again."

Parker tried.

Failure.

Anger heated his face. "Does everyone have to watch?"

Mary, who'd been leaning on the kitchen counter, raised her brows but then looked for something to do. Her eyes landed on the manila folder sitting at the edge of the counter. For a moment, Parker's heart rate spiked. That was the background check Sloan ran on Alice, but it was either let Mary look at it, or have her watch him fail. He darted his gaze to Grace on the couch and she'd already busied herself with her cell, so he went back to the bottle.

Move.

Nothing.

Again.

A twitch.

"Maybe it's broken," he offered.

"It's not broken. Your brain just needs to work out that the arm is there again after not having it." Flint picked up some tools he'd taken out and put them back in his toolbox. "Keep trying while I tidy up."

After ten more goes, Parker's frustration swelled to every cell in his body. He felt The Beast stirring, waking up as though called to defend. But there was no battle. None but the one in his mind. Cool calm washed over him. It was so sudden and instant that he knew it hadn't originated from his own body. He glanced at Sloan, who gave him a soft smile along with more of her calming gift. His sister could not only read others' emotions, but affect them too. "You can do this, Parks. Just search for that zone we find when meditating. Like your *Shifu* taught you in Fujian."

He raised a brow. "I hated mediating."

She snorted. "I know. So what do you do then?"

His mind traveled to the ropes in his room, to the knots he would form, to the way it quieted his energy and mind, but being a rigger worked best when he had a model to work on. Shibari was about the art as much as the meditation and eroticism. But he wasn't willing to share that pastime with anyone. He glanced at Mary, more specifically to the folder in her hand, and then frowned at the water bottle. He didn't need help.

"Just keep me from getting worked up," he said, and tried to pick up the bottle again.

A longer jerk this time. The hand moved. But it wasn't enough.

"Stop," Grace said, standing up. "I hope you don't mind me intervening, but I think you need to try some different exercises first."

"Like what?"

"Like simple limb recognition." She took Parker's hands, both the metal and the flesh, and held them. That's all she did. "Can you feel me holding your hands?"

"Yes," he replied.

"Good. Now what about this?" She rubbed her thumbs over his hands.

"I feel it in my actual hand."

Flint closed his aluminum suitcase. "Well, you won't get much sensation in the bionic arm. Just minimal if the simulated nerve wires are working."

"I feel pressure," Parker said.

Grace stroked up both arms until she hit his shoulders and then went back down. "How's that?"

"Good." The pressure on his bionic arm followed her touch. "I feel it."

Grace let go. "Now try using the arm. Don't think. Just do it."

He went for the bottle. The arm moved, the fingers opened, but he overshot the bottle and tipped it over. With a grunt of frustration, Parker swiftly stood. "This is going to take too long. It's all taking too long."

He swiped the bottle, knocking it to the floor. The weight of judgement followed him as he paced alongside the table. What did they know about it? All the decisions for this unit were up to him. None of them wanted to be a leader. Sloan's calming vibes were only irritating him further.

"This will take patience, *mijo*," Mary said from the kitchen, eyes still lost in the folder.

He stopped pacing. "What do you think about the alliance?"

Mary's posture stiffened, her finger paused mid-way to her mouth as she was about to lick it to turn the paper. She met his eyes, mock gasped, and touched her chest. "You're finally deigning to ask my opinion?"

"Don't get used to it," he replied.

"Well, I was going to tell you at some point. I always do."

His smiled widened. He wouldn't have it any other way. "So, Mary Lazarus. Give me your two cents. What do you think about these Sinners?"

She inhaled deeply and exhaled slowly. "To be honest, I've thought about it long and hard, and, *mijo*, I think this decision is not something I should coach you on. It's up to you and your brothers and sisters to choose."

"None of them—" He cut himself off.

"None of us what?" Sloan threw up her hands.

"None of you are telling me the truth."

She scowled at him. "Since when do you want the truth if it's not your version?"

"Try me."

"The truth is, none of us want to get in the way of you and your mate. This alliance goes hand in hand with that relationship. Anything we say can affect your choice, and I for one won't stand in the way of love—or hate. That's all on you."

His brow furrowed as he looked at his mother. "But you know the Sisterhood best."

She cocked her head. "You know Alice best."

"I only know the fake Alice."

Grace became enthralled with her cell phone. Flint cleared his throat and then thumped his chest to clear the obstruction.

"I beg to differ," he said. "When I met your mother, I knew her as a nun, but deep inside I always knew she wasn't. I connected with that hidden woman. I thought I was going to Hell for falling in love with a nun"—he laughed—"but she knew about the biggest regret in my life, that I was working there to make amends for the car accident my friend caused, and she loved me more for it. When she unloaded the truth about the lab to me, and how the Sisterhood had ordered her to assassinate you or take you to them, I knew she needed my help. But Parker"—Flint clapped him on the good shoulder—"Just so you know, we forged our own path together. A new one. Alice wouldn't be the first Sinner to break away."

"Just like that, huh?"

Flint nodded, but Parker wasn't convinced, and he told his mother. "The Sisterhood has changed since you were there. Alice said so, and you heard what claims she made about... demons." The word sounded wrong in his mouth. Parker was a science man, not religious in the slightest. He still thought it was some kind of sick joke, but he hadn't figured out why.

"The thing is, *mijo*, what Alice said about the demonic activity isn't new to the church."

"Don't tell me you believe her."

"There are things you'll never understand, and hopefully won't need to. *They* believe the threat is real. I don't know if it's going to affect us, or if we can even do anything to help them on the meta-physical front, but that's not what they're asking."

"They want help to find their missing Sinner and to eliminate the Syndicate."

She nodded. "And I suppose a truce. To be honest, they never did at the start. It was only when the chips were stacked against us that they gave the directive to assassinate you. They don't see you as the enemy anymore."

"Because they have a bigger enemy." He searched his mother's shrewd face and noticed Sloan doing the same. "You're not convinced."

Mary shrugged and added cryptically, "Not yet, but I will be."

Parker's cell phone rang. Grace jumped to her feet, her eyes wide and expectant. It was the call they'd been waiting on. Parker hit the call button and put it on speaker.

"You're good to go," he said.

Wind blew through the line, gusting into the microphone.

"Envy?" Parker prompted. "Gluttony, you there?"

More wind. *"Yeah. We're here."*

Grace slumped in relief, her hand on her face. Sloan gave her a squeeze on the shoulder.

"And?" Parker rolled his new shoulder, feeling tingling as the wiring inside kept attaching to his musculature and nervous system.

"And, you were right. It's a Syndicate base." It sounded like Tony, his teeth chattering. *"We checked it out as best we could. A butt load of replicates still in embryo tanks. No sign of Despair."*

Using their Deadly names over communications was a habit, and falling into using Despair instead of Daisy sat well with Parker. It was how it should be. With her a part of their group, code names and all.

"So what *is* there?" he asked.

"Fucking weird shit." Evan. *"And we're freezing our nuts off. We're coming home."*

A scuffling sound, and then Tony's voice came through. *"We've planted the devices you gave us, and AIMI should be patching herself in as we speak. If anything goes down, we'll know about it."*

"Good," he said. "Time to come home. Jet is fueled and ready."

After he cut the call, Flint said to him, "And it's time for you to continue the rehabilitation and calibration of the bionic connection."

seventeen

ALICE MONTGOMERY

WHEN ALICE LOGGED in on Parker's computer the following morning, a message popped up with a ping. She hadn't even had her coffee or gone through the overnight emails.

> *Parker.Lazarus@LazTech.com*
> — Cancel meetings today.

Alice frowned and replied.

> *Alice.Montgomery@LazTech.com*
> — Good morning, sunshine. I slept well. Did you?

The little dots instantly appeared, which meant Parker had been sitting by his computer waiting for her. She smiled, hating the traitorous rush of endorphins in her system.

> *Parker.Lazarus@LazTech.com*

— I slept fine. Two hours.

Alice.Montgomery@LazTech.com
— And unless you've decided to come into the office today, which you really should, you have no meetings scheduled.

Parker.Lazarus@LazTech.com
— Not me. You.

Alice.Montgomery@LazTech.com
— I don't have any meetings.

Parker.Lazarus@LazTech.com
— Good. Be ready at 8:30.

Alice.Montgomery@LazTech.com
— That's in five minutes!

She gaped. She wasn't prepared for a meeting.

Alice.Montgomery@LazTech.com
— Who am I meeting? What do I need?

Parker.Lazarus@LazTech.com
— Just yourself. I have to go.

AND WITH THAT LAST MESSAGE, Parker's icon became inactive. He'd logged out. Alice was still blinking at the screen when a phone call came from reception saying her eight-thirty was here. What the hell?

She jumped out of Parker's plush leather seat, smoothed her hair, and went to the office door. When she opened it, a man and a woman strode down the carpeted foyer toward her, both wheeling clothing racks laden with fashion.

Blood drained from her face. She recognized the man. It was Parker's tailor, and the woman was his personal shopper. She smiled tightly at them.

"Hello, George and Bridget," she greeted. "I think there's been a mixup. Mr. Lazarus isn't in the office today."

George, a tall thin man with zero facial hair, or hair on his head, leaned in to peck the air beside her cheek.

"Not to worry," he said. "We're here for you. I thought Parky boy told you."

Parky boy? Alice shook her head, supposing Parker *would* be on nickname terms with the man that built his bespoke wardrobe.

Bridget pushed up her statement bangle before folding her arms. "We're prepared."

"For what?" Alice gaped.

"Mr. Lazarus said you might resist." She gave Alice's saggy frock a scathing once over. "Frankly, I'm surprised it took him this long to call us. You're the face of his personal brand. We have a lot of work to do."

George pursed his lips and raised his brows, facial armor engaged for fashion war.

"Well, I can't afford anything," Alice said flatly, a little miffed, if she was honest. Parker knew this was a false identity. It wasn't as though she always dressed like this. "And I regret to inform you that I have no time. I'm sorry to put you out like this but you may as well return."

The two of them shared a glance, took hold of their racks, and then pushed into the office. In the foyer and down the hallway, staff and disapproving executives had poked their heads out of their offices to snoop. If she made a scene, it might reflect poorly on Parker. But, then again, if she allowed them in and to monopolize her with this sort of unethical use of work time, it could reflect even more poorly on him. Especially considering the sharks were circling and watching how Parker ran the company. There were hundreds of staff here. Millions of dollars in revenue a year. In the end, Alice went with the same office excuse she always did: If Mr. Lazarus ordered it, then so be it. She allowed them in and shut the door.

Two hours later, Alice had been poked, prodded, and measured from bust to boot. She'd been stripped down to her underwear, fitted, splayed and sprayed with perfume. Parker had ordered her a complete wardrobe makeover, and if George or Bridget failed to have the item in stock, they made a list and promised to send the rest as soon as it was tailored or ordered in. They refused to take no for an answer, even when Alice threatened to send back items she didn't approve of. By the time they'd left, she returned flustered to her seat, her stomach rumbling for food.

This showering her with gifts—at least, she thought that's what Parker was doing—was becoming a little excessive, if not endearing. No one had ever spent money on her like this and it wasn't like he'd picked out what clothing for her to wear. He'd left the style up to her. He just wanted to buy her things.

He hadn't even accepted the alliance. So what was this? A preamble? A sign? Or was he messing with her?

Shifting uncomfortably in her seat, Alice turned her attention to find a gazillion messages from executives backlogging her inbox. They'd been calling on Parker for weeks and were curious as to how she was spending her time without him in the office. Cheeks flaming, she typed back polite 'none of your business' type responses and left it at that, but during her trip to the lunch break room, she couldn't help noticing them congregating in an office and shutting the door as she walked past. Her intuition went on high alert.

Parker really needed to turn up for work.

And he needed to communicate.

Just because he'd started the company didn't mean he was immune from scrutiny and subterfuge. She returned to the computer with a mix of emotions battering her head and heart as another possibility came to mind. Was the in-house shopping Parker's way of looking out for her? Of... dare she think it, courting her?

THE FOLLOWING two days started much the same. Parker sent his fashion police, and Alice was forced to endure being picked apart and prodded. By the third day, she was ashamed to admit she kind of liked the shopping. It was a pity she wouldn't get to keep any of it, not if she ended up back at the Sisterhood. This uncertainty prompted her to call off the fashion visits once and for all.

He was buying her things, and she was starting to like it, yet he'd remained unresponsive on the office messaging system. He barely replied to her emails about the alliance and request for help to recover their missing Sinner, Prudence. It was time to talk, and it would be better if they did it in person. She was just about to send him another message when the receptionist called, announcing another visitor. *Shit.*

On her way to the office door, she imagined a beauty salon entourage about to accost her. This just wasn't her. And if Parker assumed she was the kind of woman who liked to be primped and kept, then he had another—

"Alice," Mary Lazarus greeted as Alice opened the door.

Alice's blood pumped with a singular message—*enemy, danger.*

She assessed the ex-Sinner and tried to locate a weapon. Found nothing but her fists. The last time Alice had seen Mary face to face had been a chance encounter at the front of the Cardinal City Cathedral months ago. Alice had been sure Mary recognized something familiar within Alice, even then.

"I was wondering when you'd come." Alice stepped aside. There was no point running from this.

The petite woman entered. She wore black leggings and a sports hoodie, snug and stretchy—great for extreme and explosive movement. Her long black, silver-streaked hair was in a braid that dangled between her shoulder blades. She walked on sure, silent feet like a panther perfectly balanced and ready to pounce. In her hands she carried naught but a manila folder. Coupled with the clenched jaw, Alice had to assume the woman was feeling hostile. Or at the very least, defensive.

What's in the folder?

Alice closed the door behind Mary, giving them privacy. Mary took stock of the room, noticing some of the shopping bags and clothes George and Bridget had left behind. Alice blushed and gestured at them. "Your son seems to think I need better clothes. And... er... other things."

Mary snorted, amused. "When Parker was little, he used to spend all his allowance shopping. Usually on gifts." Then she met Alice's eyes. "Let's not beat around the bush. I'm here to ask questions."

"About?"

"You." Mary walked over to the vintage leather Chesterfield and dropped the manila folder onto it. Then she sat and waited for Alice.

Oh my, Grandmother, what big teeth you have.

There were no Sinners as legendary as Mary Lazarus. She was the name whispered in the dark at night. The name used as a punishment to ward off bad behavior, and the name used in prayers of hope.

Some, maybe even Alice herself, had wished to leave the Sisterhood behind like Mary had. Maybe. A long time ago. Mary's reputation preceded her, and that's what spooked Alice the most.

As though her feet were lead, Alice joined her and sat slowly, eyes never leaving the woman who could put Alice down in a blink. She stayed vigilant. Ready. And braced for the wolf.

Mary held out her hands, palms to the ceiling. Alice raised a brow just as a *ping* sounded on the computer. The first contact from Parker in almost two days. How odd that he chose now when his mother was here... unless he was concerned.

Danger. Enemy.

Mary waited, not a movement in her chest with the intake of breath, nor a lowering of her thick dark lashes. She was silence personified as she waited for Alice to place her wrists in Mary's palms. This was an interrogation technique they'd learned in the Sisterhood —they used their own bodies like a polygraph machine. Mary wanted to see if Alice was lying via her pulse fluctuations, and no doubt, if Mary was unsatisfied in any way, she would respond appropriately, possibly with force. Except... they both knew a Sinner could school her pulse and beat this test.

Strike first.

Alice stifled her instincts, unwilling to attack the woman who'd raised Parker. Instead, she put her wrists in the woman's waiting hands. If Mary was surprised, she didn't show it. Another *ping* sounded at the computer. They ignored it. And then the phone rang.

"Do you need to get that?" Mary asked.

"It's your son," Alice replied. "I'm convinced he's monitoring me through the internal security system. Probably watching us right now."

Probably watched the entire time Alice was fitted for clothes, but she kind of liked knowing that. She may even have played into it a few times.

Mary gave a feminine grunt, then she glanced up at the camera in the corner and smiled.

Alice smirked. "He can wait until we're done."

Let him squirm.

A flicker of some unnamed emotion passed over Mary's expression. Alice wanted to believe it was respect for her, but she shoved that down deep inside. Misplaced hope could be delusional. She had to keep her wits about her. Maybe the hold-up with this alliance was that she hadn't garnered the esteem of the matriarch.

"What do you want to know?" Alice relaxed her shoulders when Mary took her wrists.

And that was her first mistake. Mary didn't want to run her own polygraph test using Alice's pulse. She wanted to fight—she yanked on Alice's wrists. Alice may have placed her hands within the woman's, but she'd also braced her foot. The moment Mary tugged, Alice rolled and evaded her grip until she ended on the other side of the Chesterfield, still ready, still a warrior in her own right.

Mary may be the legend, but Alice was the future.

Both women faced each other and circled. Neither looked away.

"It's going to be like that, huh?" Alice dropped into a defensive stance.

Mary mirrored and Alice smiled at her classic intimidation technique. Mimic the enemy. Throw them off balance. Confuse them. Alice had learned the same tactics, and then some.

Mary threw punches, strikes, jabs, all in quick succession and all on perfectly balanced feet. The woman had a few decades on Alice, but she was a machine. Alice blocked each time, her bones jarring on contact. But Mary didn't give up. She kept coming for Alice, her face calm and giving away nothing, her body language so precise and controlled that Alice could garner no intention there either. Mimicking was over. What was her motivation for this attack? Distrust? Self-preservation?

"What do you want?" Alice snapped, taking Mary's wrist and snapping it down, intending to twist their bodies and bring her to the ground.

But Mary flowed like water and slipped out of Alice's hold.

"Are you here to kill me?" Mary asked.

"You know I'm not." Alice circled her hands and body and shifted Kung-Fu stances until her fingers were claws ready to strike. Mary mirrored. Again. Alice's jaw clenched. "You know we trained under the same masters. It is stupid to fight each other."

"All I know is that you've been watching my family. You were supposed to hunt me down decades ago, yet you didn't."

Alice's fists lowered. "That's because the Sisterhood's mission has changed. I can't speak to the Reverend Mother's mission back then, but now, one AWOL Sinner is nothing in the grand scheme of things, especially one who's values are aligned with ours."

"Our values aren't aligned. I'll never condone the assassination of children."

"Neither do we," Alice shot out, taking Mary's hit on her shoulder.

Mary launched at her again, hard and fast. Alice didn't want to hurt her, just as she'd never wanted to hurt Parker on that warehouse rooftop. So she kept defending, kept blocking, and when they knocked into the desk, and Mary picked up a paper weight, Alice kept dodging. Around and round the office they went, going in circles until Alice realized something. Although she never telegraphed it, Mary had to have noticed Alice's limp—it was so obvious—but instead of using that knowledge to her advantage, like Parker had done, Mary ignored it.

This wasn't a fight. This was a test. Mary didn't want to hurt Alice anymore than Alice wanted to hurt her back. Alice wanted to show the Sisterhood had changed, and Mary wanted Alice to prove it.

"Enough." Alice dropped her hands and allowed Mary to grapple and bring Alice to the ground.

The woman pushed Alice face first into the carpet and pried her arm back. Alice winced, but didn't struggle. She tapped her hand on the floor.

"I'm not going to hurt you, Mary," she said. "Even if you hurt me first."

Mary pulled on Alice's arm, sharpening the pain.

"Do you remember life before the Sisterhood?" she asked, surprising Alice.

"I don't know. Bits and pieces. Why?"

"Why the limp?"

Alice exhaled, closing her eyes. None of this was making sense. She thought this was about Mary's relationship with the Sisterhood. "I was in a car accident as a child."

The pressure on her arm eased and then went. Mary moved to the couch, where she put her face in her hand, breathing hard. Wincing, Alice rubbed her shoulder and got to her feet. She tested her leg, putting pressure on it. Pain lanced her thigh, but she'd survive. She always did.

"What's going on?" she asked, sensing the danger was gone… if it had ever been there in the first place.

Eyes full of liquid pain met Alice's. Mary's bottom lip trembled.

"Mary?" Alice frowned. "Are you okay?"

Unable to speak, the woman shook her head. She almost lost control of her tears, but swallowed and took a deep breath. "Tell me about your childhood. Please."

Feeling more naked than when George and Bridget had stripped her, Alice hugged herself. "What's going on?"

"Please, just tell me."

"I… God, okay… I guess, I was in a car accident when I was young. Drunk driver. Lost my parents. Some distant family looked after me for a few years. When they didn't want me, I went into foster care. A few years of that and the Sisterhood found me. That's it."

Mary slumped onto the couch, her head in her hands. She started mumbling words under her breath in her native tongue.

"You're freaking me out, Mary," Alice said. "I think I liked the fighting better."

Mary barked out a pained laugh and then handed Alice the manila folder. Alice flicked through the documents, her spine stiffening with each page turned.

"Why are you showing me this?" She closed the folder and put it down. It didn't surprise her. It was just a background check. A dossier. A very detailed one, but she would have expected no less from the Lazarus family.

"I'm so sorry," Mary said. "Everything that has happened to you since you entered foster care is my fault."

Alice blinked. "What?"

"Flint was friends with the driver who crashed into you all those years ago. He hated that he never stopped his friend from getting into the car that night, and making amends was the sole reason he got a job at Biolum Tech—that's the original Syndicate lab. He was so filled with guilt that he donated most of his salary to you. For years."

Alice frowned, casting her mind back to what she could remember, but she was too young to pick up anything about money. She had vague memories of her aunt and uncle always heading out, dressed up for a party. She remembered her aunt and uncle fighting a lot, but she was so young. Her days had been filled with wishing for her parents to come back, or for finding a new family.

At the thought of Flint, the ghost of a memory flickered in her mind. Familiarity. Had she met him when she was younger?

"The money was supposed to help you." Mary took Alice's hand. This time, her grip was soft, her eyes warm. "It's because of me the money stopped coming. Because of us. After we escaped the lab, when we went into hiding and made the decision to leave all ties behind, that included you. If we had known your family shoved you into foster care when the money stopped coming, we would have done something." Mary shook her head, bitterness in her expression. "The only reason the Sisterhood found you was through Flint's money trail. They knew you were someone important to him, and thus to me. They couldn't get to me, so took you as a replacement. You're my punishment."

Alice snatched her hand back. At first, fury and denial pumped through her. The Sisterhood chose Alice because they saw potential. And they were right. So what Mary was saying didn't make sense.

Alice's fate *was not* someone else's punishment.

"I can't believe this." Alice rubbed her temples and paced, her dodgy leg hurting more than before. In her mind, she repeated everything Mary had told her. From the car crash that stole her parents' lives, to being linked to Flint, to the lack of money being the reason her selfish family gave her up, to Alice's initiation into a secret society of assassin nuns.

Alice's connection to this family had started decades ago.

"Flint wasn't driving the car that killed my parents," Alice said, turning to Mary.

"No."

"So..." That ghostly memory finally hit Alice. She'd been little and at a new school a few years after being fostered to her aunt and uncle. She hated the new school and had told her teacher she felt sick so went to the office where she sat on a bench waiting to see the nurse. It was there she'd seen the bearded man talking to the principal. He wore a checked shirt and a backward baseball hat. The man was tall, rumbly, and a little scary. But she'd overheard bits of the conversation because she'd caught her name—a name she couldn't even remember now. It hadn't been Alice. Over the years she'd assumed she imagined him because she'd wanted so desperately for someone to come for her. To whisk her away to a loving family that sings with her. Could this memory have been real? Had this been Flint checking up on her? Alice met Mary's eyes. "So he was only ever helping me."

"Yes, but, what I'm trying to say, rather unsuccessfully, is that he would have still been helping you if I hadn't come along." Mary smiled thinly. "I remember him telling me he was saving for your collage fund."

A harsh laugh ripped out of Alice. "College? Me?"

She couldn't think of anything worse.

Alice went to the windows overlooking the city. The mid-afternoon sun cast long shadows against the buildings. The world was so big out there, and yet, somehow Alice kept coming back to this family, to that feeling inside her chest that refused to go away when she thought of Parker.

"Does Parker know?" she asked. She couldn't stand it if he felt sorry for her, and that was the only reason he—she glanced at the shopping bags and winced.

"No one knows but me. I had to... I had to..." Mary scrubbed her face, guilt written all over it.

She had to protect her family first.

"That's why you fought me," Alice said. "You thought if I knew who you were and hated you for it, I wouldn't be able to hide my feelings. I'd hurt you back. I'd show my true intentions."

"And when you kept defending, never truly trying to hurt me, I knew you had no idea." Mary inhaled and exhaled. "You had no idea I was the woman who ruined your life."

Long minutes ticked by. Alice watched the world go by through the windows, people and cars like ants below in the city. To the right, below the Lazarus Tech building, cathedral spires rose into the sky like sharp weapons. Alice touched the window.

"You have one thing wrong," Alice said quietly. "My life wasn't ruined after coming to the Sisterhood."

"But they turned you into a killer, like me. They—"

Punished her? Told her she was going to Hell? This was all true, but Alice and her sisters were a unit. It was them against the world—against Hell, against fate.

"They became my family," Alice said, rounding on the woman. "They're my sisters. We look out for each other. We love each other and support each other. Wasn't it like that for you?"

"I never made friends at the Sisterhood." Mary's eyes narrowed shrewdly. "You truly don't want to kill me—us?"

"No." Alice threw up her hands in frustration, tired of giving the same answer. "I admit, there was a time the Sisterhood did. But when I came there, they were already on another path. After you defected, the Vatican found out about us. You know that, right?"

"I didn't know that."

"When you took the kids, you left a gaping hole in the Sisterhood's cover story for being at the lab. The Vatican was appalled when they found out the Sisterhood kept vital information about the future of those children from them. Everything has changed."

Mary's hands twisted in her lap. "And if we join the Sisterhood to beat the Syndicate, what will you do after the threat is neutralized? Will this alliance end? Will you leave us alone?"

"Mary, even if we neutralize the Syndicate, the Sisterhood's job is only beginning, but a future will be possible."

The phone started ringing again. Both Mary and Alice looked at it.

"It will be Parker," Mary said. "I never told him I was coming. He won't like me meddling. I should go."

Alice joined her at the door, but before Mary opened it, she looked at Alice with a deep sadness.

"When we first left the lab and finally found a home to settle into, Parker realized that he'd missed out on so many things other children took for granted. He was the last in the family to learn to ride a bike. The last on the street. And the eldest." Mary's eyes turned wistful. "I remember him being so determined to learn. It was written all over his face. But he never got on that bike because someone was always watching and judging. I always thought he'd given up, until one night, I heard a crash on the front sidewalk. When I went to investigate, I found him learning on his own. He refused help every time. He even growled for me to leave him alone.

"So I did. I left him alone, but stayed close. I watched night after night as he fell over, scraped his knees, and picked himself up to try again. Eventually he made it the length of the sidewalk but hit a tree. I ran out there, thinking the worst, and he was so ashamed. He tried to tell me he was fine, but he'd broken his arm."

"So stubborn," Alice said, her brows puckering.

"He refused to admit he was in pain, even when we set his arm, but afterward, he also refused to leave my side until he fell asleep."

Mary took Alice's hands, and this time, there was no danger, no enemy looking at her but only a woman who cared—a mother.

"Pride is a double-edged sword, Alice. It can drive someone to great heights, but it can make you lose your wings. He doesn't need someone to help him fly, he's got that down. He doesn't even need someone to break his fall. He needs someone strong enough to fly with him into the sun and hold him when it burns. Do you understand?"

Alice thought back to what she'd overheard through the bug she'd planted. Parker was a perfectionist for a reason. He was afraid no one would want him if he failed.

Mary didn't wait for Alice's response before swiftly exiting the room, shutting the door behind.

Ringing filtered back into Alice's cognition. With a sigh, Alice limped over and picked up the phone.

"Parker Lazarus's office," she said.

"Alice." His smooth, deep voice triggered butterflies in her stomach. Just one word, her name, and she was melting like a puddle.

She rapped the phone handset on her forehead, as if she could beat the stupid out. Then remembered he was probably watching so stopped. *Damn, girl.*

"Alice," Parker repeated.

"Yes."

"Are you hurt?"

"I'm fine." She paused. "Wait. Were you actually worried?"

Parker's exhale through the handset was audible, as was the string of curse words he tried to hide from her by muffling the phone. When he came back, there was an edge to his voice. "Why, pray tell, did my mother attack you?"

"So *you have* been spying on me," she said. Her pulse quickened. "Were you watching me undress and… all the shopping?"

"I had to make sure you were—"

"You can't *make* me do anything, Parker Lazarus. If I want to buy

154

clothes, I will. If I don't, I'll send them back. I'm not some sort of doll for you to play dress up with."

His voice deepened. "If I wanted to play with you, there'd be considerably less clothes."

She gaped. Made an embarrassing sound. He chuckled.

She rallied her wits. "And furthermore, if you think you can buy me, or lure me, or—"

"Be nice to you?"

"Yes! If you think you can... wait. What?"

"Alice. I just wanted you to have nice things. You deserve it."

Alice didn't know what to say.

"Alice?"

"Yeah?"

"The answer is yes."

"To what?"

A deep, velvety laugh that liquified Alice's restraint. "To the alliance. We'll work together to find your Sinner and my sister." His tone hardened. "And then we'll destroy the Syndicate."

"It's too late."

"What?"

"Well, I mean for working together. After the attack at the cathedral, the other Sinners left for the abbey. I'm the only one left."

It was only half true, but she wanted to make him sweat.

AXEL ALVARES

AT THE FRONT of the Lazarus Tech skyscraper, with his back against the cold stone wall, Axel Alvares readied himself through a breathing technique he'd learned as a CCFD cadet. He had doubts about this mission. He'd always had doubts, but he couldn't stop it, even if he wanted to.

When death put your name on his chalkboard, there was no avoiding it. But through the offer the Syndicate had given him, he might find a way around it.

His little sister, Elena, needed him.

The boss's voice in his earpiece: *"Go time."*

He checked the white plastic mask was safe and secure in his back jeans pocket, took a deep breath, and entered the building. He bumped into a petite woman coming out.

For a split second, their eyes met. He glimpsed a fit older woman, perhaps in her fifties. Long black hair, determined face. Then he kept moving.

Julius's voice burst into Axel's ear. *"Don't fuck it up this time."*

Get to the elevator.

Get this done.

For Elena.

He wasn't the only man moving toward the elevators. Members of the Faithful, all with the same hopes and dreams as Axel, moved in unison to fill elevators and stairwells. Many of them might not make it out alive, and they were happy for it.

Unease squirmed in his stomach. The elevator doors closed. He put his white Halloween mask on. When the doors opened on the top level, Axel went straight for the fire alarm and pulled the lever.

"I want this Sinner gone, and then all of them. Those bitches will ruin everything."

nineteen

PARKER LAZARUS

FROM THE PRIVACY of his bedroom, Parker watched Alice in his office through the live CCTV footage on his laptop. He'd spent every waking hour for the past few days trying to calibrate his new arm, but even as his body healed, his mind struggled to fine tune the dexterity of the bionic arm. He could punch a hole in a wall, but playing the piano was beyond him. Recovery was taking too long, and since Evan and Tony returned from their expedition, the family had been working solidly on a plan so that once they finalized the other locations, they could launch into action immediately. They could take down each Syndicate base around the world. But to do that, he needed to be in top working condition.

He'd tackled his rehabilitation with dogged determination, no matter how taxing it had become. The only source of happiness he'd received was watching Alice being fitted for clothing and shopping. It seemed that simply from looking at her visage, his inner turmoil quietened. There was something about seeing this side of Alice. She was for his eyes only. No one in the office knew the real her, and the same went for the opposite. Only she knew the real him.

Each day that went past, he poured more money into George's account, purely so he'd return the following day and make Alice smile again. The woman claimed she didn't want the gifts, that she'd return them all, but he'd caught the lift of her lips and the straightening of her spine when she touched the goods.

He wanted to shower her with gifts.

But then Mary had walked in, and they'd fought. Anger tightened his jaw just thinking on it. What had his mother been thinking? To accost his mate, on her own, in his office. Without him.

Furious did not cover the words he had for his mother. The moment it started to go down, and he realized he was helpless watching from the penthouse, he'd tried to call and break it up. When that didn't work, he'd rushed down to the basement and slipped on his Deadly battle outfit, except by the time he'd checked security footage, he'd found they'd stopped fighting and, suddenly, he'd felt like a voyeur. Like this was private Sinner business and he should leave them to it.

He'd pulled up a chair and watched.

Until Mary left, and then he'd needed to hear Alice's voice. Now here he was, back in his penthouse, still dressed in his battle suit, but smiling at her on the security footage with the phone to his ear, listening to her defy him.

"You left your answer too long," Alice said to him. "The Sisterhood doesn't wait around. The alliance stands. We won't attack you and you won't attack us, but in terms of working together, it's me for now."

"When we have the final Syndicate base locations, will you provide Sinners for our attack?"

"Well, how long will it take to finalize those locations, and what does this attack involve? What are the parameters? You need to tell me these things, Parker."

God, he loved it when she got pushy. When Alice mouthed off at him, all he could think of was how she would apply that same mouth on other parts of his body. How she would defy him then. He scrubbed his face to eliminate the image of her looking up at him from his cock, his hand fisted in her hair. Maybe he'd tie her hands behind her back. Maybe he'd—

"Parker? You still there?"

He cleared his throat. "Not too long. Maybe another week or so."

"Okay. So it will depend on the resources we have available at the time and what the plan is."

"Good. We can discuss details over drinks."

She laughed down the handset. "Smooth."

"We need to talk, so why not over drinks?"

Alice's tone sobered. "Parker, there's a lot we need to talk about. We need to talk about why the Syndicate attacked us at the cathedral. We need to talk about the stack of paperwork a mile high that you keep putting off. We need to talk about how you need to stop ignoring what's happening here at the office."

"Ignoring is the opposite of what I've been doing. Trust me. Drinks tonight, Alice."

"I'm busy."

"Yes, you are. With me."

"Maybe if you ask nicely." She twirled her finger around the telephone cord and rotated on the chair until her back was to the door. "Maybe if you get down on your knees and beg."

He opened his mouth to speak, but then froze as the office door opened. Multiple men entered the room, all wearing white Halloween masks on their faces.

Syndicate. No white robes, which meant they weren't there to make a splashy show. They were here to get in quietly, do the job, and get out without being recognized on camera. The job being Alice.

"Behind you," he barked.

Alice whirled, tossed the phone cord around the first man's neck and pulled him in to choke. Parker's mate moved with lethal precision, striking and defending as though second nature. And there was nothing he could do but stare at the CCTV video footage on his laptop and watch, his pulse rapidly rising, his heart galloping in his chest.

This was different than with Mary. Far different.

She elbowed one in the face and then kicked at a man behind. Pride swelled in his body. *Poetry in motion.*

But there were too many. How did they get through building security? What if there were more?

He had to go.

Already in his suit, already at penthouse level, all he needed to do was fit the grappling gun gauntlets to his suit and then take a running leap from his balcony and hope his bionic arm would obey his mind. Whilst fitting the clunky devices over his forearms, he realized he could build this tech into the robotic side. He made a mental note to work on it later and took a running leap from his balcony, up and over into the void beyond. His grappling hook shot to the next building and latched on, tensile cord seamlessly retracting and pulling him forward when gravity tried to take him down.

His swing worked smoothly, but passage to the next building required his left arm and if he couldn't activate the release button in synchronized time, he'd wind up slamming into a facade.

No time for mistakes.

But he made them. He slammed into five buildings like a drunken monkey, his irritation rising to boiling point each time. His only saving grace was that he'd been able to recover and move onto the next building before any tenants noticed him.

When he burst through the rooftop stairwell exit and into the

Lazarus Tech building, only one word pierced the madness of his mind. *Alice.*

He imagined the worst, replaying the way more masked men had converged on her as she'd tried to fight off three at a time.

"AIMI," he said into the inbuilt microphone in his hood.

"Yes, Pride?"

"Alert any of the team available to be on standby for backup."

"Copy that." A pause. *"Done. Gluttony and Wrath are suiting up."*

He arrived at the landing to the executive floor and paused at the door, listening to the sounds beyond. Scuffling. Shouts. People. Too many. Were they running to escape or hide? He couldn't make out anything definitive except that the danger was still present. He pulled the flexible computer screen from the forearm of his suit. It clicked into place.

"Show me the heat map for the top floor of the Lazarus Tech building on my suit screen."

"Pulling building schematics now. Accessing thermal imaging map. Heat map displayed."

Military grade thermal imaging flashed over the screen. Bodies moved around the top executive level. He located a huddle barricaded in their offices—his staff—and he located the hostiles encroaching from the elevators, down the corridors, and toward a singular office. His. "Shit."

One body moved inside the office. *One.* He frowned. Still and prone bodies around the roving heat signature. Some of the prone bodies were going cold—dead. Had Alice managed to eliminate them and lock herself in the room? If so, she was trapped, but safe. She would need his help to get out.

"AIMI," he said. "Call my office."

Alice picked up after one ring.

"Alice?" he said. "Are you okay?"

"P—"

"Pride," he said over her. While he was in his suit, it was imperative he be addressed as Pride to avoid his identity being compromised. Especially here. "Are you safe?"

She laughed, then made a wheezing sound. *She was hurt.*

Parker went cold. Empty. The urge to protect his mate, the only instinct penetrating.

"I'm okay. I took care of the ones in this room," she said, "and I locked the office door, but…"

He exhaled in relief, but tensed after glancing at the heat map. "There's more outside the office and closing in."

"Can you see them on the camera? How many?"

"I'm in the stairwell. You stay put, and I'll come to you."

"But how many?"

He slid the flexible screen back into the forearm of his suit. "Twenty hostiles and counting. More coming up the stairs. Stay safe until you get the okay."

She tried to protest, but he cut the call. He needed to concentrate, and he needed to be the one in control. Holding his bionic hand before his face, he willed the fingers to curl into a fist and then open. It took time, and the reaction was off, but it worked. He might have to keep the left for striking, and the right for dexterity. Or… he could summon The Beast.

If he did, claws would shoot out of both hands, one metal, one natural.

But that would have to be a last resort. The Beast would be messy, irrational, and instinctual. It would decimate anyone it perceived as a threat, and to that primal part of him, anyone between him and Alice was a threat, even if they were bystanders. No. It was better he handled this with as much finesse as Pride usually gave.

With class.

The sound of gun fire exploded beyond the door and an almighty roar of fury burst from him. *Fuck class.*

He pulled his face mask up, only to realize it wasn't there. Frantically, he patted about his suit, looking for it in case it had fallen. Damn it. In his haste to leave the penthouse, he'd failed to collect the purple face mask. If he went out now, he'd be recognized.

If just one person, one staff member saw his face...

More gunfire. A scream. Not Alice—

"AIMI, call 911," he said.

"On it."

"And call..." If he called in backup, he might compromise everyone's identity. And waiting for them wasn't a viable option. Alice needed assistance now.

With a plan formulating in his head, he checked his hood was up and then pushed through the door.

"Call the team and tell them to stand down," he finished. "I've got this."

twenty

ALICE MONTGOMERY

WITH HER BACK against the door, Alice jolted as the enemy tried to batter their way through. Littered around the office lay multiple men with their white masks fallen to the side. For one attacker, she'd shoved the mask into his neck, breaking his larynx. He'd passed out from the pain.

They were all sick, scarred, or deformed men. All members of the Faithful, their vulnerabilities preyed on by the Syndicate. None of them were truly a danger to her. None of them knew the first thing about hand-to-hand combat, so this first wave had been a numbers game. Come at her and try to overwhelm her.

She frowned at them, all on the floor, feeling more guilt than she'd ever felt after taking down an opponent. They had never stood a chance, and she'd shown no mercy. They were the fodder. Next came the cavalry.

Gunfire blasted the door, and she dove to the right, taking cover behind a cabinet by the wall. Screams and shouts beyond filtered through the cracks in the door. She supposed most of them looked normal, apart from minor deformities or injuries. From what she could tell, none of them were powered replicates, but the day was still young.

Goddamned Faithful. They'd somehow breached security at ground level and found their way up here to lay siege to the entire floor. Maybe one of the executives was paid off. Alice wouldn't put it past them, considering the lack of loyalty shown toward Parker in his absence.

She crawled to where the phone was on the floor and crouched behind the desk. Parker had said he was on the way, but she needed a Plan B. She dialed security. No answer. She dialed city emergency, got through immediately, but found SWAT was already in the building and apparently negotiating a surrender. Emergency tried to keep Alice on the call, but she hung up. Negotiation. Right. As if that would save her—the attackers would be in this room before that happened.

She knew why this had happened. The Faithful couldn't find her sisters who had left the city, so they'd come after her to finish the job. The Syndicate wanted Alice dead.

Maybe under duress Prudence had revealed the Sisterhood's intentions to take them down. Maybe these attacks were just retaliation for Alice's involvement at the warehouse. All she knew for sure was that the Syndicate had become an active threat against the Sisterhood.

And she was outnumbered, even with Parker somewhere in the building.

She refused to sit and wait to be rescued. So that left her with one choice. Prepare for infiltration. She tipped Parker's desk to act as a shield. The computer and stationery crashed to the ground. She wound cords around her fists to protect her knuckles. None of these Faithful had guns, only knives. They truly had been the cannon fodder—a thin attempt to get in without making a scene or causing alarm via gunshots. But now the authorities were here, they frantically tried to get into the room and end her with a bullet.

Such a Faithful thing to do. They wanted death. To them, the sacrifice of their life would be rewarded with rebirth as a powered replicate.

Crouched low, Alice limped around and scooped up discarded daggers, then returned behind the desk and waited. She took a moment to assess her injuries. Possible cracked rib. Bruised temple, sticky blood oozing but not gushing. Shallow slashes on her forearm. Again, oozing but not gushing. She'd live.

Deciding her defense was better served from the side of the door, Alice propped a body behind the desk so the top of the hair showed —hopefully a decoy. Then she took up position and waited, trying her hardest to listen to what went on outside. Shouts. Crashes. The gunfire ended. A man's scream cut off. A heavy crash against the door. And it sounded like… it sounded like… she inched closer to the door and put her ear against the wood. A low, feral snarl. The lion returned to claim his kingdom. Death incarnate. Someone was praying, over and over: *Please God. Please Go—*

A clawed metal hand burst through the door, right next to her face. It was covered in blood. Alice jolted back and gripped her daggers. The fist withdrew, leaving a hole in the door. Taking a deep breath, she summoned her courage and looked through.

On the other side, a shadow slid down the length of the door. A body, she realized. After it fell, she saw the back of broad shoulders, heaving with breath, and a Deadly Seven hood move as he surveyed the room for more enemies. There were none. He'd killed them all. Sensing her, he turned to reveal a strikingly dangerous profile, jaw tense and face hard. Parker.

"It's me," he said.

Two words and her heart burst. Alice opened the door, her daggers ready in her palms.

Parker held her gaze. "Are you hurt?"

"I'll live." Alice glanced down at his bionic hand—*that's new*—still dripping with blood, and then to the body on the floor, his chest pulverized. "You... ran your hand *through* him."

"He was in the way," Parker said, starkly serious.

In the way. To get to Alice. *Right.* Okay, well, they'd deal with that later. First, they had to get out of there and, with the authorities downstairs, they wouldn't be alone for long. Alice glanced over Parker's shoulder and her stomach dropped. Standing in the doorway to another office was one of the executives, his gaze pinned to Parker, his expression a mix of horror and shock and... smugness. When Alice looked back at Parker, she realized why. He wore no mask to hide his identity.

"You've been made," she hissed, turning the daggers in her palms, ready to take out the executive.

Parker tensed. His eyes flashed gold, and he snarled. "We have to go."

Alice tried to bring him back into the office. "We should find a scarf, or something, to hide your face."

"It's not important. Getting you out is. Let's go."

"But—" His identity!

"Now, Alice." He tugged her across the reception area until stumbling became jogging. The executive fled the moment they'd started moving, like the coward he was. Probably the one who'd been paid off to let the Faithful in.

Once inside the stairwell, Alice hesitated. All she could think of was that smug look on the executive's face.

"Alice," Parker said, a few steps up. "Come on."

She clenched the daggers, her knuckles turning white. "He *saw* your face. With everything going on here, don't you think that's a bad thing? They're already pushing for a vote of no confidence." A nod to herself. "I'm going to eliminate him."

She pulled the door halfway open before Parker slammed it shut and held it. Shocked, she looked up at him and prepared to argue, but his eyes—they sparked. And his scent, it flourished with musk.

"You would murder to protect me?" he asked, his voice turning deep.

"I am an assassin, Parker. I'm a *Sinner*. Or have you forgotten that?"

The gravity of her words showed on his face. Alice expected disgust, or at the very least disapproval. It was one thing to kill or maim in the heat of battle, but it was another to deliberately seek out and end someone's life. He said, "It was my choice to come in here without a mask. I knew what I was doing."

Alice's eyes narrowed. "You *knew* you'd compromised your identity?"

He searched her face. "I had to get to you."

"I could have handled it myself."

"I didn't care."

"But—" She glanced back at the door.

"Alice, we have to go."

"But—"

Parker's lips met hers hard and with passionate fury. His big body pushed her against the door. He kissed her like she was the air he breathed. Tasted her like she was a drug. It lasted a glorious second, and then he broke away, chest heaving, golden eyes dark with desire.

"We need to leave," he repeated, his voice rasping.

Alice nodded dumbly, his arousing scent curling around her. "Leaving is good."

He pulled her up the stairwell, and they broke out onto the

rooftop. Cool wind gusted their face. They were so fricking high, there were clouds around the buildings.

"How—?"

Parker shot Alice a wolfish grin and showed the grappling gun gauntlets on each forearm, then he tugged her close and said, "Hold on."

She placed her palms on his chest. "But, don't you usually use the wingsuit to get down from this height?"

She was sure she'd seen blurry pictures in the newspaper of one of the Deadly Seven coasting down from a building after stopping an active shooter.

He looked down at her. "There's only one wingsuit and no chute. I admit, the grappling guns take a bit of finesse, but it's better than going splat on the ground."

Shouts echoing up the stairwell jolted them.

"Activate the suit," she said, adrenaline pumping. "I'll jump on your back, rodeo style."

"Alice, do you understand the kind of training required to pull that off? Just hold onto me while I use the gun."

"There isn't time for an argument."

The door opened and SWAT poured out, guns aimed. Before they had a chance to catch Parker's identity, Alice shoved him off the edge of the roof. The look in his eyes would haunt her for the rest of her life. Horror, pain, anguish. Then he twisted like a cat and slammed his arms and his legs closed. He opened like a falling star, the wing-suit activated, and started coasting.

"Miss, don't do it," said one of the cops, but Alice was already running, launching herself off the roof in a swan dive. Ice cold wind slammed her face, watering her eyes as she descended. She focused on the gray shadow coasting a few feet below. In an effort to close the gap, she pulled her arms to her side and tipped her head down, increasing velocity. Closer and closer she went until she landed on his back, almost tipping him and losing balance. Parker recovered equilibrium, and she adjusted her balance to ride him.

It was ethereal, if only for a moment.

The wind, the clouds, the ride. She felt like a goddess in the sky aboard her warrior dragon. He craned his neck, his hood flapped off his face, and his hair billowed.

"Hold on," he shouted, his voice snatched by the air.

She gripped his hood, knowing the jolt coming next could potentially send her careening, and if it did, she would have no escape, no second chance. Her life would be over. Even the adrenaline pumping through her veins was not enough to dull that thought. She gripped his hood, engaged every muscle in her aching body, and braced.

Parker's right arm angled toward a building, a grappling hook on a thin tensile rope fired out and latched onto a building. Instantly, the rope retracted. They whiplashed, wobbled, and then their velocity clashed with gravity. Parker went forward. Alice went to the side, her stomach jumping into her throat. She slipped off his back. Her fingers cut on his hood. Parker shouted, but Alice was underwater, not in the air. Everything was distant. Time slowed as her life hurtled before her eyes. Her sins. Her future in Hell. The lack of love in her life. The family she wanted. The man who came for her, risking everything. The same man whose other arm snapped out and yanked her back to him.

Seconds.

It took mere seconds.

The wingsuit retracted, freeing Parker's mobility, and then she was back in his vice-like embrace as they swung alongside a building, clinging to him with everything she had. Metal claws embedded in the facade of a building, tearing up the brick. Eventually they came to a stop, fifty feet from the ground. Parker's deep scowl and dark eyes said it all. She looked away as he lowered them into a city alley.

The moment their feet hit the ground, he retracted the grappling hook and growled, "What were you thinking? You could have been killed!"

Rolling her shoulder, testing the muscle, to hide the fact her body trembled with the aftereffects of adrenaline, she scowled back at him. "I didn't. We both got out."

"You pushed me off the roof without knowing I could activate the suit once airborne."

"I knew."

"No, you guessed."

She shrugged. "I don't see what the big deal is. I know you. I know you think of everything, including that, as a safety, you would allow the suit to activate or deactivate mid-flight. And you did."

He pointed in her face, eyes blazing. "You could have been killed!"

She folded her arms, eyebrow raising, pretending not to be ruffled. "Were you worried about me, Lazarus?"

Parker stormed off, pacing a few feet away, his bionic fist opening and clenching. Then he rounded back on her. "When you stayed, I thought you were going to take the blame. For the body count, and —" He cut himself off, some kind of wild emotion flashing in his eyes.

"And what?"

"And it was reckless and stupid. *You* were stupid."

She recoiled. "I was the one who acted on instinct, *trusted* you, and saved our lives. Stupid is the opposite of what I am."

"You're stupid for trusting me."

"What?"

He threw up his new hand. "It's not perfect yet. I could have failed to activate the wingsuit. I could have missed catching you. I could have failed to hold on!"

I could have missed catching you. Such a far cry from his original sentiment. *You're not worth holding on to.*

Alice glanced at his new hand, only now seeing the fine motor skills were jerky and rusty. He was right. She'd assumed. She'd assumed that because he'd thrown his fist through a person, and a door, that he was ready for anything. The fear in his eyes said otherwise. Not fear for himself, but for her.

Her heart kicked against her ribcage like a mule and suddenly she couldn't breathe. She put her palm on his chest, her voice almost a whisper. "It was reckless of you to come to my aid without your mask, but you did. Now your identity is compromised. He saw your face."

His big, warm hand covered hers.

She flinched. "They'll hand you over to the police."

"They wouldn't dare."

"How can you be so cavalier about this? Liza can't save you from the authorities every time."

"These men are greedy, Alice. They won't turn me over. Trust me."

"So what, you'll bribe them?"

"No," he said, jaw tightening. "They'll blackmail me first."

A stone dropped in the pit of Alice's stomach. "They'll take your company."

The grim nod he gave made her sick to the core. Parker would lose everything. Because of her.

PARKER LAZARUS

PARKER RUSHED Alice back to the penthouse via a network of rooftops and less trodden alleys the Deadly Seven frequented for anonymity. With each passing minute since their conversation, Alice's demeanor quietened. He worried she'd injured herself more than she admitted. So when they walked through his front door, he closed it and turned to her.

Silence stretched.

"Are you injured?" he finally asked. Notwithstanding her limp, blood covered her body.

"Not badly."

"I'll run the shower."

He left her in his bathroom, told her there were clothes for her in the closet, and then went to the kitchen to remove his suit and wash his face and hands. Left standing in his boxer shorts, he braced the countertop and hung his head, replaying the events in his mind.

She'd pushed him off the roof.

She'd jumped into the air without a chute, without any safety except for him. And he hadn't known until he felt her land between his shoulder blades.

She was lucky. Damned lucky. He could have just as easily assumed she was a threat and eliminated her. The wind had stolen her scent. Only a delay in his reaction time saved her.

He exhaled, tension leaving with his breath. She could have *died*.

Never in his life had he wanted to tie up someone so badly. Usually the urge was part of the ritual, the intimate connection between rigger and the model, the absolute trust, the safety. But with Alice, he didn't give a damn about any of it. He just wanted her safe and secure where he could keep her. Where nothing could harm her. And that was fucked up because her spark, her strength, and independence were parts of what he liked about her.

He'd never felt more helpless than the moment she'd pushed him, he twisted and fell, and they'd locked eyes. His body still twitched and shuddered with adrenaline and endorphins. Even his bionic arm twitched, as though the signals from his brain were messed up. He looked at his metal hand and his lip curled in disgust. If he'd not spent two months stubbornly refusing to admit he was handicapped, he could have come up with this solution earlier. He'd have perfected the fine motor skills, and he wouldn't have run his hand clean through a man's chest.

He scrubbed his face, still trying to rein in his emotions—the confusion—the events. Alice had barely blinked at the dead body, and he'd not checked to see how the Faithful had faired within his office. If they were dead or alive, he honestly didn't care. Parker closed his eyes and all he could see was that man's eyes through his Halloween mask. All he could hear was his prayers. Parker had only meant to push him out of the way, but his arm went straight through him. His instinct to get to his mate was strong.

The worst part was, he didn't regret it. Parker would plow through a million men just to get to Alice. Even more frightening… she might feel the same way.

Alice had wanted to assassinate his executive, purely because he saw Parker's face. Was it possible Alice was as obsessive as him? Would they burn so hot together they'd turn to ash?

Would there be anything left?

The shower water faucet turned off and Parker straightened, scrubbing his face. He pulled himself together and opened the fridge to find something for Alice to eat. Plus, he didn't want to think about the things he overheard—her padding barefoot to his walk-in closet, her gasp as she discovered the entire wardrobe she'd sent back to the retailer was now in there. The sound of rollers as she opened a drawer. Her heartbeat increased as she found lingerie displayed like something in a museum. The thud of her heart grew painfully loud, even from this distance and yet, he schooled his breath so he could hear more.

The drawer slammed shut.

Fabric rasped.

Footsteps thumped carpet, getting louder.

Parker tensed, still looking into the fridge, suddenly aware he was in boxer shorts and nothing else. He reached for a Tupperware container, this morning's delivery from Alice. When his bionic hand tried to grasp the box, it slipped, and he dropped it. His cheeks heated and he slammed the fridge door shut, deciding to leave the food for later. When he turned, he found Alice staring at him, all fresh faced and wet-haired from the shower.

Brown eyes. Freckles. Pouty lips.

She wore one of his shirts. It barely covered her hips, leaving her thighs naked, a thick scar threaded on one. In her arms were blood-soaked clothes. Part of him became aroused at the sight of her in his shirt, at their scents mingling together. But the other part, the more logical part, was confused that she'd ignored his gifts.

"I should go," she said, eyes stark.

"Go where?"

"Home." Her brows lifted as though it was obvious.

"This is your home, Alice."

She laughed disparagingly. "You can't just buy me a wardrobe and call it my home, Parker. It doesn't work like that."

She tried to get to the door. Dressed like that? So the world could almost see—nope. He blocked her. "Why not?"

"Because it doesn't."

She tried to leave again, but it wasn't because she didn't want him. He smelled her arousal and heard her pulse spiking. Her eyes had softened on him. So why was she leaving? Was buying her a closet full of clothes really that bad?

Then he scented something else—metal—mixed in with the old blood on her clothes. Her knives must be in there. She avoided his gaze.

This woman never avoided his gaze, well, not since he'd learned her true identity. The real Alice never backed down, and if she wasn't going to tell him what bothered her, he had to figure it out on his own.

What had Alice been trying to tell him for the past few weeks?

To join forces with her. To trust her. That the executives at his work were trying to oust him. What would he do if someone threatened his mate's livelihood?

"You're going after the executive," he stated.

Wide eyes snapped to his. "What?" She scoffed. "No, I wasn't."

"Alice," he chided. "Don't lie to me."

A tinge of pink hit her cheeks. "Okay, fine. But if you're not going to do it, then I will. Someone has to, and it may as well be the one already going to Hell."

No. Absolutely not. She already had black stains on her heart from the work she did for the Sisterhood. He would *never* add to that tally. Ever.

"We don't know anything for sure yet. Let's just play it cool and deal with him later. I've already asked Sloan and AIMI to scrub CCTV footage showing my face. It will be his word against ours."

"And if it's not?"

"Then we'll deal with it." He looked at the kitchen. "Have something to eat."

She paused, thinking, but then nodded. He had no doubt her capitulation was purely because he'd said "we" and not "I" in that first sentence. Parker took her dirty clothes and dropped them in the waste bin, then went back to the fridge and had a second go at removing the Tupperware container. With a surge of triumph, he picked it up.

"Here's something I prepared earlier." He put the container on the counter.

She sat on a stool, her eyes twinkling. "Oh, really?"

With his good hand, he put two plates out, but when it came to opening the container, he knew there was no going around it. He had to use both hands. Damn it. He attempted to open the dish twice, but failed to grasp the edges.

"Do you need a—"

"If you say hand…"

"Sorry."

"I'm fine." But his bionic fingers wouldn't do the job.

"Parker."

"I said I'm fine." Alice jolted from the anger sharpening his tone, and he hated it. He shoved the dish away and walked out of the kitchen, shaking his head.

It shouldn't take this long for him to calibrate the arm. He knew exactly how it worked. He'd made his own adjustments, along with Flint's. Hell, he could build his own arm if he wanted to.

Alice followed him into the living area where he paced by the piano. He opened his mouth to say something, but she spoke first.

"If you say you're fine again, I'll bop you over the head."

"Bop me?" He stopped and arched a brow.

They stared at each other for a long, awkward moment, then she pointed at the piano.

"Do you play?" she asked, walking over to it.

Boxes still sat on top of it, but the keyboard was clear. She hit a key.

"Sounds in tune," she noted, then slid her eyes to him, waiting.

"Yes, I play." But never with an audience. His bionic fingers twitched.

"Show me." Alice removed the boxes and opened the piano lid to expose the strings. She took a peek inside before sitting on the bench and playing *Chopsticks*. "Something like this?"

He rolled his eyes. As if he'd be so dull as to learn that beginner rubbish.

"Move over before you hurt yourself." He sat down next to her.

He placed his fingers on the keyboard, hovered over keys—for a sheer second doubt plagued him. He'd never played to an audience because he had to be perfect. When he fucked up, he couldn't hide it. He hated it. The heat of Alice's attention burned down one side of his face.

He dropped his fingers and they came down too strong.

"Sorry," he mumbled, and flinched.

She smiled at him.

That's all it took for the sun to break the storm clouds. His fingers landed on the keys and he played the upbeat jazz tune she'd hummed in his office. He picked it because the left keys weren't too taxing, and maybe he wanted to impress her, but she slapped her palm over his. The keys smashed together, resonating discord.

"Not that one," she whispered. "Please."

Her breath hitched. He hated seeing her slouch because of something he'd done, so he shifted keys and played a version of another Nina Simone song—*Feeling Good.*

With half his mind on his mate's reaction, and the other half on the chords, this one played out with fewer errors, and when Alice started singing in a husky voice, a mix of both devil and angel, he forgot about his hands completely. He played on instinct. Together they increased tempo and volume until she matched his gusto with her own. Her voice and his music filled the penthouse with rich, unadulterated sound. She sang the final, long note and he forgot to breathe.

Alice bowed her head, her shoulders shaking. For a moment, he thought she was crying, but when he tipped her chin to see her face, he found another smile so rich and sweet. She took his robotic hand and laced her fingers with his. His robotic hand moved perfectly, no twitch. Her grin widened.

"You…" His eyes narrowed with suspicion. "You did that on purpose. The song. The singing. All of it."

She shrugged. "Well, I knew you would try to keep up with me if I sang, so… yeah. I guess I did it on purpose."

She tried to pull her hand from his, but he clenched, holding tight. Frowning, she met his eyes and tugged again. But he wasn't letting go.

"No," he said, searching her face. "It wasn't just about me. Your singing. It was new. Raw. When was the last time you sang?"

Tears glimmered in her eyes. "Can we talk about that another time?"

He gave a curt nod. If this conversation was bringing her pain, he could wait.

"So tell me this then, why are you refusing my gifts?" He glanced at his oversized shirt on her. "Why are you wearing my shirt instead of your own new clothes?"

Her breath hitched with a breath, defining hard nipples against the fabric.

"Maybe I like the way you smell," she confessed. "And maybe I kept one thing."

twenty-two

ALICE MONTGOMERY

ALICE'S HEART kicked in her chest as she held Parker's leonine stare. Her body was in turmoil. Sweet, jittery, aroused turmoil. The butterflies didn't just flutter; they danced. They sang. They hummed along every line of her body.

He'd played so beautifully, even the beats he'd missed or fumbled. The beauty was in the resilience, the ability to carry on when he'd made a mistake. There had been no hot-headed pride in those moments, he'd only kept watching her sing with awe in his eyes. That awe, that incredible window to his thoughts, had hit her harder than any words or touch could.

So she'd kept singing to see it. Singing for the first time in decades. Singing because Parker Lazarus had developed *feelings* for Alice. For *her*. Not the Sinner, or the fake assistant she pretended to be, or the killer she would become if this family turned dark. But her. The woman who hummed when she was stressed. The one who'd offered to kill for him. The one sitting next to him now, smiling like a stupid teenager at the half naked carved Adonis refusing to let go of her hand.

"What was the gift you kept, Alice?" he asked, voice deep and soft. His gaze burned through the fabric on her body, as if he could see through to the guilty pleasure encasing her intimate skin. She squirmed, her pulse throbbing.

When she'd walked into his closet, only to find it half filled with all the items she'd returned to the personal shopper, she'd forgotten to think. To breathe. To swallow. Then slowly, with careful attention, she'd inspected how each item had been placed with loving care. Shoes on racks. Jewelry in a display case. Clothing on rotating racks. But the pieces that stood out the most were the folded lingerie. An entire wall had been fitted with flat roller drawers. She pulled out each to find different types of lingerie. A red lace bra and panty set. A silk babydoll teddy. A long, purple satin gown.

It had all been too real, and before she gave in to the feelings bubbling in her body, she knew she had to secure this relationship. She would not give her heart over just to see it stomped on if Parker was arrested.

She couldn't stay the night. She had to get home and plan a way to eliminate the threat against him. Parker was a man who not only lived in luxury, but liked it. He lived for it. And he'd potentially given it all up for her. So she'd hastily put on his shirt, but not before having a moment of weakness and slipping on some lingerie. She wanted to go to sleep that night feeling close to him.

"Alice." Parker lifted her hand and guided her off the piano bench to stand before him. He pushed her gently, indicating he wanted her to take a step back.

Muscles on his tanned body twitched as he eased back on the bench to assess her, his hands by his side, legs spread wide, eyes intense and full of dark possessive desire.

"Show me," he decreed.

Alice's breath caught in her throat. Her nipples peaked, and a rush of desire warmed her intimately between the legs. Parker's nostrils flared. He inhaled, and a low rumble began at the base of his throat.

"Alice," he warned. "Show me what you kept."

She bit her lip to hold her smile. There was something about bringing a man like this to impatience, to hear his whimper of restraint, to see the arousal tenting his boxers—the same hardness he ignored in order to hold her stare. Every muscle in his body was locked and tight. Every line and curve, so damned sexy and powerful. How had she worked so closely with him for so long? Two years torturing herself, pretending to be plain and boring when she felt anything but.

That stare. It made her feel like a queen. Like she was the only person in his orbit.

Maybe that's what emboldened her to walk her fingers along the hem of her shirt, bunching the fabric in a seductive tease. He broke eye contact and leaned forward in anticipation as inches of her naked thighs were revealed. Another inch. Another inch.

And another.

Until Alice exposed the red lace, her flat stomach, her sheer bra. She lifted the shirt completely off to stand unapologetically before him.

Parker stayed forward, captivated by the sight of her body. His pheromones thickened the air, and she knew, even though he acted unaffected, his insides were fluttering just like hers. They had to be.

"Turn," he said. "Slowly."

His alluring scent infused *want* and *need* into her system. "No."

That brow arch. That cocky, incredulous ego. "No?"

She stepped closer until he sprawled back and her knees hit the bench between his widespread legs. The bastard stretched his arms and rested them on the piano keys, making them tinkle. He waited for her to assess him, too. So she did. Her eyes did a slow drag down his front, roamed over his glorious abdominals, down more, and then her mouth dried. The line of his erection was a clear outline against the silk. He was big, thick and long from the head to the base. She doubted she'd be able to accommodate him.

"Turn around, Alice. I want to see all of you."

Forcing her eyes back to his face, her lips quirked. "Do you have any idea how long I wished for you to say that? That for two years I had to be someone you didn't think twice about?"

"I want to see you now."

"And I'm telling you no. You see all of me when I want you to." What she really meant to say was that she didn't want him seeing her back.

Her insolence stoked the desire in his eyes. He pushed away from the piano, took hold of her hips, and brought her back to him. Goosebumps erupted as his breath warmed her chest. Proprietary eyes drank her in. He thought he owned her... or at the very least, that she belonged to him. And... she turned the idea over in her mind before coming to the hot, thrilling conclusion that she was okay with that. To have this man forever stare at her like she was his own personal drug, to have him want to devour her... yes, she was okay with that.

Because she felt the same.

God help any woman who smiled at him, who flipped her hair, or gave him a coy look from beneath her lashes. There would be no mercy. Alice reached around her back, intending to undo the bra clasp—

"Not yet," he rasped. This time, there was no demand in his voice, but a question... a hope. "Let me savor this."

She lowered her hands. One only savored when they appreciated... when they wanted. His lips hovered between her breasts and he shuddered, inhaling deep, making a satisfied noise that rumbled in his chest. He looked up and held her gaze. He allowed her this dominance, this power over him. Him sitting and her standing.

And she had it, she realized. He'd demanded much from her, but any time she'd resisted, he'd backed off. He'd never pushed her places she didn't want to go. Oh, sure, he tried it. But never forced it.

This moment would change everything between them and he was asking permission with his eyes, with the soft hesitant stroke of his thumb over her sensitive skin. She gave a small nod.

Hot lips landed on her skin. Her hands threaded into his silken hair. His legs caged her thighs. He kissed her all over, bare flesh and over the lace. He took it all. Tasted everything. And when he found her nipple straining through the thin fabric, he covered it with his mouth. Wet heat enveloped her as he sucked, harder and with fury. Pleasure shot to her womb and she cried out, fisting his hair. He came off, unapologetic and unreservedly aroused. He put a hand on each breast, squeezed and erotically kneaded with an expert touch until she gave herself over to the lazy bliss. He explored her body, lingering on unique feminine lines. He showered so much attention on her that she had the sense he was doing more than appreciating. He was mapping every inch so he could remember it when they were apart.

"Red looks good on you," he mumbled, running a finger along a strap, stretching it to another angle until it dented against her skin. He canted his head like an artist before a canvas and then pulled the second strap into a harness shape above her bust. He then let go slowly, dragging the elastic over her sensitized skin, watching her shiver in pleasure. "Beautiful."

But not my back.

The knowledge tugged on her heart and she rocketed out of her daze. He couldn't see the scars there. They were different. She pulled his hair, bringing his face to attention. Defiance flared in his eyes, and he dug his fingers into the fragile lace bra before ripping the fabric out of the cups with slow, methodical purpose. When he was done, all that remained were the red elastic straps containing her naked breasts.

"I thought you liked that bra," she grumbled.

"It was never about the bra, Alice. But what was beneath." Parker went back to owning her body, taking from it what he willed. He licked and laved, sucked and kissed. And she let him. Good God, she let him. His tongue was more intoxicating than his scent. It was the promise of protection, of care, of kindness and—

He lifted her leg over his shoulder and kissed her reverently along her inner thighs, not even pausing before landing at the apex, changing the mood to downright erotic. Two heavy-lidded, golden eyes met hers and challenged. When she made no response, he laved over the mound of lace. The sight stole her breath. She stared into the eyes of the lion.

"I want to hear how you sound when you feel good," he said, laving her again through the lace. "And I want to hear how you sound when you don't like it."

Rules. Directives. An image of the ropes in his room. Perhaps this was a test.

Steeling her resolve, she grasped his hair and pulled tight until his breath hitched, and then she pushed his mouth to her sex. He didn't hesitate. He kissed her there, devouring through the lace. Bliss pulsed in her body. Her standing leg weakened and, before she knew what happened, both legs were lifted around his shoulders and he held her curled around his face. The strength it took to maintain that pose was astounding. He not only maintained carriage, he feasted on her until she made the sounds he wanted to hear. Whimpers. Mewls. Gasps. Moans.

More.

She needed more.

She must have said it aloud, because he twisted and lowered her gently on the piano lid. An animalistic growl later and teeth tore through the lace, his tongue pushing through the hole he made, stroking and invading her in a way no man had ever done before.

He wasn't a man. He was a master. A god. Parker-fucking-Lazarus.

Through the haze of her desire, she managed to hold him against her sensitive flesh, to maintain some sort of agency. For someone who never gave an inch, Parker gave everything she asked, touched her in every way she needed. When she made a sound of pleasure, he increased his intensity. When she grunted with annoyance, he changed his methods. With his fingers, his lips, his tongue, he was there.

His wild scent took her to a feverish place full of ecstasy. She was his world until she felt herself tightening, until he rumbled in approval and worked her harder, until her orgasm crashed into her like a freight train, obliterating all sense.

In the languid aftermath, he kissed up her body, beard scratching over her stomach, her neck, until he nuzzled around her ear.

"Next time," he promised. "I'll have you in our bed."

A flash of when she was last there, of the ropes and bolts she'd seen above the bed, of the sensual artwork on the walls.

"In *your* bed," she breathed, correcting him.

"In knots." He kissed. "Beautiful, perfect knots."

She imagined him working over her body, attentive and tender, equal parts passion as surrender. A low, drawn-out moan of anticipation escaped her lips.

"Now?" she gasped, already feeling her body heat.

"No," he clipped, surprising her. Reality jerked her heart. Still sprawled in tattered lingerie, she blinked uncontrollably at the ceiling.

"Why not?" she blurted before she could stop herself.

"Because, my sweet little assassin," he said, grinning as he slid his palms up her thighs. "What happens in that room is about trust."

"And you don't trust me."

"No—it is you who doesn't trust me."

He supported her as she lifted into a sitting position. The sensation of one hand, cool as marble, and the other rasping from callouses, distracted her. She'd forgotten about her back.

Too late.

Parker's thumb paused over a ridge on her skin and then stroked, testing curiously. He glanced over her shoulder and couldn't hide his disapproval. "What the fuck happened?"

Panic engulfed her. She shoved him away, hard.

"None of your business." She scrambled to find the discarded shirt and put it on, covering the mess on her back—her penance. "I should go."

He took her hand. "You're staying here."

She twisted out of his grip. "Don't—"

"Alice."

"Parker."

They squared off. She refused to back down. It was stupid of her to think she could hide it from him. He was always going to find out. She'd just not prepared herself. She'd only wanted the adoration in his eyes to last a little longer, to pretend he truly worshipped her.

"Alice," he said. "That wasn't from the car accident."

She blinked. He knew about the accident? "Mary told you about that too?"

Clever eyes assessed her. "Why would *Mary* tell me about it? I ordered the background check myself."

So he didn't know about the connection to Flint? It didn't matter. None of it did. He'd been right. The scars on her back weren't from the accident. They'd come after, at the Sisterhood. But she wasn't alone in them. Every Sinner had them. They were from the whip that purged them of their shame, the one that absolved them of sin, that gave them the thinnest chance of getting into Heaven.

He took a step closer, expression already forming into defensive mode. "Tell me."

"This isn't your fight, Parker."

"When it involves my mate, it's always my fight."

"It's not!" she shouted. "You can't win every battle."

"Try me."

"Argh!" She threw her hands in the air. "You're impossible."

"You know that word is made up of the words, I'm possible."

She laughed bitterly. "There's no beating you, is there?"

Golden eyes softened.

"No," she said, pointing at him. "I don't want your pity."

"Fine." He held up his palms in surrender. "You don't have to tell me now, just… don't leave. Stay." His look of earnest gave her pause, and then he added, "It's safer here."

She rolled her eyes. "I can take care of myself. I don't need a savior."

Alice walked to the door. Parker rushed to catch up with her.

"Alice, I mean it." His fingers splayed on the door, blocking her. "Stay."

Another order? She folded her arms and gave him a look.

"Please," he gritted out.

She relaxed. "Now, was that so hard?"

His grin flashed sharp teeth, not entirely human, and if he was a dog, she was sure he'd have wagged his tail. His happiness was infectious, more so because she'd never seen him like this.

"I'll finish preparing the food." He started toward the kitchen. Paused. Looked back at her from over his shoulder. "Unless you want to order in?"

So that was it? He would give her the best oral sex of her life and then just order takeout like nothing had happened? She sensed his attention pulsing in the air. He wanted this. And she did too. *So stop being so guarded.*

"The food I made is fine."

"Good. I like your cooking."

ALICE COULDN'T SLEEP. At first, she thought she couldn't drift off because Parker had insisted he sleep in the same bed. *His* bed, which he continued to call *our* bed. Somewhere over the past few days he'd decided they belonged together, and now he only saw that. She had to admire his focus and supposed this tenacity was what made him the success story he was today.

Failure was not a word in Parker Lazarus's vocabulary.

And then there was the fact she was his mate—his sin's biological opposite, which was complete bullshit. She wasn't proud of herself for a good reason, but she wasn't humble. She wasn't a pillar of virtue in the community. She wasn't a real nun. None of the Sinners truly believed they were. How could they be if that belief ended with a fate in the fires of Hell?

So they pretended.

Parker wasn't pretending. He never did. Needing a mate was as intrinsically woven through his being as the ropes on the wall would inevitably wind around her. If she stayed here, truly gave herself over to this life, then it would be final.

It would also be devastating if she left him, whether intentionally or by accident. Alice had heard the story about what happened to Sloan when she was separated from Max for too long. Sloan had blacked out and gone berserker, attacking anyone who felt sloth. Parker had already put his fist through a body to get to her. He might tear the world apart if their mating bond couldn't keep him sane.

For the first time in her life, she doubted her true mission—to be the last stand against the Deadly Seven should the mating bonds fail. Her weapon had been violence, but maybe it should be something else. Maybe it should be love.

Maybe she couldn't sleep because of the thoughts churning about the need to protect Parker from the executives who wanted his company. She clenched her fists at the memory of the one who'd caught Parker's identity beneath the cowl of his hood. That smug smile on that man's face.

She wanted to wipe it off. Permanently.

And finally, maybe she couldn't sleep because of the long, hard length of male beside her, inches away and also pretending to be asleep. Was he waiting for her to drift off before he left her alone? What was he thinking?

It hadn't escaped her attention that their sexual encounter had finished one-sided, and *that* opened many more questions in her mind. Had her scars truly repulsed him? Did he pity her? If so, then what would he think when he learned what caused those scars?

Her stomach twisted into knots, and she squirmed. She opened her eyes to the dark shadow of Parker's muscular body next to her and sighed. He wasn't under the covers with her, and he remained in nothing but his boxer shorts. Golden eyes blinked at her, and she jolted. He was awake.

"Can't sleep?" His voice was a soothing baritone.

She shook her head, knowing he saw her in the dark.

"You said a closet full of clothes didn't make this your home. So what will?"

Alice sat up. "Were you watching me sleep?"

He joined her sitting. "You weren't asleep."

"Or are you making sure I don't leave?"

"You're avoiding the question."

"Because it's the middle of the night. It's not the time for deep and meaningful life questions."

"Then why can't you sleep?"

Her lips parted. His question speared right through to the truth. She needed answers to all her questions, and she was too afraid to ask them, so they stayed churning in her head.

"Fine," he growled. "Then let me hold you."

She tensed. "You want to hold me?"

"That's what I said." Defiance flashed in his eyes, as if simply asking to touch her put him out, but she saw through his stubborn arrogance. It was a sign of vulnerability, a defense mechanism. He was just as afraid of this kind of intimacy as she was. And he craved it just as badly.

She couldn't remember the last time someone had touched her with compassion. She couldn't remember her mother hugging her. There was no love at the foster homes, and nothing but distance at the Abbey—the nuns tried to be kind, but ultimately it all felt shallow. It was as though the Sinners were the nuns' little projects, their own penance.

If it wasn't from the brief affection from her fellow sisters, she'd be completely bereft of the good kind of human touch.

Slowly, she laid down, facing him. He shuffled closer, smoothed his hand over her hip, and held it there. For long moments she remained tense. He did too. But then he relaxed and cupped the back of her head, pulling her into the cocoon of his body. His unique male scent surrounded her, driving the tension away. On her next exhale, she melted into his side and burrowed beneath his jaw, where his soothing scent strengthened. The last thing she remembered before drifting off to sleep was a low vibrating rumble from the base of his throat that sounded suspiciously like a purr.

twenty-three

ALICE MONTGOMERY

ALICE WOKE to voices filtering through Parker's closed bedroom door. The sun shone through the windows, telling her it was mid-morning. How had she slept for so long? She threw off the covers and winced at the ache in her muscles. The days after a battle were always the hardest. She forced her limbs to move, cursed her aging body, took a hot shower, and then dressed in some of the workout attire from her side of the closet.

It still felt odd to think of it as her side, but the more she did it, the easier it became. Could this really be her life?

When she left the bedroom, she found not only Parker but other members of his family surrounding the counter in his kitchen. All of them, including their mates. The penthouse was crowded. Alice's training took over. She became still. She studied. She assessed the threat.

First, she found Parker standing tall and regal in an untied silk robe that displayed his ridged abdomen and perfect pecs. At least he'd found some navy pajama pants to cover those indecent silk boxers. His slightly damp auburn hair was tied back, and his beard was freshly trimmed and oh so kissable. He must have showered before her, and she'd slept right through it. Alice bit her bottom lip, thinking of what she might have seen if she'd awoken an hour earlier.

He looked up, caught her gaze and held. That simple connection sucked all the air out of the room. Everyone else disappeared. All sound, all sight, simply vanished.

And then someone wolf-whistled.

Alice looked around. Sitting on the large leather sectional were a group of women. The WAGS—wives and girlfriends. Freckle-faced and with blond, bouncing curls, Misha still grinned with her fingers in her lips. Next to her, Lilo rocked a newborn in her arms. Grace cooed over the baby Alice assumed was Wyatt's and Misha's. Lilo had her own slight, round belly growing the next generation Lazarus. Sloan and Bailey were deep in discussion at the end of the sectional.

In the kitchen was a feast of male testosterone. Evan, Griffin, Wyatt, Tony, Parker, Max, and Joe—Liza's mate and FBI agent. Liza stood next to him, arms folded, intense gaze looking at papers and a laptop on the counter. No Mary or Flint.

It was virtually a full house. And everyone stared at Alice. She'd never wished for her sisters more than in that moment. Misha broke from the group first and dragged Alice over to the sectional. Parker sent Alice an apologetic look, but then returned to whatever important job they discussed. *Traitor.*

"You must be Alice," Misha said, smiling. "I'm so excited—*we're* —all so excited to meet you."

Alice gave a tight smile as Misha introduced the rest, even though Alice already knew who they were. She may have avoided meeting most of them over the past two years, but she'd done her research. Bailey sized up Alice. Grace gave a kind smile, and Lilo virtually exploded with excitement. She handed baby Amari to Grace and started rapid-firing questions at Alice.

"So you're the Sinner, right?" Lilo shook Alice's hand. "I'm so intrigued. I'd love to write an article about the Sisterhood, but of course I know that it's a secret. It is right? I mean, I can't, can I? I still want to hear about everything. Is that bad?" Lilo darted a glance between the women. "It's bad, right? I'm being weird. Oh gosh, I shouldn't have said anything. It's just, these hormones make me even more cotton brained. You know?"

Alice laughed stiffly, her wide eyes searching for Parker again.

Misha stepped into Alice's vision. "Lilo's just excited. We're all excited. Before you came along, none of us had seen the inside of Parker's penthouse for months!" Misha lowered her voice, side-bar style. "And Wyatt's even easing up on my lockdown restrictions. We're allowed to go out this week!"

"Wait. What?" Alice frowned at her. "What do you mean lockdown?"

Bailey joined them. "The Syndicate tried to kidnap Misha for the fetus stem cells. She's not growing them anymore, so she's not in danger."

"Except now that's me," Lilo laughed, a little flustered. "But so far Griff has been pretty reasonable. He only follows me on outings every other day."

Alice blinked. "They're actually locking you up or stalking you?"

"Well, I can understand their concern." Lilo glanced at her feet, her expression betraying her frustration. From what Alice knew about the woman, she was not the kind to enjoy being locked up. None of these women were. They were strong and independent, but apart from Bailey, they weren't really fighters. Not the way Alice was. "Anyway," Lilo continued. "I'm so happy to meet you properly. Like, not the fake you. You know what I mean. The point is, now that you're here, everyone seems to have relaxed a little. It's good."

Lilo's cheeks went bright red, and then she rushed over to Griffin. "I can't stop talking. What's wrong with me?"

"Nothing." He pulled her under his arm and kissed the top of her head, then went back to listening to whatever Parker was saying.

"And by everyone," Sloan piped up from her spot on the couch, finishing Lilo's thoughts. "She means the men."

"Really?" Alice said, thinking the opposite. Since she'd arrived, she'd caused nothing but uncertainty and an increasing possessiveness in Parker she hadn't known existed. Probably because he'd never dated anyone.

Parker barked from the kitchen, "Get in here, Sloan. Alice, you too."

She rolled her eyes and reluctantly stood.

"That's probably our cue to leave," Misha said, taking the baby from Grace. "I don't want to know about any of this Syndicate talk. It's too stressful."

Misha, Grace and Lilo said goodbye to their mates and then left. Alice walked alongside Bailey to the kitchen, sensing a kindred spirit. The strong woman carried herself with confidence and aplomb. Her Nightingale Securities bomber jacket looked good on her, adding to the badass vibe. But then the obscenely handsome Tony waggled his brows at her approach and blew a raspberry on her neck, to which she giggled and melted into his side. So maybe she was a softie. Tony stood behind Bailey and wrapped his arms around her front before dropping his chin on her shoulder. All eyes settled on Alice as she took up a position next to Parker at the island counter.

She stiffened. Everyone was so lovey-dovey. Was this really her future? She screwed up her face. Sure, she wanted compassion. Last night, falling asleep to the sound of Parker's purring had lulled her into contentment. Suddenly, surprisingly, she couldn't think of anything she'd rather do than elicit that sound in him again. Even if that meant going all lovey-dovey with him.

Parker shifted, so he was between Alice and Tony. Then he glared at the other males. Alice could have sworn she heard a low, breathy growl in the base of his throat, and she looked around the group, worried. What was going on?

Liza scowled at her brother. "Don't be a dick, Parker. They're all mated. No one is going to beat his chest and Tarzan-steal your lady."

Steal?

"I know that," Parker snapped. "I can't help it."

Sloan snorted. "Always knew you were an animal, bras."

He pointed at her. "I'm warning you."

"Suck it. You called me a monkey when my powers came in."

"I did not. I said your powers were based in mirror neurons and monkeys had been studied—"

"Can we get to the reason we're here?" Griffin interrupted, pursing his lips.

Parker's jaw snapped shut, but he remained tense, nostrils flared. Alice tried something. She placed her palm on his arm. He visibly relaxed but refused to look at her. She would take it.

"We've isolated locations around the world," Parker told her, eyes still on the papers and laptop. "We suspect they're all Syndicate bases."

Alice nodded. "We always knew Julius had overseas investors, but since our resources don't extend further than this continent, we couldn't get information other than that."

"And the Vatican?" he asked. "You said they now know about the Sisterhood."

Alice straightened, suddenly aware of her scars pulling on her back. "They were original investors of your creation, but, as I'm sure Mary has told you, that all changed after she stole you—"

"Freed us," Liza corrected.

"Yes." Alice blushed. "The Sisterhood acknowledges and accepts that. We understand the part the Sisterhood played—"

"You mean the part where you wanted to kill children?" Wyatt's dark brows lowered as he folded his arms, pushing his biceps out.

Alice planted her feet. "For the record, the Sisterhood isn't what it used to be. I was only the same age as some of you when that all went down. Since I joined the Sisterhood, since the Vatican learned of our existence, things have been different."

The weight of scrutiny settled on her, but how could she tell them how the Sisterhood had changed? How could she explain the scars on her back, or the Sinners' penance, or the constant disgust from the clergy? Yes, the Sisterhood had changed, but Alice wasn't sure that was an entirely good thing.

She wiped clammy palms on her thighs and gave a pointed look at the maps they'd been pouring over. "Six locations?"

Parker stared at her a moment longer before gesturing at the maps. "Evan and Griffin flew to Norway to investigate the first location, and we need teams to gather intel on the others. If they're truly what we think they are, then we can strike simultaneously and destroy them all. We can even strike remotely if we're smart enough to set it up properly."

"I can provide a Sinner as backup for each location scout." The slight lowering of Parker's shoulders made Alice think that was exactly what he'd hoped for. "Six locations, two team members at a minimum, and one of them should be powered to provide a tactical advantage."

More than one family member raised a brow, probably waiting for Parker to cut down her assertiveness. But he nodded, thoughtful.

"You and I will take Columbia," he said. "Wyatt will take Asia. Evan can go back to Norway and conduct a thorough final sweep now that we have a plan. Sloan can go to Australia. Tony to Ireland. Liza to Zimbabwe. If a Sinner goes with each, then they can all search for your missing agent as well as provide backup."

"I want to go with Sloan," Max said, his Australian accent thick. "I know my way around. I'm ex-military. Why not use me?"

"Fine," Parker said. "You go with Sloan, but a Sinner will have to accompany you too."

"But we need you here," Wyatt said to Max. "Running Nightingale with Bailey and protecting our mates."

Parker shook his head. "It's highly unlikely the Syndicate will try to kidnap them again. They're all preparing for their big reveal. That was the whole reason Julius took Daisy—he's in a rush. He doesn't have time to start his research over."

"I disagree," Griffin said, making a pointed look at Parker's yin-yang tattoo. Somehow, even when they'd touched overnight, the tattoo turned heavily black. "That's your pride talking. Lilo is still in danger, and will be until the Syndicate is destroyed."

"That's why I'm allowing you to remain in Cardinal City," Parker said, his tone tight.

"You're *allowing* me?" Griffin's eyes narrowed behind his spectacles.

"Yes." Parker closed the laptop. "You'll each have access to the new AIMI via satellite. It's a reconnaissance mission. If anyone learns of the missing Sinner, or Daisy, and you can't safely infiltrate, then do not engage. Call for backup. Alice will book appropriate travel for tonight. I suggest everyone use this time to prepare."

Alice's brows went sky high. That may have been how things worked when she was his simple assistant, but now they were equals. Sensing her ire, he glanced at her and paused. She said nothing. Just waited.

"Please," Parker gritted out.

"Since you asked so nicely, sure." She gave him a sweet smile. "I'll need to borrow your phone."

"*Our* phone."

"Aww, dawg, good luck with that." Sloan thumped Parker on the back, grinning, then grabbed Max's hand and started for the door, scoffing under her breath. "Dude's finally got some manners."

"Fly out tonight," Parker called after them. "Be ready."

"Wait," Alice said, stopping everyone as they turned to leave. She met Parker's eyes. "You haven't told them about—"

"It's a non event," he insisted, jaw tight.

Fine. Don't tell them your identity was compromised, she said with her eyes. *See what keeping secrets gets you!*

She could have sworn she heard his mental *harrumph* as she kept her mouth shut. Deciding now would be a good time to start on her calls, Alice went to the living room, where she'd spotted a phone on the ridiculously ornamental side table next to the sectional. Masculine rumblings by the door prickled her senses, but she remained firm and dialed the private number for the Hildegard Abbey.

twenty-four
PARKER LAZARUS

WHILE ALICE MADE PLANS, Parker checked equipment for the mission. He wanted to help Alice, but frustratingly, he actually didn't know how to do the menial office tasks. Just like the cooking, he knew he'd come to rely on Alice in more ways than one.

She never complained, not even when he brought her a simple apple for a mid-morning snack. He couldn't cook or make a sandwich. So it was an apple. For lunch it was takeout. By the afternoon, and she was still on the phone making calls. He sat at the piano and practiced with his bionic fingers until they slipped from mental fatigue. But that was the problem with the bionic arm. While his real flesh and blood arm would continue to work on muscle memory alone, right up until a moment of failure, the left arm would fail if his mind wasn't strong. But if trained properly, could work when his body gave out. He still hadn't tested his limits. If he failed, if he held Alice in his arms again… he shook his head, unable to dwell on it.

Tonight they would fly into another country and hunt for Daisy. Tonight, they would be the bird flying over the wall to find her in captivity. They would free his sister. What she must be going through. What she *had* gone through…

The kind and caring little girl had become something unrecognizable—a heartless, cold and unfeeling thing. Until she'd sacrificed herself for Liza. Until she'd thrown out a life raft, crying out for help, and Parker hadn't been there to see it. Failing to be there for Daisy was Parker's biggest shame. He'd been so caught up with his battle against Alice—a battle that made little sense now—when he could have been down in that warehouse, backing up Liza and saving Daisy from making the second biggest mistake of her life. The first being that she tried to save their birth mother Gloria from the flames of a burning building.

Julius was a mad man. Parker had never doubted it. His pride had curdled Parker's gut any time they'd been close. Julius's pride was so bad that if Parker ever blacked out and slipped into his berserker state, Julius wouldn't be recognizable after Parker was done with him.

But the worst part was that with The Beast now pacing continuously inside Parker's body, he didn't think he needed to black out to cause destruction. That berserker state lived just beneath the surface. And if that was the case, what did it say about him? What right did he have to profess superiority? To lead?

His fingers stuttered over the keys, causing the tune to break. His fist plunged through the keyboard in frustration, exploding discord into the air. Ivory keys popped and scattered. The strings inside the baby grand snapped. The Beast roared to the surface, coloring his vision red. He looked at his inner wrist tattoo. Almost black after only hours apart from touching Alice. Hours.

It seemed the same rules of biology didn't apply to him as they did to the others, which made little sense. The research notes he'd deciphered from Gloria's laptop said nothing about him reacting this

differently. He'd always known what his genetic makeup would be…
but this reaction? He was ill prepared.

"Parker?"

He swung around to find Alice standing in the doorway to his
bedroom, his cell phone dangling in her hands. While she'd been
planning, booking appropriate travel for his family and coordinating
the Sinners, he'd tried to find protective gear for Alice but found little
beyond their Deadly suits. She probably wouldn't accept one anyway,
but he would have felt safer knowing she had bullet proof protection.
Saying that, she'd survived this long without it. She was that good.
And this was the problem. Every time he looked at her, his pride
swelled and his cock ached. The Beast, already at the surface of his
control, urged him to take her, to claim her like an animal. To lose
himself in her, whether she wanted it or not. To make it so no one,
not even her, could doubt that she belonged with him.

"Come here," he said, frustration lacing his tongue.

She strode over with concern etched in her eyes. She didn't see the
lion inside him, prowling and pacing, ready to pounce.

"What happened?" she asked.

"I need to touch you." It would soothe The Beast. He hooked
fingers into her yoga pants and tugged her close, then buried his face
in her chest and simply soaked her up, let her infuse every pore in his
body.

The moment he touched, the tattoo itched as though a thousand
ants crawled in circles. His internal sin equilibrium balanced, and he
felt at peace. Shibari, or rock-climbing, had been the old way to quiet
his mind, but now he had Alice. Her hands landed gently on his
head.

"Parker?"

"Don't worry about it."

She pushed him back, craning his neck to capture his gaze. "You put your fist through the piano. It's not nothing." She paused. "Was it what Griffin said? About your pride?"

He showed her his tattoo. "It's balanced now."

"But... never mind."

"Ask."

"I just... and maybe I'm wrong and have no clue what I'm talking about, but shouldn't you remain balanced longer than a few hours after we separate? Isn't that how the mating bond works?"

He stood. "And what will you do with this knowledge if I tell you? Pass it on to your sisters?"

Alice's expression went flat. She stilled so completely, Parker knew he'd pissed her off irrevocably. Yet he refused to bend.

"I thought we were beyond snipes like that," she said, glowering.

His jaw clenched with his shame. She was right, but he'd be damned if he admitted it.

"You claim I don't trust you, but that, Parker, that right there is why." Steel in her tone was colder than ice. "You bait me as though you expect me to do or be someone I'm not. You use anger and arrogance to distract me from my questions. You still keep the strongest part of you locked away from me."

"You hide the truth, too, Alice."

"Yeah, well the truth can be painful." She paced before him, flexing her fists.

"You're not the only one in pain."

She stopped. Blanked. Then started pacing again, grappling with her thoughts. "You're right," she said.

"I am?"

"Yes. How is my pain any more important than yours?" She faced him and lifted her chin. "One of us has to go first. One of us has to rip off the Band-Aid and be the bigger person, it may as well be me."

"Oh no. You don't get to go first. I'll go first."

"My scars are from penance!" she shouted at the same time he roared, "Every time I look at you, I feel proud."

"What?" they both said.

"You're proud of me?" she rushed. "And that's why you were out of balance so fast?"

"Yes," he ground out, then went back to her answer with a sinking feeling in his gut. "What do you mean, those scars are your penance?"

Her lashes lowered. "Any time a Sinner comes back from a mission, we must see a priest and complete our penance. Sometimes that involves physical acts of contrition. The lash, the cilices, the sack, the—"

"Those are antiquated forms of penance. I thought the church was done with those," he growled.

She shrugged. "The Sisterhood *was* done with them. They gave up trying to save our souls from the fiery pits of Hell. But now the Vatican is in our hair, they believe we have to keep trying." She turned her back and lifted her shirt, displaying the hatching of silvery scars, new and old. "This is them trying." She dropped her shirt and rounded on him. "But I can't completely blame them. I accept responsibility. I want to be saved. And if this is the way to do it, then I'll never stop trying. Your turn. Why did you break the piano?"

"Because I hate—" He bit his words off.

"You hate what? That you need me?"

They were shouting now, and The Beast wanted a say. Parker's next words came out guttural and straight from the lion's mouth. "I hate that I need you so much it hurts. That I want to fuck you senseless every time I smell you. That there's this animal part of me that cares nothing for decorum or decency. It wants to bite anyone else who comes near you. It wants to devour you and feast on you until there's nothing left." His eyes fluttered at the memory of her intimate taste, craving it with a passion that made him painfully aroused.

"What does that have to do with the piano?"

"Nothing," he snapped. "Everything!"

"So tell me. Trust me!"

"You want to know more? Fine. I hate that I feel so much pride when I see you, I'm thrown into chaos. I hate that I didn't see you sooner."

"You saw me, Parker. I was always there!"

She turned her back on him and went to the kitchen. No. They weren't done. His stride ate up the space between them, and he gripped her shoulders, shaking her. "*You* weren't there, Alice. *You* still aren't fully here."

She folded her arms. "You're doing it again. Deflecting. Answer. My. Damned. Question."

Now his chest was heaving, his breathing labored. The Beast wanted to go to bat for him, but it was Alice. *It was his mate.* He had to trust her. Or what was this all for? What was the point?

"I'm not perfect," he confessed. "My hand isn't." He threw up the bionic hand in her face. "Sometimes there's a delay and I need it to be perfect."

Her brows lifted in the middle. "And what do you think will happen if you're not perfect for once? The world will continue to turn, the—"

"I might let go of you!"

He realized this was a stupid emotion for him to have, to fear perfection when she was a Sinner—someone so used to being told she was evil that she'd just accepted it. She allowed herself to be flogged, because she probably thought she deserved it. Just like him, she was the product of another's ill-conceived machinations.

How could he rationalize that sharp tug in his chest every time he thought about making a mistake? Every time he remembered Mary slamming that close button on the elevator and leaving Daisy behind in the burning building. Every time he thought about Alice's true reason for being with him—to finish what the original Sisterhood started.

She might be his mate, but what was he to her? A failsafe?

He lifted his head, The Beast still not sated, and caught her gaze. "You're prepared to kill my family, if things go sideways. Admit it."

She stilled. And his heart dropped. She didn't need to say anything, that reaction was it.

"Yes," she admitted. "If you and your family turn to the darkness. If you reach the point of no return and become the destruction of the world… Yes. It is my job to assassinate you all. Probably while you sleep."

"We're far superior to you."

"I already beat you in a fight, Parker."

"That was before my power manifested."

"Keep telling yourself that." She shrugged, despair echoing in her eyes. "I don't know what else to tell you, but I'm the last line of defense. Someone has to be, even if it's the cost of my immortal soul."

Anguish hit him. "Alice. I'm going to spend my life proving that you're not going to Hell and Heaven is here with me. Do you understand?"

Maybe it was his animal so close to the surface, but the words shot out of him from a place of instinct. Silence filled the small space between them, expanding like an ocean. Then she smiled, and a sparkle entered her whiskey eyes.

"So… you said earlier there was an animal part of you. Which kind?" she asked, tracing a pattern on the floor with her toe.

"Which kind of…" He shook his head, flustered. "I don't know.

Too many of them. Multiple feline species, some kind of wolf, a frog... Why does it matter?"

She flicked his robe out of the way and palmed his bare chest. Instantly, his body reacted. It was more than the sin equalizing. It was the rightness. The magnetism. The primal need gathering force like a thunder storm. A coy glance from beneath her lashes.

"I guess, if it's the cuddly animal that purrs, then I'm down with that."

Cuddly animal?

She rubbed him again, stoking to life instincts he couldn't control. The need to mate with her was more than uniting with the woman who balanced him. Her next words were husky and heavy with desire. "Who am I kidding? I'll take the other animal too. The one that wants to devour me until there's nothing left."

Shock splashed through him. "You want that? The Beast?"

"Is that what you call it?" Now she was the one to purr.

"Alice." He captured her wrist before it trailed down his stomach. "You don't know what you're asking for."

She captured his gaze. "Oh, yes I do. I want all of you, just as you want all of me. Every last drop."

His heart stuttered. With a sultry glance cast over her shoulder, she walked to his bedroom, her hips swaying in a way that went straight to his dick, despite her limp. More so because of that. Her resilience. Her strength. Her sexiness. And when he heard the telltale rasp of rope being pulled off a hook, he knew this was the moment he'd dreamed about as a child staring up at the blue sky. This was how he found freedom.

ALICE TREMBLED as she sat on Parker's bed with the rope in her hands. He prowled into the room, the glow of his beast still present in his eyes. The skin was taut across his body, pulled to tension with his restraint. She'd never seen anyone more magnificent that him. Tall, proud, king of a man. Everything about him screamed virility from his thick bearded square jaw to the breadth of his shoulders, to the... her gaze traveled south, the appendage that had her mouth watering. Her breath quickened, and her pulse raced.

Mine, she thought. *All mine*.

He took the rope from her and replaced it on the hook. Then he inspected each coil, each color and thickness and softness, until he landed on a red silky length that reminded her of the bra he'd destroyed. Returning to her, he placed it on the bed.

"I can hear your pulse race, Alice," he said. "You don't have to do this."

She lifted her chin. "I want to."

"But something is bothering you. This doesn't work if you're not honest with me. I need to know you will tell me when you're uncomfortable, and I need to know what feels good so I can do more."

Her brow arched. "What you *need* is to practice those knots so your hand's coordination will improve."

"Is that why you're doing this?" He flicked the bundle of rope.

Her lashes lowered. "Like I said, I want all of it. I'm just—"

"You still don't trust me."

"No, it's not that." She bit her lip. "I don't trust myself."

"Why?" he demanded.

"I have… problems with bondage," she said. "But I want to get over them. Help me."

"The scars?" His eyes widened.

"The leg. The accident. There was a seatbelt that couldn't come off, there was…"

Alice shut her eyes at the ghostly sound of tires spinning, of the CD skipping, of something that started in laughter, ending in pain.

"Okay. We'll start slow. One rope. One scene."

Alice glanced at the pictures on the wall behind Parker. "You did those?"

"The rope art, yes. The photographs, yes. The women? No."

Her gaze flicked to his and saw the truth in them. "Have you, um… had sex with any of your models?"

"No."

"They're beautiful."

"You are too."

He said it so casually, so easily, that she had to believe him. She filled her lungs until bursting, and then exhaled slowly. She wanted to help him, and she wanted to trust him and, by God, she wanted to fuck him. But first they had to shed every last piece of emotional armor. This was as much a test for herself as it was for him. After the last drop of air left her lungs, she nodded.

"Keep your clothes on," he said.

"Aww," she whined, almost stomped her foot like a child, and his lips curved seductively.

"We start slow, Alice. Shibari isn't always about sex."

Her follow up protest was short lived as she became enthralled with his hands unwinding the bundle of rope until he flicked it out like some kind of expert cowboy. But she knew this was more than that. More than a show. It was a connection between the two of them, and her skin pulled tight in anticipation for whatever that entailed.

He removed his robe and climbed behind her on the bed to cradle her smaller body in his own. Strong arms surrounded her, holding the rope, caging her in. In silence he pulled the single cord across her chest, drawing her back to him until her head rested on his shoulder and her back was flush to the heat of his front. Calmness spread in her body, melting her bones.

"Shibari is more than knots and bondage. It's sensual. It's about this: the trust; the intimacy; the surrender."

He let go of one side of the rope and slowly dragged the length across her chest. The ridges of cord rasped over her skin, sparking sensation, melting her until she fell deeper under his hypnotic spell. He moved her hands into a praying position and bound them.

"Close your eyes," he whispered. "I've got you."

Surrender. Her lashes fluttered, and she gave herself over to the sensations. With gentle, methodical touch, Parker moved them in harmony. He would shift her chin, or arm, but shadow his own body in tandem. He arched when she arched. He supported when she fell. This was like nothing she'd imagined.

At first, it was a little unnerving. But with each caress of the rope, each soft touch from him, she was eventually lulled into submission.

It was almost like being on a boat, rocking gently in the waves. Floating.

A small sigh escaped her lips. She couldn't get any more relaxed, but then he tugged sharply on the rope, jolting her, drawing her bound hands up sharply to her chest. Her heart rate spiked. He tugged again and again. Each confident pull thrilled her like a sudden wave, and she gasped as the rope rasped lightly over her chest, her nipples, shooting pleasure into her veins.

Parker stopped. He held her by the ropes, her hands pinned to her chest and with him still behind her, cradling with his body. Lips fluttered at her ear.

"That sound," he said, "was your good sound. Am I right?"

All she could do was nod, too lost in the euphoria.

He let go of the tension. The rope slithered along her skin, sending shudders skipping through her body, and then he gently guided her into another position. This time, he raised her bound hands over her head to loop behind his own warm neck. The ropes moved with a flurry, a quickening of the sea. Line after line wrapped around her torso. She didn't even realize it also wrapped around him until he suddenly pulled tight, tugging her back against his front. Trapping them together.

Her eyes flew open on a gasp.

Trapped.

With a band around her chest.

Pinned against him. Surrounding her. Supporting her.

The sound of jazz filtered into her periphery. Tires spinning. Her mother singing. The rope became a seatbelt. Alice's pulse skyrocketed, and she struggled to breathe.

"Alice?"

But she couldn't respond. She was lost in that terrible moment and the helplessness she'd felt. Only this time, this time—

"Alice, you're making that other sound," Parker said, tensing. "You need to use your words. Are you okay?"

"I'm... I'm..." Water leaked from her eyes. Emotion clogged her mind. Small tears turned into wracking sobs, but the rope harness about her torso prevented her from gaining enough air. She gulped.

Parker's claws sprung from his fingertips—both the metal and the natural—and he shredded the rope, cutting it clear down the middle. Like a released spring, her chest inflated the moment she became free. Air filled her lungs, and she gasped as though endlessly drowning while he flung pieces of her entrapment to the side, frantic to remove every last bit.

"Your ropes!" She sobbed at the destruction.

"Fuck the ropes."

"But—"

"I don't care about the ropes, Alice. Only you." Parker moved to her front so he could cup her blotched and wet face. Intense, anguished eyes held her own. His voice softened. "I'm so sorry. I should have gone easy on you for your first time. Shibari can be intense. It can bring emotion to the surface. I—"

He shook his head in self-deprecation—an emotion Alice had never seen on him. It stabbed her in the still flurrying heart, still lost at sea. She cupped his face.

"It's okay. I'm okay. I just felt so..."

"Trapped," he said, frowning. "The accident."

Alice's forehead met his, and they stayed together, holding each other.

"No, Parker." Her throat tightened as the truth came to light. "For the first time in my life, because of you, holding me together, I felt like I could finally fall apart."

He looked up, eyes suddenly full of wonder. "You weren't afraid?"

"Not like you think. I felt the pressure, the entrapment, and I remembered the accident. I went back there to that feeling of helplessness. You know I've never cried over it? I've never had anyone to hold my hand or to hug away the pain. Until now. Feeling you against my back, around me, everywhere… I felt safe. I felt as though I could be me. Like I could… sing again."

He blinked at her.

It was stupid. *God, she was stupid for saying that.*

He gently lifted her chin, so she returned to his gaze. "What do you mean, sing again?"

She took a deep breath and let it all out on the exhale. "My parents and I were singing when we had the car accident. I always thought it was my fault because they were distracted. So I never sang again. Until… earlier with you."

"I'm sorry." He hugged her tight.

"It's okay. I guess, I feel okay about it now."

A slow, hesitant smile lifted his lips.

"So this is the real you," he murmured.

A wave of bashfulness overcame her. "Maybe."

"Then, I suppose there's only one thing to say." He paused, drawing out the moment dramatically before finally whispering, "Hello."

"Hi," she returned, her own smile gathering force.

"The Real Alice, I'm going to kiss you now."

"Okay."

He eased her back against the pillows and covered her body with his. He was like a warm blanket made of flesh, and his kiss was like whiskey that warmed her raw soul. It coaxed her desire back to life, and it made everything so much more. When he tried to pull away, she bit his lip, holding him to her. His growl was wholly inhuman, and it sent a rush of hot, wet heat between her legs.

"Alice, you're exhausted. You need to rest."

"Not yet." She arched into him.

He smooshed his face against her and rubbed where their cheeks connected. Then Parker pushed off the bed, eyes aglow with unholy fire. "You're not ready for this, Alice. Not yet."

She pushed up on her elbows. "I'm pretty sure I am."

His lips curled to reveal sharp fangs, and he hid his face in a way she could only assume was from shame.

"You need rest," he insisted. "And water. I'll get some."

He was out the bedroom door before she could protest. She stared at the empty doorway for too long, wondering what the hell had just happened. Not ready for this? How cocky could he—*oh*. He wasn't talking about his junk. His eyes. That snarl. That animalistic behavior. *Oooh*.

He didn't want her seeing him lose control. He didn't want her to see that part of him, especially when he was so used to containing everything in a nice, neat, rope-tied package. That turned her on even more.

"You know," she shouted at the door. "I showed you the real me. At some point you're going to have to do the same."

The sound of the fridge door closing filtered back to her, then his footsteps, then him. Magnificent. His brows met in the middle as he stood in the doorway, cracking the lid on a bottle of water.

"I know," he said, sitting on the bed and handing her the drink. He gently stroked her hair as she sipped. "Get some rest, Alice. We head out in a few hours."

twenty-six

PARKER LAZARUS

OVER THE ROAR of a plane engine, Parker shouted instructions at Alice on how jumping from this altitude differed from BASE jumping off a high-rise. The hold was open and ready for their launch. Cold air whipped at their faces, lashed their hair, and gusted against their goggles. His one hundred plus jumps made him far more knowledgeable in this area than whatever she had. He had to make sure she was prepared.

"Now, you may not know this," he roared against the wind. "But there is a reserve parachute located here." He pointed to the ripcord in her backpack. Alice smirked up at him, probably because she already knew, but quietly allowed him to complete his second safety check of her set up. The nap she took earlier today had returned a healthy glow to her face. He was glad he'd stopped things from getting too heated. She'd needed the rest. What came next would be intense, and with her unreliable leg, he was concerned she might land wrong. He had suggested tandem jumping, but she'd only given him the same casual smirk she gave him now. Infuriating. Impossible. Sexy.

The Syndicate base they would infiltrate was deep in Cartel territory. He tugged on the straps secured to her shoulders, just to make sure they weren't loose. He tried not to think about the rope he'd tied on her earlier and how next time he would like to see that rope against her bare skin, no clothes in the way. Maybe a purple color this time. *His* color. Maybe he would tie her within a star formation, crisscrossing all over her skin.

The pilot shouted from the cockpit that they were within range of their destination and Parker shook his head to clear his thoughts, but his urges had been nigh on impossible to ignore since he'd walked away from Alice in his bed. The Beast knew she was willing, and it wanted to unleash. Desire ran rampant in his veins and was a constant, painful companion. If he couldn't fuck her senseless, then jumping out of a plane was the next best thing. Only one of those would expose his fear.

He met Alice's sparkling eyes.

"When I say go," he shouted. "I want you to jump." She'd been pensive the entire plane ride and now raised an indignant brow. Maybe she was afraid. "If you want to hold hands, I can guide you to the drop zone."

But she didn't hold hands. She put on her goggles and kissed the air in his direction before falling backward out of the plane. Amber hair caught the golden sunset as it streamed past her face. The damned woman winked at him. He gripped the support bar and looked down to find she'd already twisted and righted her trajectory like a pro—her black clad body a lethal dart tunneling through the air.

Speechless.

And goddamned aroused. Again.

Fuck. He adjusted himself in his pants. *Get your head in the game, Parker.* Of course she knew how to sky dive. She knew how to do everything. Except the Shibari. That was a first, and he'd given it to her. The Beast's lust stirred. *Fuck!*

He jumped out.

Exhilaration. Adrenaline. Bliss.

He was flying. Free. Just like he and Daisy had dreamed about. One day he would do this with her, and they would fly together. For now he focused on the Columbian land mass drawing closer by the second, and his mate rotating in the air below to blow him another cheeky kiss before using hand signals to direct *him* to the drop zone. As if he didn't know.

He flipped his middle finger up. Her eyes crinkled, and she returned to the task at hand. Too soon they reached the correct altitude to pull their ripcords, their chutes filling with air and slowing their descent.

As silent as they could be, they landed in a dry field and quickly cut their spent chutes. The sun had just gone down. The low twilight visibility and tall dead grass were on their side. Together, they rushed to a set of trees on the outskirts and regrouped.

Alice checked her weapons—short sword at her back, daggers and other blades around her belt and boots. In her full Sinner getup, Parker thought she looked deadly enough to be the woman with his family's fate in her hands. They'd not spoken about her confession, her final kill-switch orders, but the truth of it weighed heavily on his mind. She was right. Someone had to be the final stand against them in case things went wrong, and it was better for this person to be someone close—someone who knew them. Mary had spent her life training her children to avoid this devastating future, but the fact was, they would always be a threat, and Mary loved them too much to kill them if it came to it.

Alice was more than his mate. She was his Do Not Resuscitate order.

Good thing he didn't plan on dying any time soon.

As to the quality of that life, and whether he would keep Lazarus Tech, he'd deal with that later. The Board had been calling him, and he'd continued to ignore them. *They wouldn't dare.*

"AIMI," he said into the microphone in his hood. "Please respond."

A crackle came through the speaker, but AIMI responded. *"Yes, Pride. I am here."*

He relaxed an iota. He'd made a fairly good hypothesis about AIMI's range using the satellite link he'd set up, but there was always a margin of error. Hopefully because of his success, the other teams would have communications up and running too.

"Can you zero in on Despair's tracking signal through the receiver in my suit?" Even though Daisy had never been one of the Deadly Seven, using her sin's name in the field as code was safer for everyone. Whether she wanted to join their crime fighting team was another question, and one he couldn't answer without his sister. He wouldn't blame her if she decided to leave the game altogether after they found her. But they *would* find her.

A band constricted around his chest.

Alice's eyes met his and held. They both held their breath. The plan was for each member of the Deadly Seven to use their new proximity to search for Daisy's tracking signal. They'd hoped that, perhaps, the reason they couldn't get an accurate log onto Daisy since AIMI's rebirth was because of distance.

"She's either not there, or her signal is blocked," AIMI said. *"I'm not picking up anything within a twenty-mile radius."*

"Can you search further?"

"Checking now. Thirty miles miles... Negative. Fifty miles... negative." AIMI paused. *"I'm sorry, Pride. I know you were hoping to find her here."*

Parker straightened. AIMI was sorry? That was an odd thing for her to say. He'd not allowed Sloan near AIMI's base personality programming like he had last time. She shouldn't be saying things like that. But he had programmed her to learn for herself. Was it possible she was developing a personality of her own?

"Update me if you hear from any of the other team members," he said.

"Will do."

The connection cut.

There went that hope. This game of cat and mouse was becoming tedious. Parker was ready to take the situation into his own hands. He was done playing. This was the beginning of the end for the Syndicate.

"Let's go," he said to Alice and gestured due east. "One click that way."

She nodded and lifted her hood.

"How's your leg?" he asked, as casually as he could.

Her eyes crinkled over her scarf. "I've been through a lot worse than landing from fourteen thousand feet. My leg is fine. But thanks for caring."

"Just making sure you're in shape for the mission."

"Right." She rolled her shoulders, cracking her neck. "And for the record, I've had almost two hundred jumps. This leg hasn't given out yet."

Fuck. His pants tightened. His mate loved adrenaline as much as he did. She was perfect for him. When they got home, there would be no more waiting. He would claim her. Maybe he wouldn't wait until they got home. There was always the jet ride back.

He covered his mouth and nose with his mask, and then they set off. From what limited intel he gathered about the target site, its function was similar to the one in the States. But rather than operating on an old army base, this black site was a farm surrounded by long grass and the odd tree. There was one big farmhouse, a smaller outhouse, and a barn. There were even a few stray cows around to make it look legit. It was simple enough, but satellite thermal imaging had already confirmed the underground maze filled with multiple heat signatures. All Parker and Alice needed to do was get eyes inside the base and to create an uplink on their computer system to send data to AIMI.

They stopped beside a tree and crouched until the tall dry grass hid them.

"Two guards near the farmhouse door," Alice murmured, her voice muffled by her mask.

He dropped his mask to his mouth and tipped his unhindered nose, scenting the air. "There's plenty more around." He pulled the mask back up. "We wait for darkness."

"Agreed."

Complete nightfall was only a few minutes away. Parker used the time checking on the functionality of the small drone he'd brought. Alice swept the perimeter, staying on their line of communication the entire time. When she returned, night hid her shadow, but he scented and heard her movement.

"There's a back entrance and an open window at the farmhouse," she said, coming up to him, quiet as a wraith.

"Guards?"

"A lot. Maybe fifty."

"Easy."

She snorted. "But they're reckless, untrained and irreverent. Some are shooting tins and drinking."

"Idiots."

"Maybe. Prudence said there were some sites where the security was shit. I guess they rely heavily on this territory being run by Cartel."

She was probably right. More fun for Parker, then.

"Window." He pointed at the farmhouse.

Without another word, they crouched low and hid behind shrubs along the fenced property line, then deployed the palm sized drone he'd packed. Each team deployed around the world with a similar device. They were all under strict instructions that this would be a reconnaissance mission and to only engage if it was safe.

The drone whispered into the air and zoomed through the open window. AIMI had been installed on the drone along with manual override. For now, he kept control. There might come a time when the signal would cut, and AIMI would have to take over. With any luck, they'd be in and out of there with their intel and no trouble.

Unless, of course, they found Daisy. Or Prudence. Then trouble would find them because, despite Parker's instructions to the rest of the team to wait for backup, he never followed his own rules.

On the drone's controller screen, they watched the scene play out. The warehouse was empty except for an industrial elevator at the back. Parker piloted the drone to sit on top of the metal cage and waited until someone walked in and activated it.

"Biometric access," Alice mumbled. "Eye and palm print. We're definitely in the right place."

"Agreed. In line with what they've used at the other sites. Getting one of us down into the basement won't be as easy."

They were lucky the elevator was a cage. The drone was as stealthy as you could get, but it wasn't invisible. They had to rely on skill to keep it out of sight. Alice and Parker both counted the floors as the elevator descended. There had to be at least five levels, possibly more. With each level of descent, AIMI used the drone to map the layout. The worker stepped out and Parker maneuvered the drone through the tight space between the cage and door before it closed.

"Nice work," Alice said.

"I know."

"Looks like your fine motor skills have improved."

He paused. "Shibari helped." And the piano. And... her.

"Any time."

He wanted to smile, but something on the screen stole their attention. The glow of dormant replicate tanks, all filled with full grown bodies.

"Fuck, that's a lot," he said, and piloted the drone around the room. "At least a thousand."

"Jesus Christ, there are more behind those locked doors. Look at the power cables leading into those rooms."

"Enough juice to power an army."

"Looks like a closed-circuit computer system down here. Just like they had at the other base."

"Meaning..." Alice thought about it. "Oh shit. That means we can't hack into it over Wi-Fi."

"Correct. We'll have to infiltrate and access the system in person. But we prepared for it this time."

The Deadly Seven had brought back a number of replicate tanks from the recent warehouse battle to study at their headquarters. Well, Flint had studied them while Parker had rebuilt AIMI and recovered from his amputation. Julius and that Faithful from a few days ago had controlled the replicates using a smart device or tablet. It was possible that the entire community of replicates was centrally controlled. The entire world's worth of replicates might be disarmed by a single kill code.

An idea came to him, and he landed the drone near where the worker had gone to sit—next to a row of computers.

"AIMI," he said. "Use the drone to read data from nearby computers."

"Putting feelers out now."

"Upload to the cloud."

"Sure."

"ETA?"

"T-Minus twenty minutes."

"Let me know if you find anything interesting."

"Such as?"

"Blue prints. Base schematics. Prisoner manifests." It was unlikely they'd find the kill code on the system, but they would take what they could get.

"Understood."

Parker stood back with Alice and waited. After a time she whispered to him, "AIMI is incredible."

There was a time when he would have made some kind of arrogant comment about his genius, but he knew it took more than one person to make AIMI what she was today. She was a family effort. Hell, she *was* part of the family.

"I've found something interesting," AIMI said.

"What is it?"

"There are three more sub levels from this one. Each one houses a different species of bio-weapon."

"Different species?" For a moment his pulse hammered, thinking there were more warped creations in the Syndicate cannon they hadn't come across yet.

"Correct. Animals. Beasts. I believe they're programmed to hunt sin."

Parker exhaled. They knew about those. "They're caged?"

"Correct. There are also mechanical weapons of a similar technology to your arm. Except an entire exoskeleton."

"Interesting," he murmured. "Perhaps they're for enhancing the replicates."

"Or for regular humans," Alice offered.

He nodded. "What else, AIMI?"

She paused. *"I know where they're keeping prisoners."*

Alice's gaze whipped to Parker's.

"Is there a manifest?" he asked AIMI.

"Record keeping is lacking, but I found something." She rattled off a few names, none of which he knew. But there was one unidentified female. Whether it was Daisy, Prudence, or someone else, they wouldn't know until they found her.

"Directions?" he asked.

"In a barn, southeast end of the farm."

"Above ground?"

"Affirmative."

"ETA on the data upload."

"Another fifteen minutes and counting."

Alice grabbed his arm. "We can wait fifteen minutes."

"I never wait."

twenty-seven
ALICE MONTGOMERY

ALICE SWORE under her breath as Parker shoved the drone controller into her hands and took off in the direction of the barn. *Goddamned cowboy!*

She looked at the controller. If she put it down and someone found it, would their data be lost? Or hadn't Parker asked AIMI to upload it to the cloud? Yes, he had. That meant the controller was only needed to extract the drone, but then again, AIMI could also take over piloting it. Decision made, she hid the device behind some grass and unpinned two long razor needles from her hair. For stealth missions, these were her favorite assassin's tool of the trade.

A quiet stab into a vital artery, and her victim bled out before anyone knew what happened. Stab into the spinal cord, and she could paralyze.

She wasn't about to let Parker have all the fun, but even more concerning was that if they had to return to this base at another time to infiltrate and disarm all the replicate tanks, they wouldn't be able to if he got caught rescuing the prisoner.

But if Alice was caught, the Syndicate might only think it was retaliation from the Sisterhood for their recent attacks. She could act as a distraction until the big plan reveal. Parker hadn't thought of that before running headlong into danger.

The man might be bullet proof with that Deadly suit on, but she wasn't. It was better if she covertly attacked rather than went in, guns blazing, so to speak. Parker was anything but subtle, not with those animal instincts. Alice dropped her face mask and tugged the bottom up to reverse it—now it was black side out, red side in. With frustration skipping up her spine, she crept toward the barn, making sure to stay hidden in the long grass or through sticking to the darkest shadows. A rusted tractor sat collecting weeds near the barn. By the wheel was a darker, human shaped blob. *Parker.*

His head swiveled her way, his eyes glowing gold in the dark like a wild cat. Then they narrowed.

Screw you, Parker Lazarus. They were here as a team.

Keeping low, she dashed over to him and leaned against the cool metal surface.

"I told you to stay put," he grumbled into the dark.

"You didn't," she mumbled back. "But that's beside the point. We're here as a team. We do this together, or at the very least discuss a plan together."

She heard his teeth grinding behind his mask. "Very well. What's your suggestion?"

Alice wanted to laugh. He didn't ask for her plan, but her suggestion.

"If this goes pear-shaped, it's better for the long-term mission that I'm discovered, not you."

"No one is getting captured."

"I didn't say captured."

He stared at her. "You want me to stay hidden."

"Yes."

"And I'm supposed to allow my mate to head into certain danger without protection."

This time it was her turn to stare at him, all angry eyed. "You know the kind of person I am. I don't need protection. I need your trust."

He looked away, eyes searching the darkness, before he cursed and punched the dirt.

"Good man." She gave him a patronizing pat, much to his chagrin.

"Only because this plan makes sense," he said, pointing at her. "And only because I sense a ridiculous amount of pride coming from these guards—it could mean they won't see you coming." He paused and canted his head, listening. "There's something else. They're talking…"

Alice hushed and waited patiently, feeling slightly awed at the godlike man next to her. He could hear a mile away if he wanted. What she wouldn't give to have an ability like that. All the missions she could have used it on. Parker's eyes skated back to her.

"What is it?" she asked.

"They're talking about their boss, José… he told them the American boss—"

"Julius?"

"Maybe. He said the American has no clue what's happening down here and they'll get away with whatever they want. Soon their plans will be executed, with or without approval from the American."

Alice frowned. "I thought Julius was a control freak."

"So did I."

"Do you think what's happened with Despair had somehow affected his leadership status? Do you think there's dissent within the Syndicate ranks?"

"I don't know." Parker rubbed his chin through the mask. "We assumed Julius was the leader because he used to be back when we were created. Hell, he was the sperm donor, for Christ's sake. But maybe he's just a means to an end for these other Syndicate leaders."

They were silent for a moment, processing the new information. Parker looked thoughtful, his clever eyes focused inward as he was, no doubt, planning something dastardly. Alice had never thought the Syndicate—or Julius, rather—would spend resources hunting down the Sisterhood. They'd also let a few replicates get caught, and caused mass chaos at Lazarus Tech. The police were chasing Alice and Parker for a statement, but they'd managed to put them off. Not for long.

And if what these guards said was true, then Julius wasn't in charge. He was just another cog in the broken machine.

"All right," Parker said. "You go in first. I want you to see that I trust you."

Something warm and pleasant unfurled in Alice's chest. He couldn't see her lips stretch into a smile, but he noticed her eyes crinkle.

"If you don't hear from me five minutes after entry," she started.

"I'm coming in after you, and I won't be held responsible for what happens to anyone in my way."

She nodded, and then moved. But he yanked her back to him, tugged both their masks down and kissed her like the world was on fire. Hot, salty man invaded her in every sense. That delicious, spiced musk of his curled around them as he plundered her mouth with his tongue. When he broke away, he left her breathless and shaky. The smile he gave was pure masculine ego.

"What was that for?" she whispered.

"So you know I'm serious. Five minutes and then I'm coming for you."

CLOSE TO THE BARN, four guards in filthy clothes sat around a table laughing and carousing. Although Alice's Spanish was passable, she concentrated more on their body language—they assumed they were safe. Certainly safe enough to get drunk and play games at this isolated farm.

Grubby shot glasses filled with *guaro* sat next to an empty bottle, tipped over. Glassy eyes tracked movement as they played with a deck of cards. This wasn't going to be a problem.

Parker spoke through her earpiece. *"What's taking so long?"*

"Shut up." She tugged her mask down to reveal her face and then unclipped her weapon's holster, dropping it to the ground.

"What are you doing?"

"Shhh."

Alice checked the poison-laced pins in her hair and then fluffed her locks and sauntered toward the guards, doing her best to hide her limp with a sashay. The skydive drop had irritated it, despite what she'd told Parker, but she didn't want him to think she wasn't capable.

She unzipped her jacket to show the lingerie beneath, breasts pushed up enticingly. She had to admit, when she'd picked this particular bra from Parker's closet, she hadn't thought these men would be the first to see it on her. As suspected, each alcohol ridden set of eyes landed on the vicinity of her chest and leered.

Alice fanned herself and told them in Spanish that she was lost and thirsty before pouting like a femme fatale. *Can anyone help?*

One of the guards, a man with a thin mustache, raised incredulous brows. Alice never really expected them to believe an innocent woman would stumble into this remote facility, but the worst case scenario was that she'd put them off guard. Best case was she'd distract them all enough to take them down.

The mustached man said to another in Spanish, "Should we shoot her?"

"Nah," said the other. "Let's use her first, *then* shoot her."

Alice grinned.

Best case scenario.

The men tripped over each other to get to her. She waggled her finger at all but one of them and took him around to the side of the barn where she promptly put pressure on his carotid and sent him to sleep. *Too easy.* He crumpled to the ground, and she cried out for help. The bastards didn't come. They laughed. Clearly they assumed the jerk she'd KO'd was having his way with her, so she stepped out from the shelter of the barn and called for help again, pointing, indicating the fallen comrade they couldn't see behind the corner. It was unexpected enough that another jogged over, and the third and fourth collected their guns. She tugged the first into the shadows and whipped the edge of her hand down on his neck, squashing that vital spot. Zipping her jacket back up, she made short work of taking the remaining two guards out with her sharp pins—the paralytic toxin working fast to drop them.

"I can't believe that worked," Parker said through the comms.

"You wouldn't believe how often men underestimate a woman," she mumbled, dragging the bodies together to make a pile. "Honey, I have a gift for you. Now, it's not Shibari, but tying up this lot should keep you occupied until I get out."

Parker's humored snort came through the comms and, it was stupid, but that little acknowledgment made her go all warm and fuzzy inside.

When she straightened, he was there—eyebrow arched so high it half disappeared beneath his hood.

"Thought you didn't want me to get caught," he said, amused eyes twinkling.

"Who's going to catch you now?" She gestured at them. "They're all out. Right?"

For due diligence's sake, Parker scented the air and canted his head, making her wait until he scoped the area with his senses. Alice listened keenly for any other sounds that might indicate hostiles. Nothing.

"I think we're good," Parker said. "But it stinks in there. Stay frosty."

She nodded and strapped her holster back on, then unsheathed her sword, just in case. The first thing she noticed after rolling the heavy barn door open was the stench. Urine, feces, blood. She scanned the darkened room, looking for hostiles, and found none. These prisoners mustn't be worth much, or again, these guards had truly believed they were untouchable in this area. The hairs on the back of Alice's neck prickled. Perhaps they should have researched the Cartel controlling this area before dropping into it. For these guards to be so nonchalant about a woman walking into their territory, they must feel secure. She shook off the dread and searched the barn.

Bales of hay, half moldy and rotten, were scattered about. Long pitchforks. High exposed beams with large chains and meat hooks dangling from them. Any floor not covered in hay was sticky. It was definitely a torture chamber. All she had to do was find the victims. Further toward the back of the barn were shoulder high animal pens. Rustling made her tense until a cow popped her head through the slatted fence.

Alice's heart dropped. It was thin, too thin. Large liquid eyes glistened, and it didn't even have the strength to moo at her. She shut her eyes and shook her head, then kept moving. It was ruthless, but the cow wouldn't be the only one she'd have to ignore. This wasn't a rescue mission for multiple people—their resources didn't extend that far. Continuing down the line, she peeked over the top of each pen to search inside. She passed two, each with a prone man—she thought.

It was hard to tell amongst the blood, hay, and dirt. It was even harder to tell if they were alive. Inside the third pen was a woman.

Alice stared for a moment, trying to ascertain her identity. Daisy had silver hair. This woman's hair was too dirty to tell the color. She was also naked from the waist down. There was one way to tell if she was from the Sisterhood.

"Bless me, father," Alice whispered, praying with more than her words.

The figure roused and then looked up—swollen eyes peeking out from beneath a curtain of stringy dark hair.

"For I have sinned," the woman croaked.

Alice's throat closed up. Tears burned her eyes, and she internally rejoiced. "Sister Prudence."

The Sinner tried to stand, but she was injured in too many ways for Alice to count. "Wait there," Alice said, and searched for a latch. It wasn't even locked. Shock pounded into her chest.

These prisoners had been treated so poorly that they'd stopped trying to escape.

"Four minutes." Pride's voice through the comms.

She squeezed her eyes shut, knowing he'd have hoped for a different outcome. "It's my Sinner."

A pause, then, *"Do you need help?"*

Alice wanted to say no, that she was strong enough to carry Prudence on her own, but she wasn't sure if her soul could take it. The woman was beat up bad. Blood streaked down her naked legs.

"Yes," she whispered. "And bring pants."

A minute later, Parker jogged into the barn. Alice waved him down to her pen and then went inside to crouch beside Prudence. Sinners were bred tough. Many of them had suffered torture, assault, and much more, but never this bad. Never for this long. Prudence was older than Alice by half a decade. She was reaching her expiry date. Death was around the corner for all of them, but closer for the older ones. Some of them tried to run from Hell, but others, like Prudence, seemed to run toward it. They put their hand up for all the dangerous missions, often not coming back. Parker slowed to a stop next to Alice, took one look at the poor woman laying battered and broken on the floor, and then handed Alice the pants before turning his back and standing guard at the pen door.

"I took them from a guard," he said, facing outward to give them privacy.

Alice showed Prudence the pants to warn her about what was coming next—touch. Then she eased them on the woman and tried not to look at all the hand sized bruises on her thighs.

Alice should have killed the guards. She wanted to kill them now.

Parker turned back around and held Alice's eyes. "I'll carry her out."

Alice nodded grimly, then faced Prudence. "We're taking you home. You're safe now."

Prudence flinched upon recognizing Parker.

"Don't worry," he said. "My family has pledged an alliance with the Sisterhood."

Together, Alice and Parker helped Prudence stand. Then he collected the fragile woman in his arms and carried her with an ease and gentleness that Alice had never seen in the man. She watched him leave, his head bent low and intimate as he whispered calming assurances to Prudence. His comms were still on.

You're safe now.
We'll protect you.
I won't let go.

twenty-eight
PARKER LAZARUS

AFTER ARRIVING at the Hildegard Sisterhood Abbey, a few hours by plane from Cardinal City, Parker Lazarus did his best to remain calm. Their journey from the Columbian Syndicate site included an hour-long walk across land and two consecutive plane transfers until they ended in the Lazarus Tech jet, flying back Stateside. Each minute had been nerve racking, for both Parker and Alice, but especially for Prudence. Parker had tried to calm her and set her at ease, but the longer he'd held her, the worse her anxiety got. Men had done this to her. He'd never felt more helpless than he did then, and never more proud of Alice. So much that he touched her in small ways, just to balance his sin.

Alice stayed with Prudence during the jet ride while he'd busied himself with getting out of his Deadly suit and into civilian clothing. He'd wanted to take Prudence to Lazarus House, but could appreciate her need to be among her own people, her sisters, her home. And since Alice and he were the first team back from the coordinated reconnaissance mission, he had time to kill before he rendezvoused with family to discuss intel.

It was after midnight when they arrived, and from the moment they'd crossed through the giant wrought-iron gates of the abbey, Parker felt ill at ease. The picturesque grounds were a mask over the true, sinister nature of this place. The virtuous nuns with their vows of silence hid more than their voices. The vine-covered limestone monstrosity of a building may have looked like something from a child's fairytale book, but these same fairytales had twisted origins. It didn't sit right that the same people who had flogged Alice could also be a source of solace for her.

Prudence had recovered enough to walk herself along the long driveway, up the high steps leading to the building. She was proud, and walking in on her own two feet meant something.

The Reverend Mother waited on the steps, along with the other Sinners and a few nuns in habits. Like a host of deadly butterflies, the Sinners swarmed on their missing agent and swallowed her whole. They moved as a group, providing a guard of honor, until they disappeared into the building. The Reverend Mother somehow managed to look down her nose at Parker, despite being over a head smaller than him.

"We owe you a debt of gratitude, Mr. Lazarus."

He blinked, surprised. He'd expected some snark, considering the way he'd treated her last time—at the very least a cold shoulder. But he could see the truth in her eyes. No longer did they hold thinly veiled resistance.

"Of course." He inclined his head.

Alice touched his arm gently. "She means it. If you ever need anything from the Sisterhood, we will be there."

"You mean *they* will be there," he pointed out. Alice would be with him, not part of this poor excuse for an organization.

An unnamed emotion passed over Alice's features, and every

instinct in his body woke up, alert. Her jaw hardened, and she turned to her superior. "There is much to talk about."

The Reverend Mother's eyes crinkled as she took in Alice's dirty attire. "I'm sure you want to clean up first." She assessed Parker. "And your companion might like a tour of the facilities."

He shook his head. "I'm fine."

"Well, you could always come and sit with us while we say our novenas for dear Sister Prudence in the chapel."

God, no. He gave her a tight, polite smile. "I'll stick with Alice."

The older nun huffed as though she expected that and was pleased. "Sister Alice, I'm sure you're exhausted. I will speak with you in the morning after first meal."

Then, with a brisk nod, she went back inside, leaving Alice and Parker alone on the doorstep. He put his hands in his pockets and frowned at the front door before looking at his mate with a smile. "A tour with you sounds good, though."

"Tour-schmour," Alice groused. "The Rev's offer wasn't sincere. She has her own agenda. Don't believe that sweet as pie old lady face."

Her own agenda? Parker surveyed the grounds and narrowed his eyes, waiting for an army of Sinners to jump him. Perhaps they should have returned to Cardinal City after all.

"Come on." Alice sighed and took him inside.

Every step he made across the plush carpeted lobby lifted the hairs on his arms. There was a vibe about this place, and he couldn't put his finger on it. It was more than the vintage architecture and creepy oil portraits of female saints on the walls. A smell permeated the air... musky, like incense, candle wax and old, dangerous things. He felt watched, despite the late night hour and deserted hallways.

Up a creaky staircase, Alice guided Parker through a corridor flanked by doors on either side. Living quarters, he realized. She stopped beside a door on the far left and stared at him.

"This is my cell," she said in monotone and then limply gestured to the doors. "The other Sinners live there."

A monastic cell… This had been her home for decades? This little room? He glanced up and down the hallway, expecting to see someone lurking, but they were alone.

"Curfew was a few hours ago," she explained. "Prudence is being looked after. If I'm not in the chapel, I should be in my room."

She opened the door to a tiny room. The cot was made with clean bedding. Facing a wall was a polished cedar pew, big enough for one. Next to it was an old record player with a small stack of jazz on vinyl. A window overlooked the midnight gardens. During the day it would be a visual feast, but all he could see was the tiny table next to the bed, scattered with torture devices. A small ropy whip with knotted tails, spiked chain cilices, a sponge with metal studs, rosary beads, and a Bible. No, not the Bible—he read the gilded title and tensed. *The Raccolta*. A Prayer book.

Alice winced as he picked up the whip and counted the tails. Seven.

"They represent the seven deadly sins," she explained, shutting the door so their voices wouldn't carry. "It's called a discipline."

He put it down and then touched the spiked metal rings.

"They're chain cilices. They go around the thigh."

They were fucking torture devices, as far as he was concerned.

"You disapprove," she said. "But mortification of the flesh rituals are as old as the Bible. Jesus invites all Christians to help him carry the cross, but we Sinners have a heavier load to bear, especially if we want the kind of absolution that frees our souls. We repent the sins of the flesh so the spirit may be sanctified."

"Mary never did this," he gritted out. "You shouldn't have to punish yourself."

"Forget it." She took the chains from him. "I don't expect you to understand."

"I understand plenty." Fury blinded him. "I understand that you've been brainwashed into believing you're so inherently evil that the only way your soul will be saved is if you physically suffer. I understand that you believe you're going to Hell, but still strive for forgiveness. I understand that it's not through your own choice that you are this way. And I know—"

"You know nothing!" she snapped, eyes bright like the heavens.

He opened his mouth to continue, but she beat him to it.

"I don't need another person disappointed with me, Parker," she said, the fire leaving her voice. "Please. Not from you too."

"Alice… I'm not disappointed in you, but them. The system. The pressure they put on you. The *lies* they tell you about yourself."

"They're not lies, Parker. You of all people should understand that. I *have* sinned. I *am* going to Hell. There's no sugar coating it. Excuses or blame don't work here. The only thing that does work are prayers for forgiveness."

He ground his teeth so hard it stirred the primal part within, filling him with an obsessive need to protect his mate, even from the bite of false beliefs. Where was the woman who'd trusted him enough to come undone in his ropes? Why couldn't she see the truth in his eyes when he told her… but he hadn't, had he? He hadn't told her how beautiful she was, not beyond words. Or how proud of her he was, or how smitten, how aroused he felt every time he looked at her. How… comforted.

How hopelessly in love.

So he held up his wrist and showed her the tattoo. Since they'd left the plane a few hours ago, he'd not touched her once. It showed. Her eyes went sad as she took in the almost dark Yin-Yang symbol.

"You need me to touch you," she said, and offered her hand.

"No, Alice. I'm showing you how proud of you I am. So much that it fills me every minute of the day to the brink and I spill over and reach for your calming touch. Don't you understand?"

She lifted her chin, the eternal warrior. "All I'm doing is being near you, Parker. I'm not actually *doing* anything."

He grazed his knuckles along her cheek and felt the sin ease from his body like an exhale. "My darling Alice. All you need to do is exist and I'm falling into you. Falling in love with you."

Glistening eyes searched his face, still not comprehending.

"You're a miracle, Alice," he said. "Not a sin. Not evil. Not anything but pure perfection."

He took her face in his hands and lowered reverent lips to hers. The only reason he could be this gentle with his bionic hand was because of her.

Their soft kiss sent sparks shooting down his spine, waking up any sense not already at attention. Another dip against her lips, a little more pressure, a lick along the plump bottom, and she let out a sound that would haunt his dreams forever. A whimper, a sigh, perhaps a need. Any or all, it didn't matter. His mate didn't hide from what they shared. She lit up with desire and tugged him hard against her lips to kiss him with an urgency he'd never seen—hunger.

And he loved it. *Christ*, he loved it.

She was his shining star on a stormy night, and he wanted to take it slow, to show his respect, his affection, her beauty. But The Beast had other ideas. It had waited too long. The moment she brushed open his collar and her sweet kiss moved down his jaw, lust tore through his veins like napalm. The erection that had plagued him all day came back with a vengeance, hard and painful and unrepentant. His teeth elongated in his mouth. Even the claws pricked beneath his fingertips, begging to get out.

He wrenched away from Alice and hid his face. *No. Not now.* Not when he wanted to show her he was in control, that he could be her safety, her new church. Her everything. Not some kind of damned animal that should be locked in a cage and studied. He braced himself against the back of her door and hung his head in shame, breathing through his changes. He was no better than the boy in the lab, just a freak show.

twenty-nine

ALICE MONTGOMERY

ALICE'S HEART broke as Parker shunned her. He leaned against her door, breathing hard, yet trying to not breathe at all. Through his shirt, muscles rippled and tensed. A flush colored his neck. He pounded softly on the door in frustration.

But it wasn't at her.

He reacted like this every time that wild part of him broke free. Was this shame? Embarrassment? The knowledge released something in Alice. Shame she could deal with. Embarrassment, she had an answer for. A finger in his belt loop, and she dragged him back to her.

"Alice," Parker warned, shaking his head.

"Shut up and kiss me."

He tried to pull away, to hide his face, but she kept drawing him back to her until eventually she smacked him across the cheek. The wild scowl he shot her did nothing to quench his energy, but it changed the mood. A growl slipped out of his lips, and it sounded neither human nor animal but something between. Something only this man could be.

"You talk about trust, Parker, but you don't trust me enough to reveal this part of you." She pushed his pecs until she backed him up against the door. "You talk about falling in love, but you won't let me love you back. Well, I'm sorry, but this is my choice, not yours."

"You've truly reached a new low, Alice. To want something as disgusting as this." He bared his fangs.

Like a hit to the solar plexus, his words robbed her of breath. Until she saw them for what they were... a cry for help. Parker, the tall brave genius who had the world wrapped around his finger, didn't think he was good enough for *her*, the Sinner.

"God, we're a pair, aren't we?" She raked her nails along his short beard and shivered at the texture. He leaned in to her touch. "I think you've spent so long trying to be perfect that you've forgotten it's okay to be something else."

"Says the woman who flogs herself for absolution." His tone was ice.

"That's different."

"Is it?"

This was the last of his defense. She could see it crumbling behind his eyes. This was Parker Lazarus burning.

A glance at the tray of tools and then she did something she'd never thought she'd do. She tossed them aside and watched them scatter to the floor. She was taking this leap with him. If they burned, then so be it. They would burn together.

"I want you, Parker Lazarus. Every part of you." She unbuttoned his shirt, starting slowly at the top. "Even the parts you think are wrong. *Especially* those parts. I've wanted you like this for years. What you've become has only increased that desire. I will never think that part of me needs absolution. You are not my sin. You're my salvation. My..." Her throat clogged and she couldn't finish, so she kissed him over the heart.

His breathing quickened, as though he couldn't quite believe her words. He gripped her hands as she opened his shirt, but didn't stop her. He stayed with her as she explored him, as she soaked up the masculine beauty of his body—strong, powerful, hard. With every inch she discovered with her lips, her body grew hot with need until eventually she realized he was guiding her touch, taking her hands places she was too afraid to go.

He lowered them, golden eyes intently watching her reaction. As her fingers brushed the coarse hair of his lower abdomen, he sucked in a shaky breath, almost nervously.

She plunged her fingers into his waistband and went straight for the thick erection pushing against the trappings of fabric. A whimper of need shot out of her as she clenched around him, but the sound Parker made—the grunt of abandon—it sent a bolt of white hot heat between her legs.

"Damned belt," she snarled. It was in the way. Then it wasn't. She unzipped the fly and dropped his pants around his ankles. Naked. No boxers. Nothing but a proud, jutting cock, rock-hard and begging for her lips.

She wasn't sure what came first—landing on her knees, taking him into her mouth, or his fingers spearing into her hair and pulling tight. He held onto her as though he'd fall. It didn't matter. They'd already fallen. Now they were on fire. The taste and feel of him consumed her. With every lick, nip, or suck, the man came undone. What started as her advances ended with his. He threw his head back against the door and thrust into her mouth, taking his pleasure in her, giving himself over to her.

Every time she looked up from beneath her lashes, she saw a flushed and feverish man in the throes of pleasure. Sweat dappled his brow and plastered strands of hair around his chiseled face. As she pumped his length, his top lip drew back, and she glimpsed fang. It only made her hotter, needier. She pressed her thighs together and gripped his hips, opened her throat, and took him deeper.

He pushed her off him and growled, low and deep.

"Stop," he said with a ragged breath. But he didn't pull his pants up. He didn't pack himself away.

Determination straightening her spine, she tugged off her shirt, and tossed it on the floor.

"Alice," he said, eyes burning with wildfire. "If we keep going, I won't be able to contain myself. Do you understand?"

"This is my favorite version of you." She slid off her pants. Now she stood only in the lingerie she'd taken from his place. *Their* place.

Those luminous eyes flared with hunger, with surrender. She pushed him. With his pants around his ankles, he fell back onto her tiny cot. She didn't care.

"I'll hurt you," he snarled, his fangs showing.

"You know I can take it."

He sat up as she straddled him and removed her bra. They came together like crashing waves, hard at first but then melting into each other, becoming one. Alice's body was a hurricane of sensation. Everywhere they met, she was on fire. His mouth on her breast, his hands at her back, the heat of his cock rubbing between her legs, only a thin scrap of fabric keeping it from where it needed to be. She was damp and ready, but he tested her with two fingers sliding past the edge of her panties.

She gasped and arched into him.

"*Christ*, Alice," he cursed, stroking her from the inside. "You're soaked."

She had no words. Could only move on his fingers, riding him.

"Parker, I need…"

"Me."

"Yes," she gasped. "Top drawer. Condom."

He reached out and rifled around until he found it, gave her a sinful look, and then ripped the foil packet with those sharp fangs before rolling it on himself. "Do I want to know why you keep condoms in your drawer here?"

"No. Hurry."

A guttural sound and he yanked her panties to the side, then positioned himself and sank her onto his length. He filled her, stretched her to the limits. She held onto him and shuddered as the sensations threatened to obliterate all that she was. Every bit of her focus zeroed in on that joining. They panted together, chest to chest, her head in the crook of his neck. Masculine sweat and aftershave. For a tiny moment she was back in that safe place on his bed, hearing his soul-shattering purr, and knew that home was with him.

"Move," he demanded. "Baby, move now."

Baby.

One word and she was gone, his forever. She rode him, hitting the spot at her apex with every plunge. Soon she chanted his name under her breath. It was too much, his size, his strength, her sensations. Alice surrendered as he gripped her hips and thrust from beneath.

"More," he ground out, ripping her underwear clean from her body and throwing it against the wall.

She sensed the struggle in him, still afraid to unleash it all, so she gripped sweaty hair at his nape and bit the thick column of his neck, right over a vein. That was it. Explosion. He threw her back on the cot and rose over her like some kind of war god. He yanked her arms over her head and clamped hard on her wrists. A look. Solid gold masculine entitlement, and she squirmed, writhing beneath the heat of his desire. Then, still holding her gaze, he continued his onslaught, pounding so hard and rough that they rocked the cot into the wall.

They were so loud, so relentless, that she feared the entire abbey would wake. And she didn't care. Not one fuck. She wanted him badly. When her climax tore through her, he had the sense to cover her mouth until she bit his fingers, and then he swallowed her scream with a kiss.

After that, she was nothing but a mess of liquid sensation floating in clouds, but Parker... he was just getting started. He threw her ankles over his shoulders and gripped her thighs, rearing back to thrust into her with single-minded tenacity. He was glorious, skin pulled taut over slabs of hard muscle. That powerful metallic arm on one side, his smooth bulk on the other. Molten eyes that never released her own. The sight of him stole her breath, so much so that she felt the need building in her again.

"Yes, Alice. Come again," he grunted, seeing the change in her expression, the small sounds she made. A burst of pheromones hit her, driving into her lungs, firing her synapses, heating every nerve ending until she exploded around him for the second time. "Come for me, baby."

This time, there was no sound. She could do nothing but open her mouth and arch her back as bliss rolled through her. He pumped one more time and then threw his head back to snarl his release at the ceiling.

Afterward, they lay entwined for a long, hot minute, catching their breath.

And then someone shouted from the next room, *"Assholes! Some of us are trying to sleep."*

"Some of us have blue beans over here!"

That was probably Mercy. Parker's eyes widened, and he looked at Alice. She bit her lip to stop a smile.

"You could have at least invited one of us to join in!" shouted another.

Nope. *That* was Mercy.

Alice giggled.

thirty

PARKER LAZARUS

SOMETHING HAD SHIFTED in Parker overnight. His sweet assassin had taken everything he'd given and wanted more. They'd made love again, more quietly the second time, and only after he was certain every prying nearby Sinner was fast asleep. Then they'd laid in her tiny cot, him on the bottom and her sprawled over his sweaty body, staring into the shadows and murmuring secrets into the darkness.

"I like it when you hold me," she whispered. "I like it even more when you tie me up. I want you to tie me without clothes next time. Like the woman in your pictures."

He tightened his embrace, squeezing her to him. "I like tying you, too. It makes me…"

"What?" She patted his chest.

"It makes me feel like I can contain you. Like you're mine and you won't go anywhere." His voice deepened. "Yes, I'd like to tie you naked. And we will make new pictures together. No one will see them but me."

She propped herself and looked down at him, her lustrous hair flowing down to tickle him. Moonlight limned her head like a halo. How could she think she was evil when she was the very essence of virtue to him? He tucked hair behind her ear. If God existed, he gave her to him.

"I'm not leaving you, if that's what you meant about containing me." She smiled softly and trailed a finger idly over his chest. "When you tie me, I feel… safe. Secure. Like the world could be crumbling outside and it won't touch me. Like when you look at me I'm the only person who exists. There is no Hell. No sin. No punishment. Just you wanting me. You *seeing* me as something beautiful."

She sighed and rested her head over his heart, listening to it beat. He stroked her hair, feeling the tug of uncertainty pull inside his gut. Her words echoed sharply in his head. *Punishment. Sin.*

That had been her life here at the abbey. It had been her life for two decades, if not more. Possibly in this tiny room with scratches on the walls and punishment etched into its soul. Shame. He never wanted her to feel it again, and to do that, she had to stop looking back.

"Alice. From now on, you won't think about the things you've done in the past." He felt her tense, so he gripped her hair in his fist. "No looking back. Just forward. Promise me."

The air left her, and she sank into him before nodding quietly. But he wasn't sure he believed her. For now, it was enough. He rested his head back on the hard pillow and curled his lip in disgust at the tiny room. She deserved so much more. He would cover her in gold and diamonds when they returned. He would spend his life showing her how much she was worth.

Her feminine sigh triggered every instinct deep inside. A low vibrating rumble started in the base of his throat. The first time he'd purred, she'd been thankfully asleep. This time, he didn't try to hide it and was glad. She climbed up his body and kissed his throat, right where the sound was thickest, and then she dropped to press her ear against his chest.

The intimate moment was as binding as a rope coiled around them. She fell asleep to the purring lullaby of his contentment. He drifted off, stroking her hair, thinking about all the ways he could tighten that rope, knot it in a way it could never be undone.

PARKER WOKE SUDDENLY to the feeling of feathers fluttering all over his face. For a moment he thought he was back on that rooftop with Daisy, staring up at wings against the blue sky. But then he opened his eyes to the sun streaming in and the soft sound of Alice's even breaths, strands of her wayward hair tickling him. She'd used him as a mattress. His legs didn't fit on the one-person cot. As carefully as he could, he eased himself out from beneath her and dressed back into his pants and shirt.

At the window, down the four of five floors, the nuns were going about their morning work in the gardens. It couldn't be more than a few minutes after dawn—the sky still had that otherworldly color. Pink, purple, orange and gold glowed around the nuns' habits. He watched them for a long moment and knew he should simply appreciate the beauty, but all he could think was that the purity of it would haunt the Sinners, forever taunting them with a heavenly life they would never receive.

It disgusted him.

He searched the small room for any belongings of worth that Alice might want to bring to his place. He doubted she would see this cell again. Never if he had his way. There were no belongings except the record player. Nothing personal. No picture frames or special mementos. Nothing but instruments of torture.

A band constricted around his chest at the mortification of the flesh tools scattered on the ground. That ritual would need to stop. He would not allow his mate to punish herself. He picked up the discipline. This was her belief. Still… he ripped it to shreds and then tossed it into the trash. He crushed the barbed chain cilices in his metal palm. The rosary beads he pocketed.

He would burn this entire place down if she let him, but a part of him knew she would never forgive him. As twisted as he thought this place was, it meant something. He looked outside and saw the pristine gardens as a taunt. She probably saw them as a sanctuary. He had to respect that.

His cell phone buzzed with an incoming message. He checked it, saw it was the Lazarus Tech Board representative, and then put it back in his pocket, ignored.

"That's been going off all morning," Alice mumbled.

He whirled. She was still half asleep, hair adorably mussed, lips extra pouty from all the kissing. She'd managed to roll her naked form within a modest blanket. God, she had no idea how gorgeous she was. Already he needed to touch her, to set his soul at ease.

"You should still be sleeping," he replied.

She raised a brow, clearly unconvinced that answer suited her question. "Like you, I don't sleep so much."

He grunted.

Alice patted the bed. "Sit with me."

"I was looking for personal items to bring home with us." He held his breath, waiting for her push back. "Jazz records, and that's it."

"I don't have anything else. Never have."

"Nothing?"

She sat up with a sigh. "Nope. And don't go blaming Flint. It's not his fault."

Alarm bells went off in Parker's mind. His jaw locked.

"Flint?" he ground out. "My father?"

Her eyes widened. "Mary didn't tell you?"

"Tell me what?"

"Oh. Well, maybe she was waiting—"

"Alice," he clipped. "What has my father to do with all this?"

"That's a long story, but I guess you'll find out, eventually. Apparently he was friends with the drunk driver who crashed into my car when I was little, killing my parents."

"I'm still not following."

"Mary told me he blamed himself for knowing his friend was about to drive and not stopping him." She scratched her head and sat up, pulling the blanket to cover herself. "I think he made some kind of trust fund for me when I was young, but I never saw it. Much of it anyway. I got put into foster care and then the Sisterhood found me —something Mary believes is her fault."

Parker stared blankly as he processed her words. Alice had been linked to his family since they were kids? Alice's fate—here at this horrible place—was all because... his mind traveled back further to when Mary and Flint had rescued them from the lab. He remembered that overheard conversation between his parents while he'd been climbing the tree. Flint was upset he had to cut himself off from someone he'd been helping. Mary was sorry too, but they both knew that, for the survival of the Lazarus children, both of them had to restart their lives and assume new identities.

It couldn't be a coincidence Alice was taken in by the Sisterhood. Was she a replacement for Mary? Was all this pain in Alice's life caused by Parker's family? The need to care for her became even greater. But then a thought occurred to him.

"Is that why you fought Mary? Because we're at fault for all of this?" He gestured about the tiny room.

"Sort of. Look, maybe I've said too much."

He sat down next to her and squeezed her arm. "If Mary attacked you, then I need to know about it so I can make it right. You're number one in my life now. More than anyone else. Do you understand?"

Her expression deadpanned in that way he always assumed was her calculating face. The one she gave the enemy when she wanted to hide her true thoughts. But she softened and exhaled. "Mary attacked me because she wanted to make sure I wasn't there to hurt her or Flint because of what happened. She needed to know the alliance was real, just like you did. I get that. To be honest, I would have done the same thing."

He rubbed his forehead. "Right."

Silence stretched between them.

"Parker," she asked. "Are we okay?"

"Tell me one thing. Last night I asked you to forget the past and look forward, but is that what you want? Will you leave the Sisterhood behind?" Maybe he'd gotten it all wrong. Maybe he'd projected his own feelings about this place. When she didn't answer, he added, "What kind of future do you see for yourself?"

She went to the window and pointed at a tree outside. "There used to be an opossum family in that tree. When I first got here as a child, I watched it grow from a pregnant mother to a litter of young. Every night I came to this window and watched them grow. I watched them leave. I watched them die." She looked at Parker. "Since I met you, I realized I don't want to die here. I want to grow. I want to look forward, not back. I want a life beyond these walls that isn't about death."

His cell phone buzzed again, and he yanked it out of his pocket, ready to hang up on the caller. But it was a message from home.

"We'll have to go soon," he said. "There's news."

"Do I have time to check on Prudence?" she asked. "And I want to make a quick stop to deliver some things to Tawny's room."

"Whatever you need."

PARKER AND ALICE met the Sinners at the breakfast table in the large dining hall. He was surprised to see Prudence up and eating with the rest of them. As it turned out, she had brown hair and smile lines around her eyes, none of which he'd been able to see when she'd been covered in dirt and blood.

From the look of her sweat stained clothes, she'd already been working out. Bruises colored her pale skin, and her eyes were still puffy, but she'd returned to her normal routine, resilient to the core.

Except those smile wrinkles looked flat.

The long table was filled with the same women he'd met at the cathedral. Four of them, not including Prudence. The Reverend Mother and their weapon's master Leila were nowhere in sight. She might still be on the mission with one of the Deadly Seven. He should really check his messages, but he'd wanted last night to be about Alice. If the rest of the Sinners had returned, some possibly before Parker last night, and some after, then most of Parker's siblings would also be home.

Alice took him to the table and sat him down next to the peaches and cream blond, Tawny.

"I'll get us some food from the kitchen. Be nice," Alice said.

"I'll try," he replied.

She grinned. "I was talking to the girls."

Shrewd female eyes landed on Parker. He stared back. For the first time, he realized that none of them held any pride. That sickly feeling normally in his gut simply wasn't there.

The psychic Sinner eyed him warily from across the table. Parker thought she would feel more at home in his club, Hell, rather than in a convent. Gothic makeup, piercings and rainbow streaks in her hair.

Raven sucked her teeth at him and plucked a cigarette from her pocket, tapped it on the table and then stuck it on her bottom lip. She stared at Parker, challenging him with her eyes.

The red-headed femme fatale gave him a saucy look. "What's up, Magic Mike?"

"Mercy," he greeted. He wouldn't dignify her comment with an eye roll. She clearly referred to their louder than planned sexual activities the previous night. "I hate to burst your daydream but there was no dancing involved."

"What about the horizontal mambo?" Thea added with a smirk before shoving a spoon of oatmeal into her mouth.

Mercy made a kissing face. "What about, 'ooh, ooh, *oooh* Parker. That's the spot. That's the spot'."

Tawny slapped Mercy on the chest and then gave a little nod toward Prudence. Mercy had the decency to look ashamed. Thea did, too. Suddenly the sound of spoons tinkling against china bowls was the loudest sound in the room.

Parker cleared his throat and faced Prudence. "How are you feeling, Sister Prudence?"

Empty eyes flicked to him, then away. She took a moment and lifted her chin before meeting his gaze again.

"As good as I can be," she replied.

Alice returned from the kitchen and placed a bowl before him. Oatmeal. He tried not to grimace and wondered where she had learned to cook because it wasn't from this place. She said, "If you don't like it, I'll make you something else when we get home."

All spoons dropped and gazes zipped Alice's way, even Prudence's.

"You'll *make* him something?" Thea blinked.

"I like cooking. So sue me."

But while they stared at her, agape, Parker's heart lifted out of his chest. She'd said *home*. Their home. It was one thing for her to not comment when he'd said it, but to accept it herself. He was feeling ridiculously happy about it and covered by coughing and thumping his chest. The smile he gave her was small, but appreciative. "I look forward to it."

Without looking at her sisters, Alice said, "Shut it. You all knew this was coming, especially you, Raven."

Next to Alice, Tawny's eyes glistened. "But now? For good?"

Alice touched her. "I'll only be a few hours away if you ever need me. And that record collection I lent you, I want you to keep it."

Tawny's eyes widened. "But they're your favorite. They're vintage."

"And now they're yours. I've already delivered them to your cell."

The mood turned solemn, and Parker shifted in his seat. He felt it was worth saying more to them.

"Further to what Alice said about needing her, I'd like to formally extend that offer from my family, too." Whether he liked these women, or this organization, he knew that Alice did. If they needed her, Alice would go in a heartbeat. Parker would be a few steps behind. Or perhaps in front, if he had his way. He shoveled a spoon of oatmeal into his mouth and immediately regretted it. The sooner they got out of there, the better. The jet was already on standby.

"Prudence," Alice said. "Is there anything you can add that might help us take down the Syndicate?"

Prudence looked down and played with her food. "I've been thinking on it all night and I think you know much of what I know. They have bases around the world. Each base has a different leader, but it seems Julius Allcott was the one who spearheaded the research while they funded and controlled it. I can give you a list of these leaders' names. It might help consolidate what you already know."

"Did you see Daisy?" Parker asked, unable to help himself. "Or Despair as you might know her."

"We called her Falcon a few years ago. Julius called her Despair. And yes, I saw her recently. In fact, she was the reason I was captured."

Parker's eyes closed, and he rubbed his temples. "I'm sorry."

"No, you misunderstand me." Prudence pushed her bowl away. "She wasn't at fault. I tried to help her and thus exposed my cover."

"When was this?" Parker's spine stiffened.

"About two months ago, give or take. I lost track of time in that place. I was a guard on duty at one of their bases when I'd heard she'd been taken around the world to visit all the sites. The other guards laughed about it. With each trip, her treatment worsened. Julius paraded her around like some kind of sick freak show. He's not all there. I mean, I don't think he ever was, but since he took Daisy, he's truly lost it. I think he's been tapping her spinal fluid. I overhead the scientist—Van Jansen is his name—murmuring about it. The poor woman was nothing but a shell when she got to Columbia and I couldn't take it. I tried to free her but... yeah." Her face crumpled. "They, um, tortured me but I never gave away anything, even though I feared death would bring me closer to Hell."

Alice went to Prudence and hugged her. She whispered something Parker had trouble hearing, even with his advantage, and then Alice kissed Prudence on the cheek before giving Parker a nod, indicating it was time for them to leave.

Each Sinner stood as he did. There was an air of finality that twinged Parker's chest.

"One last question," he said to Prudence. "Do you have any guesses as to where Julius took Daisy?"

"I can't say for sure, but my gut says she's back in the States. There were a few random facilities that I can list for you. I don't think she'll be there, as he seemed to want to keep her close. Like a pet. It was why he paraded her around."

He gave Prudence a nod, and then took his mate by the nape and laid his lips on the top of her head. Later, when they were alone, he would show her exactly how much he thanked her for giving up her life here. And to the women, he gave them a dignified nod. The respect of a fellow warrior. Each of them felt familiar to him, whether it was because he'd been raised by one of their own, or because a Sinner was now his purpose for living. He sensed a greatness in store for them. They had their own story to tell, and it was only beginning.

thirty-one

ALICE MONTGOMERY

ALICE WAS quiet as she dressed in Parker's penthouse bedroom later that afternoon. Before they'd left the abbey, she'd found the Reverend Mother, and they'd said their final goodbyes. It was surreal. No one in the history of the Sisterhood had simply been allowed to walk away. Mary had escaped and evaded. That was different. The Rev said this wasn't walking away. This was the Long Job. Alice was expected to continue her mission until her dying breath. If the Deadly Seven ever turned, she would take them down. No mercy.

The Rev knew it.

Alice knew it.

And Parker knew it.

She wasn't hiding the truth, so why did she feel so icky? Why did she feel as though this tainted her relationship with Parker? Would they ever be so completely pure and in love like his siblings were with their partners? Or maybe it was that this *was* her dream... but at some point, dreams ended with waking up.

"You ready?" Parker asked from the doorway.

As always, he looked impeccable and delicious all at once. Pressed slacks, a shirt tailored to hug his musculature and accentuate those broad shoulders and tapered waist. A purple silk tie. Square jaw she wanted to lick. The bionic hand gave a dangerous edge to the luxury package.

But there was work to do.

They were about to go downstairs to the basement for a family meeting, and they were late. This was Alice's second official appearance at their table, not just representing an alliance, but also as his mate. That word meant more than partner. She was his number one —he'd said so himself.

For her entire life, that's all she'd wanted.

But now that she seemingly had it, she started to doubt it. How real could it be when he had no choice? This pairing was etched into his DNA. His scent was designed to lure her in. Her, the broken, evil thing used by the virtuously worthy so they didn't have to get their hands dirty. When the previous Reverend Mother had found Alice in foster care, she'd said Alice was already going to Hell—no one wanted her, that's why she was there. It's what she told all the new recruits. So… if Alice was already on her way down, why not do some good on the journey. Why not save lives? To a lonely teenager, that had sounded like a good plan.

The previous Reverend Mother had lied. Alice hadn't been going to Hell, but everything she did afterward paved the way. The only reason she was in the Sisterhood was because they wanted a replacement for Mary. She believed that now.

Alice's spine straightened as another thought hit her. The Sisterhood had psychics. Maybe someone had a premonition that Alice would one day be Parker's mate. Maybe they'd planned to train her, give her the tools to kill, and then plant her right where she needed to be to finish the job Mary couldn't all those years ago.

She closed her eyes and started tapping the beat to her favorite

Nina Simone song on her thigh. But it didn't bring the same solace it used to… *My baby don't care for—*

"Alice?"

She smoothed her hands down her simple stretch singlet and jeans. "Let's go."

Parker stopped her through the doorway and pushed her against the frame, one arm braced overhead.

"I don't want to go anywhere," he said, voice deep and oh so intimate as he looked down at her. "I'd rather stay here. Tell me you want the same."

"I…"

"What's wrong?" He trailed a finger along her neck, causing a shiver.

She shook her head.

"Liar."

And that was the crux of the matter. She was so good at lying, she couldn't tell if she was lying to herself. Should she be here, with him, when it felt like none of it had been of her choosing?

"Your family is waiting for us," she said.

"They can wait." He lowered his lips to her ear. "If you're keeping secrets from me, I'll find out."

She pressed against his hard front and almost wished she hadn't. The connection to him zinged down her arms, causing a gasp. There was no denying she wanted him. So why keep second guessing it?

"You're protecting yourself," he guessed.

She blanched. Was he right, was all this overthinking her way of self-sabotaging? Of punishing herself?

"This look in your eyes, it's the same one you get when going into battle. The same one you gave me on that rooftop. With your head covered by a hood, and half your face covered by the mask, your eyes were all I could see of you. I paid close attention."

"But back then I was asking for an alliance. I didn't think you were my enemy, so you're wrong about that. You were the one who attacked me."

"Are you worried I'll attack you?"

"No! I don't... I don't know why I'm like this right now."

"All I can say is that it's not the way you looked at me last night." He continued to graze his knuckles down her neck. "When will you see I'm not the enemy?"

"It's not that," she said, eyes downcast.

"Then what?"

"You won't understand. You've had everything you've ever wanted."

His silence caused her to look up and gasp at the raw longing in his eyes.

"I've never truly wanted anything until you."

"And that's what scares me," she whispered.

"You're scared of me wanting you?"

"I'm scared of losing you. I'm scared this is my punishment." Her fingers wrapped around his wrist and she pushed his sleeve back to view his tattoo. It was balanced now, but he had to touch her multiple times during the day. "Parker, I'm the poison, as much as your cure. If I have to kill the person I'm falling in love with, what will be left of me?"

At any time, any of them could lose control of their balance and turn dark.

Any time.

"I handled myself before we connected. Just because I like any excuse to touch you now doesn't mean I can't stop and balance myself."

"So what's your plan?" she asked. "If we're separated."

"It won't happen."

"I'm serious."

"So am I. Heaven help the poor fool who tries to come between us."

Alice pressed her lips together and raised a brow. "Your plan?"

"Tie you to me."

That sounded awfully prideful to Alice. She gave a disparaging shake of the head, and Parker was having none of it. He chucked her under the chin, forcing her to meet his worried eyes.

"Alice. Listen to me now. I never want you to feel like this is your punishment, or that you need it for any reason. Promise me if you do, you'll come to me first. You won't find another torture device and hurt yourself. Look forward, sweetheart. Not back."

"I can't help how I feel sometimes."

"You feel naughty, you come to me."

She smirked. "Naughty?"

"You know what I mean."

"You'll tie me up again?"

"Never to punish you, but if you need it, I will be your safety net."

He kissed her gently, and then tugged her toward the front door. With a sigh of capitulation, she could do nothing but follow.

They were downstairs and in the basement a few minutes later. Every member of the Lazarus family was down there, surrounding the operations table in what she thought of as the war room. Screens on one wall depicted news stories from around the city. Glass cabinets housed dormant Deadly suits. The long glass table had a screen beneath it. When she walked in, she held her chin high and tried to keep her limp to a minimum.

Out of the mates, only Max was there with his arm around Sloan as she sucked on a lollipop of some sort. Mary and Flint were also at the table among their children. Flint's intense gaze followed Alice from the moment she'd stepped into the room. Mary must have told him.

Suddenly unable to meet anyone else's eyes, Alice turned to Parker. He placed his warm palm on her nape and led them to the table. Safety net engaged, warmth spread outward from her heart.

"Finally," Liza said and gestured at Sloan. "Do your computer thing."

Sloan left the lollipop in her mouth and tapped the table a few times. Alice realized there was a touch screen keyboard beneath the glass. Multiple virtual digital files popped up along the table as though someone had dropped in a physical copy. Each folder opened to display field reports they'd all made—or AIMI had done for them.

"This everything?" Parker asked.

"Yep," Sloan replied. "These reports are the result of our reconnaissance missions, and with the names Prudence gave us, we've cross-referenced them with what we individually discovered. They check out. Each of these names controls one of the sites around the world. Together, they are the Syndicate, which makes them the big targets. We get their biometrics, we gain access to the sites, we take them down."

"They go to prison," Liza added.

"What about Julius?" Parker asked.

"He's still in Cardinal City."

"I guessed that," he replied. "I'm asking what link he has to all these people. Where does he fit in?"

Max visibly bristled at Parker's tone toward his wife. Parker's fingers clenched around Alice's neck, and the two men glared at each other.

"No one needs to have a pissing contest," Liza said, eyeing them both. "It looks like he's not the one in charge, if that's what you're getting at, Parks."

He ground his teeth. "So if we take them all out, he's going to be severely impacted. Can I have confirmation everyone has placed their charges?"

Alice's gaze whipped to him. Charges. As in explosives? Was that why Parker had been so agreeable to her entering the barn on her own, because he was laying his own explosive charges about?

"We have," Tony replied. "But I still don't see why, since we want to get inside each site."

"And we can't blow them up," Evan added. "Not with innocents inside. We need extraction plans."

"We get the biometrics," Parker said. "That's still the plan. But the charges are backup. If we can't get back there, then we can remote detonate. It sounds harsh, but this might be our only chance of eradicating this threat."

"You would kill innocent people?" Mary said, frowning at her son.

"Innocent is debatable."

"Flint was innocent," Mary stated. "He had no idea what went on behind closed doors at the lab."

"These people do. Even the guards in Columbia spoke about the boss's big plan. But it won't come to that," Parker insisted. "We'll get their biometrics."

"How?"

Parker's cell phone buzzed again. He slammed it on the table, irritated. Alice surreptitiously checked the caller ID. The office. Alarm bells prickled. He'd said everything was fine, but his pride had made him stubborn. Maybe it wasn't fine. Without waiting for his permission, she picked it up.

"No," he said, eyes wide, but she turned her back and answered the call.

"Parker Lazarus's office. Can I help you?"

The caller hesitated before speaking. "Miss Montgomery?"

"That's right."

"I need to speak with Mr. Lazarus. It's imperative."

"Whatever you have to say to him, you can say to me. I will pass on the message."

A frustrated grunt, a curse word, and Alice prepared to go to bat for Parker, but the man himself took the handset from her.

"Lazarus speaking." His face turned to stone as he listened to what the caller said. He looked at the files still open on the table and then met Alice's eyes. "Fine. But on one condition. I leave on a bang. I want an exit party. My assistant will handle the guest list. At the end of the night, I'll sign."

He cut the call, oblivious to all the gaping faces around him.

"AIMI," he said, bracing his hands on the table and frowning at the data.

"Yes, Parker."

"Start my succession planning protocol for Lazarus Tech."

"On it."

"You going to fucking fill us in, bro, or are you going to leave us all standing here with our dicks in our hands?" Liza cocked her head.

"Dicks?" Sloan snorted. "You have multiple dicks?"

"Shut up," Liza shot back. "You know what I mean."

Alice wanted to laugh. She'd always liked Liza, but even more when she talked like a trucker. Raven would get along with her like a church on fire.

"We're going to have a party," Parker declared.

"Are you kidding me?" Wyatt's brows slammed down. "I don't think this is the right time for a—"

"Wait!" Evan held up his tattooed hand. He looked down, his eyes darting about as he tried to recall something. "I had a dream about a party. A big one. A rooftop somewhere. Fancy. I thought it was just a dream because Julius was there. One of those party-with-all-your-enemies dreams and then you walk in naked."

Tony snort laughed, but Evan had psychic dreams. Some of it could be true. Still, none of this explained what Parker had said—that this was his exit party. A coldness spread over Alice, and the walls closed in. *Exit.* The board had asked him to resign.

"They're blackmailing you," she whispered.

He gave a wolfish grin, as though this was just another Wednesday at the office.

"Parker, this is serious. Your identity was compromised."

Liza blurted, "Is this about the attack at your office? I never got any reports it was you."

"Who's blackmailing you?" asked Wyatt.

Everyone in the room started talking, protesting, and arguing over each other.

"Why is this the first time we're hearing of this?" Griffin shouted. It was so unlike him that everyone stopped, and then Alice remembered he had a baby on the way. If Parker's identity was in question, then his was too. They'd all committed crimes against civilians. Not everyone would consider the Lazarus family justice as righteous. They could all go to jail. There would be no one left to protect Griffin's mate or his unborn child.

"Because I have it handled," Parker said.

"You've gone too far this time, Parker," Griffin replied, every muscle in his body tensing. The smart business shirt he wore could not hold his bulging muscles, or keep every piece of metal in the room from vibrating. "You should have told us the moment you knew."

"I said I have it sorted."

"And when are you going to let us in on your plan?" Mary asked.

"You've endangered not only every one of your siblings, but their mates and their children. Even Flint and myself."

"They're not going to the authorities," Parker insisted, nodding at Liza for confirmation. "Just like I knew they wouldn't."

Liza shrugged in agreement. "This is the first I'm hearing about blackmail."

"So they're just going to take your company, and that's okay? When did this happen?" Mary shot back. "Why haven't you told me or your father?"

"Mary, wait." Alice put up her hand and refused to shrink under the animosity. "After you visited me at the office, the Syndicate arrived and attacked. Parker saw it unfold on camera and came over. There was no time to waste. He forgot his mask and one of the executives saw."

"I was probably still in the neighborhood," Mary said, folding her arms before glaring at Parker. "You could have told me to head back."

He narrowed his eyes at his mother. "You had just *attacked* my mate."

"Whoa, whoa, whoa." Sloan put up her hands. "Everyone chill. The important thing is that I scrubbed all the footage. There's no proof of Parker being Pride, and Alice acted in self-defense."

"That's right," Parker said, giving everyone a look that said they should just calm the fuck down. "They can accuse me all they want, but it's this executive's word against mine. I'm just using this opportunity to our advantage."

"I don't like it," Wyatt thumped his fist on the table. "You should have told us."

Parker rolled his eyes. "If I told you every one of my machinations, you'd get bored. As I am right now. Moving on. I'm holding a retirement party. I'll invite the new investors."

"I still don't understand how this is going to help us," Liza said.

A slow, smug smile stretched Parker's lips, as though he never expected anyone to understand his diabolical level of planning. "The executive who is blackmailing me was paid off by the Syndicate to get into the building. The Syndicate want their claws in my company. The new buyers of my shares will be the leaders Prudence gave us. They never needed to take my company. They're poised to destroy the world. We all saw their replicate tanks ready to be deployed. So what have they been waiting for?" Everyone looked at each other, unsure. "I'll tell you what," Parker continued. "They've been waiting to take my company, to watch me fall, to crush us first."

"That's a bit of a leap," Flint said.

"They'll come," Parker replied. "Trust me. I know pride. We've been a thorn in their side for years. They'll come to gloat. To rub some salt in. Especially Julius Allcott, isn't that right, Evan?"

Evan shrugged and nodded and looked at the data files of the Syndicate leaders. "I think he's right. I mean, I'll try to see if any of my sketches can give us more detail, but I have to admit, I saw the party. I might even recognize some of these faces. It's going to happen."

"And while you distract them with their egos," Max said, narrowing his eyes. "The rest of us will grab their biometrics, just like we did with Barry Pinkerton at that charity ball."

Sloan ditched her empty lollipop stick at Parker. "Only you, bras. Only you would bring the enemy to you instead of chasing after them."

Tony smacked her over the head and scowled. "Stop calling people lady's undergarments."

They all laughed, and it was Alice's worst nightmare. Couldn't any of them see the potential for disaster here? Was she the only one who knew how much his sin had been overwhelming him when they weren't touching? Parker could lose everything. The Syndicate would come, like he said, because they were so sure they would win. And they were probably right.

She wanted so desperately to say just set off the explosives. Be done with it. Save the world, but knew the biometrics could save the world and save innocent bystanders caught in the crossfire.

"And when we get a face-to-face with Julius," Parker added, his tone suddenly solemn. "I'll trade something he's always wanted in return for Daisy's release."

"What's that?" Mary asked.

"Immortality."

The laughter stopped.

"That's assuming he still wants it," Liza said. "Daisy destroyed any chance he had of replicating his original family. Maybe he just wants to watch the world burn."

Parker tapped the data files on the world Syndicate leaders, a glint in his eyes. "Except he's not in control, like he led us to believe. They are. What Julius wants is personal, and we'll dangle it in front of him before taking it all down."

thirty-two

JULIUS ALLCOTT

"YOU NEED TO SEE THIS."

Julius ignored Van Jansen and put his Glock down to wash his hands under the stream of water in the bathroom sink. He scrubbed, turned the faucet off, and then dried his hands. *Can't even take a dump without being interrupted.* He stared at his fingers—the lock of hair had fallen off. Washed down the drain. Again. *Damn it.* A quick dip into his pocket and he pulled out the manicure scissors. A glance into the mirror and he snipped a longish chunk of white hair before tying it to his index finger.

Much better.

He finally turned to Van Jansen, standing at the bathroom door, and caught the scientist's alarmed gaze locked onto Julius's head. The *nerve* of him to interrupt here, of all places. Julius picked up the gun. Van Jansen quickly blurted his reason for being there.

"I looked into what the Sinner told us, and I think maybe she's right. I know you said not to waste my time, but I tested the theory out, and, well… come. You *must* see this. Before we lose them."

Julius tried to understand what the man was talking about. Something the Sinner had said? Which one? Who? Where? They'd failed in containing a single one of those bitches. He tuned back into what Van Jansen said.

"… the one in custody in Columbia. She said some things when we were there. Do you remember? About the action of the uncontrolled replicates, ja?" At Julius's blank look, Van Jansen elaborated. "The Sisterhood thinks the replicates are trying to get to Hell."

Oh. The Sinner in Columbia. Julius stifled an eye roll. He was not in the mood for theological theatrics. Not now. Not when nothing seemed to be working. Julius tucked the gun into the back of his waistband and then hid the firearm with his jacket.

"You must come quickly," Van Jansen insisted.

"There is no Hell," Julius gritted out. "There never has been. Now, don't you have another treatment to administer? And"—he slammed his palm on the bathroom mirror, shattering the glass—"why haven't we found a new enforcer? Where are the damned Faithful?"

Van Jansen jerked back, blinking. "That is not my department."

"Right." Julius tapped his chest. "Right. That was my darling's department." He shook his head, clearing the fog. Despair was out of commission. She'd betrayed him. Someone else had been helping. What was his name again? The fireman? "But he messed up. Again."

"Julius," Van Jansen said. "Listen to me."

"There is no Hell!" Julius slammed his palm, cutting it on the broken mirror. If Julius believed in Hell, then he might believe in Heaven. Then his wife and daughter would never return to him because they were *there*. And there was no way to bring someone from *there* to *here*.

"Aah." Van Jansen put up a finger, recklessly excited. "But alternate dimensions have long been postulated over in the scientific community…. Quickly. Follow me."

The scientist rushed off, his white lab coat flapping.

Julius put his hair-tied-finger on his lips, then touched his heart and prayed for patience before following the white coat through corridors of their building, down the rabbit hole into their basement, past the replicate tanks gurgling and bubbling, all the way to the darkened back end and through a strange hole in the wall that hadn't been there before.

Blood smeared scratches around the edges. Had fingernails made those? *Impossible.*

Footsteps echoed through the hole in a short tunnel that ended in what, he guessed, was the underground sewage network of the city. Water dripped from the ceiling and splashed onto the muddy floor where footprints paved the way forward.

What the...

"Hurry, or we will miss them." Van Jansen's voice bounced off the tunnel walls.

Julius chased his lead scientist through the rat-riddled maze until they found them—four replicates. Each more crazed and decrepit than the first, and each trying to dig their way down into a muddy part of the sewer. With their fingers. Which were now bony stumps.

"What is the meaning of this?" Julius asked, easing his firearm out of his waistband.

"Look." Van Jansen pointed into the murky water.

Something glowed down there. A small, thin light. A torch? A fallen lamp? A drowning firefly? Julius glanced at Van Jansen, who held some kind of electrical device beeping and whirring, collecting data. The scientist's eyes were manic as he held the device toward the water, heedless of the replicates splashing him with sewage.

"The readings," Van Jansen laughed. "Look at them. There is something there. They found it!"

"Found what?" Julius shouted.

Another crazed laugh from the scientist. The whites of eyes in the dim, dank space. "Who knows? Maybe Hell. Maybe Heaven. Maybe something else. All we know is there is much sin there, ja? Enough for the replicates to hunt and find."

Julius held his breath and stared at the water, at that small glowing light. Like the miracle of a lost soul blinking in the darkness. The hair around his finger felt tight. Hot. The hair on his arms pricked up as though electricity surged in the air.

Heaven? Hell? Something else?

"Do you mean..." he said, throat dry, hardly able to contain the kernel of long denied hope growing in his heart. "Do you mean that my wife and daughter could be on the other side?"

Van Jansen shot him an incredulous look. A frown. "That might be a thin theory, but—"

"But it's possible?"

"I suppose. Unlikely but, yes."

A voice called from the distance, underwater. It called Julius's name.

"Joseline?" he murmured. Had that been his wife?

"I'm sorry, what?" Van Jansen asked.

"I wasn't talking to you."

A presence prickled over Julius's skin. He felt something. Maybe someone.

Julius... save me.

Joseline? His heart leaped into his throat. His wife was down there. His wife!

The scientist gave him an odd look. "I hear no one. Are you okay?"

Julius lifted his gun and shot Van Jansen right between the eyes. Triumphant purpose filled him anew. *Hope.* And no one, not even the scientist who discovered this, would get in the way. Julius tossed the gun and tapped his finger to his heart.

"Not long now, my loves." He tapped again, and then shouted to the replicates, "Keep digging!"

Not long.

The replicates continued to dig, indifferent to the corpse bumping past them as it floated away.

thirty-three

PARKER LAZARUS

THE NIGHT of the party came around too quickly. Parker spent the week putting his plan into place, including the part where he hosted the event at his own penthouse—in the building he'd previously been so strict about protecting. It would be unexpected. It would throw anyone doubting his intentions off the mark. The Syndicate leaders needed to think Parker and his family were clueless to their identity, after all, why would he knowingly invite the enemy into his abode? All these things worked perfectly in his favor.

During the past week, Parker's beautiful Sinner spent the time working as his assistant, calling the catering company, hiring the quartet, alerting the media so he could retire in style across the social pages of the local paper in the morning. Nightingale Security would be there in an official capacity. Liza and Joe had invited some of their cop and FBI buddies. And the press was there. If the Syndicate tried to do anything untoward, they risked outing themselves on national television. It was a gamble Parker was willing to bet would pay off.

All his ducks were lined up. The enemy would come. His family would secure their biometrics, and the Syndicate would see him sign away his company. But most importantly, Julius would be intrigued enough that he'd accept Parker's invitation. The Syndicate might be run by multiple people around the world, but it was Julius's brain-child. It would be a blow to his pride that Parker had invited the rest of them and not him.

Julius hated the idea of being obsolete. Of being left alone. This notion bled into every action the man had ever taken, from the creation of the replicates to keeping his progeny close by as a pet. Julius needed to feel important. He wanted power.

And Parker was going to dangle it in front of him—Gloria Godi-va's original research. She was the lead geneticist who created the Seven. Julius had originally wanted to create replicates so he and his family could live again in a new utopia of his making. Daisy had stolen that dream from him, but Prudence said he'd been tapping into Daisy's spinal fluid, probably to harvest stem cells. Parker's bet was Julius still planned on bringing that family back somehow, and he would do anything to realize that dream.

Finding the Syndicate sites, yet not finding Daisy, had been a red flag. It was too convenient, as far as Parker was concerned. Julius prided himself on being one step ahead of the rest.

As Parker finished his tie before the bathroom mirror, he heard Alice in their closet. She sang her favorite song under her breath. But he also heard the distinct metallic sound of weapons moving. He'd told her not to wear any tonight, and the guests were arriving. Conversation filtered into the room from the terrace only a few feet away.

The string quartet and press had arrived twenty minutes ago. As far as the public believed, Parker was retiring because he wanted to travel with his brother, Tony. Everyone knew they liked to chase adrenaline seeking adventure together, so it wasn't a far stretch to believe the corporate life bored him. Unless you really knew him. Any

Syndicate leaders arriving, and of course the blackmailer, would be expecting a different reason for tonight's events. His big announcement would happen about two hours after the party had started. That left them two hours to mingle and gather biometrics.

Tightening the knot on his tie, he gave his reflection a nod. His bionic hand worked perfectly. The Windsor knot was flawless. His stylish suit was impeccable, and the purple rose corsage matched the one he would pin to Alice's breast. There would be no doubt in anyone's mind that she was with him.

He found her exactly where he'd suspected, the large walk-in closet, sitting down on the chaise. Behind her was a long display cabinet that housed his ties, watches, and now her jewelry—none of which she'd touched. Beyond that was the gauzy curtain covering the window separating them from guests. Since Lazarus House wasn't the highest building in the neighborhood, every single penthouse window was mirror tinted for privacy. The light was dim in here, they could see out, but none could see in.

In only her underwear, Alice looked down as she stroked the short sword on her lap. But there were no holsters strapped to her skin, just two garters holding her pantyhose.

Her tightly coiled chignon contrasted with the weapon in her lap and the seductive silk lingerie. She was a queen, a beauty, but a deadly one. Respect and admiration poured through him. This woman was a chameleon for everyone else. To him, she was simply Alice. His mate.

He unzipped the dress bag and his breath hitched. Inside was a floor-length gown made from sparkling diamonds. The dress was worth more than the gross domestic product of a small country. He'd wanted her to know she was worth more than any of this, and that he'd never put her in jeopardy. But she wasn't impressed. She'd not even noticed him unzipping the dress bag.

"Alice," he said.

Someone laughed boisterously outside, drawing his brief attention. Shadows moved outside the window.

"I know," she replied without looking up, her gaze locked on her reflection in her sword. "We need to get out there. First impressions are everything."

"Look at me."

She didn't. Her shoulders hunched and for a moment, he thought it was the dress. *Too much.* Would it show her back and the scars? No, he'd told the designer exactly what he'd expected, and it was perfect.

He kneeled and palmed her thighs. She tried to lift him up.

"You'll wrinkle your suit," she said.

"What is it?" he asked, searching her face.

Her expression shut down. So this was about him.

"You need to trust me, Alice." He pushed her knees apart and moved closer.

"Of course I do."

"But…"

"But why won't you tell me what you have planned, because I know you're not really planning on handing over your company."

He grinned. "If I tell you, you'll find a way to dissuade me."

"Now I'm really concerned."

"Alice," he chided. "This is something I need to do on my own. That's all. Please."

He was pushing the limits of their new relationship, but the more people that knew about his plan, the more variables he had to be mindful of, and the more ways it could all burn to the ground if he wasn't careful.

"There's more, isn't there?" he asked. "What is it?"

"I guess I'm questioning everything about myself."

"Did you have a chance to speak with Flint?"

She shook her head. "I've been avoiding him. Keeping busy with prep for this event. But it's not him. It's me."

"You're perfect."

"You're just saying that because I'm your mate."

"You think I'd lie?"

She narrowed her eyes at him. Her makeup was smokey, and the lips were glossy. The raspberry flavor watered his mouth.

"I don't know, Parker. Would you?"

"I don't need to lie, Alice."

Only those afraid lied. Parker managed expectations.

"Not only do I think you've got ulterior motives for tonight, but you still haven't told me what your plan is if we're separated. Don't tell me some bullshit about not needing one because you've got everything under control."

"But I do." He grinned and toyed with her garter, letting a single claw distend from his fingertip to tickle over her skin.

She shook her head and lifted her eyes to the ceiling, but he caught the glimmer in them. The unshed tears. His claws retracted.

"I just have this feeling I can't shake." Her brows puckered in the middle. "You're so sure everything will go according to plan?"

"You've known me for two years, Alice. When have my plans failed?"

"Um. The night you let go of my hand on that rooftop."

"That's different."

"You're right. Forget it," she said, sighing. "This is your plan, not mine. Stupid me for thinking we were equals. Who do you need me to be tonight?"

He stared at her, letting her words sink in. This would all make sense by the end of the night, and then she would see he trusted her the most.

"Alice, up until now you may have lived your life according to what others wanted, but I only need you to be you. That's the only person I want you to be. Are you sure you're okay?"

"I'm fine."

Her posture said anything but, and he needed to set her right. He couldn't have his stoic warrior queen go out like this. His eyes darted to where his bionic hand gripped her gently and suddenly all he could think of was how he'd lost that arm in the first place—his stubborn pride. Maybe she'd been a little right. He'd never planned to lose the arm. His plan had been to take Alice down with him, at the very least, but then their mating bond triggered, and he'd forgotten which way was up.

But it was too late to doubt himself now, and if things didn't go according to plan, then Alice would remain in the dark. This was for her benefit.

His bionic hand traced down her stomach and skimmed over the silk waistband of her underwear.

She sucked in a breath. "What are you doing?"

"Demonstrating my perfectly fine motor skills—how well this hand works now."

"Parker," she gasped as he traced lower over her mound, pressing in to tease her sensitive flesh over the silk. He kissed between her breasts, right on the clasp of her bra. "I've got it all sorted, Alice. You know me. Let me take care of this. Trust me."

"But—"

He softly circled his metal finger over her sweet spot, eliciting a small whimper from her. A wiggle. An arch into him.

"I want you to relax tonight," he said, nuzzling into her neck, nipping at her ear lobe. "Nothing will go wrong. These people will leave, and we'll have their biometrics."

She started panting, gripping his hair. He loved how responsive she was to him, how every bit of tension in her body released, how she gave herself over to him. This language was one he'd always understood. She might worry, but when he had her like this, he knew exactly where her heart lied.

"I'm going to get you off, Alice," he said, increasing the tempo of his finger. "And then I'm going to fuck you, right here, right now, while our enemies are walking around on that terrace a few feet away. That's how confident I am of tonight's plan." They locked eyes, hers feverish and his steady. "You trust me, don't you?"

She nodded. "Of course."

"Then let me take care of things. Of you."

He kept his touch gentle but firm, never once faulting. But it wasn't enough. He needed to taste her. So he slid the silk down her hips and laid her on the chaise. He found her sex wet as he licked straight down the middle. She came apart under his tongue in minutes. He was inside her moments later. His slow thrusts turned into fast, passionate love making until his release barreled through him.

When they were both spent, his mate's fire returned to her. As he helped her dress, she looked at him with the same snarky spark in her eyes that he'd fallen in love with. She was once again the same woman who'd air-kissed him as she fell backward out of a plane. He was sure she had words for him about his impromptu claiming, but she kept them to herself. She let him have this moment, and in turn let herself have it too.

She placed her hands in his and he gripped them tight, knowing that this woman was worth holding on to. He only hoped she felt the same way when the night was done.

thirty-four

ALICE MONTGOMERY

ALICE HAD NEVER FELT SO out of place in her life as she did on that penthouse terrace by the balcony. Her dress weighed on her. The shoes pinched. Tasteful fairy lights draped around poles and columns, and the stars twinkled in the sky, but she couldn't shake her grumpy mood. Parker had convinced her to leave her weapons in the dressing room, stating that any battle tonight would be one of words, not fists.

So she endured without her sword.

The night was clear and crisp. A pool stretched across the roof and a pop-up bar was set up on one side. Parker had told Alice that a few months ago the Syndicate tried to kidnap Misha from here. They'd even attempted to land a helicopter. Wyatt had destroyed the elevator in his efforts to get to his mate. Not even a scar remained on either Wyatt or the elevator.

It was now champagne and caviar. The rich and the richer. Standing in her skintight, sparkling sheath, Alice couldn't believe Parker had been right. Each of the Syndicate leaders waltzed in without a care in the world, despite knowing they walked into enemy territory. But then again, that was exactly what Parker had done when he'd walked into the cathedral and a room full of Sinners. To be fair, his arrogance had been justified.

That's what worried her.

In a room full of prideful arrogance, whose would come first?

To everyone else, Parker looked like a dignified king as he moved about the room socializing. To her, she saw the heavy head beneath the crown, from the pinch of his eyes to the press of his lips. More than once he'd touched her, whether a brush at the elbow or his favorite spot at the back of her neck. He tried to hide his release of tension, but she felt it in the air. The pride in the room must be suffocating.

Part of her felt honored to be that steady rock for him. He, the heroic vigilante. He, the billionaire visionary. He, the savior. In a room full of gut-wrenching pain, he came to her for relief. Her nails dug into her palms. It was this same system that could work against him and trigger his doom. She guessed there was no way of knowing for certain what the future held. Even their psychics had foretold two different futures, any of which could become reality.

Parker came up behind her and touched her elbow. "You ready?"

The leather glove on one hand only added to the suave, enigmatic air he always seemed to exude. She relaxed her fingers. "Let's do this."

"Good." He lowered his lips to her ear and spoke quietly. "Next up is Brigit Johansen. She's the CEO of venture capitalist company Erobre. Definitely Syndicate. She's not even trying to hide it."

Alice's eyes narrowed at the skinny blond in her sixties. "She doesn't have a drink. Let's bring her one."

A flash of teeth. "That's my girl."

They collected champagne from the bartender and joined the Norwegian and her entourage, a tall buff bodyguard, and a shorter man with a weaselly face.

"Brigit Johansen," Parker said as they arrived. "May I introduce Alice Montgomery, the future of Lazarus Tech."

Alice blushed and laughed at Parker. "You're being silly. I'm just his assistant. Here, I brought you a drink for the toast."

Brigit smiled tightly as she accepted the champagne, the warmth never entering her eyes. She flat out dismissed Alice and turned to Parker.

"And when will your announcement be?" she asked, her accent thick.

"Later." He stared blankly.

"How does it feel to have something you've worked for your entire life taken away from you?"

Wow. No sugar coating from this woman. Parker's lip twitched and his eyes danced with humor.

"Why, Brigit? Nothing has been taken away from me yet."

Brigit grunted and took a sip from her glass. Parker put his ungloved hand on Alice's elbow, taking advantage of their connection. The woman's pride must be through the roof.

"Yet," Brigit agreed.

While Parker spoke briefly with the woman about the weather, Alice imagined stabbing her in the eyes. Parker excelled in diplomatic chit-chat. When they moved to the other leaders, it was much of the same. Parker introduced Alice. They promptly ignored her and made some kind of derogatory or snide comment to Parker about his upcoming "retirement."

Through it all, Parker remained stoic and unwavering.

Alice dropped off a fingerprinted glass behind the bar for one of the Lazarus siblings to collect. She smiled politely at the bartender and accepted another glass of champagne, then stood back and watched as Parker took his second spin about the terrace, this time making a point to talk to the executives who blackmailed him. He did this all with a half smile on his face, as though he knew a secret none of them did.

If only he'd let Alice in on that secret, she'd feel a lot more at ease about the night. Damned Parker Lazarus and his magic tongue, distracting her in the dressing room when she should have been insisting he reveal his plan.

The rest of the Lazarus family and their mates milled about, dispersed at random intervals. There was a tension only select people felt. Alice kept checking doors and wished she'd brought at least one Sinner with her, but this was her life now. Every time she looked at Parker, she couldn't exactly complain.

There was one thing to say for him choosing this location, his complete and utter control of the security system. AIMI scanned and recorded each individual as they arrived. She could lock down the entire building if she needed, or open the front door to guests. The only way out would be to fly off the roof, and as Parker had already told her, landing a helicopter was difficult.

So he was right. No one would be leaving in a body bag. They were all too smug and prideful to start trouble. They truly wanted to see Parker lose everything because the Lazarus family had taken so much from them. That's all this night was for. Gloating.

You trust me, don't you?

Her nails dug into her palms again.

"Tough crowd, huh?" Flint asked, coming up next to Alice. His glass of champagne remained untouched. Without his usual baseball cap, his silver streaked hair, trim beard, and suit looked rather dapper. It hadn't struck Alice before how similar that beard was to Parker's. Short, trimmed, and razored in a way that accentuated their jaw.

This was the first time Alice had seen Flint since she'd found out the news about their history. She'd passed it off as unimportant, but suddenly seeing his face now compounded the memory of the man in the principal's office all those years ago. Her childhood longing rushed to the surface.

"You get used to it," Flint said.

"What?"

"Them." He nodded toward Tony and Parker as they told a boisterous story a few feet away to some avid businessmen. "Their act."

"Oh, I'm not worried about that." Alice knew Parker put on airs and sometimes frivolity for his cover identity to steer the conversation away from the possibility of him being a vigilante. Misdirection at its finest.

Flint glanced at Alice's empty glass and asked if she wanted another. Her throat was suddenly parched. She nodded gratefully, and he flagged down the barman. When the drink returned, Flint handed it to Alice and stared at her. *Here it comes.*

"Alice, I want to say something to you and I hope I'm not being too forward or inappropriate."

"Flint," she said, heading off the conversation. "You don't have to. Mary explained."

"I want to." He took her hand, pain echoing in his brown eyes. "I have to apologize for what happened. For leaving you to fend for yourself as a child. It's not an excuse, but I thought the money I left you had actually gone to you. I had no idea your family was so greedy."

"It's water under the bridge. You never owed me anything."

"If I had known the Sisterhood—"

"Flint. Please." She smiled gently and squeezed his hand. "A wise person recently told me to stop looking back and start looking forward. Who I am today is because of what happened in the past. I'm grateful for that. I'm grateful I am a woman who can stand by Parker's side with my head held high." Her throat tightened. "I'm also grateful this family has welcomed me."

His eyes turned glossy, and he nodded.

The truth of Alice's words rang through her. She wasn't sure if she'd believed it before, but now, saying it aloud, she lifted her chin. A few months ago, she didn't believe she was worthy of being in this relationship. But now she had the love of an incredible man. Alice searched the room for Parker and found him already looking at her. She smiled fondly. The concern in his eyes turned to affection. Her diamond dress felt lighter, like it fit.

"Two," said a man to Alice's left.

When she caught his profile, she stilled. *Julius*. He'd come.

His face was haggard, his suit hung off his tall frame as though he'd lost weight, and chunks of white hair had been hacked from his head. Alice glanced down and found why—he'd tied a lock of pale hair around his index finger. *Weird*. Warning bells rang in her gut.

This man was deranged.

Flint cursed next to Alice and shifted closer to her, as if to protect her.

Next to Julius was another face she recognized. A handsome, tall man with short hair. Unlike Julius, whose expensive suit swam on his frame, this one's muscles threatened to split the thrift shop seams. Large brown eyes surrounded by thick black lashes she might be a little envious of. He was the Faithful who'd attacked her at the cathedral, the one controlling the replicates. And the only Faithful who'd escaped.

Was he Julius's protection? A bodyguard?

Alice's grip tightened around her champagne flute, and she calculated the time it would take to smash and stab into Julius's carotid.

"Ms. Montgomery," Julius drawled, accepting his champagne from the bartender. "I'm surprised to see you. Alive."

Her brow arched. The tall companion's lips flattened in what looked like frustration.

"And I'm surprised to see you had the balls to come," she replied. "I mean, I thought you'd have been licking your wounds after what Daisy did to you."

Anger fired in Julius's eyes. He tapped his hair entwined finger to his chest and mumbled something she couldn't quite catch. Then he darted a glance to the other Syndicate members and calmed himself. Alice inwardly smiled. Once again, Parker had been right. They'd thought this man had more influence with the organization than he did.

A warm hand slid over Alice's nape, and then a brazen kiss below her ear. Parker leveled his stare at Julius. Seeing them side by side, Alice could tell they were biologically related.

"Julius Allcott," Parker stated. "I don't remember putting your name on the guest list."

Julius visibly prickled, but held his tongue, preferring the language of ego and entitlement. The derangement melted away and was replaced with a shadow of the formidable man he used to be. Alice saw how this man had convinced investors to take a chance on his dream. With a simple look, he seemed to suck all the air out of the room.

Just as she'd thought about his influence, he proved her wrong by tapping his chest again as he mumbled something like a madman. Hadn't Daisy snatched a locket containing his wife and daughter's hair? Was he still so obsessed with bringing them back?

More alarm bells rang in Alice's head. It was one thing to battle a sane psychopath, but one without logic would be unpredictable. Parker must have known this, Alice realized, and she felt foolish for not picking up this nuance sooner. It made sense now why he knew Julius would take the bait. Not just pride, but obsession.

"You've aged since I last saw you, Julius," Parker noted.

"You can thank your incompetent sister for that," Julius quipped.

Parker's fingers tightened around Alice's nape.

"Where is she?" he demanded.

Julius smirked until Parker grabbed his arm, bionic fingers tightening. The movement exposed metallic workings beneath Parker's sleeve. The bodyguard intercepted, but Julius halted him, and instead pried off Parker's fingers himself. His strength shocked Alice, and when she looked at Parker, she found him with the same expression.

"You didn't think you were the only ones to receive gene therapy, did you?" Julius taunted, then gave Parker a dismissive look. "At least your sister has been good for something."

"You bastard," Parker said. "You treated your own daughter like a pet, no, worse than one. Torturing her and then parading her around like some kind of exhibit. Her cells won't get you where you need to be. You know that. Not while they're in the state they—"

He cut himself off, as though he'd spoken too much. Turning to the bar, Parker took another flute of champagne and guzzled it down.

"I'll swap Despair for Gloria's research," Julius offered, taking the bait.

Only Alice caught Parker's small smile before he removed it and returned to face Julius. Parker narrowed his eyes, pretending to consider the proposal.

"I want proof of life," he demanded.

Julius nodded to his companion, who pulled a smart phone from his pocket and thumbed the screen. He showed Parker the live video feed, bumping rudely into Alice as he moved.

Alice's body went on high alert, ready to retaliate if necessary, but then she felt something strange. He shoved paper into her hand. *Odd.* Holding her breath, she curled her fist around the note, and then made a show of looking at the screen as though nothing had happened.

Could this be a message?

The bodyguard continued to ignore her and looked at the video of a dirty, silver-haired woman prone on the ground against a curved concrete wall, and then the phone was put away.

"That doesn't prove she's alive," Parker said. "I want to speak with her."

"First, I need to see the laptop, and that it's been decrypted." Julius shrugged.

"It's all in here." Parker tapped his temple. "The laptop has degraded too much to be of use. So you take me to Daisy, and I'll write everything down."

Julius glanced around the room with the same bored expression Alice had seen on Parker so many times. "I know what you're doing here, and it won't work."

"And what's that?" Parker folded his arms.

"Cut the heads off the snake and it will all disappear. The Syndicate is bigger than these people."

"I know," Parker replied. "It's worldwide. Norway, Columbia, Ireland, Australia, Japan, Africa and here."

The two men stared at each other, neither willing to give an inch but both knowing Parker had revealed every single Syndicate location. The paper burned a hole in Alice's hand and she itched to read what it said. She glanced at the bodyguard, but he kept his hard gaze on Parker, as did Julius. Something flickered in Julius's expression. Recognition.

"But if you want to bring *them* back," Parker said with a pointed look where Julius's locket used to be. "You need me."

Surely he was bluffing. No one could replicate a person without the right DNA samples.

"It was never about them." The glint in Julius's eye rivaled the stars as he subconsciously tapped his chest, but before he could speak, Parker echoed the man's tap on the collarbone.

They never had a chance to continue their conversation because Liza came jogging up, Joe at her side. He wasn't in fancy clothes but his FBI jacket, an exasperated expression on his face. They both sent a worried glance toward Julius and tried to pull Parker away. But he stood firm.

"You need to leave, bro," Liza said.

"What is it?" he asked.

"They're coming for you," Joe said.

The police.

Parker gave a flat smile. "Then it's time for my announcement. Alice…"

He offered his crooked elbow to her, as though they were about to take an afternoon stroll in the countryside.

Liza stage whispered, "Are you mad? Go!"

Parker met Alices's eyes. *You trust me, don't you?*

She took his elbow, and they walked to the balcony where a small dais was set up with a podium overlooking the night cityscape. Alice's panic surged. She wanted to do what Liza had said —leave. Take Parker and go anywhere law enforcement wouldn't find them.

But she forced herself to trust him. He wasn't nervous. She shouldn't be.

There must be a plan.

"Ladies and Gentlemen." Parker's voice rose above the crowd. The string quartet cut off. Suddenly hushed and murmuring voices seemed loud in the night. "It's time for me to retire."

Brigit Johansen's bodyguard pushed through the crowd to make way for his charge. They stood at the front of the crowd before the dais, eager looks on their faces. They reminded Alice of a starving dog about to get a bone. She let her gaze pan over the crowd. The executives were there, also smug. The Lazarus family all looked worried.

Evan scowled from a corner, Grace by his side. Liza and Joe looked tense. Flint had found Mary. And Julius looked curious.

"Many of you know I built Lazarus Tech from the ground up," Parker said, deep voice booming. "It all started with a little invention in my early twenties and has grown to the empire it is today. But it's time for me to move on and name my successor." He smiled at Alice as though he had all the time in the world. As though the police weren't bursting through the front door.

The executive who'd blackmailed Parker stepped forward. A few other men clapped him on the back, but Parker turned to Alice.

"As I've been eager to tell anyone with ears tonight, Alice Montgomery is the future of Lazarus Tech. The woman who has kept the company afloat during my injury. The woman who has kept *me* afloat. My future wife. I trust no one more to look after the company while I'm off exploring the world."

"What?" she blinked. *Future wife?*

He grinned. "My company is yours now."

Crickets chirped. Traffic blared from the streets below. Somewhere in the distance, a cat hissed and called. And the pounding on the front door of Parker's penthouse made Alice jolt.

Brigit stepped forward. "You're making a big mistake."

Four armed police walked onto the terrace, barging their way through. Camera flashes popped in quick succession, capturing everything. No one quite understood what was happening, especially Alice. *Future wife?* But Parker still remained unruffled, and his family took their cue from him. That playboy mask he'd been wearing most of the night around Tony came back into full effect as he glared at the police.

"What is the meaning of this?" he blurted.

"Parker Lazarus, you're under arrest for acts of vigilantism and—"

The police continued to recite a list of crimes a mile long, but Alice tuned out.

She gaped at Parker and hissed, "You said to *trust* you."

He nuzzled near her ear, inhaled deeply and whispered, "Part of the plan, baby."

Parker stepped down off the dais, found Julius in the crowd, and tapped his chest in the same spot as Julius had moments earlier. Then he allowed himself to be handcuffed and taken away.

thirty-five

PARKER LAZARUS

SITTING in the back of a police wagon, driving through Cardinal City on the way to the station, Parker mentally recited what he knew for sure.

One, his family would be arguing over whose fault this was and whether they should have blindly followed his ridiculous plan in the first place.

Two, the biometrics would all be collected and, if his family were worth their salt, they'd be actioning the part of the plan he'd included them in on—infiltrating the Syndicate and shutting down systems from within.

Three, Julius would break him out because he wanted what was in Parker's brain.

Four, Daisy was alive.

Five, after what happened at Lazarus Tech, Parker knew there were too many people vying for control of his company. Even though Sloan had scrubbed the CCTV footage, there could always be other damning evidence out there. He always knew one day his identity would be compromised. They'd known for years the FBI was building a case against them. Liza's mate Joe had been able to distract the Feds for a while, but being charged for vigilantism was always a possibility.

With the easy way the Syndicate leaders had accepted Parker's invitation, he'd guessed the night of his reckoning would be the retirement party. The moment Parker had accepted it, he came up with a plan to beat it. If he could make the law charge him for this particular incident, he knew the variables. He could work toward acquittal from all charges, and then no matter what happened later, under the Double Jeopardy clause, he wouldn't be tried for the same crime again. He could essentially be a vigilante, and there was nothing anyone could do about it. The same didn't apply to his family unless they were also acquitted, but he hoped it wouldn't get to that point. Soon the trouble with the Syndicate and Julius would be over.

That left him with the sixth thing he knew for sure. Alice would be extremely angry with him. But if he'd told Alice the plan, she would have begged to be included and where he was going, where Daisy was, he wouldn't wish that on anyone, especially his mate. Or future wife, rather. Alice was now in charge of his company. She was safe, and she had control of his finances to support herself and his family. The moment they were alone, they could be married. And then, as his spouse, Alice wouldn't have to testify against him. She would forgive him for this. He hoped.

Worst-case scenario, if she left him and he lost his freedom, then at least he did everything he could to save Daisy. What was a little jail time when Daisy had been a prisoner for thirty years?

Alice would understand.

She would.

He sighed and leaned his head back on the seat before glancing at the officer on each side of him. They'd cuffed him, but he could break out of them. He might not need to, depending on how and when Julius showed up to extract him. At least this way, with Parker's showy arrest in front of the press, and subsequent kidnapping by the *real* criminal, Parker could plead his innocence later in court.

As long as everything kept going according to plan, things would work out fine.

HOURS LATER, Parker lay on the solitary bench in the local police station's holding cell. Dawn wasn't far away. He thought Julius would have tried to break him out by now. But nothing.

Crickets.

The stinky, toothless hobo on the other side of the cell had pustules over his bare feet. No one had spoken to Parker or even offered him a phone call since he'd arrived, and he knew he'd be transferred as soon as the district attorney's office was opened. That left barely an hour to get out of there.

Julius should have wanted Gloria's research so badly that he'd break Parker out. Julius's decline in mental health hadn't been something Parker had factored into his plan. He'd wanted Gloria's research. Hadn't he?

Or had Alice been right and Parker's pride was clouding his judgement?

In the darkness, with only the stench of the hobo to keep him company, Parker's memories haunted him. Smoke and chemicals singed his nostrils. He was seven. Evan had just been born and they were running out of a burning building, escaping the only home they'd ever known—the Syndicate lab. Parker and Daisy went into the elevator, squishing in with the others, but she faced the open doors with anguish in her eyes. Someone was out there, in the fire, and Daisy wanted to go to her before it was too late. She sensed despair and her first instinct was to comfort. Parker could have stopped her. He'd seen that look in her eyes. It was the same look she had when staring up at the sky. Longing. Pain. Sadness.

Daisy dashed past them as the doors closed. All that was left of his sister was her little bonsai plant on the floor.

Mary and Flint argued whether to go back into the burning building for Daisy, but then Mary made the decision that changed everything. If she went back for Daisy, they'd all get caught. So she left her behind.

One life wasn't important when the fate of the world was at stake.

Was that what was happening now? He sat up and glared at the wall.

It *should* be what was happening. His family *should* be forgetting about him. They should be out there on planes, flying back to the sites across the world, infiltrating the systems and shutting down everything they could. They should be gathering evidence to send to prosecutors, evacuating innocent personnel, and then setting off the charges—destroying the bases, the replicates, the weapons... everything.

That's what he'd told them to do. That was the plan.

Parker had thought he'd blinked the memory away, but the acrid smell of smoke remained. He lifted his nose and sniffed again. There was definitely the taint of fire in the air. But where was it coming from? He went to the bars and looked out, but couldn't see much down the dark hallway.

The fire alarm went off and Parker's lips curved. *This is it. Julius's team is here.*

Two officers ran down the hallway, their keys jangling. One of them opened the door while the other handcuffed Parker before leading him out, cursing softly under his breath, complaining he didn't get paid enough for this.

Police were everywhere, shouting and barking orders. Other cells were opened and prisoners hauled out. In the blink of an eye the station became chaos. Fire. Heat. Smoke.

The officer leading him inhaled smoke and coughed horrendously.

"We need to get low." Parker urged him down.

The smoke was so thick they couldn't see five feet in front. Parker was just about ready to snap his cuffs when a fireman appeared like an apparition. Their savior's identity was hidden by full protective gear, face mask and helmet. He stared for a split second at Parker and then handed the officer an oxygen mask before beckoning.

They followed, with Parker taking up the rear. He took not two steps before someone tugged him from behind. He rounded and found another fireman taking Parker's bare hand, and all the sin in the room popped out of existence. His eyes snapped to those blinking at him from behind the fireman's goggles—firewoman. *Alice.*

His heart hammered fast. What was she doing here? It was supposed to be Julius... or at least one of the Faithful. That was the plan. Parker had worked it all out in his head. Julius was filled with deadly pride, and Parker knew what that did to someone... didn't he?

Alice guided him furiously in the chaos, weaving expertly through smoke. Eventually they burst through a less used fire exit and onto an empty side street where Alice had stashed more bunker gear. Water drops landed heavily and Parker couldn't tell if it was the rain or from a fire hose. Alice pointed at the gear, but he shook his head.

This isn't how it's supposed to go.

"Hurry!" she shouted.

Grinding his teeth, he snapped the cuffs and then dressed in protective gear, including the goggles and breathing apparatus to conceal his identity. Alice took him down the alley and they burst out onto the street where fire trucks and emergency services were in full force, swarming and saving.

Alice continued to guide him until they cleared the area and found a quiet spot behind a Dumpster a few blocks away. She pulled off her headgear and threw it on the floor.

"What were you thinking?" she snapped.

"That Julius would break me out and take me to Daisy. You ruined it."

She scoffed. "I ruined it? You almost cost your family their lives. They barely got out of the country to finish the job. Cops have been knocking on everyone's doors. Do you have any idea what's happening?"

"I had it under control, Alice."

"No, you didn't." She pushed him. "If you had the presence of mind to consult your family, or me, you might have—*God!* You're impossible."

Light rain fell from the sky, making it the weather, not the fire hose he'd felt earlier. Parker stepped out of the last of his gear and pinched the bridge of his nose. "Julius—"

"Julius didn't give a shit. He was there to gloat. You got that part right. We haven't seen a sign of him."

"The rest of the family?"

Alice's nostrils flared. "They're fine. No one has been arrested. There's no warrant. They just want to talk to all of them."

"I thought…" He blinked, turning over the events in his mind. Julius should have broken Parker out.

"You thought wrong but"—Alice sighed and showed him a piece of paper—"maybe all isn't lost."

There was a message scrawled onto it: *I can take you to Daisy.*

There was more to it, a name—Axel Alvares—and a meeting place and time. The Cardinal City Fire Department, an hour ago.

"He was Julius's bodyguard," Alice said. "He said Julius has gone mad, that he's been talking to people who aren't there. He wants to help us rescue Daisy."

"And you believed him?"

"Well, he helped me get you out of jail, and, yeah, there's something about him. I don't think he meant to get as embroiled with the Syndicate, but he did."

Parker grew quiet. Had he really been so far from the truth? Did Julius have zero intention of taking him, or would he have turned up, eventually? Was Parker's pride truly blinding him?

"Parker," Alice said softly. "You need to let others help out sometimes. We can share the load. You can't do it all on your own."

"I shared my company with you."

"I don't want money. I want you!"

He scrubbed his face. He wanted Alice too, but he needed to prove he could save his sister and then destroy Julius. He had to fix his mistake. He put his hand out. "Do you have the address for where Daisy is?"

She lifted her chin. "If you think you're going without me, just forget it."

"This is my battle, Alice. Not yours."

"Except it's not. I'm your mate. Apparently your future wife! It's always going to be *our* battle. And if you ever try to keep me from fighting at your side again, I'll… I'll…"

He raised his brows indignantly. "You'll what?"

"I'll sneak into your room and cut all your hair off while you're sleeping!" She held his gaze, never backing down.

She'd do it too.

Alice was the sort of woman who would stand by his side and not only support him, but improve him. This was one of those moments. Away from her, he was half a man. Together, they could be invincible. His lips tugged up on one side.

"Does this mean you accept my proposal?"

She put her hands on her hips. "No, it doesn't. That was a shitty proposal. Do better!"

"I bought you an entire closet, and you tried to send it back. I didn't exactly think you were the flowers and chocolate type."

She dug into her pocket and threw something in his face. He caught it, opened his fingers. It was a Chinese Flower Knot made from purple rope. He frowned. Hadn't that been in his office desk drawer?

"Not a flowers kinda girl, huh?" She scowled. "I've been carrying that around in my pocket for days. Whatever. Let's go."

His cheeks heated, and he hated getting it so wrong. Everything was wrong. He pocketed the flower, resolving to deal with it later.

"So they all got out of the country all right?" he asked, squinting up at the wet sky. "Tell me at least that part of my plan worked."

"I've been a little busy trying to get you out of here, but as far as I know, each leader's biometrics were captured. AIMI has been working to disable their systems. I asked the Sinners to provide back up one last time, and as before, one has partnered with each of your family to visit each site."

"Even Griffin?"

She nodded. "They all decided this was the make-or-break moment. All hands on deck."

"Good. And what happened after I was arrested? Did the Syndicate leave the penthouse without drama?"

"One of them said something cryptic to Wyatt as they left. Something about this being the beginning of the end for us."

"What do you think?"

"I think Julius is keeping a lot of knowledge to himself. Axel said he's been ignoring Syndicate calls. The attacks on the cathedral were all Julius. He went through a phase of blaming the Sisterhood for all his problems and just wanted retribution. It had nothing to do with the grander Syndicate plan. Now he's moved onto something else. Something he won't share with Axel or the rest of them, only his lead scientist."

"And you trust this Axel guy?"

Alice bit her lip. "I think he's sick. Dying. And somehow he thought his only hope was to work with the Syndicate so his younger sister won't go into foster care when he dies. He's had his hopes twisted, just like all the Faithful. I don't think he's a bad man, just someone in a crappy situation. I've done bad things in order to survive. So have you. He knows it's not right, and he's trying to correct it."

Interesting. Parker searched his partner's face and knew she believed it.

"Where is he now?"

"He's waiting for us somewhere near the docks." She shook her head. "I think Daisy is underground in the sewers."

"So Daisy has been under our noses the entire time. Makes sense why the tracking wasn't working. We should have searched for them earlier." Parker wanted to be sick. Julius had somehow managed to evade Parker for years. This time, he wouldn't get away. This time, Parker was going to end things for good. "We go and save Daisy. The family will take down the international Syndicate machine and we destroy Julius."

"Hopefully by the day's end, we'll be done with the bastards, once and for all."

"Alice," he said, and lifted her chin so their eyes met. "Thank you."

"For what?"

"For never giving up."

"You'd do the same for me. You *have* done the same."

His mind went back to the man his fist went through and couldn't rouse an inch of regret. "I would do it again."

Even if it landed him in prison.

thirty-six

ALICE MONTGOMERY

IT WAS mid-morning as Alice and Parker walked along the docks. Seagulls squawked from their hidden perches on walls, their wings flapping about in the increasing rain. Wind buffeted. Ocean waves crashed against the harbor rocks. The day was turning out to be miserable, and Alice was not looking forward to where they had to go.

Parker removed his jacket. He tried to offer it to Alice, but she ignored him so he tossed it into a trash can and then rolled up his shirt sleeves to bare one metallic arm, one flesh and tattooed. The Yin-Yang symbol was balanced. Alice had foregone her Sinner uniform and simply wore black athletic attire, her hair poison-pinned into a low bun. Her short sword was strapped between her shoulder blades and gave her a sense of comfort. Parker continued to touch her in small ways, and she continued to swat him, despite knowing he probably needed her balancing influence. She was still passively pissed off at him.

Future wife.

Pfft.

First, he had to *ask* said future wife for her consent, not just *decree* it so. This wasn't Medieval England. She rolled her eyes and stuffed her anger deep down, vowing to deal with it after they rescued Daisy.

This sister meant a lot to Parker, and Alice knew a thing or two about never leaving a sister behind. So she was all in. The rest of the Lazarus siblings were still abroad, infiltrating and dismantling the overseas Syndicate bases, each with a Sinner to help. Joe had told Alice the Feds watched Lazarus House, so going back there to regroup was impossible. Alice had broken Parker out of prison, and they were about to rescue Daisy, but neither of them talked about what would happen after.

Even if they did succeed and saved Daisy, Parker's identity—and the rest of the family's—had been compromised. She'd broken him out of custody. That was a felony. If caught, they'd both go to prison for a very long time. The Sisterhood had a contingency plan, which was basically to fall on her sword and go to Hell, but she refused to go there—literally and figuratively. Not now when she had hope in her life, so she'd already come up with multiple options. They could leave the country. She could have one of the other family members dress up as Pride while Parker was incarcerated, proving that they couldn't be the same person. They could bribe a judge. There were so many scenarios running through her head that she almost missed the landmark where Axel said to meet.

"There's supposed to be a storm drain around here somewhere," she murmured, scanning the rocky embankment below the docks.

A few fishermen walked around, still left from the early morning markets, but none had eyes on Alice or Parker. It seemed like a storm was coming, and everyone was finishing up. He hopped down onto the rocky bank and held out his hand to her.

She ignored him and lowered herself. His jaw clenched at her dismissal. They picked their way across the boulders and jagged limestone, avoiding the crashing waves, until they found the large storm drain dribbling water into the ocean. Surrounded by cobblestone bricks, the tunnel was big enough for a tall man to fit. An iron grate stopped wayward people walking into the underground system. The light tang of sewage and acrid mold wafted out, making Alice crinkle her nose.

"Cardinal City has a combined waste system. Both storm and sewage." Parker scratched his scruff. With a sharp gaze, he searched around. "Interesting place for a Syndicate base."

"Julius is insane. Maybe he moved Daisy here because he's gone out on his own. He's already ignored the Syndicate's directives. He's obsessing over the past—coming after us Sinners, blaming us for it all going wrong in the first place. And he's been taking some kind of serum. What did he call it at the party?"

"Gene therapy," Parker answered dryly.

"You all were created in a petri-dish, right?"

He arched a brow. "That's a gross over simplification. *Gene therapy* isn't exactly the same thing as what happened to us. It's possible Julius has been taking a modified version of the greed serum, making him strong and potentially able to sense sin."

A rogue wave buffeted the rocks, spraying mist onto their faces. Along with the rain from the sky, they were well and truly soaked.

"Greed serum?" Alice frowned and cast her mind back over the reconnaissance she'd done for the Sisterhood and remembered an incident with Lilo and Griffin near the monorail. And a beast of some sort. "Wait. That *thing-man* that kidnapped Lilo had the serum?"

"Correct. It's nasty stuff. It allows the recipient to sense sin, but also amplifies every other sense. The user would become extra strong, extra irrational, and basically the sin incarnate. But the user would also burn up all their cells and die from serum. It didn't take long for Donald Doppenger to die after ingesting too much serum. Days, if not hours after his overdose at the end. He still became a force before his final breath."

"*Jesus.* I wonder if this serum is making Julius delusional. Axel said he's been talking about seeing his family again." The dead one.

Parker canted his head and squinted up at the rocky horizon to the docks. "Someone is coming."

Alice couldn't see anything yet, but then boots dangled over the embankment and Axel hopped down onto the rocks on the other side of the drain. She looked at her partner—fiancé, if he had his way—and wondered how far those senses could reach.

"Hey," Axel greeted grimly, still in his CCFD T-shirt. Soot smudged his cheeks. The light rain had caused tracks of black to run down his skin, but Alice couldn't blame the soot for the dark circles beneath his eyes. There was a sadness in the soul-deep brown depths. He flicked the torch on and scanned the drain through the grate.

Parker glared at him. "So what's your deal?"

"He means, thank you for helping him out of jail," she added quickly.

Parker cleared his throat and folded his arms, but gave a short curt nod.

"Don't mention it." Axel exhaled. "Look, my deal is that in a moment of weakness I signed up for something I shouldn't have and have been regretting it ever since."

Parker's voice turned hard. "And that means we should just trust you?"

Alice thwacked him on the chest. "He helped you get out of jail. Have a little faith."

"No, it's okay," Axel said to her. "I get it. I wouldn't trust me either. All I can say is I'm the only one who can take you to Despair. So you're stuck with me."

"Daisy," Parker corrected.

Axel stared at him and then nodded. For some reason, this made Parker tense and narrow his eyes.

"Why are you doing this?" he pressed.

Lines etched around Axel's eyes and bracketed his mouth before he answered. "When I first heard about this replication offer from the Syndicate, it seemed too good to be true. I mean, a chance to cheat death? Who wouldn't want that? And the fact the recruiter was hot didn't hurt things."

"You better not be talking about my sister," Parker warned.

Axel ignored him. He'd made it sound like the choice was no big deal, but Alice knew there was more to it.

She lifted her chin. "You should tell Parker why you're really doing this."

Axel's eyes darted nervously to Parker. He hesitated. So Alice spoke first.

"He's protecting his little sister," she said.

Parker's eyes whipped to Alice's. "We all have shit going on. Doesn't mean we join a radical terrorist cell intent on taking down the world."

"I made a bad choice," Axel agreed. "And I'm trying to fix it."

"Are you sure you're not doing this for revenge?" Parker leaned forward and bared his sharp teeth. "I mean, suddenly you're helping us when your boss has failed to hold up his end of the bargain. What's to say you don't betray us the moment you get a better offer?"

"We don't have time to debate." Alice tugged Parker. "Let's go and find Daisy."

He looked like he trusted Axel about as far as he could throw him, but nodded. They were running out of time. Alice felt it in her bones. The rain came down harder, and the water running from the drain had increased.

"First, we need to get through the grate," Axel said. "I didn't realize it was rusted shut. The only other way into this system was via Syndicate Tower and I wouldn't want to go there. Too much trouble with other members of the Faithful still guarding. If we can get in here, we have about a thirty-minute walk."

While Alice and Axel searched the grate for weak spots, Parker simply grabbed two bars, tensed until his muscles bulged obscenely in his shirt, and pulled. Metal creaked. Groaned. The rust crumbled, and he opened the grate, heedless of the gushing water flooding his designer shoes.

"Let's go," Parker said.

Together they followed Axel further into the system. The tunnel walls were made from a combination of bricks and concrete pipe. Cobwebs and moss covered everything. Critters crawled. The smell made Alice want to puke, but she kept going. The water wasn't so bad with the fresh rain.

As they walked deeper into underground Cardinal City, Parker became increasingly agitated. They came to an intersection, and he put his hand on a metal vent-like contraption on the wall, next to some smaller pipes and an old lever, pausing to think.

"What?" she whispered, hardly able to see in the dark. Axel was the only one with a torch.

"It's a sluice gate," Parker explained. "We've passed a few already. They stop or allow the flow of water."

"Is there water on the other side?"

"I can hear it." He nodded grimly. "We need to be careful. Despite what you may think, these sewers aren't safe. There are multiple layers and levels of pipes and tunnels. The city has over thirty-five-hundred miles of pipes, and not all of them are walkable like this one. Some of them old. Some of them new. If anyone activates the sluice gates, this can be flooded, especially on a day like this."

"I've been down here a few times for work. The rain has just started. We'll be fine for an hour or two," Axel said. "As long as we hurry."

They rushed after him, Parker seeing better than either of them and keeping Alice from falling down when she lost her footing. Begrudgingly, she accepted his help. If she hurt her leg now, she would impede the rescue mission.

After fifteen minutes of silence, Axel said, "So… you saw Julius at the retirement party… he's not the same."

"What happened to his hair?" Parker asked.

"He keeps cutting bits and tying them on his finger. I have no idea why. But he's been increasingly secretive and erratic over the past few days. I caught him moving Syndicate equipment late at night through a weird hole in the basement wall. The morning before the party, he moved Daisy out of her usual holding cell. I only know because I followed him when he wasn't looking. He almost shot my head off when he found me. I managed to convince him I was on his side, but… he's gone crazy. Don't expect to reason with him."

"Replicate tanks?" Parker asked. "Where is the American base, because it's not at Syndicate Tower. I know this much. We've had eyes on it for years. It's mainly office space."

"You're right," Axel confirmed. "The Tower is a front. Mostly. There are a few handfuls of tanks, mainly for demonstration purposes for recruitment of the Faithful. It can be destroyed easily and covered up if the authorities raid. There were also a few closed off rooms in the basement I never got to see, so I can't say what was in there. Van Jansen—the scientist—used to head off daily to an undisclosed location somewhere nearby, but they never told me where. I was still yet to prove my loyalty enough to satisfy Julius."

"Attempted murder wasn't enough?" Parker scoffed.

"No," Axel replied darkly.

"Maybe we find this scientist and ask him," Alice suggested.

"Can't." Axel shone the torch at her and she flinched. "Julius killed him."

Alice blocked the light. "Killed his own lead scientist?"

"Well, he's disappeared." Axel shrugged and continued walking. "I'm assuming it's not good."

They all took a moment to let that sink in. If Julius had picked off his main scientist, then he no longer needed him. This was the beginning of the end.

thirty-seven
PARKER LAZARUS

PARKER LIFTED his nose as a familiar scent hit. Above the acrid stench of the tunnels, he smelled family, and fear. He couldn't understand the logic, but the base part of him belonging to The Beast knew the scent was from his own kin—Daisy. And she was afraid.

He ran.

"*Shit.*" Alice stumbled behind him and then shouted for him to not be a cowboy and do something stupid.

But he had to. Every instinct in his body knew his sister needed him. These same instincts knew Alice would be okay. The danger was ahead, not behind.

That scent of Daisy's fear traveled over the water, prickling his nerves. He pushed onward, knowing the sooner he got to her, the better. He squelched through gushing water. He bounded over ridges and debris. Minutes felt like hours. He lost his companions and soon the sound became just wet steps and his breath filling the tunnels. When Daisy's scent grew strongest, he slowed to a silent stalk. Claws sprung from his fingertips, his teeth elongated, his vision and hearing strained. For the first time since he'd developed his new abilities, he was thankful for them.

Drip, drip, drip.

Splashing.

Rodents scurrying.

Breathing.

At a four-way tunnel intersection, he heard the mumbling curses of a man. The sense of pride—*sin*... so much it cramped Parker's stomach. *Julius.* He was down the left tunnel. Daisy's scent was to the right. Straight ahead sounded like—he cocked his head—it sounded like people working. Shuffling. Rhythmic thudding. Splashing. Could there be service workers here, now, during a storm?

Keeping his steps quiet, Parker turned right and went for Daisy. He almost missed the sound of her breathing through an offshoot of narrow pipe. He had to crouch to get to her. When he emerged through the pipe and into another small circular space, he found her chained to a rusted ladder.

"Daisy," he whispered and squatted as water rained down in streams from a drain opening two levels above. She was half submerged, head slumped, silver hair floating where it met the water. Cold to the touch, but her heartbeat was strong. "Hey."

He shifted hair from her face. Long eyelashes fluttered. Eyes opened and focused on him. No obvious injuries. Just exhaustion, dehydration, and malnutrition. Possible internal damage, considering what Axel and Prudence had said about Daisy's treatment by Julius. She needed a hospital.

"Pigeon?" Daisy whispered, her voice a rasp.

He paused, his mind going back to their rooftop with the birds. He'd told no one her nickname for him. Had always hated it, but now there was no sweeter word.

"Yeah, I'm here. I'm going to take you home."

"You shouldn't have come," she mumbled. "I don't deserve it."

"Of course I should," he clipped. "I won't leave you again."

"You don't understand," she said. "I'm bait."

"Then we better hurry." He picked up her chains and yanked until they snapped, his metal fingers making quick work of crushing them. Daisy gave his bionic hand a quick, curious look. She'd missed so much while entrapped by Julius.

Snarls somewhere behind him.

Little hairs on the back of his neck stood on end. He checked down the solitary pipe he'd come. If whatever had snarled came through here, there would be nowhere to hide and little room to fight. The sense of Julius's deadly pride *surged* in Parker's gut.

"Can you move?" he asked his sister.

She nodded, but when she tried to stand, she couldn't. Concern bloomed in Parker's chest. "Stay here, D. Stay safe. Alice is coming. She's my mate. You can trust her. I'll be back."

Then he ducked back through the pipe and followed the snarling and sense of pride until he made it back to the intersection. Alice's and Axel's footsteps drew closer, but were still a few minutes out. He must have run fast to create such a big lead... or Alice's leg was bothering her. He frowned as worry for her wrapped around his heart.

Better deal with Julius and whatever belonged to those snarls before she arrived.

A shadow emerged from the gloom of one tunnel. A tall, pale man with a head of uneven white hair. The chunks cut out were worse. Almost no hair was left. *Julius.* Dirty suit—the same one he wore at Parker's party. Probably hadn't slept. Probably because he was down here, messing with things he shouldn't. The iPad in his hands blinked with a running software program.

The replicate program?

Parker glanced down the tunnel with snarls and workers. Not workers. Replicates.

"I thought you were in jail," Julius said casually, his hair-tied index finger inching toward a button on the device's screen.

"Touch it, and you die."

Julius launched into fits of laughter. "You won't win. You can't."

"And why not? I can rip those replicates apart with my hands. And then I'm coming for you. Surrender."

More laughter. Parker bared his teeth and snarled.

"Whoops." Julius lifted the iPad as Parker stepped forward, ready to decimate. "I wouldn't come closer if I were you."

"You're a dead man." Parker hurtled forward, reached with his bionic hand, wrapped it around Julius's throat and just when Parker's fingers should have crushed the man's windpipe, Julius tapped his screen. A tap. That's all it took, and Parker's metal arm became a dead weight, dropping to his side.

What the hell?

Shock barreled through him as he tried to lift his arm. It wouldn't respond. His wild eyes shot to Julius's satisfied face.

"You see, *boy*, you had your reasons for coming to that party, and I had mine. And they weren't to get Gloria's research. Maybe they were a bonus, but I'm beyond her now." His lips curved. "I wanted to know who I was up against and how to beat you."

He tapped the iPad again. Parker's arm made whirring sounds. The lights along the seams glowed in warning. The same thing happened when he serviced it. Cold horror washed through Parker. Was Julius controlling his arm? "What did you do?"

"How could you forget that arm came from a Syndicate lab? I recognized it the moment you attacked me at the party. I thought you were the one to beat. The king of the Lazarus family. But you'll always be the apple that fell far from my tree."

Parker blinked, still disbelieving. He had completely rewired and recoded the technology. Hadn't he? Or hadn't Flint or Sloan? *Goddamn it.* This was what happened when someone else took over a job *he* could do better. Loopholes. Weak spots to exploit. There must have been a back door.

Parker's pride took a serious hit. His Yin-Yang tattoo itched like hell as it adjusted to his new equilibrium. He wanted to roar his furious shame through the tunnel, but bit his tongue until it bled.

"Oh," Julius laughed. "And don't forget this part, too."

He tapped the screen and then Parker's arm detached from his stump and dangled in Parker's torn shirt. Then the shirt ripped under the weight and the arm splashed into the waste water. Like blind snakes, wires in his stump searched for the couplings they just lost. Nausea washed over him as the metal arm sank. *This can't be happening.* How could he not have predicted this? Or planned for it? Or made the arm goddamned unhackable?

Because you've been too busy trying to do everything yourself.

Just like Alice had warned him. But… letting people help got his arm hacked. If Parker had taken the time to assess the bionic arm himself, surely he would have found the security leak. Surely.

A stream of torchlight hit them from behind. Alice and Axel. That simple light leading to his mate reminded him of how he'd lost his arm in the first place. Pride.

Shit happened when he accepted help, but it was worse when he tried to do it on his own.

Julius's face contorted into something ugly, and he cursed at their intrusion. He lifted a gun. Aimed. Parker snapped out of his shock and dropped to the water, searching for his arm. If he could get it reattached… His fingers brushed metal—

"Look out!" Alice shouted.

Gunfire. Concrete crumbled. Water splashed. Something snarled. Was Alice okay?

He searched behind him—glimpsed her pointing her sword at a figure near him, and then a dark shape hit Parker, knocking him to his side. His head submerged, and all he could think of was Alice. He rolled to his feet. Instinct saved him. His good arm whipped out, the heel of his palm hit the body—a replicate—recoiling him. One after another, more figures arrived and Parker hit them, sending them flying backward. Four... five... six. They weren't right. Half were naked, the other half had clothing hanging from them in tatters. His hits would have stopped a normal man, but these replicates picked themselves up like zombies. Scratched faces and bloody stumps for fingers. But it was their eyes that horrified Parker. Life and acknowledgment existed there. Trapped. They knew what was happening to them. These people had been remade and reborn from Faithful donated DNA. They'd thought their new lives would be glorious, but they were puppets on Julius's strings.

The man himself was already disappearing down a tunnel, the glow from his device glancing off the curved walls as he ran to a safe distance. When he turned back, the glow lit up his sinister face from beneath.

"Like I said to your sister," Julius shouted, his voice echoing. "Your hope is futile. You can't win. I've planned for all variables."

Parker pushed a replicate underwater until he ran out of breath. His resistance was strong, but not enough for the strength pumping through Parker's arm.

"You didn't plan for us tracking you around the world," Parker shot back, unable to stop himself from returning a taunt. Maybe if he could keep Julius here, he could finish these replicates and deal with him once and for all. He kicked out as a second replicate came for him and connected.

In his periphery, Axel jammed a knife into a replicate's eye, and Alice sliced through a third replicate. He smiled at her form. *Magnificent.* His tattoo itched, pride shooting higher. Maybe that's what he needed, to turn into a mindless pride monster and just obliterate Julius.

"Didn't I?" Julius shouted, a manic grin on his face as he tapped away on that cursed iPad. "I knew exactly what would happen when I dragged her around, all tortured and full of despair."

A replicate's punch to Parker's face sent him reeling, just as Julius's words had done. He knew?

And then from his memory, Julius's words at the party came back. "*It was never about them.*" At the time Parker had thought Julius meant his family—the wife and daughter he was trying to raise from the dead. They were his sole purpose for doing all of this. But those words hadn't quite made sense in the context, and now he realized why. Just before Julius had spoken those words, Parker had mentioned every Syndicate base location.

It was never about them.

Meaning, never about the Syndicate. By dragging Daisy around to the sites, suspecting she had a tracking device on her, Julius ensured the doom and destruction of the greater Syndicate operation. He'd planned for their demise.

"You wanted them destroyed," Parker revealed. "Why?"

"They thought they could control me," he shouted. "Me! The man who started all this. They wanted me to give up my—" Julius cut himself off, closed his eyes and tapped his collarbone. "*Not long, my loves.*" Julius took a deep breath, rallied, and met Parker's eyes. "I don't need them anymore to get what I want. You see, your sister did me a favor when she destroyed the last piece of DNA from my wife and child. I realize that now. She showed me what truly mattered, and it wasn't a world without sin, it was simply them. I just want *them.* And now, with these uncontrolled replicates, through a miracle, I can find them again. I don't need to bring them to me when it's far easier for me to go to them!"

He was talking about what Alice had claimed, what the Sinners had warned about. Parker gaped. But that was insane. Wasn't it? "Hell isn't real, Julius. You've gone mad."

"It's not Hell." He jerked, affronted. "It's just another dimension where souls go after here."

"And you have proof of that?"

"The only proof I need is in my heart." He tapped his chest. "I know they're waiting for me. I heard her."

Alarmed, Parker met Alice's eyes across the intersection. Hearing his dead wife? Even if there was another dimension, there was no proof there were souls on the other side. There was no proof it was Hell. Damn it, there was no proof of *anything.* For all they knew, it was a glitch in the replicate programming.

Parker didn't give a fuck what it was. That wasn't his job. His job was to stop Julius, to stop sin in *this* world. Here and now. And for that, he needed his arm. Alice jumped into the water to help him search, but the moment they dropped their guard, more replicates surged down the tunnel, barreling past Julius, almost bowling him over.

And then he felt it. A tingle in the air. An electrical current. One of these replicates was powered—the same as Evan. *Electricity.*

"Got it!" Alice lifted his bionic arm.

"Get out of the water!" he shouted at her. "They're powered."

With the grace of a dancer, Alice jumped backward and clung to a ridge on the wall. Parker dove into the smaller tunnel leading to Daisy. He would survive a jolt of electricity, but if he wanted to reinstall his arm, he couldn't afford to fry the wires at his stump.

Lightning surged through the water, electrocuting anything it touched. Including all the other replicates. They cooked. Steam rose.

Stupid, Parker thought. Julius had just wiped out his own army. Julius realized the same thing and worked on his iPad again. Parker expected more replicates to arrive, but he must have exhausted his supply. A sluice gate separating the offshoot pipe from the intersection dropped, blocking Parker from Alice.

"No!" he shouted, and hit the gate. "Alice!"

The metal wall was solid. No way through. He searched around and found no lever. It must be on the other side, or it was all run by a computer system. That's how Julius had triggered it. Another wave of electricity surged, this time conducting through the metal sluice gate, zapping Parker's hand. He jerked back with a wince.

Silence beyond.

"Alice!"

His heart stopped. It broke. This was his fault. All of it. Alice had followed him into this tunnel to save Daisy. She'd told him not to run off on his own, and look what happened. Julius outmaneuvered him at every corner. His tattoo itched as his internal sin balance shifted. Pride plummeted and shame rose. He hit himself in the head. *Stupid.*

His balance was changing too fast. It was Parker who'd invented the bio-indicator ink Evan used in the tattoo. This system was of his devising. He knew the consequences of ignoring it but all he could think of was the biggest shame in his life. That moment, thirty years ago, when Daisy had rushed out of the elevator and into the flame riddled room. He could have stopped her. He'd seen her lower the bonsai plant. He had time to stop her as she brushed past him, but he'd been afraid. A coward.

Parker continued down the narrow pipe to emerge in the curved, tall drain cavity. Still weak, Daisy kept her head above the increasing water by holding onto the ladder.

That's why he'd raced ahead of Alice to get here. He had to prove that one was worth the many. They all were.

And now Alice might be dead. The sluice gate was closed, the water fell from the sky, and they were trapped. In his efforts to save one, he might have killed them all.

"Pigeon?" Daisy asked. "What happened to your arm?"

Shame exploded in Parker, tipping his internal sin equilibrium to unstable. Blackness clouded his vision and the sin in the vicinity amplified. *Pride.* It choked him. He sensed it pulsing somewhere in the tunnels behind the sluice gate, and all he could think was to eradicate it. Eliminate the deadly sin. There was no thought. No reason. Just instinct—Kill.

thirty-eight

DAISY LAZARUS

DAISY WATCHED as the change came over Parker. It started out as a small thing. He shook his head, blinked a few times, and then used his beard to scratch his inner wrist, right over the Yin-Yang tattoo. But she knew those movements. She'd felt them herself. He was blacking out, succumbing to that darker side they all held within —the uncontrolled berserker that needed to eradicate anyone with the sin of pride coursing through their veins.

When Daisy had seen his arm was missing, and that he'd come back here—for her—pride had swelled in her body. He'd grown into a hero. Her little brother, her Pigeon, saving her. This was the same little brother who'd stubbornly insisted on doing things his way, but always forgot about his ego when she called him to adventure. He'd hated how she'd called him Pigeon, thinking it was because of the way he ate. But she'd called him that because he reminded her not only of the freedom birds they played with, but of a story about Parker's favorite inventor—Nikola Tesla.

She still remembered the two of them giggling over the book. Nikola Tesla had nursed a pigeon back to health and then fallen in love with it. Nikola claimed the bird was the love and joy of his life, that as long as she was around, there was purpose in his life. Parker had liked the story because he learned about, in his opinion, the greatest inventor of all time. She'd liked the story because it made her realize what her purpose was. The joy of her family, starting with the obsessively serious, first little brother. Her pigeon. Her purpose. She knew if she could bring joy to his life, she could bring joy to all of them.

And now he stared at her like he wanted to rip her to shreds.

She glanced down at her own Yin-Yang tattoo, only just shy of the balance line. She could thank Parker for that. He'd insisted she get the tattoo to keep herself in check and she'd used the markers frequently while captive to keep herself from disappearing into nothingness.

Parker stalked her through water pouring from the storm drain above. He was no longer her sweet, stubborn pigeon. He was a hunter. A beast. But he still needed her help.

She emptied her mind of all prideful things. She thought about birds flapping their wings above her in the dawn sky. Of stars twinkling. Of freedom. She closed her eyes and winced, knowing there was nothing else she could do to protect herself from an attack in this state. Maybe a few weeks ago she could, but Julius had drained her dry with his experiments and, right now, she barely had the energy to keep herself afloat.

She held her breath and waited for his attack. It was what she deserved, anyway. She should just let him take her. But the image of a pigeon kept invading her mind. Parker was her purpose—her family. She opened her eyes and found now that she felt zero pride, he'd given up on her and had crouched to get back through the offshoot pipe. The water was rising. He would drown if he went down there.

"Parker," she said. "Stop."

He faced her with eyes of luminous gold. His tattoo still said it had too much light in it. That meant a lack of pride. Shame. So she had to make him feel something other than that. She had to make him feel pride. So she listed his accomplishments.

"You're the leader of the Deadly Seven. You kept your family alive when I couldn't. You created a Fortune 500 company. You invented many things, just like Nikola Tesla. You did it, Parker. You found your freedom." She fired off anything she could think of, which wasn't much. Parker advanced on her slowly, like a cat in the grass, stalking its prey. Nothing was getting through to him, but she had to keep trying. "You found your mate. You said her name is Alice." He was inches away from her, heedless of the rain gushing down his face and splashing in the water level, now rising faster and up to his thighs. "She must be amazing. She's a Sinner, right? Like Mary? She must be—"

He snapped at her face. She jerked back as his fangs missed her nose. Trembling, she couldn't look at him. Instead, she kept her eyes down to the water rising and the cord of purple rope floating by his pants. The length led to an intricately knotted flower, half tucked into his pants. It was such an odd thing for him to carry that she hoped it meant something to him. She yanked it and held it before his face like a shield.

Golden eyes flickered. He frowned at the knotted flower and took it from her hands.

"Alice," he mumbled.

"Did she do that?" Daisy asked.

"No. But she—" he squeezed his eyes shut and clenched his fist around the knot.

Thick despair rolled into Daisy, and she almost swooned from the drag of it. He was sad. So, so sad. It was the same despair she felt daily from Julius. It was dangerous.

"Tell me about her."

"She's dead."

"I don't believe that."

His eyes met hers. "She was out there with a powered replicate."

"But she's your mate. She must be incredible."

He stilled. He glanced at the flower. Daisy could have sworn she felt his joy like a warm drink on a chilly night. Then he straightened his spine. "She *is* incredible. She beat me in a battle. I lost my arm because I was too proud to admit how incredible she was. And now because of my pride, she might be lost to me."

"Then you should tell her."

"Didn't you just hear what I said? She might be dead."

"She's alive. If she can beat you, she can handle one replicate."

Coming back to himself, he nodded, eyes now full of sharp purpose. "You're right. She can handle herself. But us..." He glanced at the rising water level and at the offshoot pipe, now submerged. "We need to survive."

Relief washed through her and she slumped, her fingers slipping on the ladder. She wasn't sure if she had the energy to do as he said, but he must have known that. He held out the knotted flower to her.

"Help me unravel it."

"Why?"

"I only have one arm, so if I'm climbing the ladder I can't hold on to you. I'm hoping the rope is long enough to tie you to me so, if you can't hold on, it will keep you afloat."

Within the short time it took them to unravel the rope, the water had risen to their chins. The rope was long enough to loop around their bodies. It hurt under Daisy's arms, and her lips chattered from the cold. But they weren't dead yet.

She looked up at her little brother.

"What?" He took hold of the ladder rung.

"Don't leave me behind," she whispered, the horrors of last time igniting in her mind, hot like the flames that engulfed her birth mother.

"Never again."

Their ascent was painstakingly slow. A one-armed man and a woman at death's door. Every labored step Daisy took up the ladder, the water did the same. It was like a breath on the back of her neck, following her, holding her trembling nerves for ransom. Parker tried to help her, but he was losing his own battle to despair. More than once she'd seen him glance at his missing arm with frustration.

"You should just let me go," Daisy said, her teeth chattering. "I'm slowing you down."

"Stop it," he said. "We'll make it."

But the water level was rising faster than they could climb. Her numb fingers slipped on the metal rung and she almost fell. The rope under her arms burned, holding her to Parker. He looked down at the water, eyes full of calculations.

"Maybe we let go and float up." He winced and looked up. "A grate covers the drain. If we can't get out, then hopefully we can still access air."

Hopefully.

He said the words but didn't feel them, she would sense it. She slumped with nothing left to give. She hadn't for a long time. Maybe not since she'd chased after a woman whose despair had been a close companion of Daisy's her entire life. For years she'd sensed Gloria Godiva's joy and despair fluctuate from beyond a two-way mirror. Daisy was different to her siblings. She felt their joy as well as their sin. So when she'd seen the woman with her own eyes, and thought maybe if she could get to her and give her a cuddle, then she would be happy. It had always worked.

But the flames had other ideas.

Closing her eyes, she heard her birth mother's voice whisper from the smokey shadows of her memory. *Live, special one. Live.* But Daisy wasn't special. Like Julius had said, she was the test run. The prototype the rest of them were made from.

"You're not the test run," Parker gaped.

She must have said that aloud. "But I am. Julius said it all the time. I was the first. The imperfect prototype."

Water surrounded them, lifting them like the tide. Parker's legs wrapped around her, a safety net in case the rope failed. With only five feet left to go before they hit the storm grate blocking the street, they knew they were out of time. The gaps between the iron were too small for a hand to fit through. Water was coming in from above at an alarming rate, and once it overflowed, they would drown.

His jaw worked, his teeth ground, and his eyes were fierce and lit with the kind of spirit she'd only ever dreamed of.

"Listen to me, Daisy, when I say this. I read Gloria's research. I committed it to memory and then I destroyed it because I was ashamed of this"—he flinched—"beast she made of me. I should never have hid the truth from my family, you included. I was jealous because the truth was, she started with perfect. You got the best. She made you the strongest." His eyes were suns breaking clouds through the storm. "Do you understand? She made *you* perfect."

Her throat clogged. Her eyes burned. "But I'm not."

"What you are is a Lazarus. And we never quit. Come on." He looked up and started climbing again. Even if she wasn't sure if she believed Parker's words, he did. And the damned bastard was usually right. Daisy rallied her strength and put her hands back on the rungs.

"Look, Daisy," he said as his face tilted toward the grate, two feet away. "What do you see?"

Daisy followed his stare and latched onto a small patch of blue sky struggling to hold its own against the storm. Her lips curved. "I see freedom."

thirty-nine

ALICE MONTGOMERY

"THIS WAY," Axel said to Alice and beckoned her toward a ladder leading up to a manhole.

Her leg was killing her and the robotic arm weighed a ton, but she refused to let Axel carry it. She had no idea how Parker had lived with it attached to his body. Would *still* live, she promised herself. Not *had* lived. Never that. She was willing to bet her life that he was okay on the other side of that sluice gate.

He was too stubborn to die.

They were a block from where the powered replicate had tried to electrocute them. The second wave of voltage wasn't as powerful as the first. She'd survived. And then she'd run her sword through the clone's neck.

Julius fled the moment he realized most of his replicates were taken out by one of his own. She wasn't even sure he'd shut the sluice gate. It could have been an automatic city process activated by the storm. Whoever was at fault, the outcome remained the same. She'd been cut off from Parker. The tunnels were flooding, and Julius was gone. There was nothing they could do but get out and hope Parker and Daisy had the same opportunity.

Axel shoved the manhole lid aside, and they emerged onto a city street. Frigid rain poured down from the cloud riddled sky. It was so dark it felt like the evening, not mid-afternoon. A car slid to a stop, narrowly missing hitting them. The driver, an elderly man, gaped at them through the windshield.

"Sorry!" Axel held out his palm.

Once on the street, Axel and Alice moved the manhole cover back into position and they jogged to the side, taking cover from the rain beneath a closed bakery awning.

"Is your cell working?" Alice asked him. Her own was waterlogged.

He pulled his out. "It's waterproof."

"I need to make a call." Without waiting for permission, she took the cell and dialed Parker's number. Dead. Next she dialed Mary's and made a silent prayer of gratitude that she'd memorized it when working as Parker's assistant. Mary picked up after two rings.

"Yes?" Mary answered.

"Mary, it's Alice."

A pause. "Alice?"

In the background, a baby cried. Must be Amari.

"Have you heard from Parker?" she asked.

Another pause. "No… was I supposed to?"

Shit.

It's fine. It meant nothing. Parker could still be fine. "We've had a situation," she explained. "I need his watch tracked."

"Hold on."

Two seconds later, Flint spoke. "Alice, it's Flint. What do you need?"

For some stupid reason, it was the deep timbre of his voice that threatened to undo Alice. He would do everything in his power to save his family... and she was part of it. She almost choked on her next words. "Parker is stuck down a drain with Daisy. I don't know where they are. I have his arm. I'm on a borrowed cell. Julius... he—I don't know if they're okay."

"I'm on it." A long, drawn out pause. "AIMI said he's about a block east of you. Keep me on the line."

They jogged down the street in the direction Flint gave, talking as they went. "Is anyone back from the mission?" Alice asked.

"No. But all are safe. All are on their way back."

"And the Sinners?"

"Safe too. Alice... it was a success."

She swallowed as she ran. Hopefully this would be too. She turned a corner and Flint shot out. "You're about five feet away from the tracking beacon in his watch."

She searched the street. Traffic was low because of the rain and most people were indoors, but the storm was easing and a few were coming out of the residential buildings. It should have been easy to spot Parker.

"He's not here," she said.

"The drain." Axel pointed.

At the corner of two streets was a cast iron grate with puddles dribbling into it, and three sets of fingers gripping onto the bars. Alice's heart surged in her chest. They were alive. But as they ran, water bubbled up and over from inside the grate. They wouldn't be alive for long if they couldn't open it.

"Parker," Alice shouted, dropping the cell and running to him. Two pale faces tilted to the grate, trying to breathe through the water gushing around them. There was too much for him to talk clearly, but she saw the relief in his eyes as she arrived. "I'm here."

Placing the bionic arm down, she gripped the grate and pulled, but it was stuck tight. Axel joined her and yanked as hard as he could. She unsheathed her sword and stabbed the edges, trying to break any attachment between the iron and the asphalt, but her attempts were in vain.

"It's no use," Axel said, pushing to a stand. "It's welded shut. I'll see if I can get an angle grinder from a resident."

"Parker, you need to push!" she shouted into the drain. "Push as hard as you can, just like you did by the ocean."

Doubt flickered in Parker's golden eyes and Daisy spluttered, choking as water entered her mouth. Alarmed, Alice slammed her fist on the grate and lowered her face until she was inches from Parker. They locked eyes. She touched his fingers with her own, seeing the visible reaction come over him as his internal sin equalized.

"I know you want to suppress that part of you," she rasped. "But you need to use it. Forget about how it made you feel in the past. Look forward, not back. Use The Beast, Parker. Even with one hand you have the strength to bust this wide open. Stop holding back and *use* him. You still owe me flowers, damn it!"

Claws sprung from Parker's fingertips. His eyes glowed as he unleashed a wet snarl.

"That's right, baby. More. Let him in more. You know I love him too." Parker startled. He blinked at her through spiked lashes, and she realized she'd said she loved him. She loved all of him. And she loved how right those words had felt. *"Come on!"*

Alice planted her feet, looped her fingers around the grate and when Parker's growl became a restrained roar, when she heard the iron groaning in resistance, she added her strength, as meager as it was because she knew they would always be a team. If he went down, she would too. They'd fall or fly together.

Daisy's pale, slender fingers slotted through the gaps and pushed.

Axel came running back, minus a grinder, and skidded to his knees. Together, they all strained against the barrier.

And then it broke.

More than broke. The iron grate exploded outward, throwing Alice and Axel backward. Axel shoved the bent and twisted grate aside while Alice scrambled to her knees and reached down into the water to grip her lover under the shoulders. Axel did the same for Daisy. The rising water made the lift easy and before long they were all lying on the street, lungs heaving, staring at the rain trickling from the sky.

Alice gripped Parker's face between her hands and kissed him, tears in her eyes. Then she showed him the bionic arm. "I brought you a hand, but you didn't need it."

Parker Lazarus blushed. He *blushed*. Affection washed through his expression, and he stroked her cheek before leaning forward to kiss her again. When they pulled away, he rolled to check on his sister.

Alice couldn't believe it. No gloat. No snide comment, something like "I know I'm the best." Just a humble blush and a kiss. Her heart melted.

"Daisy?" Parker's tone held a note of strain.

Daisy lay in Axel's arms, staring up at his face, her breath a wet wheeze.

"You," she whispered. "I remember you."

"Get away from her." Parker went for Axel's hand, but Daisy stopped him.

"No," she said. "He was good to me. He brought me food. I just... never saw your face until now. It's... nice."

"You recruited me," he said, frowning. "You don't remember?"

She shook her head, confused. Still holding Daisy's gaze, Axel lifted her effortlessly, determination all over his face. If Alice didn't know any better, she'd say he had the look of a man enthralled.

Daisy burst into a coughing fit, rolling her head to the side to vomit water. When she was done, Axel pulled her to his chest and gave them a grim look.

"She needs a hospital."

"She needs to come home," Parker shot back. He picked up his bionic arm. The wires were still searching, the arm still functioned, but he didn't reattach it. Maybe he wouldn't until he was certain it was unhackable.

Home.

Flint.

Alice had dropped the cell phone. She found it on the street, still connected to the call, and put it to her ear. "Flint?"

"Thank Christ. Is everyone okay?"

"So far, but—"

Parker gestured for Alice to hand him the phone. The stern look in his eyes held no room for argument so she gave it over.

"Flint," Parker said. "We have Daisy but she's sick. We're coming home."

The private conversation that came next turned every muscle in Parker's shoulders to stone. Alice had thought their troubles were over, but seeing the look on his face made her guts turn to jelly. By the time Parker cut the call two minutes later, Alice's heart kicked in her chest like a wild stallion.

"What is it?"

He flattened his lips. "We take Daisy to the hospital."

"Why?"

"It's not safe at home."

Realization hit. "It's still being watched by the Feds."

Grim eyes met hers. "That... and Wyatt is back. He's destroyed the med lab."

"What?" she blustered. "Why?"

The baby crying in the background. "Is Amari...?"

"She's fine but… Mary was babysitting when—" Parker glanced to Axel, who still held Daisy tight to his chest. Primal fury darkened Parker's face. Cold, hard intent speared Axel. "I'm going to ask you a question. And you better pray you give the right answer. Did you know?"

Axel's dark brows pinched together. "About what?"

"While my family were off following the crumbs Julius left, every one of my siblings' mates were taken." Parker's eyes were soulless when they locked on Alice. "Lilo, Misha and Bailey were out having coffee. Max and some of his crew were watching them, but they've all gone missing. Grace and Joe never showed for work."

"I didn't know," Axel blurted. "I swear."

Daisy's eyelids fluttered, and she rested her head against Axel's chest. "Julius always said doomsday meant turning you all dark. It was the reason he made me take Max that first time. I thought with everything going on that he'd given up on that plan."

"Shit." Parker scrubbed his face. "Griffin is going to kill me."

Parker had trouble breathing. He roared his pain and dropped to a crouch, his head in his hand.

"This is my fault," he murmured. "I thought I had it all worked out. The Syndicate was going down and so I loosened security restrictions early. I was that cocky. That stupid."

"No one could account for Julius's madness."

"But this was my madness. His plan never wavered. His goal was always his wife and daughter and stupid me—"

"Hey. Stop that. We will get them all back, safe and sound. You have my word that the Sisterhood will back you up. And you have something Julius never accounted for."

"What's that?"

Alice looked at Daisy. "Her."

Parker stilled, staring at his sister. He straightened. "You're right.

339

Like you said, Daisy. He thinks you're the trial run, but you're not. You're the strongest one of us all. You're our secret weapon. We just need you to find your mate."

Axel glared at them. "She's not anything unless we get her to a hospital."

"They're alive," Daisy rasped through a shuddering breath.

"How can you know?" Parker asked.

"Because I spent decades learning the ins and outs of Julius's mind, and there was one thing he loved to toy with—hope. For years he taunted me with something he would never give"—her face twisted into disgust—"calling me his darling, as though he loved me. Believe me when I say, they're still alive because so long as there is hope, there is suffering. And he wants us to suffer worse than he has."

forty

ALICE MONTGOMERY

TWO NIGHTS LATER, Alice sat at a booth in Heaven. Parker was playing a solemn song on the piano, and it set the mood for the night. He refused to open the restaurant or the nightclub next door until they were done with Julius and everyone was safe and back home.

"So it wasn't you?" Liza asked from across the table. A glass of whiskey sat untouched between her hands. She was talking about the surprise death of the executive who'd leaked footage of Parker dressed as Pride. They'd only just found out a few hours ago. Tony and Sloan also sat at the table, nursing drinks. Wyatt was in the kitchen keeping busy, his baby in a sling, keeping his wrath from slipping simply because she made him happy. Evan and Griffin were still out searching the streets. *They'd all* been out, but now needed a break and some food. Griffin refused to stop, and Evan refused to leave him alone.

"I *wish* it was me," Alice answered Liza. "I mean, I *wanted* to kill him, but Parker stopped me."

They all glanced at the man as he played morosely, but beautifully.

He'd reattached his arm after he and Flint had severed the weak security link and made adjustments to accommodate his regenerating limb. They'd added more layers of impenetrable technology, preventing Julius from ever gaining control again. More than that, they'd reverse engineered some sort of Wi-Fi coupling Julius had used to control the arm. Apparently, if he tried it again, they could use it as a weapon. They had to find him first.

"Who was it then?" Tony asked. His glowing complexion had taken a sallow turn. Alice didn't think he was eating. "Because even though the murder doesn't look good for Parker, it helps his case."

She pushed her bowl of nuts over, but he ignored them and itched his Yin-Yang tattoo. With every single mate missing, it would be up to Parker and Alice to keep the heroes in balance.

"Eat it," Alice insisted. "For Bailey."

He shot her a flat look, but picked at the nuts. "So who do you think it was, then?"

"I don't know." She thought about who would have the power to order a hit in a high profile case like that. It didn't look good for Parker, but he'd posted bail. His plan remained to be acquitted of all charges in order to add a layer of protection for the future. He couldn't be charged twice for the same thing. "I keep thinking it was the remaining members of the Syndicate. The heads were in town, and the death happened before they knew their bases had been destroyed. But, I don't know. Maybe they're cutting their losses and eliminating anyone that can be traced back to them."

"Could be," Liza said. "Thanks to Axel's and Daisy's intel, CCPD and the Feds have raided Syndicate Tower and the basement. It all adds up with Parker's story about being kidnapped from the local holding cell." She then turned toward the stage and shouted, "Hey, dickhead. How about playing something that doesn't make me want to slit my wrists?"

Parker scowled back at her, but adjusted his rhythm to something jazzy. Alice realized how much he'd changed in the past few weeks. Not only was he comfortable playing in front of his family, he was taking requests. She only wished it were under happier circumstances.

Maybe seeing his effort to open himself up was what made her do the same. She used to love singing. Then the accident happened. Then she sang for Parker. Now... she slid out of the booth and shoved Parker aside on the piano bench. When he gave her a curious look, she said softly, "Will you play Nina for me?"

"Are you sure?"

She nodded. "I'm ready."

Parker seamlessly switched to playing *My Baby Just Cares for Me*. Alice tapped the piano lid for percussion. She started singing softly, but with each verse she increased her volume until she was belting it out at the top of her lungs and they both had grins on their faces. Tony joined in until the last note died and Parker leaned in to kiss her beneath the ear.

"When I get you alone," he murmured. "There will be flowers."

"I love you," she whispered.

"I love you too."

Liza made a vomit sound but stood and clapped loudly.

"Fucking brilliant! But now your lust is killing me. Quick, I need innocent baby cuddles."

She dashed to the kitchen where Wyatt stood watching with a sad look on his face, and Alice realized that, perhaps, singing about love was the wrong song choice.

"Dinner is ready," he said, and handed the baby to Liza.

Alice turned around and found Mary, Flint, and Daisy had walked in. They'd just picked her up from the hospital. Alice glanced back at Wyatt in the kitchen, but he was busy dishing up.

"Will he be okay?" Alice asked Parker.

Daisy had tried to kidnap Misha when nine months pregnant, and hurt her. A fall had sent Misha into labor. Alice suspected the reason they couldn't come back to Lazarus House after rescuing Daisy was because Wyatt had just returned home from the mission, already out of balance, only to find that Misha was missing. He'd lost his temper and had taken it out on the basement.

"He's fine. He's calmed down," Parker replied quietly. "He knows this time Daisy had nothing to do with it."

"And last time?"

"He's got Amari to worry about now. She's keeping his sin in check."

Evan and Griffin strode in wearing their Deadly gear, their hoods pooled around their shoulders. Griffin's face was haggard, and Evan's was bleak. A simple shake of Evan's head meant they hadn't found a sign of their mates. Griffin didn't make eye contact.

Parker sighed. "Let's head to the dining room."

"Good idea. You need to say a few words while everyone is here."

"I do?"

"Absolutely."

"But I messed up."

She flashed him a smile. "Exactly. Now, you think about what you're going to say, and I'll go help Wyatt with the plates."

A few minutes later, they all sat around the family table in the private dining room. A few table place settings stayed vacant, a visual reminder of the missing family. Daisy stood at the doorway, hesitant to come in.

Parker took her to her seat. "Your place has been set since we found out you were alive."

Silver hair covered her face as she looked down. Parker pulled out her chair for her and then stood at the head of the table behind Mary and Flint.

"And we will leave Grace's, Lilo's, Misha's, Max's, Bailey's, and Joe's place as a reminder we will see them again. They're family. They're also Lazaruses. And they won't quit."

Murmurs of agreement around the room. Amari made a cooing gurgle. Wyatt retrieved her from Liza, much to her annoyance. Parker cleared his throat, recapturing everyone's attention.

"I just need to say a few more things. First, I apologize for my behavior over the past few weeks. I'm sure you all know I was reckless, proud and, for lack of a better word—"

"A dickhead," Liza finished for him.

Parker nodded. Wow. When Alice had asked him to say a few words, she didn't think he'd be so humble doing it. There was more. He put his hand on Alice's shoulder.

"Second, Griff, you need to slow down. You're no good to anyone if you run yourself ragged. We will take turns out on patrol and sweep the city, above and below ground in a methodical manner. Evan, you need to sleep. We need your visions and you don't dream them if you're awake." Evan nodded sleepily. "And you should work with the psychic at the Sisterhood to compare notes." He looked in turn to each of the glum faces around the table. "We'll find them safe, I promise. And I'm not saying that from some prideful, conceited place. I'm saying that because I have faith in all of you. We're finally together as Gloria intended. The only way for us to fail now is to lose hope."

"Easy for you to say," Griffin grumbled. "It's not your pregnant wife missing."

Wyatt narrowed his eyes at Alice. "In fact, your mate just happens to be the only one still with us."

"Be careful of what you imply," Parker warned. "I'll let your attitude slide because I understand what you must be feeling. But if it wasn't for Alice and her Sinners, the Syndicate would still be ready to deploy thousands of replicates around the world, and Daisy would be dead. We had a loss, people, but we also had a big win. I'm not detracting from the loss but I think it's important to remember we've also done good."

Griffin scrubbed his face, and shook his head, but settled down.

Parker pulled out his seat and sat down. "We'll start the hunt for Daisy's mate tomorrow."

Daisy cleared her throat. All eyes turned to her.

"There's no need," she said. "I know who he is."

"Axel?" Alice blurted, her mind going back to the way he'd looked at Daisy.

Daisy gave a thin smile, one that still didn't reach her eyes. Alice wondered if the woman would ever smile properly again.

"Yes, Axel. He doesn't know." Daisy picked up her fork and stabbed a carrot. With a breath, and without removing her eyes from her plate, she continued. "He doesn't know because I don't think my power triggered. I feel nothing except my sin equalizing."

"You have a gift," Parker insisted. "I know what it is."

"It doesn't matter." Daisy lifted the carrot to her mouth and paused before eating to say, "It doesn't matter because Axel was a member of the Faithful. And he's dying."

And then she ate.

The entire table stilled. They were all sad they were missing their mates, yet Daisy had finally found hers and he was dying. Mary mumbled a prayer and made the sign of the cross. Flint poured water into a glass and gave it to Daisy. Parker tapped his finger on a napkin, thinking.

Alice should say something. Shouldn't she?

"It's going to be fine," Parker insisted. "I don't know how, but I do know we can't solve the world's problems tonight. Let's eat. Tomorrow, we fight."

Every single person in that room lifted their forks and dug into their meals. It brought tears to Alice's eyes because she knew, without a doubt, that even though she'd signed on to be the last line of defense against the Lazarus family if they ever turned dark, it would never happen. They had each other's backs. And they would fight for love until their dying breaths.

IN A DARK, abandoned waste-water facility, Julius Allcott rushed between the computers he'd set up on a rusted metal platform. Cords and wires snaked everywhere and he had to hop to avoid catching his feet. He checked on the status of the replicate tanks he'd positioned around the city. Good to go. He checked on the Faithful teams in place, waiting with detonators at each bridge leading into the city.

"Is it ready?" his wife said to him.

"Almost, my love," he replied. "I've done exactly as you said. The plan is ready to execute."

Kidnap the mates. Destroy the bridges. Lock down Cardinal City so no one can get in or out. Loose the replicates and other weapons. Watch the city burn and destroy itself. Watch sin finally have its day. And then while that was all happening, while the Deadly Seven were distracted or falling into sin themselves, he would be underground, back at that same spot, burrowing deep into the spirit dimension, bringing his wife and daughter back to him.

She was close, already speaking to him through the void. The moment he'd heard her in that tunnel, he'd almost wet himself with joy. But she'd told him that until the gate was open, she wouldn't be fully here.

"Then what are you waiting for?" his wife asked. "Detonate."

Julius opened a line of communication with his team and spoke. "It's time."

The city foundations rocked. One by one, each bridge was taken out. It was time for everyone to finally see what Julius had always known—there was no escaping deadly sin.

bonus extended epilogue

Bleary-eyed, Alice summoned patience of steel and followed Parker into his office at four thirty in the morning. They shouldn't be there at all, let alone at this ungodly hour. He was still on bail for vigilantism and being watched like a hawk by prosecutors and the Feds. But Parker Lazarus never walked to anyone else's tune, so why would he start now?

"Remind me again why we're here—*oof!*" She slammed into his broad-shouldered back as he stopped just inside the threshold.

He'd forgone the business suit this morning, and wore a designer T-shirt that hugged his torso and accentuated defined abs. Alice was sure he wore the hoodie open just, so she'd see his stomach flex and bend every time he moved. Considering his attire and the duffel bag in his hand, she'd assumed they were going to work out in the in-house gym. But the man dropped the bag, tugged her inside, and then shut the door behind them—locking it. The hole he'd put in the door with his bionic fist had been repaired, and the office furniture had all been replaced and fixed. Nobody would have known a week ago a band of white-masked terrorists had tried to kill Alice there.

She shivered and rubbed her arms. The yoga jacket she'd put on felt too thin.

Without a word, Parker checked the heating gauge, adjusted the temperature, and then directed her to stand before the large floor-to-ceiling windows showing the view of Cardinal City in lights, seventy-five floors below.

"Parker Pride Lazarus," she warned. "If you don't tell me what's going on right now, I'll follow through with my promise to cut your hair while you sleep. Maybe I'll even give you a bowl cut."

A deep chuckle behind her. A gentle touch on either side of her jaw as he ensured she faced the city opposite. His lips beside her ear. "Patience is a virtue, my little assassin."

She clenched her teeth. Funny how, when someone told her to be patient, her body revolted. It was also funny how, since falling in love with Parker Lazarus, Alice was struggling with calm. Even now, her insides flipped and twisted at the very smell of him. That masculine scent underlying any cologne or laundry soap. It was him. Musky, heady, heavenly. And all hers.

He bent and opened a hatch on the floor to expose two exposed bolts, about shoulder width apart. She narrowed her eyes and studied. They were looped for tying rope. Instantly, her pulse quickened. Her nipples hardened. Shibari? Here? Now?

She squeezed her eyes shut and prayed. Please. Holy mother in heaven, yes please. She'd missed that quiet submission she'd felt when in his care. That floating haze of euphoria she could only get from being lulled by his strong arms. The containment of her big emotions. The safety of being allowed to let go and know she wouldn't fall apart.

But... she glanced at the locked door, and then over at Parker as he picked up his duffel bag, who gave her a disapproving stare because she wasn't staring out the window. Her subsequent cheeky wink turned that disapproval into something hot and needy—God, she hoped this session involved less clothing than last time. She hoped it wasn't all rope tying and knots. Well, unless she counted the knots in her stomach from wanting his touch.

It had been too long since she and Parker had been intimate. With so many loved ones missing, it had been disrespectful to even think about sex in the same building as someone who could sense lust. They'd spent every waking hour combing the city streets for the missing, and only catching sleep when they could.

"Face the front," he grumbled.

Was it bad to want a little private touch time with Parker? Without being judged? Alice hugged herself to stop the trembles of anticipation and stared ahead at the dark city. The light pollution drowned out the stars, but she felt them in her bones, twinkling and shining in anticipation, waiting for Parker to confirm her suspicion.

He dropped the bag behind her. The thud sent a shiver down her spine. The zip opening made her nipples harden. The rasp of rope caused a moan to slip out of her mouth.

"Are we…" She couldn't finish the thought in case this turned out to be a dream.

"Undress," he said by her ear.

Alice divested her jacket and lifted her shirt over her head. Parker's hands stopped her. "Slowly. Look at your reflection in the glass. Look how beautiful you are."

She swallowed and looked up. She'd been too wound tight to realize this was why he'd brought her here at this hour. It was dark enough outside that the windows were almost a mirror, and if she focused on her reflection, the city lights turned to a bokeh of twinkling stars around her. Magical.

Over her shoulder, she glimpsed Parker's eyes glowing gold with his animal instinct. The lion about to pounce. Their gazes held. Alice resumed undressing. Slower this time. She hooked her fingers on her waistband and slid her pants down her hips, desperately trying to summon any seduction lessons she'd learned from Mercy, but failing miserably in her eagerness. After she'd kicked her shoes and pants off, she straightened and met his watchful eyes, waiting for further instructions.

"All of it," he said with a pointed look at her underwear.

Alice stilled, afraid to unleash her excitement. They'd never done this with her completely naked. The very thought of his ropes sliding over her skin, his firm and steady touch, the rhythmic pull and push—wet heat rushed between her legs and she let a whimper loose.

Parker rumbled and then teeth clamped down on her bare shoulder. He inhaled deeply. His mating pheromones exploded, shrouding her as tight as any rope. The urge to turn, grab his aroused cock, and put it in her mouth was undeniable.

He gripped her wrists as she tried to do just that and gave a low warning growl. "This is why we're using the ropes. I can't control my scent. You can't control yourself. It would be over in seconds."

Alice gave a frustrated whine. She didn't care. But she did. He was right. Damn it.

Parker flicked her bra open and released her breasts with a sharp inhale of appreciation. But he didn't touch. He walked to her front, held her gaze and tugged her wrists together before winding a long length of soft purple cord around and around her forearms.

"I know you've enjoyed this in the past," he said, studying her face. "But tonight I want you to use a safe word."

Her gaze snapped to his. They'd never needed one before, but she supposed the last time she was in his ropes, she'd broken down in tears and he had to slice the cords to get her out. It had been good, though. Cathartic. She'd slept for hours afterward.

"How about Pride," she suggested.

His lips curved into a smile, humor twinkled in his eyes. "Pride it is. Any time you want to stop. Any time you reach a hard limit, you say that word. Understood?"

She nodded. Then frowned. Safe word? Hard limits? "What are you going to do to me?"

He trailed his hand around her stomach and side as he returned to stand behind her.

"You wanted flowers, Alice. I'm going to give them to you."

Parker had been planning this excursion for days. Days and nights. It had been the only thing keeping him sane over the past few days since Daisy's rescue, and subsequent kidnapping of the rest of his siblings' mates. Sleeping next to Alice, scenting her, had been a wet dream he couldn't awaken from. All he'd wanted to do was bury himself in her tight, slick center and forget about the world. She was his escape, his solace, his drug. Yet he couldn't use any of it without hurting his family.

He couldn't kiss her around them. He could barely touch her to reset his internal sin-balance. The only option was to go somewhere no one would see them. He could have taken her to a hotel, but knew the bolts were already installed in this office. He'd always had them there as an option for his skills. Sometimes he practiced on his own. Never had he had a woman up here, and now he was eager to fulfill that fantasy with the one woman he loved more than anything. The one woman who challenged him as much as accepted him. He knew she felt the same. From lingering glances across the room, to reaching for him in her sleep. They needed to get this obsession for each other out of their systems. At the very least, release some pressure.

She'd told him she wanted flowers. A better proposal. Romance.

Parker Lazarus didn't do romance. Not without tying his little assassin up first, ensuring she couldn't escape. Alice had denied his extravagant gifts. She wasn't impressed with diamonds. So he would give her his heart and his body. And he'd bring her to orgasm so many times she would realize she couldn't live without him, either.

With her hands bound, Alice couldn't touch Parker as he made his way about her mostly naked body, sliding rope and knotting patterns. Watching him work through their reflection in the window was mesmerizing. Every so often, he would pause to lick or kiss her. A simple, short lave down a portion of her flesh. Or a quick, tongue twirling kiss to induce goosebumps. Every time was accompanied by a male breathy groan of need. It was as though he was too hungry to wait, and tasting her was the only way he could assuage his appetite. When his touch slid down her stomach and out to her hips, he slid her panties off and then went back to methodical work, covering her body with a harness pattern that reminded her of diamonds. He coiled rope strategically around her neck and other parts of her body. Then he delved into his duffel bag and pulled out a series of pre-knotted shapes.

Flowers.

Alice gasped.

She held her breath as he wove the flower-knots into place about her body. Over her heart. At her navel. All down her spine.

Not only was he a genius, a vigilante hero, and a god between the sheets, but Parker Lazarus was an artist. A giver. He blocked her reflection and gave a deep grunt of approval as he put the finishing touches on his design. Alice's breasts swelled under his attention. Her nipples grew even harder, a fact he zeroed in on. Without her panties, the air tickled her damp entrance, making her squirm with need until she pressed her thighs together. Gold, heat filled eyes met hers.

"Stunning," he said, and stepped to the side.

Sliding her gaze to her reflection, her pulse stuttered. She was not Alice Montgomery. She was not a Sinner. She was a woman, in perfect balance—equal parts rope and flesh. Parker watched intently as she inspected herself.

Her hands were bound before her but loose at her front. The rope harness fit over her collarbone and around her naked breasts. It moved around her thighs and above her knees. In fact, it looked strategically placed, like it had a purpose.

"Are you going to suspend me?" she asked.

Sensuous lips curved upward. "Clever girl. But I have one more rope to tie."

Deft fingers weaved a small knot in a long line of purple cord. Just one knot, two long thin lines on either side. Then he kneeled before her.

"You smell so good," he murmured and licked between her legs. "I can't—"

His tongue darted into her folds, sending pleasure shooting up her spine. Alice whimpered as he kissed her intimately, fast and hard, tongue darting to flick against her clit. She cried out as a zap of pure bliss rocketed from his contact. He pulled back, chest heaving. A frown marred his handsome face.

"Go slow," he mumbled to himself, like a mantra. "Make it last."

"No, no, no," she groaned. "Faster. More."

"Trust me, Alice."

She tried to pull him back, but he ducked her touch and placed the knotted rope right over where she was most sensitive and then secured the line to run straight from the rope under her navel and looped it between her legs to her rear, fitting it between her bottom to tie at her lower back. Then he pulled the cord tight so it fit snuggly, pressing on her clit, making her eyes flutter as sensation hit. He dipped his finger between her legs, wet himself in her juices, and lubricated the knot. She couldn't help rocking and moving her hips to trigger the friction.

Parker clicked his tongue in disapproval. "Slow."

"Bastard."

He arched his eyebrow and then sucked her taste from his finger.

Then he straightened, unzipped his hoodie and pulled his shirt off. The sight of him, all hard slabs of muscle and metal gleaming in the dim light, made her rock against the knot again. It felt good, but it wasn't him. She looked at him with a plea in her eyes.

"I'm ready, Parker."

He cupped her between the legs and pressed the heel of his palm against the knot, making her squirm with feeling.

"Almost done, love." He dug into his pocket and pulled something out. "Last thing."

Alice threw her head back in frustration to stare at the ceiling. Her body was about to burst out of her skin. She needed him to touch her, to satisfy that need. His erection strained in his sweat pants, proving he felt the same way.

He lifted her bound hands to his lips and kissed her knuckles. The golden-eyed hero had a flicker of doubt in his eyes. She tensed.

"Parker?"

"You said you wanted flowers, Alice." He took a deep breath and exhaled. "So here they are. All over you. I want you to be my wife. I should have asked you the right way from the start." He slipped something over her ring finger. "It's not diamonds, but I made it, and it represents exactly how I feel about you."

It was a thin, woven band made from a cord of purple satin. An intricately knotted flower graced the top. He'd made his own engagement ring... that had a flower as the center piece? No one had ever made her something before—like actually spent time thinking about what would make her happy. What would be better than diamonds and shallow gifts? Hot tears prickled Alice's eyes. She swallowed over the lump in her throat to stay the emotion.

He was perfect.

"Alice Montgomery, I've never met a woman like you. Not only do you bring harmony to my raging insides, but you're able to stare my beast in the face without an ounce of fear. You—" His eyes darted from side to side as he struggled to come up with words. "You make me whole, you... you tame me."

Oh God, she was going to cry. Here, in an office at five am, naked and in ropes before a window facing the city. With the love of her life kneeling before her, holding her bound hands to his cheek.

"Alice?" he asked nervously. His brow furrowed, and he refused to look up. The set of his shoulders was hard, tense. The rasp of his beard against her fingers prickled.

No wonder he'd tied her up for this. The man was afraid she'd reject him again. The thought made guilt flash in her heart. Yes, the bastard had just assumed she'd marry him. And yes, she'd been a little abrupt with her protest. But...

"Yes," she blurted. "Yes, I'll marry you, Parker Lazarus."

Relief loosened his posture. He clutched her rope tied stomach to his face. She looped her bound hands over his head and tried to hold him closer, but all she'd managed to do was rock her body more, triggering the friction against that special knot. A small moan slipped out.

His gaze snapped up, caught hers and held. Solid gold satisfaction flashed. "Get ready, Alice."

"For what?" she gasped.

"For a long life filled with pleasure."

When he stood, he dominated her with his size and presence. Strong fingers dug into the harness at her chest and yanked her closer. He kissed her roughly for a long, fast minute and then pushed her away, a glint of fire in his eyes.

"Now comes the fun part," he said.

"God, yes. Hurry." Every time he moved her, the pleasure knot tweaked and rolled in her desire, sliding and slipping, winding her tighter. He opened his mouth to speak, but she glared at him. "If you say patience, one more time, I'm going to use the safe word."

He bit his lip, and she wanted to die from how fuckable he looked. His auburn hair was all mussed from how he'd rubbed his face against her stomach. She gave a moan of frustration, of need. Without another word, he gathered more rope and then used his office chair to tie three lengths to a bolt in the ceiling. Then he tied the other ends strategically around the harness on her body. In the end, he covered the floor bolts and mumbled that he changed his mind and wouldn't need them.

Once the rope was in place, he pulled the lengths, and she became weightless. He hoisted her into the air. With so many points of contact on her body, she was surprised at how comfortable the harness was. And then he folded her legs into a kneeling position and adjusted the rope to keep her feet against her bottom. Every time he walked past her front, he displaced air and it brushed cooly against her hot center, teasing her enough to elicit a rock of the hips and a breathy moan.

Lastly, he lifted the rope attached to her hands and her arms raised over her head. She was floating in a kneeling position, her knees splayed wide, exposing her most intimate parts. She threw her head back in abandon and undulated her hips, pleasuring herself. The sense of falling made her swoon, only for a second, and then she became distracted as Parker stood before her and admired his work, his expression dripping with male appreciation, especially when his gaze dipped between her legs. She was his toy to play with now.

"Parker," she whimpered, rocking her hips. "I need you now."

"You'll get me when you're screaming my name, begging for it."

Fuck. Damn bastard.

But she loved it. She wanted it to last, like he'd said, and she had zero patience.

The look of need on his face had morphed into stubborn pride. He wouldn't bend until he was ready. Until whatever plan he'd concocted in his mind came to fruition. It made her squirm even more in her bondage. Her lashes fluttered closed as she gave herself over to the sensations, to the experience. Alice bit her bottom lip and waited.

Parker came closer until he stood between her knees. He glanced down, frowned, and then hoisted until she lifted higher, higher, and her hips were at eye level to him. When she was secured, he gripped her bottom, plumped the exposed flesh between the pattern of cord, and lowered his mouth to her hot, needy center. A wet slide of his tongue, straight down the middle and back up to swirl around the knot. His tongue danced around the rope. He flicked the knot over her clit and toyed with her, winding her up until she tightened, and then moved on to kiss her inner thighs as she whimpered hotly for more.

He blew on her wet core, causing her to release a frustrated groan of tension. "Parker."

"Nope." He went back to working on her sex with teasing licks. "That wasn't a scream."

Bound, she couldn't grab his head and hold him there. She couldn't do anything but rock her hips, but even that was difficult, bound as she was. He slid a thick finger inside her and she gasped, her eyes rolling from the sensation.

"The last time we fucked, Alice," he said, voice low and almost inaudible as he studied his fingers sliding around her desire. "You prayed using my name. Over and over you said it as I thrust into you. What will it take for you to pray to me again, little Sinner?"

Alice was floating, wrapped in his control, at the mercy of his whims and devious intentions. And she never wanted to leave. She would stay here forever, but the sun was rising. The sky lightened into purples and pinks over his shoulder.

"You know what it takes," she rasped.

With a grunt of approval, he removed his fingers from her. She whimpered her protest.

"What does it take?" he asked again.

"You," she gasped. "Always you."

Pleased with her response, her arrogant beast released tension on the ropes, loosening her position and lowering her, watching intently for signs of distress or pain. First he unfolded her legs, then her arms, and then her body. There was no pain. She was either numb or over-taken with pleasure. She felt nothing but a desire to have him inside her.

He kept lowering her until her heels hit the floor.

"Are we done?" she pouted.

A wolfish grin was her answer as claws severed her from the suspension ropes. But the rope wrapping her body remained.

"We're not done," he said, his voice sounding unnatural, his expression almost pained. "But The Beast is impatient. I can't have you five feet from the ground with me like this."

The gold in his eyes was luminous. Sweat dappled his brow.

Tension pulled skin taut over muscle. Veins protruded over his neck and arms. He was right. The strain it was taking to control himself was too much. He didn't trust himself.

But Alice did, and she didn't want control.

Parker tried to gently unwind the rope from her body, but it was too intricate for him. His fingers trembled and fumbled. She didn't want to wait an hour. She wanted now. So she pushed him. Hard. She taunted The Beast. He stumbled back, eyes wide and curious. Her brows lowered, and she charged at him, lowering her shoulder and hitting him squarely in the hard chest.

A snarl ripped out of him and he took her by the harness at the chest, then yanked her close so they stared eye to eye. The strength in his single hand moved her like a rag doll and she couldn't be more attracted to him than in that moment.

"I know what you're doing," he said, a wild grin forming on his lips. "Instead of using the safe word, you're trying to get me to surrender first. But why?"

Alice licked her lips, adrenaline pumping in her blood. "Because I want The Beast again, Parker. I love that passion. I loved how you took from me at the abbey. I don't want you to hold back, and with me secured like this, you won't think I'm capable of protecting myself. You'll deny me what I want."

"So say the safe word and I'll cut you out."

"Never." She kicked him.

Or she tried. The harness around her thigh prevented her from striking out properly. But it did the job. Just like her bite against his neck had the first time they'd made love, defiance brought his inner warrior god out to play. Lust bloomed in his eyes. Claws—both metal and natural—flashed as he started shredding her bindings, slicing through the pressure, releasing her until she was free everywhere but her wrists. *Still wants me bound. Still wants some level of control.* Then he tossed her over his shoulder and slapped her ass. Hard. She squealed in delight and kicked her legs. He slapped her again and stalked to his couch, where he dropped her on the leather.

Parker Lazarus loomed over her, hair wild and untamed, eyes flashing with purpose, hands dipping into his sweatpants. He pulled his heavy, hard length out and squeezed it in his fist.

"Hands behind you," he demanded.

She slid her bound wrists over her knees and under her legs until they were behind her back.

"Turn over." He stroked himself again.

Alice rolled to her front and presented her bottom. He gripped her hips and lifted so she arched over the back of the couch, her feet on the carpet, her face angled down into the seat. With her hands bound behind her back, she was helpless, and horny as hell.

Wiggling her ass at him, she whimpered into the couch. The blunt head of his cock pressed against her entrance, but he didn't push in. Instead, he stroked up and down her slick, swollen center, teasing her again.

Fuck it. Fine. *Have it your way, you arrogant bastard.*

She shouted his name over her shoulder. "Parker. Now!"

A stroke of approval across her ass and then he pushed inside her. She couldn't help it. She moaned long and hard. The sensation of him filling her, of finally fitting where he belonged, it was too much. He stilled completely.

"Christ, Alice."

"What?"

He sliced the bindings on her wrists, releasing her arms. "You're going to need to hold on for this."

Then he let the animal out and fucked her. It was hard, fast and greedy. All she could do was clutch the couch and submit. She held on as he slammed into her, rocking her body and couch forward. He braced around her chest, trying to hold her closer. The slap of flesh connecting filled the room. He pulled her this way and that to accommodate his insatiable mood. She held on, as he'd asked, but not her scream as her orgasm ripped through her body, claiming her sense, her vision, and her reason. One last thrust and he seated himself deep inside her with a feral snarl of satisfaction as he reached his climax.

Together, they collapsed on the couch. Her bones were made of liquid, something warm and whiskey-like as he moved her so they could both lie on their sides. She basked in his soft kisses at her neck, his gentle strokes along her arms.

"You didn't use the safe word," he grumbled, annoyed.

"Didn't need to."

He made a strange sound—something caught between an angry grunt and whine—it was enough to worry her into facing him. Dawn washed into the room, casting his face in soft hues and revealing the concern and guilt in his eyes. She touched his cheek and smiled.

"I'm fine, Parker."

"But..."

She kissed him reverently on the lips. "I love you," she whispered, and then stared at her ring made of rope and twine. "And I love this ring."

Her eyes burned, and she dashed away the tears.

"Hey," he rumbled, frowning. "No looking back."

"I just... never thought I'd get this far. Be with someone I love who fits me perfectly."

Golden eyes softened. "I love you too. Future wife."

He tightened his embrace, and she squirmed in his arms. "How much time do you think we have before everyone arrives for the day?"

A wild, toothy grin. "Enough for one more round."

This time, Alice not only screamed Parker's name. She prayed it. Just like he'd wanted.

The End.
(Of Parker's and Alice's story)
To get first dibs on more super secret sealed sections, make sure you're subscribed to Lana's email newsletter.
Visit subscribe.lanapecherczyk.com to join.

join lana's vips

Subscribe to Lana's newsletter and receive a free box set, first dibs on giveaways, special printable freebies and more. You won't want to miss out.

subscribe.lanapecherczyk.com

On Facebook? Join Lana's Angels Reader Group https://www.facebook.com/groups/lanasangels

OMG! How do you say my name?

Lana (straight forward enough - Lah-nah) **Pecherczyk** (this is where it gets tricky - Pe-her-chick).

I've been called Lana Price-Check, Lana Pera-Chickywack, Lana Pressed Chicken, Lana Pech...*that girl!* You name it, they said it. So if it's so hard to spell, why on earth would I use this name instead of an easy pen name?

To put it simply, it belonged to my mother. And she was my dream champion. For most of my life, I've been good at one thing – art. The world around me saw my work, and said I should do more of it, so I did. But, when at the age of eight, I said I wanted to write stories, and even though we were poor, my mother came home with a blank notebook and a pencil saying I should follow my dreams, no matter where they take me for they will make me happy. I wasn't very good at it, but it didn't matter because I had her support and I liked it.

She died when I was thirteen, and left her four daughters orphaned. Suddenly, I had lost my dream champion, I was split from my youngest two sisters and had no one to talk to about the challenge of life.

So, I wrote in secret. I poured my heart out daily to a diary and sometimes imagined that she would listen. At the end of the day, even if she couldn't hear, writing kept that dream alive.

Eventually, after having my own children (two firecrackers in the guise of little boys) and ignoring my inner voice for too long, I decided to lead by example. How could I teach my children to follow their dreams if I wasn't? I became my own dream champion and the rest is history, here I am.

When I'm not writing the next great action-packed romantic novel, or wrangling the rug rats, or rescuing GI Joe from the jaws of my Kelpie, I fight evil by moonlight, win love by daylight and never run from a real fight. I live in Australia, but I'm up for a chat anytime online. Come and find me.

Subscribe & Follow
subscribe.lanapecherczyk.com
lp@lanapecherczyk.com

facebook.com/lanapecherczykauthor

instagram.com/lana_p_author

amazon.com/-/e/B00V2TP0HG

bookbub.com/profile/lana-pecherczyk

tiktok.com/@lanapauthor

goodreads.com/lana_p_author